Catherine Cookson was born in East Jarrow and the place of her birth provides the background she so vividly creates in many of her novels. Although acclaimed as a regional writer – her novel THE ROUND TOWER won the Winifred Holtby Award for the best regional novel of 1968 – her readership spreads throughout the world. Her work has been translated into twelve languages and Corgi alone has 30,000,000 of her novels in print, including those written under the name of Catherine Marchant.

Mrs Cookson was born the illegitimate daughter of a poverty-stricken woman, Kate, whom she believed to be her older sister. Catherine began work in service but eventually moved south to Hastings where she met and married a local grammar school master. At the age of forty she began writing with great success about the lives of the working class people of the North-East with whom she had grown up, including her intriguing autobiography, OUR KATE. More recently her many bestselling novels have established her as one of the most popular of contemporary women novelists.

Mrs Cookson now lives in Northumberland.

Catherine Cookson

The Gambling Man

CORGI BOOKS

THE GAMBLING MAN
A CORGI BOOK 0 552 10450 7

Originally published in Great Britain by
William Heinemann Ltd.

PRINTING HISTORY
William Heinemann edition published 1975
Corgi edition published 1976
Corgi edition reprinted 1977 (twice)
Corgi edition reprinted 1978
Corgi edition reissued 1980
Corgi edition reprinted 1981
Corgi edition reprinted 1982
Corgi edition reprinted 1984
Corgi edition reprinted 1985

This book is set in Times

Corgi Books are published by
Transworld Publishers Ltd.,
Century House, 61–63 Uxbridge Road,
Ealing, London W5 5SA

Printed and bound in Great Britain by
Cox & Wyman Ltd., Reading, Berks.

Contents

THE CONNORS

Paddy Connor *a steelworker*
Ruth Connor *his wife*
Rory Connor *their elder son, a rent collector*
Jimmy Connor *their younger son, apprenticed to a boat builder*
Nellie Burke *their only daughter, married to Charlie Burke*
Lizzie O'Dowd *Paddy Connor's half-cousin*

THE WAGGETTS

Bill Waggett *a widowed docker*
Janie Waggett *his daughter, a nursemaid and engaged to marry
Rory Connor*
Gran Waggett *his mother*

THE LEARYS

Collum Leary *a coal miner*
Kathleen Leary *his wife*
*Nine surviving children of whom three have emigrated to
America*

John George Armstrong *Rory's friend and fellow rent collector*

Septimus Kean *a property owner*
Charlotte Kean *his only daughter*

PART ONE

1875 Rory Connor

Tyne Dock was deserted. It was Sunday and the hour when the long dusk was ending and the night beginning. Moreover, it was bitterly cold and the first flat flakes of snow were falling at spaced intervals, dropping to rest in their white purity on the greasy, coal-dust, spit-smeared flags.

The five arches leading from the dock gates towards the Jarrow Road showed streaks of dull green water running down from their domes. Beneath the arches the silence and desolation of the docks was intensified; they, too, seemed to be resting, drawing breath as it were, before taking again the weight of the wagons which, with the dawn, would rumble over four of them from the coal staithes that lay beyond the brick wall linking them together. Beyond the fifth arch the road divided, one section mounting to Simonside, the other leading to Jarrow.

The road to Jarrow was a grim road, a desolate road, and a stretch of it bordered the slakes at East Jarrow, the great open stretch of mud which in turn bordered the river Tyne.

There was nothing grim about the road to Simonside, for as soon as you mounted the bank Tyne Dock and East Jarrow were forgotten, and you were in the country. Up and up the hill you went and there to the left, lying back in their well-tended gardens, were large houses; past the farm, and now you were among green fields and open land as far as the eye could see. Of course, if you looked back you would glimpse the masts of the ships lying all along the river, but looking ahead even in the falling twilight you knew this was a pleasant place, a place different from Tyne Dock, or East Jarrow, or Jarrow itself; this was the country. The road, like any country road, was rough, and the farther you walked along it the narrower it became until finally petering out into a mere cart track running between fields.

Strangers were always surprised when, walking along this track, they came upon the cottages. There were three cottages, but they were approached by a single gate leading from the track and bordered on each side by an untidy tangled hedge of hawthorn and bramble.

The cottages lay in a slight hollow about twenty feet from the gate, and half this distance was covered by a brick path which then divided into three uneven parts, each leading to a cottage door. The cottages were numbered 1, 2 and 3 but were always called No. 1 The Cottages, No. 2 The Cottages, and No. 3 The Cottages.

In No. 1 lived the Waggetts, in No. 2 the Connors, and in No. 3 the Learys. But, as this was Sunday, all the Waggett family and three of the Learys were in the Connors' cottage, and they were playing cards.

'In the name of God, did you ever see the likes! He's won again. How much is it I owe you this time?'

'Twelve and fourpence.'

'Twelve an' fourpence! Will you have it now or will you wait till ye get it?'

'I'll wait till I get it.'

'Ta, you've got a kind heart. Although you're a rent man you've got a kind heart. I'll say that for you, Rory.'

'Ah, shut up Bill. Are you goin' to have another game?'

'No, begod! I'm not. I've only half a dozen monkey nuts left, an' Janie there loves monkey nuts. Don't you, lass?'

Bill Waggett turned round from the table and looked towards his only daughter, who was sitting with the women who were gathered to one side of the fire cutting clippings for a mat, and Janie laughed back at him, saying, 'Aw, let him have the monkey nuts; 'cos if you don't, he'll have your shirt.' She now exchanged a deep knowing look with Rory Connor, who had half turned from the table, and when he said, 'Do you want me to come there and skelp your lug?' she tossed her head and cried back at him, 'Try it on, lad. Try it on.' And all those about the fire laughed as if she had said something extremely witty.

Her grannie laughed, her wrinkled lips drawn back from her toothless gums, her mouth wide and her tongue flicking in and out with the action of the aged; she laughed as she said, 'That's it. That's it. Start the way you mean to go on. Married sixty-five years me afore he went; never lifted a hand to me; didn't get the chance.' The cavity of her mouth became wider.

Ruth Connor laughed, but hers was a quiet, subdued sound that seemed to suit her small, thin body and her pointed face and black hair combed back from the middle parting over each side of her head.

Her daughter, Nellie, laughed. Nellie had been married for three years and her name now was Mrs Burke. Nellie, like her mother, was small and thin but her hair was fair. The word puny would describe her whole appearance.

And Lizzie O'Dowd laughed. Lizzie O'Dowd was of the Connor family. She was Paddy Connor's half-cousin. She was now forty-one years old but had lived with them since she had come over from Ireland at the age of seventeen. Lizzie's laugh was big, deep and hearty; her body was fat, her hair brown and thick; her eyes brown and round. Lizzie O'Dowd looked entirely different from the rest of the women seated near the fire, particularly the last, who was Kathleen Leary from No. 3 The Cottages. Kathleen's laugh had a weary sound. Perhaps it was because after bearing sixteen children her body was tired. It was no consolation that seven were dead and the eldest three in America for she still had six at home and the youngest was but two years old.

It was now Paddy Connor, Rory's father, who said, 'You were talkin' of another game, lad. Well then, come on, get on with it.'

Paddy was a steelworker in Palmer's shipyard in Jarrow. For the past fifteen years he had worked in the blast furnaces, and every inch of skin on his face was red, a dull red, like overcooked beetroot. He had three children, Rory being the eldest was twenty-three.

Rory was taller than his father. He was thickset with a head that inclined to be square. He did not take after either his mother or his father in looks for his hair was a dark brown and his skin, although thick of texture, was fresh looking. His eyes, too, were brown but of a much deeper tone than his hair. His lips were not full as might have been expected to go with the shape of his face but were thin and wide. Even in his shirt sleeves he looked smart, and cleaner than the rest of the men seated around the table.

Jimmy, the younger son, had fair hair that sprang like fine silk from double crowns on his head. His face had the young look of a boy of fourteen yet he was nineteen years old. His skin was as fair as his hair and his grey eyes seemed over-big for his face. His body looked straight and well formed, until he stood up, and then you saw that his legs were badly bowed, so much so that he was known as Bandy Connor.

Paddy's third child was Nellie, Mrs Burke, who was next in age to Rory.

Bill Waggett from No. 1 The Cottages, the son of Gran Waggett and the father of Janie, worked in the docks. He was fifty years old but could have been taken for sixty. His wife had died six years before, bearing her seventh child. Janie was the only one they had managed to rear and he adored her.

Bill's love for her had been such that he did not demand that she stay at home to keep house for him when his wife died but had let her go into service as a nursemaid, even though this meant that once again

14

he would be treated as a young nipper by his mother who was then in her seventy-ninth year. But he, like all those in the cottages, gave her respect if only for the fact that now at eighty-five she still did a full day's work.

Collum Leary was a miner. He was now forty-eight but had been down the pit since he was seven years old. His initiation had been to sit twelve hours a day in total blackness. At eight he had graduated to crawling on his hands and knees with a chain between his legs, which was attached to a bogie load of coal, while his blood brother pushed it from behind. He could not remember his mother, only his father who had come from Ireland when he himself was a boy. The nearest Collum had ever got to Ireland was the Irish quarter in Jarrow and as he himself said, who would bother crossing the seas when almost every man-jack of them were on your doorstep?

Collum at forty-eight was a wizened, prematurely aged man who carried the trade-mark of his following on his skin, for his face and body were scarred as with pocks by blue marks left by the imprint of the coal. But Collum was happy. He went to confession once a twelve-month, and now and again he would follow it by Communion, and he did his duty by God as the priest dictated and saw to it that his wife gave birth every year, at least almost every year. Those years in which she failed to become pregnant were the times he took Communion.

'How's the shipbuilding goin', Jimmy?' Collum Leary now poked his head forward across the table.

'Oh, grand, fine, Mr Leary.'

'When are you goin' to build your own boat?'

'That'll be the day, but I will sometime.' Jimmy nodded now. Then catching Rory's eye, he smiled widely. 'I said I will, an' I will, won't I, Rory?' The boy appealed to his older brother as to one in authority.

Rory, shuffling the cards, glanced sideways at

Jimmy and there was a softness in his expression that wasn't usual except when perhaps he looked at Janie.

'You'll soon be out of your time, won't you, Jimmy?'

Jimmy now turned towards Bill Waggett, answering, 'Aye, beginnin' of the year, Mr Waggett. And that's what I'm feared of. They turn you out, you know, once your time's up.'

'Aw, they won't turn you out.' Bill Waggett pursed his lips. 'You hear things around the docks you know; there's more things come up on the tide than rotten cabbages. I hear tell you're the best 'prentice Baker's ever had in his yard; a natural they say you are, Jimmy; mould a bit of wood with your hands, they say.'

'Aw, go on with you.' Jimmy turned his head to the side, his lips pressed tight but his whole face failing to suppress his pleasure at the compliment. Then looking at Bill Waggett again and his expression changing, he said, 'But I'll tell you somethin', I wouldn't be able to finish me time if old Baker saw what I was doin' at this minute.'

'You mean havin' a game?' Rory had stopped shuffling the pack and Jimmy nodded at him, saying, 'Aye. Well, you know what some of them's like. But now there's a notice come out. Didn't I tell you?'

'No, you didn't. A notice? What kind of a notice?'

'Well it says that anybody that's found playin' cards on a Sunday'll lose their jobs, an' if you know about somebody having a game an' don't let on, why then you'll lose your job an' all.'

Rory slapped his hand of cards on to the table. 'Is that a fact?'

'Aye, Rory.'

'My God!' Rory now looked round at the rest of the men, and they stared back at him without speaking until his father said, 'You don't know you're born, lad.' There was a slight touch of resentment in the tone and the look they exchanged had no friendliness in it. Then Paddy, nodding towards Bill

Waggett, said, 'What did you tell me the other day about when you worked in the soda works, Bill?'

'Oh that. Well'—Bill brought his eyes to rest on Rory—'couldn't breathe there. If you were a few minutes late you were fined, and if it was a quarter of an hour, like it might be in winter when you couldn't fight your way through the snow, why man, they stopped a quarter day's pay. And if you dared to talk about your work outside you were fined ten bob the first time, then given the push if it happened twice. That's a fact. It is, it is. An' you might be sayin' nowt of any account. And if anybody covered up for you when you were late . . . oh my God! they were in for it. You know what? They had to pay the fine, the same fine as you paid. You were treated like a lot of bairns: back-chat the foreman and it was half a dollar fine. My God! I had to get out of there. You see, Rory, as your da says, you don't know you're born being a rent collector. Your da did something for you lettin' you learn to read. By! aye, he did. It's somethin' when you can earn your livin' without dirtyin' your hands.'

Rory was flicking the cards over the flowered oilcloth that covered the wooden table. His head was lowered and his lids were lowered, the expression in his eyes was hidden, but his lips were set straight.

Jimmy, as always sensing his brother's mood, turned to Collum Leary and said, 'It's a pity our Rory isn't in America along with your Michael and James and on one of them boats that ply the river, like Michael said, where they can gamble in the open.'

'Aye, it is that, Jimmy,' Collum laughed at him. 'He'd make his fortune.' He turned and pushed Rory in the shoulder with his doubled fist, adding, 'Why don't you go to America, Rory, now why don't you?'

'I just might, I just might.' Rory was now fanning out the cards in his hand. 'It would suit me that, down to the ground it would. A gamblin' boat. . . .'

'Gamblin', cards, fortunes made in America, that's all you hear.' With the exception of Rory the men turned and looked towards Lizzie O'Dowd, where she had risen from her chair, and she nodded at them, continuing, 'Nobody is ever satisfied. Take what God sends an' be thankful.' Then her tone changing, she laughed as she added, 'He's gona send you cold brisket this minute. Who wants pickled onions with it?'

There were gabbled answers and laughter from the table and when she turned away and walked down the room past the chiffonier, past the dess-bed that stood in an alcove, and into the scullery, Janie, too, turned and followed her into the cluttered cramped space and closed the door after her.

Hunching her shoulders upwards against the cold, Janie picked up a knife and began cutting thick slices off a large crusty loaf. She had almost finished cutting the bread before she spoke. Her head still bent, she said quietly, 'Don't worry, Lizzie, he won't go to America.'

'Aw, I know that, lass, I know that. It's me temper gets the better of me.' She turned from hacking lumps of meat from the brisket bone and, looking full at Janie, she said, 'It's funny, isn't it, it's funny, but you understand, lass, don't you?'

'Aye, I understand, Lizzie. Aw, don't worry, he understands an' all.'

'I wish I could think so.'

'He does, he does.'

Lizzie now put the knife down on the table and, bringing one plump hand up, she pressed it tightly across her chin as she remarked, 'I'm not a bad woman, Janie, I never was.'

'Aw, Lizzie, Lizzie.' Janie, her arms outstretched now, put them around the fat warm body of Lizzie O'Dowd, whom she had known and loved since she was a child; even before her own mother had died she had loved Lizzie O'Dowd as if she were a second mother, or perhaps she had placed her first, she was never quite certain in her own mind; and now, their cheeks pressed close for a moment, she whispered,

'It'll all come right. It'll all come right in the end, you'll see.'

'Aye, yes. Yes, you're right, lass.' Lizzie turned her head away as she roughly swept the tears from her cheeks with the side of her finger. Then picking up the knife again and her head bowed once more, she muttered, 'I think the world of Ruth an' I always have. She's the best of women. . . . Life isn't easy, Janie.'

'I know it isn't, Lizzie. And Ruth's fond of you, you know she is. She couldn't do without you. None of us could do without you.'

'Ah, lass.' Lizzie was smiling now, a denigrating smile. 'Everybody can be done without.' She gave a short laugh. 'Have a walk around the cemetery the next time you're out.'

'Aw, Lizzie—' Janie was leaning against her shoulder now laughing—'you're the limit. You know, every time I feel down I think of you.'

'Huh, that's a left-handed compliment if ever I heard one: When you're down you think of me. You can't get much lower than down, can you?'

'You!' Janie now pushed her. 'You know what I mean. Look, is that enough bread?'

'That! It wouldn't fill a holey tooth; you'd better start on another loaf. . . How is that nice family of yours?'

'Oh, lovely as always, lovely. Eeh! you know I often wonder what would have become of me, I mean what kind of job I would've got in the end. I'd likely have landed up in some factory, like most others, if I hadn't had that bit of luck. Life's so different there, the furniture, the food, everything. The way they talk, the master and mistress, I mean. Do you under-stand, Lizzie? You know I'm not bein' an upstart but I like bein' there. Mind you, that's not to say I don't like comin' home; I love coming home, even when I know me grannie is goin' to choke me with words and her bloomin' old sayin's. Eeh! the things that she remembers.' They were laughing again. Then she ended, 'But there's different kinds of life . . . I mean livin', Lizzie. You know what I mean?'

'Aye, lass, I know what you mean, although I've never lived any other kind of life but this and I don't want to, not for meself I don't, but for you and . . . and others. Yes, yes, I know what you mean.' She now placed portions of the meat on the slices of dry bread which she then stacked on a plate. Patting the last one, she exclaimed, 'Well now, let's go and feed the five thousand an' find out if it's tea they want or if they're goin' to get the cans on.'

In the kitchen once more, Lizzie slapped down the heaped plate of meat and bread in the middle of the table, saying, 'Is it tea or are you gettin' the cans on?'

The men glanced furtively from one to the other, their eyes asking a question. Then Paddy and Bill turned simultaneously and looked towards the women, and as usual it was Lizzie who answered them, crying loudly now, 'There's none of us goin' trapesing down there the night an' it fit to cut the lugs off you. If you want your beer there's the cans.' She thrust out her thick arm and pointed towards four assorted cans, their lids dangling by pieces of string from the handles.

The men made no answer but still continued to look towards the women, and then Ruth spoke. Quietly and in levelled tones, she said, 'It's Sunday.'

The men sighed and turned back to the table again, and Bill Waggett muttered under his breath, 'An' that's that then. Bloody Sunday. You know'—he glanced up from the cards and, catching Jimmy's attention, he nodded at him, saying softly, 'I hate Sundays. I always have hated Sundays ever since I was a lad 'cos she kept me going harder on a Sunday than when I was at work.' He had inclined his head backwards towards the fire-place and had hardly finished speaking when his mother, her dewlap chin wobbling, cried across the room, 'Lazy bugger! you always were. Wouldn't even kick when you were born; slid out like a dead fly on hot fat.'

As the roars of laughter filled the kitchen Bill Waggett turned towards his mother and yelled, 'That's a fine thing to say; you should be ashamed of yersel.' He now looked towards Ruth as if apologizing, but she was being forced to smile, and Ruth rarely smiled or laughed at ribaldry.

'Remember the day he was born.' Old Mrs Waggett had got their attention now. 'Me mother an' me grannie pulled him out, an' I remember me grannie's very words. "Like a Saturday night rabbit he is," she said. You know'—she turned towards Janie—'when the last of the rabbits are left in the market, all weary skin an' bone? "You'll never rear him," she said; "he'll go along with the other five." But I never had no luck, he didn't.'

She now glanced in impish affection towards her son, where he was sitting, his head bowed, moving it slowly from side to side. The movement had a despairing finality about it. His mother had started and it would take some kind of an event to stop her, especially when as now she had the ears of everyone in the room. He could never understand why people liked listening to her.

'And it was me own mother who looked at him lying across her hands an' said, "I don't think you need worry about the press gang ever chasin' him, Nancy." An' you know somethin'? The press gang nearly got me dad once. Around seventeen ninety it was. I'm not sure of the year, one, two or three, but I do know that all the lads of the Tyne, the sailors like, put their heads together; they were havin' no more of it. They ran the press gang out of the town, North Shields that is, not this side. Then in come the regiment. Barricaded the town, they did, an' forced the lads on board the ships. But me dad managed to get over to this side of the water; he said himself he never knew how.'

'He walked on it.'

There were loud guffaws of laughter now and Gran cried back at her son, 'Aye, an' he could have done that an' all, for at one time you could walk across the river. Oh aye, they once made a bridge with boats, me mother said, and laid planks over 'em, and a whole regiment passed over. The river's changed.' She nodded from one to the other. 'You know, me grannie once told me they caught so much salmon on the Tyne that it was sold at a farthin' a pound. It was, it was. Can you believe that? A farthin' a pound!'

'Yes, yes, Gran.' All except her son were nodding at her.

'And I don't need to go as far back as me grannie's or even me mother's time to remember the great shoals of fish that were caught in these waters. An' there were nowt but keels and sailin' ships takin' the coal away then. None of your Palmer's iron boats. What did you say, our Bill?' She frowned towards her son. ' "Oh my God!" that's what you said. Well, I'm glad you think of Him as yours.'

She joined in the titter that now went round the room. Then nodding her head from one to the other, she went on, 'Talkin' of coal. I can remember as far back as when Simon Temple opened his pit at Jarrow. I was only eight at the time but by! I remember that do. The militia was marching, the bands playing, an' when he got to Shields market the lads pulled the horses from his carriage and drew him themselves. His sons were with him and his old dad. They pulled them all the way to the Don Bridge, where the gentlemen of Jarrow met him. And that was the day they laid the stone for the school for the bairns of his workmen. By! I remember it as if it was yesterday. Simon Temple.' She shook her head and lapsed for a moment into the memory of one of the rare days of jollification in her childhood.

In the pause that followed Collum Leary put in, 'Simon Temple. Aye, an' all the bloody coal owners. Grand lads, grand fellows, great gentlemen. Oh aye, especially when they're shedding crocodile tears over

22

the dead. Ninety-nine men and lads lost in the Fellon pit and over twenty at Harrington. . . .'

'That was a long time ago, Collum.' Grannie Waggett thrust her chin out at the small man who had usurped her position of storyteller and he turned on her, no longer jocular as he cried, 'Don't be daft, Gran. It's happenin' almost every month in one pit or t'other. Don't be daft, woman.'

'Leave be. Leave be.' It was the first time Kathleen Leary had spoken and her husband looked at her as he repeated, 'Leave be, leave be, you say. Bloody coal owners!'

The mood of the kitchen had changed as it nearly always did when the subject of work was brought up, whether it was Paddy Connor talking of the steel works or Bill Waggett of the conditions in the docks, or Collum Leary of the soul destroying work in the mines; and nearly always it was on a Sunday when the atmosphere would become charged with bitterness because nearly always on a Sunday Grannie Waggett was present.

'Come on, Gran.' Janie had taken hold of her grandmother's arm.

'What! What you after? Leave me be.'

'It's time we were goin' in.' Janie nodded towards the wall. 'An' I'll soon be making for the road.'

Grannie Waggett stared up into Janie's face for a moment. Then her head nodding, she said, 'Aye, aye, lass; I forgot you'll soon be making for the road. Well—' She pulled herself up out of the chair saying now, 'Where's me shawl?'

Janie brought the big black shawl from where it had been draped over the head of a three-seated wooden saddle standing against the far wall pressed between a battered chest of drawers and a surprisingly fine Dutch wardrobe.

The old woman now nodded, first to Ruth, then to Nellie, then to Lizzie, and finally to Kathleen Leary, and to each she said, 'So long,' and each answered her kindly, saying, 'So long, Gran,' and as she made for the door with Janie behind her, Lizzie called to her, 'Put the oven shelf in the bed, you'll need it the night.'

'I will, I will. Oh my God! look at that,' she cried, as she opened the door. 'It's comin' down thicker than ever.' She turned her head and looked into the room again. 'We're in for it, another window-sill winter. I can smell it.'

Janie had taken an old coat from the back of the door and as she hugged it around her she glanced back towards the table and Rory, and when she said, 'Half an hour?' he smiled and nodded at her.

'Go on, Gran, go on; you'll blow them all out.' Janie went to press her grandmother on to the outer step, but the old lady resisted firmly, saying, 'Stop a minute. Stop a minute. Look, there's somebody coming in at the gate.'

Janie went to her side and peered into the darkness. Then again looking back into the room, she cried, 'It's John George.'

Rising slowly from the table and coming towards the door, Rory said, 'He wasn't coming the night; he mustn't have been able to see her.'

'Hello, John George.'

'Hello there, Janie.' John George Armstrong stood scraping his boots on the iron ring attached to the wall as he added, 'Hello there, Gran.'

And Gran's reply was, 'Well, come on in if you're comin' an' let us out, else I'll be frozen stiffer than a corpse.'

Janie now pressed her grannie none too gently over the step and as she passed John George she said, 'See you later, John George.'

'Aye, see you later, Janie,' he replied before entering the kitchen and closing the door behind him and replying to a barrage of greetings.

Having hung his coat and hard hat on the back of the door he took his place at the table, and Rory asked briefly, 'What went wrong?'

'Oh, the usual. . . . You playing cards?' The

obvious statement was a polite way of telling the company that he didn't wish to discuss the reason for his unexpected presence among them tonight, and they accepted this.

'Want to come in?'

'What do you think?'

As John George and Rory exchanged a tight smile Bill Waggett said, 'You'd better tighten your belt, lad, an' hang on to your trousers 'cos he's in form the night. Cleared me out of monkey nuts.'

'No!'

'Oh aye. We were sayin' he should go to America and make his fortune on one of them boats.'

'He needn't go as far as that, Mr Waggett, there's plenty of games goin' on in Shields and across the water, and they tell me that fortunes are made up in Newcastle.'

'Gamblin'! That's all anybody hears in this house, gamblin'. Do you want a mug of tea?' Lizzie was bending over John George, and he turned his long thin face up to her and smiled at her kindly as he answered, 'It would be grand, Lizzie.'

'Have you had anything to eat?'

'I've had me tea.'

'When was that?'

'Oh. Oh, not so long ago.'

'Have you a corner for a bite?'

'I've always got a corner for a bite, Lizzie.' Again he smiled kindly at her, and she pushed him roughly, saying, 'Death warmed up, that's what you look like. Good food's lost on you. Where does it go? You haven't a pick on your bones.'

'Thoroughbreds are always lean, Lizzie.'

As she turned and walked away towards the scullery she said, 'They should have put a brick on yer head when you were young to make you grow sideways instead of up.'

The game proceeded with its usual banter until the door opened again and Janie entered, fully dressed now for the road in a long brown cloth coat to which was attached a shoulder cape of the same material. It was an elegant coat and like all the clothes she now wore had been passed on to her from her mistress. Her hat, a brown velour, with a small flat brim, was perched high on the top of her head, and its colour merged with the shining coils of her hair. The hat was held in place by two velvet ribbons coming from beneath the brim and tied under her chin. She had fine woollen gloves on her hands. The only articles of her apparel which did not point to taste were her boots. These were heavy-looking and buttoned at the side. It was very unfortunate, Jane considered, that her feet should be two sizes bigger than her mistress's, yet she always comforted herself with the thought that her skirt and coat covered most parts of her boots and there was ever only the toes showing, except when she was crossing the muddy roads and the wheels of the carts and carriages were spraying clarts all over the place.

'Eeh! by! you look bonny.' Lizzie came towards her, but before reaching her she turned to Rory, who was rising from the table, saying, 'You going to keep her waiting all night? Get a move on.'

The quick jerk of Rory's head, the flash of his eyes and the further straightening of his lips caused Janie to say quickly, 'There's plenty of time, there's plenty of time. I've got a full hour afore I'm due in. Look, it's only eight o'clock.'

'It'll take you all that to walk from here to Westoe an' the streets covered.'

'No, it won't, Lizzie. When I get goin' George Wilson, the Newcastle walker, or me grannie's fusiliers aren't in it.' She now swung her arms and did a standing march and ended, 'Grenadier Waggett, the woman walker from Wallsend!' Then stopping abruptly amid the laughter, she looked to where John George was taking his coat from the back of the door, and she asked flatly, 'You're not comin' surely? You haven't been here five minutes.'

'I've got to get back, Janie, me Uncle Willy's not too good.'

'Was he ever?'

The aside came from Lizzie and as Ruth went to admonish her with a quick shake of her head Rory turned on her a look that could only be described as rage, for it was contorting his features. He did not shout at her, but his low tone conveyed his feelings more than if he had bawled as he said, 'Will you hold your tongue, woman, an' mind your own business for once!'

Strangely Lizzie did not turn on him, but she looked at him levelly for a moment and countered his anger with almost a placid expression as she said, 'I've spent me life mindin' me own business, lad, an' me own business is to take care of those I'm concerned for, and I'm concerned for John George there. That uncle and aunt of his live off him. And what I'm sayin' now I've said afore to his face, haven't I, John George?'

'You have that, Lizzie. And I like you mindin' me business, it's a comforter.'

'There you are.' She nodded towards Rory, who now had his back to her as he made his way down the long narrow room towards the ladder at the end that led into the loft, which place was Jimmy's and his bedroom and had been since they were children, one end of it at one time having been curtained off to accommodate Nellie.

With no further words, Lizzie now went into the scullery, and Janie began saying her good-byes. When she came to Nellie she bent over her and said below her breath, 'You all right, Nellie?'

'Aye. Aye, Janie, I'm all right.'

Janie stared down into the peaked face; she knew Nellie wasn't all right, she had never been all right since she married. Nellie's marriage frightened her. Charlie Burke had courted Nellie for four years and was never off the doorstep, and Sunday after Sunday they had laughed and larked on like bairns in this

27

very room. But not any more, not since she had been married but a few months. It was something to do with—the bedroom. Neither her grannie nor Lizzie had spoken to her about it and, of course, it went without saying that Ruth wouldn't mention any such thing. But from little bits that she had overheard between Lizzie and her grannie she knew Nellie's trouble lay in—the bedroom, and the fact that she had not fallen with a bairn and her all of three years married. Charlie Burke rarely came up to the house any more on a Sunday. Of course he had an excuse; he worked on the coal boats and so could be called out at any time to take a load up the river.

Janie now went into the kitchen to say good-bye to Lizzie.

Lizzie was standing with her hands holding the rim of the tin dish that rested on a little table under the window, which sloped to the side as if following the line of the roof.

'I'm off then Lizzie.'

Without turning and her voice thick and holding a slight tremor, Lizzie said in answer, 'He's a bloody upstart. Do you know that, Janie? He's a bloody snot. I'm sorry to say this, lass, but he is.'

'He's not; you know he's not, Lizzie.' She shook her head at the older woman. 'An' you're as much to blame as he is. Now yes you are.' She bent sidewards and wagged her finger into the fat face, and Lizzie, her eyes blinking rapidly, put out her hand and touched the cream skin that glowed with health and youth and said, 'Lass, you're too good for him. And it isn't the day or yesterday I've said it, now is it? He's damned lucky.'

'So am I, Lizzie.'

'Aw, lass.' Lizzie smiled wryly. 'You'd say thank you if you were dished up with a meat puddin' made of lights, you would that.'

'Well, and why not? And it wouldn't be the first time I've eaten lights.'

They pushed against each other with their hands;

then Janie said, 'Remember that starving Christmas? How old was I? Ten, eleven? No work, strikes, trouble. Eeh! we had lights all right then. Me grannie cooked them seven different ways every week.' She paused and they looked at each other. 'Bye-bye, Lizzie.'

Spontaneously now Janie put her arms around Lizzie and kissed her, and Lizzie hugged her to herself. It was an unusual demonstration of affection. People didn't go kissing and clarting on in public, it wasn't proper; everybody knew that, even among engaged couples kissing and clarting on was kept for the dark country lanes, or if you were from the town, and common, a back lane or shop doorway; the only proper place for kissing and clarting on was a front room, if you had one; if not, well then you had to wait for the bedroom, as every respectable person knew. She was going to wait for the bedroom, by aye she was that, even although she wasn't all that taken with what she understood happened in the bedroom.

She now disengaged herself and went hurriedly from the scullery, leaving Lizzie once more gripping each side of the tin dish.

Rory and John George were already dressed for outdoors and waiting for her, Rory, although not short by any means, being all of five foot ten, looking small against John George's lean six foot.

John George wore a black overcoat that had definitely not been made for him. Although the length was correct, being well below his knees, the shoulders were too broad, and the sleeves too short, his hands and arms hanging so far out of them that they drew attention to their thin nakedness. There was a distinct crack above the toecap of one of his well-polished boots and a patch in a similar place on the other. His hard hat was well brushed but had a slight greeny tinge to it. His whole appearance gave the impression of clean seediness, yet his position as rent collector in the firm of Septimus Kean was superior to that of Rory, for whereas Rory had only worked for Mr Kean for four years John George had been with him for eight. Now, at twenty-two years of age and a year younger than Rory, he showed none of the other's comparative opulence for Rory wore a dark grey overcoat over a blue suit, and he had a collar to his shirt, and he did not wear his scarf like a muffler but overlapping on his chest like a business gentleman would have worn it. And although he wore a cap—he only wore his hard hat for business—it wasn't like a working man's cap, perhaps it was only the angle at which he wore it that made it appear different.

Looking at him as always with a feeling of pride welling in her, Janie thought, He can get himself up as good as the master.

'Well then, off you go.' Ruth seemed to come to the fore for the first time. She escorted them all to the door and there she patted Janie on the back, saying, 'Until next Sunday then, lass?'

'Yes, Mrs Connor, until next Sunday. You'll give a look in on her?' She nodded towards the next cottage and Ruth said, 'Of course, of course. Don't worry about her. You know'—she smiled faintly—'I think she'll still be here when we're all pushing the daisies up.'

'I shouldn't wonder.' Janie went out laughing, calling over her shoulder, 'Ta-rah. Ta-rah everybody. Ta-rah.'

Out in the black darkness they had difficulty in picking their way in single file down the narrow rutted lane. When they reached the broader road they stopped for a moment and Rory, kicking the snow aside with his foot, said, 'By! it's thick. If it goes on like this we'll have a happy day the morrow, eh?'

'I'd rather have it than rain,' John George replied; 'at least it's dry for a time. It's the wet that gets me down, day after day, day after day.'

'Here, hang on.' Rory now pulled Janie close to

him and linked her arm in his. 'It's comin' down thicker than ever. Can't even see a light in the docks. We'll find ourselves in the ditch if we're not careful.'

Stumbling on, her side now pressed close to Rory's, Janie began to giggle; then turning her head, she cried, 'Where are you, John George?'

'I'm here.' The voice came from behind them and she answered, 'Give me your hand. Come on.'

As she put her hand out gropingly and felt John George grip it, Rory said, 'Let him fend for himself, he's big enough. You keep your feet, else I'm tellin' you we'll be in the ditch.'

It took them all of twenty minutes before they reached Tyne Dock, and there, taking shelter under the last arch, they stopped and drew their breath, and Janie, looking towards a street lamp opposite the dock gates, said, 'Isn't it nice to see a light?'

'And you can just see it and that's all. Come on, we'd better be goin'. It's no use standin', we soon won't be able to get through.'

As Rory went to pull Janie forward she checked him, saying, 'Look, wait a minute. It's daft, you know, you walkin' all the way to Westoe, you've only got to tramp all the way back. It isn't so bad in the town 'cos there's the lights, but from the bottom of the bank up to our place . . . well, we've just had some, haven't we? An' if it keeps on, as you say it'll get worse underfoot, so what's the sense of trapesing all the way there with me when John George's place is only five minutes away?'

'She's right, Rory. It's daft to tramp down all the way to Westoe for it'll be another couple of hours afore you get back. And then with it coming down like this. Well, as Janie says . . .'

Rory peered from one to the other before he answered, 'Imagine the reception I'd get if I told them back there I'd left you at the arches. They'd wipe the kitchen with me.'

'But you're not leavin' me at the arches; John George'll see me right to the door. Look.' She turned and pushed John George away, saying, 'Go on, walk on a bit, I'll catch up with you in a minute at the Dock gates.'

When John George walked swiftly from the shelter of the arch Rory called, 'Hold your hand a minute . . .'

'Now just you look here.' Janie pulled at the lapels of his coat. 'Don't be such a fathead; I'd rather know you were safely back home in the dry than have you set me to the door.'

'But I won't see you for another week.'

'That didn't seem to bother you all afternoon, 'cos you've done nowt but play cards.'

'Well, what can you do back there? I ask you, what can you do? There's no place to talk and I couldn't ask you out in the freezing cold or they'd've been at me. And I wanted to talk to you, seriously like 'cos it's . . . it's time we thought about doin' something. Don't you think it is?'

She kept her head on the level, her eyes looking into his as she replied, 'If you want a straight answer, Mr Connor, aye, I do.'

'Aw, Janie!' He pulled her roughly to him and pressed his mouth on hers and when she over-balanced and her back touched the curved wall of the arch she pulled herself from him, saying, 'Eeh! me coat, it'll get all muck.'

'Blast your coat!'

Her voice soft now, she said, 'Aye, blast me coat,' then she put her mouth to his again and they stood, their arms gripped tight around each other, their faces merged.

When again she withdrew herself from him he was trembling and he gulped in his throat before saying, 'Think about it this week, will you?'

'It's you that's got to do the thinking, Rory. We've got to get a place an' furniture 'cos there's one thing I can tell you sure, I'm not livin' in with me dad and grannie. I'm not startin' that way up in the loft. I

32

want a house that I can make nice with things an'
that . . .'

'As if I would ask you. What do you take me for?'

'I'm only tellin' you, I want a decent place . . .'

'I'm with you there all the way. I'm not for one
room an' a shakydown either, I can tell you that . . .
I've got something in me napper.'

'Gamblin'?'

'Well, aye. And don't say it like that; I haven't
done too badly out of it, have I now? But what I'm
after is to get set on in a good school . . . A big
school. And there's plenty about. But you've got to
be in the know.'

'What! be in the know afore you can get into a
gamblin' school?' Her voice was scornful. 'Why,
you've been up at Boldon Colliery where they have
schools . . .'

'Aye in the back yards an' in the wash-houses. I
know all about Boldon Colliery and the games there,
but they're tin pot compared to what I'm after. The
places I mean are where you start with a pound, not
with a penny hoping to win a tanner. Oh, aye, I
know, there's times when there's been ten pounds in
a kitty, but them times are few and far between I'm
telling you. No, what I'm after is getting set on in a
real school, but it's difficult because of the polis,
they're always on the look out—it's a tricky business
even for the back-laners. That's funny,' he laughed,
'a tricky business, but it is. Remember what Jimmy
said the night about notices in the works? They try
everything to catch you out: spies, plain-clothes
bobbies, touts. It's odd, you know; they don't run
you in for drinking, but you touch a card or flick a
coin and you're for it . . . Anyway, as I said, I've got
something in me napper, and if it works out . . .'

'Be careful, Rory. I . . . I get worried about your
gamin'. Even years ago when you used to play chucks
and always won, I used to wonder how you did it.
And it used to worry me; I mean 'cos you always won.'

'I don't always win now.'

'You do pretty often, even if it's only me da's monkey nuts.'

They both made small audible sounds, then moved aside to let a couple of men pass. And now she said, 'I'll have to be goin', John George'll get soaking wet . . . Eeh! I always feel sorry for John George.'

'Your pity's wasted, he's too soft to clag holes with, I'm always telling him. It's right what she said'—he jerked his head—'those two old leeches suck him dry. He gets two shillings a week more than me and yet look at him, you'd think he got his togs from Paddy's market. And he might as well for he picks them up from the second-hand stalls. And this lass he's after . . . he would pick on a ranter, wouldn't he?'

'Well, he's not a Catholic.'

'No, I know he's not. He's not anything in that line, but he goes and takes up with one from the narrowest end of the Nonconformists, Baptist-cum-Methodist-cum . . .'

'What's she like?'

'I don't know.'

'Doesn't he talk about her at all?'

'Oh, he never stops talkin' about her. By the sound of it she should be a nun.'

'Oh Rory!'

'She should, she's so bloomin' good by all his accounts. She's been unpaid housekeeper to a sick mother, her dad, two sisters and a brother since she was ten. And now she's twenty, and she daresn't move across the door for fear of her old man. He even escorts his other two lasses to work. They're in a chemist's shop and he's there when it closes to fetch them home.'

'What is he?'

'He's got a little tailor's business, so I understand. But look, forget about John George for a minute. Come here.' Once again they were close, and when finally they parted he said, 'Remember what I said. Think on it and we'll settle it next Sunday, eh?'

'Yes, Rory.' Her voice was soft. 'I'm ready anytime

34

you are, I've been ready for a long time. Oh, a long time . . . I want a home of me own . . .'

He took her face gently between his hands and as gently kissed her, and she, after staring at him for a moment, turned swiftly and ran from under the arch and over the snow-covered flags until she came to John George, who was standing pressed tight against the dock wall. She did not speak to him and together they turned and hurried on, past a line of bars arrayed on the opposite side of the road, and so into Eldon Street.

Her throat was full. It was strange but she always wanted to cry when Rory was tender with her. Generally, there was a fierceness about his love-making that frightened her at times, it was when he was tender that she loved him best.

'Daft of him wanting to come all this way.'

'Yes, it was, John George.'

'Of course I was just thinking that if I hadn't have come along he would have taken you all the way, and that, after all, was what he wanted. I'm blind about some things some times.'

She was kind enough to say, 'Not you, John George,' for she had thought it a bit short-sighted of him to accompany them in the first place, and she added, 'Don't worry. And you know what? We're goin' to settle something next Sunday.'

'You are? Oh, I'm glad, Janie. I'm glad. I've thought for a long time he should have a place of his own 'cos he doesn't seem quite happy back there. And yet I can't understand it for they're a good family, all of them, and I like nothing better than being among them.'

'Oh! What makes you think that? What makes you think he's not happy at home, John George?'

'Well, he's surly like at times. And I get vexed inside when I hear the way he speaks to Lizzie 'cos she's a nice body, isn't she . . . Lizzie? I like her . . . motherly, comfortable. Yet . . . yet at times he treats her like dirt. And I can't understand it, 'cos he's not

35

like that outside, I mean when he's collecting; he's civility's own self, and all the women like him. You know that, don't you? All the women like him, 'cos he's got a way with him. But the way he speaks to Lizzie . . .'

Janie paused in her walk and, putting her hand on John George's arm, she drew him to a stop. Then flicking the falling snow away from her eyes, she asked quietly, 'Don't you know why he goes on at Lizzie like that?'

'No.'

'He's never told you?'

'No.'

'You mean he's never told you an' you've been workin' with him and coming up to the house for . . . how many years?'

'Four and over.'

'Eeh! I can't believe it. I thought you knew.'

'Knew what?'

'Well, that . . . that Lizzie, she's . . . she's his mother.'

'*Lizzie*?' He bent his long length down to her. 'Lizzie Rory's mother? No! How does that come about? I don't believe it.'

'It's true. It's true. Come on, don't let us stand here, we'll be soaked.'

'What . . . what about Mrs Connor? I mean . . . his mother . . . I mean.'

'It's all very simple, John George, when you know the ins and outs of it. You see they were married, Mr and Mrs Connor for six years an' there was no sign of any bairn. Then Mr Connor gets a letter from Ireland from a half-cousin he had never seen. Her name was Lizzie O'Dowd. Her ma and da had died— as far as I can gather from starvation. It was one of those times when the taties went bad, you know, and this lass was left with nobody, and she asked if she could come over here and would he find her a job. Everybody seemed to be comin' to England, particularly to Jarrow. They were leaving Ireland in boatloads. So what does Mr Connor do but say come right over. By the way, she had got the priest to write 'cos she couldn't write a scribe and Mr Connor went to a fellow in Jarrow who made a sort of livin' at writing letters an' sent her the answer. It was this by the way, Mr Connor having to go an' get this letter written, that later made him see to it that Rory could read and write. Anyway, Lizzie O'Dowd arrives at the cottage. She's seventeen an' bonny, although you mightn't think it by the look of her now. But I'm goin' by what me grannie told me. And what's more she was full of life and gay like. Anyway, the long and the short of it is that she and Mr Connor . . . Well, I don't need to tell you any more, do I? And so Rory came about. But this is the funny part about it. Almost a year later Ruth had her first bairn. That was Nellie. And then she has another. That was Jimmy. Would you believe it? After nothing for seven years! Eeh! it was odd. And, of course, we were all brought up as one family. You could say the three families in the row were all dragged up together.'

As she laughed John George said solemnly, 'You surprise me, Janie. It's quite a gliff.'

'But you don't think any the worse of Lizzie, do you?'

'Me think any the worse of . . . ? Don't be daft. Of course I don't. But at the same time I'm back where I started for I understand less now than I did afore, Rory speaking to her like that and her his mother.'

'But he didn't always know that she was his mother. It was funny that.' She was silent for a moment, before going on, 'There was us, all the squad of the Learys, me da, me ma, and me grannie. Well, you know me grannie, her tongue would clip clouts. But nobody, not one of us, ever hinted to him that Mrs Connor wasn't his mother, it never struck us. I think we sort of thought that he knew, that somebody must have told him earlier on. But nobody had; not until six years ago when he was seventeen and it was Lizzie herself who let the cat out of the bag. You know, Lizzie is one of those women who can't carry drink. Give her a couple of gins and she's away; she'll argue with her own fingernails after a couple of gins. And it was on a New Year's Eve, and you know what it's like on a New Year's Eve. She got as full as a gun an' started bubbling, and Rory, who up till that time had been very fond of her, even close to her, when she hadn't got a drink on her, 'cos this is another funny thing about him, he can't stand women in drink. Well, I don't remember much about it 'cos I was only a lass at the time, but as I recall, we were all in the Connors' kitchen. It was around three o'clock in the morning and I was nearly asleep when I hear Lizzie blurting out, "Don't speak to me like that, you young . . . !" She called him a name. And then she yelled, "I'm your mother! Her there, Ruth there, never had it in her to give breath to a deaf mute till I went an' had you." And that was that. From then on he never has been able to stand her. An' the pity of it is she loves him. He went missing for a week after that. Then he turned up one night half starved, frozen, and in the end he had the pneumonia. He had been sleeping rough, and in January mind. It's a wonder it didn't kill him. Now do you begin to understand?'

'I'm flabbergasted, Janie. To think that I've known him all this time and he's never let on. And we talk you know, we do; I thought we knew everything there was to know about each other. Me, I tell him everything.' The tall length drooped forward. His head bent against the driving snow, he muttered now, 'I'm that fond of Rory, Janie, 'cos, well, he's all I'd like to be and never will.'

'You're all right as you are, John George; I wouldn't have you changed.' Her voice was loud and strong in his defence.

'You wouldn't, Janie?' The question was almost eager, and she answered, 'No, I wouldn't, John George, because your heart's in the right place. An' that's something to be proud of.'

They walked on some way in silence now before she said quietly, 'I hope you don't mind me askin', but the lass you're gone on, why don't you bring her up to the kitchen?'

He didn't answer immediately but took her arm and led her across the road and up the street towards the beginning of Westoe and the select section of the town, where the big houses were bordered by their white railings and the roads were broad enough to take two carriages passing, and he said now, 'I wish I could, oh I wish I could 'cos she's nice, Janie, and bonny. Not as bonny as you, but she's bonny. And she's had a life of it. Aye, one hell of a life. And still has. Her da's got religion on the brain I think. Her mother's bedridden, and, you know, they spend Sunday praying round her bed, taking turns. The only time she's allowed out is on a Saturday afternoon when she's sent to Gateshead to visit an aunt who's dying and who seems to have a bit of money. Her da wants to make sure of who she's leaving it to and as he can't go up himself and the other two lasses are in jobs—there was a brother, Leonard, but he ran off to sea, and good luck to him I say— Anyway, Maggie is allowed to go to Gateshead on a Saturday afternoon. That's how I met her first, on one of me Saturday train jaunts.'

'You go on a train to Gateshead every Saturday? I didn't know that. Eeh! on a train . . .'

'Well'—he laughed self-consciously—'not every Saturday, only when funds allow. And then not to Gateshead, but Newcastle. I take the train up half-way, say to Pelaw, and walk the rest. I love Newcastle. Aw, lad, if I had the money I'd live there; I wouldn't mind rent collecting around Newcastle.'

'Aren't there any slums up there then?'

'Oh aye, Janie, plenty. But I don't look at the slums, it's the buildings I look at. There's some beautiful places, Janie. Haven't you ever been to Newcastle?'

'No, I've been across the water to North Shields

and Cullercoats, and once I went as far as Felling on this side, but no, I've never been to either Gateshead or Newcastle.'

'Rory should take you up, he should take you to a theatre.'

'There's a good theatre here, I mean in Shields.'

'Oh aye, it's all right, but it isn't like Newcastle.'

'They get the same turns, only a little later.'

'Oh, I'm not thinkin' about the turns, nothing like that, it's the buildings you know. I suppose it was a wrong thing to say that he should take you to a theatre, but I think he should take you up to Newcastle to see the lovely places there, the streets and buildings.'

'I never knew you liked that kind of thing, John George?'

'Oh aye, an' have ever since I was a lad. It was me da who started it. On holiday week-ends we'd walk up there. Me mother never came, she couldn't stand the distance and she wasn't interested in buildings. It was because of me da's interest in buildings and such that I was taught to read and write. He was standing looking up at a lovely front door once. They're called Regency. It was off Westgate Hill; it was a bonny piece of work with a lovely fanlight and the windows above had iron balconies to them when a man came alongside of us and started crackin'. And it turned out he worked in an architect's office and he seemed over the moon when he knew me da was interested in masonry and such and was leading me along the same lines. That was the first time I heard the name Grainger mentioned. He was the great builder of Newcastle. And John Dobson, he used to design for Grainger and others. I'd heard of the Grainger Market, and had been through it, but you don't think of who built these places. And then there's Grey Street. Eeh! there's a street for you. The best time to see it is on a Sunday when there's no carts or carriages packing it out and few people about.

By! it's a sight. As me da once said, that's what one man's imagination could do for a town.'

Janie now blew at the snow that was dusting her lips and turned her head towards him and blinked as she said, 'You're a surprise packet you are, John George. Do you ever talk to Rory about it?'

'Aye, sometimes. But Rory's not really interested in Newcastle or buildings and such.'

'No, no, he's not.' Janie's voice held a dull note now as she added, 'Cards, that's Rory's interest, cards. Eeh! he seems to think of nothing else.'

'He thinks of you.'

'Aye, he does, I must admit.' She was smiling at him through the falling snow and she added now, 'You've got me interested in Newcastle. I'll tell him . . . I'll tell him he's got to take me up.'

'Do that, Janie. Aye, do that. Tell him you want to see Jesmond. By! Jesmond's bonny. And the houses on the way . . . Eeh! lad, you see nothing like them here.'

'I think I'd like to see the bridges. I heard me da say there's some fine bridges. Funny me never ever havin' seen Newcastle and it only seven miles off. And there's me grannie. She worked there at one time, she was in service at a place overlooking the river. She used to keep talking about the boats laden down with coal going up to London. It was funny, she never liked Newcastle. She still speaks of the people there as if they were foreigners; she's always sayin' they kept the South Shields men down, wouldn't let them have their own shipping rights or nothing until a few years back. It's funny when you come to think of it, John George, we know more about the people from Ireland, like the Learys and Rory's folks, than we do about them up in Newcastle. I'm beginning to see the sense of some of me grannie's sayings; she always used to be saying, "You could be closer to a square head from Sweden than you could to a man with a barrow from Jarrow."'

41

John George laughed now, saying, 'I've never heard that one afore.'

'Oh, I think it's one of me grannie's make-up ones. You know, half the things she says I think she makes up. If she had ever been able to read or write she would have been a story teller. I've said that to her. Oh—' She sighed now and shook her gloved hands to bring the circulation back into her fingers as she said, 'We're nearly there.' Then on a little giggle, she added, 'If the missis was to see you she'd think I was leading a double life and she'd raise the riot act on me.'

As they stopped before a side gate that was picked out by the light from a street lamp she looked at John George, now blowing on his hands, and said with deep concern, 'Oh, you must be frozen stiff, John George. And no gloves.'

'Gloves!' His voice was high. 'You can see me wearin' gloves, I'd be taken for a dandy.'

'Don't be silly. You need gloves, especially goin' round in this weather, scribbling in rent books. At least you want mittens. I'll knit you a pair.'

He stood looking down on her for a long moment before saying, 'Well, if you knit me a pair of mittens, Janie, I'll wear them.'

'That's a bargain?'

'That's a bargain.'

'Thanks for comin' all this way, John George.'

'It's been my pleasure, Janie.'

'I . . . I hope you see your girl next week.'

'I hope so an' all. I . . . I'd like you to meet her. You'd like her, I know you'd like her, and what's more, well, being you you'd bring her out, 'cos she's quiet. You have that habit, you know, of bringing people out, making people talk. You got me talkin' the night all right about Newcastle.'

Janie stood for a moment blinking up at him and slightly embarrassed and affected by the tenderness of this lanky, kindly young fellow. His simple talking was having the same effect on her as Rory's gentle

42

touch had done. She felt near tears, she had the silly desire to lean forward and kiss him on the cheek just like a sister might. But that was daft; there was no such thing as sisterly kisses. That was another thing her grannie had said and she believed her. There were mothers' kisses and lovers' kisses but no sisterly kisses, not between a man and woman who weren't related anyway . . . Yet the master kissed his sister-in-law, she had seen him. Eeh! what was she standing here for? She said in a rush, 'Good night, John George. And thanks again, I'll see you next Sunday. Ta-rah.'

'Ta-rah, Janie.'

She hurried up the side path, but before opening the kitchen door she glanced back towards the gate and saw the dim outline of his figure silhouetted against the lamplight, and she waved to it; and he waved back; then she went into the house . . .

Mrs Tyler, the cook, turned from her seat before the fire, looked at Janie, then looked at the clock above the mantelpiece before saying, 'You've just made it.'

'There's three minutes to go yet.' Her retort was perky.

She wasn't very fond of Mrs Tyler. She had only been cook in the Buckhams' household for eighteen months but from the first she had acted as if she had grown up with the family. And what was more, Janie knew she was jealous of her own standing with the master and mistress.

The cook never said anything outright to her but she would talk at her through Bessie Rice, the housemaid, making asides such as 'Some people take advantage of good nature, they don't know their place. Don't you ever get like that, Bessie now. In Lady Beckett's household, where I did my trainin', the nursemaid might have her quarters up on the attic floor but below stairs she was considered bottom cellar steps. Of course, a governess was different. They were educated like. Why, in Lady

43

Beckett's the still-room maid sat well above the nursemaid.'

On the occasion when this particular remark was made, Janie had had more than enough of Lady Beckett for one day and so, walking out of the kitchen, she remarked to no one in particular, 'Lady Betty's backside!'

Of course she should never have said such a thing and she regretted it as soon as she was out of the door, and before she had reached the nursery she knew that the cook was knocking on the parlour door asking to speak to the mistress. Ten minutes later the mistress was up in the nursery looking terribly, terribly hurt as she said, 'Janie, I'm surprised at what the cook has been telling me. You must not use such expressions, because they may become a habit. Now just imagine what would happen if you said something like that in front of the children.' She had gulped and stood speechless before the young woman who had shown her nothing but kindness and when the mistress had gone she had laid her head in her arms on the table and cried her heart out until young Master David had started to cry with her, and then Margaret, and lastly the baby.

She looked back on that day as the most miserable in her life, and yet when she went to bed that night she had had to bury her head in the pillow to smother her laughter. Having earlier decided that feeling as she did she'd get no rest, she had gone downstairs to apologize to the mistress and to tell her that never again would she use such an expression in her house, and that she need not have any fear that the children's minds would ever be sullied by one word that she would utter.

She had reached the main landing when she was stopped by the sound of smothered laughter coming from the mistress's bedroom. The door was ajar and she could hear the master saying, 'Stop it. Stop it, Alicia, I can't hear you . . . what did she say?'

She had become still and stiff within an arm's

44

length of the door as her mistress's voice came to her spluttering with laughter the while she made an effort to repeat slowly: 'She ... said ... you ... can ... kiss ... Lady ... Beckett's ... backside.'

'She didn't!'

The laughter was joined now, high, spluttering; it was the kind of laughter that one heard in the Connors' kitchen when Lizzie said something funny.

'Well done, Waggett!'

There was more laughter, then the master's voice again saying, 'I can't stand Tyler. You want to get rid of her.'

'Oh, she's a good cook; I can't do that, David. And Janie mustn't be allowed to say things like that. But oh, I don't know how I kept my face straight.'

She had backed slowly towards the stairs, and when she reached the nursery floor her face split into one wide amazed grin; yet her mind was saying indignantly, 'I didn't say that. It's just like cook to stretch things. But eeh! the master, I've never heard him laugh like that afore. Nor the missis. They sounded like a young couple.'

It wasn't until she was in bed that she thought to herself, Well, I suppose they are a young couple. Yet at the same time it was strange to her to realize that people of their class could laugh together, spluttering laughter; for they always acted so very correct in front of other folk, even when the sister came. But then the sister was married to a man who had a cousin with a title, a sir, or a lord, or something, and, of course, she wouldn't expect them to act in any way but refinedly. But, anyway, they had laughed, and the mistress actually repeated what she herself had said, only, of course, with a bit added on by the cook.

And that night she had told herself yet once again that she liked her master and mistress, she did, she did, and she would do anything for them. And as she had recalled their laughter the bubbling had grown inside her, and to stop an hysterical outburst

45

she had turned and pressed her face tightly into the pillow. And her last thought before going to sleep had been, I'll have them roaring in the kitchen next Sunday. And she had.

2

It was the Saturday before Christmas; the sky lay low over the town and the masts of the ships were lost in grey mist.

Rory shivered as he walked up the church bank and entered Jarrow. He passed the row of white-washed cottages, then went on towards the main thoroughfare of Ellison Street. He hated this walk; he hated Saturday mornings; Saturday mornings meant Pilbey Street and Saltbank Row. Pilbey Street was bad enough but the Row was worse.

He had six calls in Pilbey Street and fifteen in the Row, and as always when he entered the street he steeled himself, put on a grim expression and squared his shoulders, while at the same time thinking, Old Kean and those other landlords he represents should be lynched for daring to ask rent for these places.

For four years now he had collected the rents in these two streets. In the ordinary way he should have collected them on Monday, Tuesday or Wednesday because on these days he came this way collecting, and right on into Hebburn, but you couldn't get a penny out of anybody in Pilbey Street or the Row on any other day but a Saturday morning. And you were lucky if you managed to get anything then; it was only fear of the bums that made them tip up.

He lifted the iron knocker and rapped on the paint-cracked knobless door. There was a noise of children either fighting or playing coming from behind it, and after a few minutes it was opened and three pairs of eyes from three filthy faces peered up at him. All had running noses, all had scabs around their mouths and styes on their eyes. The eldest, about five, said in the voice of an adult, 'Aw, the rent man.' Then scrambling away through the room with the others following him, he shouted, 'The rent man, Ma! 'Tis the rent man, Ma!'

'Tell the bugger I'm not in.'

The woman's voice came clearly to Rory and when the child came back and, looking up at him, said, 'She's not in,' Rory looked down on the child and as if addressing an adult said, 'Tell her the bugger wants the rent, and somethin' off the back, or else it's the bums Monday.'

The child gazed at him for a moment longer before once more scrambling away through the room, and when his thin high voice came back to him, saying, 'He says, the bugger wants the rent,' Rory closed his eyes, bowed his head and pressed his hand over his mouth, knowing that it would be fatal to let a smile appear on his face with the two pairs of eyes survey-ing him. If he once cracked a smile in this street he'd never get a penny.

It was almost three minutes later when the woman stood before him. She had a black shawl crossed over her sagging breasts, the ends were tucked into a filthy ragged skirt, and in a whining tone and a smile widening her flat face she exclaimed, 'Aw begod! it's you, Mr Connor. Is it the rent you're after? Well now. Well now. You know it's near Christmas it is, and you know what Christmas is for money. Chews it, it does, chews it. An' look at the bairns. There's not a stitch to their arses an' himself been out of work these last three weeks.'

Without seeming to move a muscle of his face Rory said, 'He's in the rolling mills and never lost a day this six months, I've checked. You're ten weeks in arrears not countin' the day. Give me five shillings and I'll say nothing more 'til next week when I want the same and every week after that until you get your book clear. If not, I go to Palmer's and he'll get the push.'

It was an idle threat, yet she half believed him because rent men had power, rent men were rich; rent men were a different species, not really human.

They stared at each other. Then the smile sliding from her face, she turned abruptly from him and went through the room, shouting, 'You Willy! You Willy!' And the eldest child followed her, to return a moment later with two half-crowns and the rent book.

Rory took the money, signed the book, marked it in his own hard-backed pocket ledger, then went on to the next house. Here he pushed open the bottom door and called up the dark well of the staircase, 'Rent!' and after a moment a man's voice came back to him shouting, 'Fetch it up.'

His nose wrinkled in distaste. If he had a penny for every time that worn-out quip had been thrown at him he considered he'd be able to buy a house of his own. After a moment of silence he again shouted, 'Rent, or it's the bums Monday.'

The moleskin-trousered bulky figure appeared on the stairhead and after throwing the rent book and a half-crown down the stairs he yelled, 'You know what you and the bloody bums can do, don't you?' then as Rory picked up the money and the book and entered in the amount the man proceeded to elaborate on what he and the bums could do.

Without uttering a word now Rory threw the book on to the bottom stair, looked up at the man still standing on the landing, then turned about and went towards the end of the street.

There was no answer whatever from the next three doors he knocked on, but he had scarcely raised the knocker on the fourth when it was opened and Mrs Fawcett stood there, her rent book in one hand, the half-crown extended in the other, and without any greeting she began, 'You won't get any change out of them lot.' She nodded to one side of her. 'Nor to this one next door.' Her head moved the other way. 'Off to Shields they are, the lot of them, to the market and they won't come back with a penny, not if I know them. Lazy Irish scum. And I'll tell you somethin'.' She leant her peevish face towards him. 'Her, Flaherty, she's got her front room packed with beds, and lettin' them out by the shift; as one lot staggers out another lot drops in. Great Irish navvies with not a drop on their faces from Monday mornin' till Saturda' night, but Sunday, oh, that's different, away to Mass they are, and straight out and into the bars. Disgrace!'

Rory closed her rent book, handed it to her, looked at her straight in the eye, then turned and walked away. He did not bother knocking at the door next to hers for he believed what she had said, they were all away on a spending spree. It was odd, she was the only good payer in the street; she'd always had a clear rent book; but of the lot of them, scum Irish they might be, he preferred any one of them to Mrs Fawcett.

Pilbey Street was bad but Saltbank Row was worse. Here it was the stench that got him. The dry middens at the back of the Row, dry being a mere courtesy title, seeped away under the stone floors of the two-roomed cottages, and the dirt in front of the cottages was always wet to the feet. In winter the stench was bad enough but in summer it was unbearable. Why the Town Corporation did not condemn the place he didn't know. Vested interests he supposed; in any case anything was good enough for the Irish immigrants, and they didn't seem to mind, for as it was well known they had been used to sleeping among the pigs and the chickens in their tiny hovel huts over in Ireland.

Yet there were Irish in the town among Palmer's men whom he had heard were buying their own houses. That had come from old Kean himself, and the old boy didn't like it.

His own father had worked in Palmer's for years,

but there was no sign of him being able to buy his own house. Likely because he didn't want to; his father spent as he went, he ate well and drank as much as he could hold almost every day in the week, because his body was so dried up with the heat from the furnaces.

Drinking was one thing he didn't blame his father for, but he did blame him for his carry-on with her . . . Lizzie. He supposed it was by way of compensation that he'd had him sent to the penny school but he didn't thank him for that either, for he hadn't attended long enough to take in much beyond reading, writing and reckoning up. When funds were low the last thing to be considered was the penny fee. And he wouldn't go to school without it. Nor would his father have his name put down on the parish list so that he could send him free—not him.

Anyway, his reading and writing had enabled him finally to become a rent collector with a wage of fifteen shillings a week. He was told from all quarters that he was damned lucky to be in such a job. Fifteen shillings for neither bending his back nor soiling his hands. And his employer, more than others, emphasized this statement.

Mr Kean owned about half the cottages in Saltbank Row, and the rent of each was two shillings a week, but when he reached the end of the Row all he had in the back section of his leather bag was twenty-five shillings and sixpence.

It was just turned twelve o'clock when he reached the main street and joined the stream of men pouring out of Palmer's and the various side streets which led to different yards on the river. They were like streams of black lava joining the main flow, faces grey, froth-specked with their sweat. He was carried along in the throng until he reached the church bank again by which time the blackness had dwindled into individual pockets of men.

He reckoned he should be back at the office by one o'clock. He never carried a watch, not on his rounds, because it could be nicked in the time he blinked an eyelid. A gang of lads supposedly playing Tiggy could rough you up. He had seen it done. But he told himself as he paused for a moment on the Don bridge and looked down at the narrow mud-walled banks of the river that there was no immediate hurry today, for old Kean was off on one of his duty trips to Hexham to see his old father. When this happened the day's takings were locked up until Monday. Saturday's takings didn't amount to very much, not on his part anyway. John George took more, for he did the Tyne Dock area and the better part of Stanhope Road.

He was getting a bit worried about John George. There was something on his mind; he supposed it was that damned ranter's lass he had taken up with. Only last night he had told him to think hard about this business, for being her father's daughter, she might turn out to be a chip off the old block and be 'God-mad' like the rest of them.

The whole of Shields was becoming 'God-mad'; there were chapels springing up all over the place and the more of them there were the greater the outcry against drink and gambling. And them that made the fuss, what were they? Bloody hypocrites half of them. Oh, he knew a thing or two about some of them. That's why he had warned John George.

As he walked on into Tyne Dock he forgot about John George and his troubles for his mind was taken up with the evening's prospects. He had heard tell of a square-head, a Swede who lived down Corstorphine Town way. He was known as Fair Square; he did summer trips there and back to Norway and Sweden, but in the winter he stayed put somewhere along the waterfront and ran a school, so he understood, and not just an ordinary one, a big one, for captains and such. But as little Joe, the tout, had said, they didn't often let foreigners in . . . That was funny that was, a Swede calling an Englishman a foreigner, and in his own town at that.

Anyway, little Joe had promised to work him in somewhere.

He felt a stir of excitement in his stomach at the thought of getting set-in in a big school; none of your tanner pitch and tosses or find the lady, but banker with a kitty up to twenty pounds a go. By, that was talking. Twenty pounds a go. Once in there it wouldn't be long afore he could set up house—he and Janie, setting up house. He wanted to get married, he ached for Janie. And that was the right word, ached. At night he would toss and turn until he would have to get up and put the soles of his feet on the ice-cold square of lino that stood between the beds.

He'd see her the morrow. Just to be with her lifted him out of the doldrums; just to look at her pulled at his heart, 'cos she was bonny, beautiful. And he wasn't spending the whole afternoon the morrow playing cards for monkey nuts. Huh! He wondered why he let himself in for it Sunday after Sunday. No, hail, rain or shine they'd go out up the lanes, and he'd settle things in his own way. Aye he would.

'Rory! Rory!'

He turned swiftly and looked up the dock bank to see John George pushing his way through a press of men towards him, and when he came up Rory stared at him saying, 'You're late, aren't you? You're generally done around twelve.'

'I know, but there was an accident back there at the Boldon Lane toll-gate. I helped to sort the carts out. A young lad got crushed. Toll's finished next year they say, an' a good thing an' all.'

'Getting into a throng with money in your bag, you must be mad . . . And where did you get that?'

Rory was now looking John George over from head to foot. 'You knock somebody down?'

Stroking the lapels of a thick brown overcoat that, although a little short, fitted his thin body, John George said, 'I picked it up last Saturday in New-castle, in the market.'

'What did you give for it?'

'Half a dollar.'

'Well you weren't robbed, it's good material. You should have got yourself some boots while you were on.' He glanced down at the cracked toecaps. 'It's a wonder the old fellow hasn't spotted them and pulled you up. You know what he is for appearances.'

'I'm going to see about a pair the day when I'm up there.'

'You're going to Newcastle again?'

'Aye.' John George now turned his head and smiled at Rory. 'I'm meeting her on the three o'clock train an' I'm going to show her round. Look'—he thrust his hand into the overcoat pocket, then brought out a small box wrapped in tissue paper—'I bought her this for Christmas. What do you think of it?'

When Rory took the lid off the box and looked at the heart-shaped locket and chain he stared at it for some seconds before turning to John George again and asking quietly, 'What did you give for it?'

'Not . . . not what it's worth, it's second-hand. It's a good one.'

'What did you give for it?'

'Seven and six.'

'Seven and six! Are you mad? How can you afford seven and six? You tell me that your Aunt Meg needs every penny to keep the house goin' and three bob's as much as you can keep back.'

'Well, it's . . . it's true. But . . . but I worked out a system.'

'You worked out a system, you!' Rory screwed up his face. 'You worked out a system! On what? Tell me on what?'

'Aw, not now, man, not now. I'll . . . I'll tell you after . . . later on. I wanted to have a word with you about something else . . . You see I'm thinking of moving, trying to get a better job. I could never hope to get Maggie away on the wage I've got and having to see to them at home and . . .'

'Where could you get a better job than what you've got?'

'There's places in Newcastle.'

'Aye, I know there's places in Newcastle, but them chaps don't get even as much as we do. There's no trade unions yelling for us. I'm not satisfied, but I know damn well that if I want more money I won't get it at rent clerking. Look, are you in some kind of fix?'

'No, no.' John George shook his head too vigorously and Rory, eyeing him from the side, shook his head also. They walked on in silence, taking short cuts until they came to the market, then they wound their way between the conglomeration of stalls, turned down a narrow side lane known as Tangard Street, and past what appeared to be the window of an empty shop, except that the bottom half, which was painted black, had written across it: Septimus Kean, Estate Agent, Valuer, and Rent Collector. Next to the window was a heavy door with a brass knob that had never seen polish, and above it a keyhole.

As John George was about to insert his key into the lock the door was pulled open from inside and they were both confronted by Mr Kean himself.

'Oh!... Oh! Mr Kean. We thought you were away.'

The small, heavy-jowled man looked at Rory and barked, 'Evidently. Do you know what time it is?' He pulled out a watch, snapped open the case and turned the face towards Rory. 'Ten minutes past one. When the cat's away the mice can play.'

'But we finish at one.' Rory's voice was harsh, the muscles of his neck were standing out and his face was flushed with sudden temper.

'Be careful, Connor, be careful. Mind who you're speaking to. You know what happens to cheeky individuals; there's never an empty place that cannot be filled. I know that you're finished at one, and damned lucky you are to be finished at one, but you should have been back here before one and your book settled, and then you could have been finished at one . . . And what's the matter with you?' He was now glaring at John George. 'You sick or something?'

John George gulped, shook his head, and remained standing where he was on the threshold of the door.

And this caused Mr Kean to yell, 'Well, come in, man! What's come over you? Close the door before we're all blown out. And let me have your books; I want to get away.'

With this, Mr Kean turned about and went through a door into another room. The door was half glass, but it was clear glass, clear in order that the master could look through it at any time and see that his two clerks weren't idling at their desks.

'What is it? What's the matter?' Rory had taken hold of John George's shoulder. 'You look like death, what is it?'

John George gulped twice in his throat before he whispered, 'Lend . . . lend me ten bob.'

'Lend you ten bob?'

'Aye. Look, just for now, I'll have it for you Monday mornin'. Just . . . just lend it me. Aw, Rory, lend it me. For God's sake, lend it me.'

Rory looked towards the glass door and as he put his hand into his pocket, he hissed, 'You were paid last night.'

'Aye, I know, but I'll explain, I'll explain in a minute or two.' The hand he held out was trembling and when Rory put the gold half sovereign on to the palm John George's fingers pressed over it tightly for a moment before swiftly dropping it into the leather bag which he still held in his hand.

'*Come on, come on.*'

They exchanged glances before John George turned away and almost stumbled across the room and into his master's office.

Rory remained gazing at the half open door . . . He was on the fiddle. The damn fool was on the fiddle. It was that lass. God, if he hadn't been here and old Kean had found him ten shillings short!

Mr Kean's voice came bawling out of the room

again, saying, 'What's the matter with you, Armstrong? You look as if you're going to throw up.' Then John George's voice, thin and trembling, 'Bit of a chill, sir. Got a cold I think.'

There was a pause, then Mr Kean's observation: 'That coat's new, isn't it? You shouldn't feel cold in that. About time you did smarten yourself up. Bad impression to go around the doors looking like a rag man.' Another pause before his voice again rasped, 'Mrs Arnold, she's paid nothing off the back for four weeks. Why haven't you seen to it?'

'She's been bad. She . . . she took to her bed a few weeks ago. But she says she'll clear it up soon because her girl's got set on across the water at Haggie's . . . the Ropery you know.'

'Yes, I know, I know the Ropery. And I know the type that works there. She'll likely drink her pay before she gets back across the water. She's got others working, hasn't she?'

'Yes. Yes, she's got a lad down the pit. But . . . but he's only a nipper, he's not getting more than tenpence a day. She's . . . she's had hard times since her man went.'

'That's neither my business nor yours, I don't want the family history, I only want the rent and the back rent. Now you see to it. You're getting slack, Armstrong. I've noticed it of late.'

There followed another silence before John George returned to the outer office, his face looking bleak, his eyes wide and in their depth a misery that caused Rory to turn away, pick up his bag and go into the other room.

When he had placed the money from the bag on the table, Mr Kean separated each single coin with his forefinger, then after counting them he raised his eyes without lifting his head and said, 'You mean to tell me this is the result of a morning's work?'

'It was Saltbank Row and Pilbey Street.'

'I know damned well it was Saltbank Row and Pilbey Street, it's always Saltbank Row and Pilbey

Street on a Saturday, but what I'm saying to you is, do you mean to tell me that's all you got out of them?'

Rory moved one lip over the other before replying, 'It's always the same near Christmas.'

'Look!' The thick neck was thrust forward, then the head went back on the shoulders and Mr Kean directed an enraged stare on to Rory's grim face as he cried, 'One gives me family histories, the other festival dates as excuses. Now look, I'm telling you they're not good enough, neither one nor the other, Christmas or no Christmas. If that sum'—he now dug his finger on to one coin after another—'if it isn't doubled at the next collection then there'll be a lot of barrows needed to shift their muck. You tell them that from me. And that's final.' Again he stabbed the coins. 'Double that amount or it's the bums for the lot of 'em.'

When Rory turned abruptly from the table Mr Kean barked at him, 'Answer me when I'm speaking to you!'

Rory stopped, but it was a few seconds before he turned to face Mr Kean again, and then he said slowly, 'Yes, sir.'

Seconds again passed before Mr Kean said, 'There's going to be changes here, Connor,' and again Rory said, 'Yes, sir.'

'Get yourself out.'

The buttons on Rory's coat strained as he drew in a deep breath before turning round and leaving the room, closing the door after him.

John George was standing by his narrow, high desk. A little colour had returned to his face and he was about to speak when the outer door opened and they both looked towards it and at Miss Charlotte Kean.

Charlotte was Kean's only child but she bore no resemblance to him, being tall, extremely tall for a woman, all of five foot eight and thin with it. Moreover, she had what was commonly called a neb on her. Her nose was large; her mouth, too, was

57

large but in proportion to her face. Her eyes were a greeny grey and her hair was black. She was an ugly young woman yet in some strange way she had just missed being beautiful for each feature taken by itself was good even though, together, one cancelled another out. Her features gave the impression of strength, even of masculinity. It was understood in the office that she knew as much about the business as did her father, yet she rarely came here. Rory hadn't seen her but half a dozen times in four years, and each appearance had given him material for jokes in the kitchen, especially at the Sunday gatherings.

He had from time to time openly teased John George about her. John George had said he felt sorry for her, because a young woman like her had little chance of being married. His words had proved true, for here she was at twenty-eight and still on the shelf.

But there was one thing his master's daughter possessed that he couldn't make game of, in fact it had the power to make him feel ill at ease, and that was her voice. There was no hint of the Tyneside twang about it. This he understood had come about by her being sent away to one of those posh schools when she was no more than ten, from which she hadn't come back to Shields for good until she was turned seventeen.

She gave them no greeting—one didn't greet clerks —but stared at Rory before demanding briefly, 'My father in?'

'Yes, miss.' Rory inclined his head towards the door.

She stood for a moment longer looking from one to the other. Then her eyes resting once more on Rory, she surveyed him from head to toe, as he said bitterly afterwards, 'Like some bloody buyer at a livestock show.' But he wasn't going to be intimidated by any look she could cast over him, and so he returned it. His eyes ranged from her fur-trimmed hat down over her grey velour coat with its brown fur collar, right to her feet encased in narrow-toed brown kid boots. He had noticed her feet before. They were so narrow he wondered how she balanced on them, how she got boots to fit them. But when you had money you could be fitted from top to toe and inside an' all, but he'd like to bet with that face her habit shirts would be made of calico, unbleached at that, no lace camisoles for her. Anyway, she had nothing to push in them.

As she went towards the door he looked at her back. It was like a ramrod, she wasn't like a woman at all. He beckoned to John George, who seemed to be glued to his desk, and as he opened the door he heard her say, 'You'll be late for the ferry, I came with the trap. Come along or you'll never get there.'

The old man always went by ferry up to Newcastle; he didn't like the trains although he had to take one from Newcastle to Hexham. When he went on his usual trips there he generally left early on a Saturday morning. What had stopped him this time? Anyway, whatever had stopped him had also nearly stopped John George's breath.

They were crossing the market again before he said, 'Well now, come on, spit it out.'

'I'll . . . I'll give you it back, I . . . I can give you six bob of it now. I'll get it from home and . . . and the rest on Monday.'

'What were you up to?'

'Aw'—John George wagged his head from side to side—'I . . . I wanted to give Maggie something and it had to be the day, it's the only time I can see her. I mightn't see her again until after the holiday and so, thinkin' he wouldn't be in till Monday, I . . . I took the loan of ten bob out of the . . .'

'You bloody fool!'

'Aye, I know, I know I am.'

'But . . . but how did you expect to put it back by Monday if you haven't got it now?'

'Aw well, man'—again his head was wagging—'I . . . I usually put me good suit in and me watch and bits of things . . .'

'You usually do? You mean you've done this afore?'

John George nodded his head slowly. 'Aye. Aye, a few times. The times that he goes off at the week-ends and doesn't count up till Monday. I . . . I thought I'd drop down dead when I saw him standing there.'

'You deserve to drop down dead, you bloody fool you. Do you know he could have you up? And he's the one to do it an' all; he'd have you along the line afore you could whistle. You must be up the pole, man.'

'I think I'll go up the pole soon if things don't change.'

'What you want to do is to pull yourself together, get things worked out straight. Leave your Uncle Willy and Aunt Meg, he's able to work, he's nothin' but a scrounger, and take a place on your own.'

'What!' John George turned his face sharply towards him. 'Take the furniture and leave them with three bare rooms or tell him to get out? What you don't understand, Rory, is that there's such a thing as gratitude. I don't forget that they were both good to me mother after me da died, aye, and long afore that; and they helped to nurse him the two years he lay bedridden.'

'Well, they've been damned well paid for it since, if you ask me . . . All right then, say you can't do anything about them, an' you want that lass . . . well then, ask her to marry you and bring her into the house.'

'That's easier said than done. If I took her away her father would likely go straight to old Kean and denounce me.' He now put his hand to his brow, which, in spite of the raw cold, was running with sweat, and muttered, 'But I'll have to do something, and soon, 'cos . . . oh my God! I'm in a right pickle . . . Rory.'

'Aye, I'm still here, what is it?'

'There's something else.'

'Aw.' Rory now closed his eyes and put his hand

across his mouth, then grabbed at his hard hat to save it from being whipped by the wind from his head. 'Well, go on.'

'It doesn't matter. Another time, another time; you're not in the mood . . . Look—' he pointed suddenly—'Isn't that Jimmy?'

They were passing the road that led to the Mill Dam and the river front. Rory stopped and said, 'Yes that's our Jimmy . . . Jimmy!' he shouted down the lane, and Jimmy who had been walking with his eyes cast down looked upwards, then came dashing up the slope at his wobbling gait.

'Why, fancy seein' you, I mean both of you. An' I was just thinking of you, our Rory.'

'You were? Why? You another one that wants a sub?'

'No, man.' Jimmy laughed. 'But I was thinkin' that when I got home I'd ask you to come down here again. Now wasn't that funny.'

'I can't see much to laugh at in that, not yet anyway.'

'Well, it was something I wanted to show you down on the front.' He nodded towards the river. 'Come on.' He again indicated the river with his head, then added, 'And you an' all, John George.'

'I can't, Jimmy, I'm sorry. I'm . . . I'm on me way home.'

'Aw, all right, John George, I understand, it's your day for Newcastle.' He laughed.

John George didn't laugh with him, but he repeated, 'Aye. Aye, Jimmy, it's me day for Newcastle.' Then nodding at him, he said, 'Be seeing you. So long. And so long, Rory. Aw, I forgot. What about the other, I mean. . . ?'

'Leave it till Monday. And mind, don't do any more damn fool things until then.'

'I'll try not to. But what's done's done. Nevertheless thanks, thanks. You'll have it on Monday. So long.'

'So long.'

'What's up with him?' Jimmy asked as they went down towards the road that bordered the river.

'He's been a damned fool, he's mad.'

'What's he been and gone and done?'

'Nothing . . . I'll tell you some other time. What do you want me down here for?'

'I want to show you something.'

'A boat?'

'Aye, a boat. An' something more than that.'

Rory looked down into the young face. It was always hard for him to believe that Jimmy was nineteen years old, for he still looked upon him as a nipper. He was more than fond of Jimmy, half-brothers though they were; he liked him the best of the bunch.

'Where we going?'

'Just along the front, then down the Cut.'

'There's nothing but warehouses along there.'

'Aye, I know. But past them, past Snowdon's, on a bit, you'll see.'

After some walking they had turned from the road that bordered the warehouse and wharf-strewn river front and were clambering over what looked like a piece of spare ground except that it was dotted here and there with mounds of rusty chains, anchors and the keels and ribs of small decaying boats, when Jimmy, squeezing his way between a narrow aperture in a rough fence made up of oddments of thick black timber, said, 'Through here.'

Rory had some difficulty in squeezing himself between the planks, but when once through he looked about him on to what appeared to be a miniature boatyard. A half-finished skeleton of a small boat was lying aslant some rough stocks and around it lay pieces of wood of all shapes and sizes. A few feet beyond the boat was the beginning of a slipway bordered by a jetty and he walked towards the edge of it and leant over the rail and looked down into the water; then from there he turned and surveyed the building at the far end of the yard.

It wasn't unlike any of the other warehouses cluttering the river bank except that it had three windows in the upper part of it, and they were big windows, one on each side of the door and one fitting into the apex of the roof. There was no name on the front of the structure like there was on the rest of the boatyards and warehouses, and Rory now turned and looked into Jimmy's bright eyes and said, 'Well?'

'It's a little boatyard.'

'I can see that but I wouldn't say it was a prosperous one. You're not going to leave Baker's for here, are you?'

'No, man, no. I'm not going to leave Baker's at all. I wish I could. At the same time I'm terrified of being stood off. No, I just want you to see it.'

'Why?'

'Oh, 'cos . . . it's up for sale.'

'Up for sale?'

'Aye.'

'Well, what's that got to do with us?'

'Nowt . . . nowt, man.'

Rory watched the light slowly fade from Jimmy's face. He watched him turn away and look at the river, then up at the house, and lastly at the boat on the stocks, and he said softly now, 'I know what you're thinkin', but it's like a dream, lad, that's all, it can never come true.'

'I know.'

'Then what did you bring me here for?'

'I just wanted you to see it, just to show you.'

'What good is that going to do you or anybody else?'

'Well, I just wanted to show you that a man could start on almost nowt an' build up. They've done it all along the river. The Pittie Brothers, they started from nowt. A sculler among the three of them, and now they've got the run of the place, or they think they have. But there's always room for another one or two. Some say the keelman's day is over since they've widened the river and the boats can go farther up and pick up their coal straight from the staithes, but as Mr Kilpatrick used to say there's other things to be carted besides coal. Anyway, I'd never aim to be a keelman 'cos it's as tight to get in as a secret society, an' they're a tough lot, by aye! Nor do I want to build keels, with a cabin an' hold, 'cos it takes all of three men to manage a keel. No; but I've got something in me mind's eye; it'd be under thirty foot but with space for timber, packages and such, something I could manage meself or, at a push, just two of us. Mr Kilpatrick used to say he could design . . .'

'Who's Mr Kilpatrick?'

'The old fellow who owned this place.'

'Did you know him?'

'Aye, in a way. I used to pop in in me bait time. He's always given me tips, things that you don't come by only by experience. He used to take the wood from the river'—he pointed to the wood scattered around the boat—'and when he was finished with it, it was as good as new. He had a way with wood. He said I had an' all.'

'And he's dead?'

'Aye.'

'Who's sellin' it then?'

'His son. Well, he's selling the goodwill.'

'Goodwill!' Rory gave a short laugh. 'What goodwill is there here? The back end of a boat and wood you can pick up from the river.'

'There's a house up there and there's some decent pieces of furniture in it. And then there's his tools. And he's got a bond on the place for the next ten years.'

'You mean it's just rented?'

'Aye.'

'How much is it a week?'

'Three and a tanner.'

'Huh!' The sound was sarcastic. 'They're not asking much, three and a tanner for this!'

'But everything is included. And a permit to ferry stuff up and down the river.'

'And what's the son wanting for it?'

'Thirty-five pounds.'

'*What!*' It was a shout. 'You havin' me on?'

'No, I'm not, that's cheap. There's the boat, and all the wood. And you haven't seen his tools. Then there's the furniture. There's three rooms up there, I've been in them. He used to give me a cup of tea now and again. He lived on his own. They're big rooms. You don't get much of an idea from here.'

'But there's no boat, he must have had a boat.'

'Aye, his son took that.'

'That son knows what he's doing. Has he been pumping you?'

'No. Why no, man, why would he pump me? Only that he knew I used to talk to his old man. He came here once or twice when I was in the yard and when he saw me t'other day he told me. He said—' Now Jimmy turned away and walked up towards the house, his body seeming to rock more than his bowed legs and Rory called after him, 'Well, go on, finish telling me what he said.'

'It doesn't matter; as you said, it's a dream.' And now he swung round and stabbed his finger towards Rory as he ended, 'But some day, mark my words, I'll make it come true. I don't know how but I will. I'll have a place of me own where I can build a boat an' ply a trade. You'll see. You'll see.'

'All right, all right.' Rory walked towards him now. 'No need to bawl your head off.'

'You bawled first.'

'Well, I had a right.' He now passed Jimmy and walked up and into the end of the slipway, over which the building extended, and looked towards the ladder that was fixed to the wall and ended in a trap-door, and he called back over his shoulder in an amused tone, 'Is this how you get in?'

'No, of course, it isn't,' Jimmy said scornfully; 'there's steps up and a door, you saw them. But—'

And now his eyes were bright again as he went on, 'I can show you inside, I know how to get in through the hatch.'

'What we waitin' for, then, if it's going to cost us nothin'? So go on, get up.'

The desire was strong in him to please this brother of his and to keep his dream alive for a little longer. He watched him run up the vertical ladder with the agility of a monkey. He saw him put his flat hand in the middle of the trap-door, jerk it twice to the side, and then push it upwards. He stood at the foot of the ladder and watched him disappear through the hole. Then he was climbing upwards, but with no agility. He wasn't used to crawling up walls he told himself.

When he emerged into the room he straightened up and looked about him but said nothing. Just as Jimmy had said, there were some good pieces of furniture here. He was amazed at the comfort of the room. The whole floor space was covered with rope mats fashioned in intricate patterns. There was a high-barred fireplace with an oven to the side of it and a hook above it for a spit or kettle. A good chest of drawers stood against one wall, and by it a black oak chest with brass bindings. There was a big oval table with a central leg in the middle of the room, and the top had been polished to show the grain. There were three straight-backed wooden chairs and a rocking chair, and all around the walls hung relics from ships: brass compasses, wheels, old charts. He walked slowly towards the door that led into the next room. It was a bedroom. There was a plank bed in one corner but slung between the walls was a hammock. And here was another seaman's chest, not a common seaman's chest but something that a man of captain's rank might have used, and taking up most of the opposite end of the room was a tallboy.

'It's good stuff, isn't it? Look at his tools.' Jimmy heaved up the lid of the chest to show an array of shining tools hung meticulously in order around the sides of the chest.

'Aye, it's good stuff. He was no dock scum was your Mr Kilpatrick. Everything orderly and ship-shape.'

'Of course he wasn't dock scum. He was a gentleman . . . well, I mean not gentry, but a gentleman. He had been to sea in his young days, ran off, so he told me. His people were comfortable. They took his son when his wife died, that's why the son doesn't want anything to do with the water front. He's in business, drapery.'

'What's up above?'

'It's a long room, it runs over both of these. It's full of all kinds of things, maps and papers and books and things. He could read. Oh, he was a great reader.'

Rory looked down on Jimmy. He looked at him for a long moment before he was able to say, 'I'm sorry.'

'What've you to be sorry for?' Jimmy had turned away and walked towards the window where he stood looking out on to the river.

'You know what I'm sorry for, I'm sorry you can't have it. If I had the money I'd buy it for you this minute, I would.'

He watched his brother's face slowly turn towards him. The expression was soft again, his tone warm. 'I know you would. That's why I wanted you to see it an' to hear you say that, 'cos I know if you had it you would give it me, lend it me.'

Rory went and sat in the rocking chair and began to push himself slowly backwards and forwards. Thirty-five pounds. A few nights of good play some-where and he could make that. He once made thirteen pounds at one sitting, but had lost it afore he left. But if he were to win again he'd smilingly take his leave. That's if he wasn't playing against sailors, for some of them would cut you up for tuppence.

67

Suddenly jumping up from the chair, he said, 'Come on.'

'Where?'

'Never mind where. Just come on, let's get out of here.' But before dropping down through the trapdoor he looked about him once again as he thought, It'll kill two birds with the one stone. Janie. Janie would love it here, she would be in her element. There was the room up there, that would do Jimmy. He closed his eyes and shook his head. He was getting as barmy as Jimmy . . . But there was nothing like trying.

When they were out of the yard and on the road again he stopped and, looking down at Jimmy, said, 'Now I want you to go straight home. You can say that you saw me, and I was with a fellow. We . . . we were going to see the turns later on. Aye, that's what to say, say we were going to the theatre later on.'

'You're goin' in a game?'

'Aye, if I can find a good one.'

'Aw, Rory.'

'Now, now, don't get bright-eyed, nowt may come of it. But I'll have a try. And if we could put something down to secure it—' he punched Jimmy on the shoulder—'the fellow might wait, take it in bits like, eh? If he's not short of a bob he could wait, couldn't he? And it isn't everybody that's going to jump at a place like that. But . . . but as I said, don't get too bright-eyed. Just tell them what I told you, and if I shouldn't be back afore they go to bed, tell them . . . well, tell them not to wait up.'

'Aye, Rory, aye, I'll do that. And . . . and you be careful.'

'What have I got to be careful of?'

'You hear things, I mean along the front, about the schools an' things. There are some rough customers about.'

'I'm a bit of one meself.'

'You're all right.'

They looked at each other, the undersized bow-

68

legged boy with the angelic face and his thick-set straight-backed, arrogantly attractive-looking half-brother, and each liked what he saw: Rory, the blind admiration in the boy's face, and Jimmy, the strength, determination and apparent fearlessness in this man he loved above all others.

'Go on with you, go on.' Rory thrust out his hand, and Jimmy turned away. Again he was running, and not until he had disappeared from view into the main thoroughfare did Rory swing about and stride along the waterfront in the direction of the pier. But before he came to the high bank known as the Lawe, on which stood the superior houses with their view of the sea and the North and South piers, and which were occupied by ships' captains and respectable merchants of the town, he turned off and into a street which, from its disreputable appearance, should never have been allowed to lie at the skirt of such a neighbourhood as the Lawe. There were only eight houses in this street and they all had walled back yards and all the doors were locked. It was on the third yard door that he knocked, a sharp knock, rat-tat a-tat, tat-tat, and after some minutes it was furtively opened by a man hardly bigger than a dwarf.

'Hello, Joe.'

'Oh. Oh, it's you, Mr Connor?'

'Aye, Joe. I wanted a word with you.'

'Oh well, Mr Connor, I'm off on a message you see.' He brought his two unusually long and fine-shaped hands in a sweeping movement down the front of his short coat, and Rory, nodding, smiled and said, 'Aye, you've got your best toggery on, must be some special message.'

He had never before seen little Joe dressed like this. He had never imagined he had any other clothes but the greasy little moleskin trousers and the old broadcloth coat he usually wore. Not that he couldn't afford to buy a new suit because he must do pretty well on the side; besides being a bookie's runner, little Joe could be called upon to negotiate odd jobs, very odd jobs, along the waterfront. Last year it was said he almost went along the line when two lasses went missing. They couldn't prove anything against him for he was a wily little beggar. But the case recalled the outcry of a few years earlier when some lasses were shipped off. Afterwards of course this line of business had of necessity quietened down for a time, but nature being what it is a demand for young lasses, especially young white lasses, was always there, and so was Joe.

He said to him now, 'I want you to get me in some place the night, Joe, like you promised. But no back-yard dos.'

'Aw, it'll take time, Mr Connor, an' I told you.' He came out into the lane now and pulled the door closed, and as he walked away Rory suited his steps to the shorter ones.

'Now you can if you like, Joe. You said . . .'

'I told you, Mr Connor, it takes time that kind of thing. And they're on to us . . . coppers; they're hot all round the place.'

'You have ways and means, you know you have, Joe. An' I'd make it worth your while, you know that.'

'Oh, I know that, Mr Connor. You're not tight when it comes to payin' up. Oh, I know that. And if I could, I would . . . There's Riley's.'

'I don't like that lot, I told you last time.'

'Well, I'll admit it, they're a bit rough.'

'And twisted.'

'Aw well, you see, I don't play meself, Mr Connor, so I wouldn't know.'

'There's other places, Joe.'

'But you've got to be known, Mr Connor, an' . . . an' it's me livelihood you know.'

'You could do it, Joe.'

And so the conversation went on, flattery pressing against caution; but by the time they parted caution had won.

'I'm sorry, Mr Connor, but . . . but I'll let you know.

I'll take a walk around your office as soon as I can manage anything for you. That's a promise; it is.'

Rory nodded, and as he stood and watched the small shambling figure hurry away and disappear around the bottom of the street he repeated bitterly, 'That's a promise.' Then he asked himself the question, 'Where's he off to, rigged out like that?' He wouldn't need to dress up to go round his usual haunts. He was going some place special?

As if he had been pushed from behind he sprang forward, but when he came out into the main street he slowed to a walk. Little Joe was well ahead, but he kept him in sight until he turned into Fowler Street.

There he was impeded in his walking by a number of people who had stepped hastily up on to the pavement from the road to allow a private coach and a dray-cart to pass each other. There were angry shouts and strong language among those who had their clothes bespattered with mud, and as he didn't want his own mucked up, he kept as near as he could to the wall, and because of the press he was only just in time to see little Joe turn off into Ogle Terrace.

Ogle Terrace, apart from Westoe, was in the best end of the town. Who was he going to see up there? On the small figure hurried until at the top of Plynlimmon Way he disappeared from view.

Rory, now about to set off at a run towards the end of the terrace, was impeded for a second time by a party of ladies coming through an iron gateway and making for a carriage standing at the kerb.

When he eventually reached the top corner of Plynlimmon Way there was no sight of little Joe.

He stood breathing deeply, working things out. Joe wouldn't have had access to a front door, not around here he wouldn't, yet it was into one of these houses he had disappeared. So the place to wait was the back lane.

The back lane was cleaner than many front streets.

It was servant territory this, at least two or three maids to a house, hired coaches from the livery stables for the owners and trips abroad in the fashionable months. And little Joe was in one of these houses delivering a message. He was on to something here.

When a back door opened and a man wearing a leather-fronted waistcoat swept some dust into the back lane, he did a brisk walk past the end of the lane and as briskly returned. The man was no longer in sight, all the back gates were closed. He moved up slowly now, past the first one, and the second, then stood between it and the third. It was as he paused that the third door opened and out stepped little Joe.

The small man stood perfectly still and gazed at Rory with a pained expression before he said, 'You shouldn've, Mr Connor. Now you shouldn've. You don't know what you're at.' He cast a glance back to the door he had just closed, then hurried on down the lane. And Rory hurried with him.

They were in the main street before the little man slowed his pace, and then Rory said, 'Well now, Joe, what about it?'

And again Joe said, his tone surly now, 'You don't know what you're at, you don't.'

'I know what I'm at, Joe.' Rory's voice was grim. 'The buggers that live along there are like those in their mansions up Westoe, they run this town; they control the polis, the shippin', they own the breweries, an' have fingers in the glassworks, chemical works . . . Aye, the chemical works on the Jarrow road. There's one in Ogle Terrace who's on the board. You forget I'm a rent collector, Joe. There's no rent collected in this area. No, they're all owned. But I know about them. Who doesn't? By the morrow I'll find out who's in that particular number and that's all I'll need to know because now I know he's on the fiddle. What is it, Joe? Gamin' or girls . . . lasses?'

'Mr Connor, you'd better mind yourself, aye you'd

better.' Little Joe's voice held a note of awe now. 'You want to be careful what you say, he's . . .'

'Aye, aye, I've got the message, Joe, he's powerful. Well now, let's sort this thing out, eh? He's one of two things: he's a man who likes a game or he's a man who runs a game. We'll leave the lasses out of it for the time being, eh? Now havin' the kind of mind I have, Joe, I would say he's a man who runs a game, and likely in that house, 'cos if he wanted to go some place else for a game he wouldn't need you as a runner. A man in his position would have a key to open any door, even the ones in Newcastle. And there's some big games there, aren't there, Joe? No pitch an' toss, Joe, it's Twenty-Ones, or Black Jack, whatever name they care to call it; isn't it, Joe?'

He looked down on the little man, and although the twilight was bringing with it an icy blast Joe was sweating. He now said in some agitation, 'Let's get out of this crush.'

'Anything you say, Joe. Where you makin' for now?'

'I've got to go up Mile End Road.'

'Another message?'

'No, no.' The little man now turned on him and, his tone for the first time really nasty, he said, 'An' there's one thing I'm gona tell you. Whatever comes of this you'd better not let on 'cos . . . an' I'm not funnin', Mr Connor, with what I'm about to say, but things could happen, aye, things could happen.'

'I've no doubt of it, Joe.'

'Don't be funny, Mr Connor.'

'I'm not being funny, Joe, believe you me. Things are happenin' all the time along the waterfront an' I should imagine in Plynlimmon Way an' all. Now, you know me, Joe, I'm as good as me word. If I've owed you a couple of bob in the past you've got it, haven't you, with a bit tacked on? And I've never had a win on a race but I've seen you all right, haven't I? And I haven't got a loose tongue either. So look, Joe.' He stopped and bent down to the little man. 'All I

73

want from you is to get me set on in a decent school.'

'They go in for big stakes, Mr Connor.' The little fellow's voice was quiet again.

'That's what I want, Joe.'

'But you haven't got that kind of ready. You couldn't start in some of them under ten quid, an' that's so much hen grit.'

'You say some of them, there must be a few who start on less. I'll come to t'others later on. Aye, Joe, the big ones, I'll come to them later on, but in the meantime . . .'

The little man blinked, gnawed at his lip, looked down to the cobbles on which they were standing, as if considering. Then his eyes narrowing, he squinted up into Rory's face, saying conspiratorially, 'There's one in Corstorphine Town I might manage; it's not all that cop but they can rise to five quid a night.'

'It'll do to start with, Joe.'

'An' you'll say nowt about?' He jerked his head backwards.

'No, Joe, I'll say nowt about . . .' Now Rory imitated Joe's gesture, then added, 'Until you take me in there.'

'That'll be the day, Mr Connor.'

'Aye, that'll be the day, Joe. An' it mightn't be far ahead.'

'You worry me, Mr Connor.'

'I won't get you into any trouble, Joe, don't you worry.' Rory's tone was kindly now.

'Oh, it isn't that that worries me, it's what'll happen to you, if you take a wrong step. You don't know this game, Mr Connor.'

'I can play cards, Joe.'

'Aye, I've heard tell you can. But there's rules, Mr Connor, rules.'

'I'll stick to the rules, Joe.'

'But what if you come up against those who don't stick to them, Mr Connor?'

'I'll deal with them when I come to them, Joe. Now this place in Corstorphine Town.'

'What time is it now?' Joe looked up into the darkening sky, then stated, 'On four I should say.'

'Aye, on four, Joe.'

'Well on seven, meet me at the dock gates.'

'Seven, Joe, at the dock gates. I'll be there. And thanks.' He bent down to him. 'You won't regret it. I'll see to you, you won't regret it.'

Once again Rory watched the little man hurry away, his feet, like those of a child, almost tripping over each other. Then almost on the point of a run himself he made for home.

When he entered the kitchen Jimmy stared at him, exclaiming almost on a stutter, 'I told them—' he indicated both his mother and Lizzie with a wave of his hand—'I told them you met a fellow an' you were going to . . . to see the turns.'

'So I am, but it was so bloomin' cold walkin' around waiting, he's gone home for his tea. I was going to ask him up but thought the better of it. But I wouldn't mind something.' He looked towards Ruth. 'I'm froze inside and out. I'm meeting him at seven again.'

'Aw—' Jimmy smiled broadly now—'you're meeting him at seven? And you're going to see the turns?'

'Aye, we're going to see the turns.'

As Lizzie, walking into the scullery, repeated as if to herself, 'Going to see the turns,' Rory cast a hard glance towards her. She knew what turns he was going to see; you couldn't hoodwink her, blast her. But Ruth believed him. She came to him now, smiling and saying, 'Give me your coat and come to the fire; I'll have something on the table for you in a minute or so.'

He grinned at Ruth. He liked her, aye, you could say he loved her. Why couldn't she have been his mother? Blast the other one. And blast his da. They were a couple of whoring nowts. Aw, what did it matter? He had got his foot in, and Jimmy would get his yard, and he and Janie would be married and they would live in that house overlooking the water.

75

And Jimmy would build up a business and he would help him. Aye, with every spare minute he had he'd help him. He knew nowt about boats but he'd learn, he was quick to learn anything, and he'd have his game and he'd have Janie. Aye, he'd have Janie.

It did not occur to him that he had placed her after the game.

3

All the while she kept looking from one to the other of them, but they remained smilingly silent. Then she burst out, 'But the money! You've got the money to buy this?' Flinging both arms wide as with joy she gazed about the long room.

'Well—' Rory pursed his lips—'enough, enough to put down as a deposit.'

'He didn't get in till six this mornin'.' Jimmy was nodding up at her, and she turned to Rory and said, 'Gamin'?'

'Yes. Yes, Miss Waggett, that's what they call it, gamin'.'

'And you won?'

'I wouldn't be here showing you this else.'

'How much?'

'Aw well'—he looked away to the side—'almost eleven pounds at the beginning, but'—he gnawed on his lip for a moment—'I couldn't manage to get away then, I had to stay on and play. But I was six up anyway when I left.'

'Six pounds?'

'Aye, six pounds.'

'And this place is costin' thirty-five?'

'Aye. But five pounds'll act as a starter. Jimmy's goin' to get the address of the son and I'll write to him the morrow.'

There was silence between them for a moment until Rory, looking at Janie's profile, said, 'What is it?'

'The waterfront, it's . . . it's mostly scum down here.'

'Not this end.'

She turned to Jimmy, 'No?'

'No, they're respectable businesses. You know, woodyards, repair shops, an' things like that. An' there's very few live above the shops. There's nobody on yon side of us, an' just that bit of rough land on the other. Eeh!' he laughed, 'I'm sayin' us, as if we had it already . . .'

'What do you think?' Rory was gazing at her.

'Eeh!' She walked the length of the room, put her hand out and touched the chest of drawers, then the brass hinges on the oak chest, then the table, and lastly the rocking chair, and her eyes bright, she looked from one to the other and said, 'Eeh! it's amazing. You would never think from the outside it could be like this 'cos it looks ramshackle. But it's lovely, homely.'

'Look in t'other room.'

She went into the bedroom, then laughed and said, 'That'll come down for a start.'

She was pointing to the hammock, and Rory answered teasingly, 'No. Why, no. Our Jimmy's going to swing in that and we'll lie underneath.'

'Aw you!' Jimmy pushed at the air with his flat hand, then said, 'I'll be upstairs, I'll make that grand. Come on, come on up and have a look. Can you manage the ladder?'

Janie managed the ladder, and then she was standing under the sloping roof looking from one end of the attic to the other and she exclaimed again, 'Eeh! my! did you ever see so many bits of paper and maps and books and things? There's more books here than there are in the master's cases in his study.'

'Aye.' Jimmy now walked up and down the room as if he were already in possession of the place,

77

saying, 'By the time I get this lot sorted out I'll be able to read all right.'

'Talkin' of reading.' Janie turned to Rory. 'The mistress is having a teacher come in for the children, sort of part time daily governess. She said I could sit in with them. What do you think of that?'

'You won't be sittin' in with them long enough to learn the alphabet. And anyway, I'll teach you all you want to know once I get you here, an' you won't have any spare time for reading.'

'Rory!' She glanced in mock indignation from him to Jimmy, and Jimmy, his head slightly bowed and his lids lowered, made for the ladder, muttering, 'I'm goin' to see if there's any wood drifted up.'

Alone together, they looked at each other; then with a swift movement he pulled her into his arms and kissed her. He kissed her long and hard and, her eyes closed tightly, she responded to him, that was until his hand slid to her buttocks, and then with an effort she slowly but firmly withdrew from him, and they stood, their faces red and hot, staring at each other.

'I want you, Janie.' His voice was thick.

Her eyes were closed again and her head was nodding in small jerks and her fingers were moving round her lips wiping the moisture from them as she muttered softly through them, 'I know, I know, but . . . but not until . . . no, no, not until. I'd . . . I'd be frightened.'

'There's nothing to be frightened of. You know me, you're the only one for me, always have been, an' ever will be. There's nothing to be frightened . . .'

'I know, I know, Rory, but I can't, I daren't.' She was flapping both hands at him now. 'There's me da, an' me grannie, and all the others.'

He was making to hold her again. 'Nothing'll happen, just once.'

'Aw—' she now actually laughed in his face—'me grannie's always told me, she fell the first night. An' you can, you can . . . Eeh!' She now pressed her fingers tightly across her mouth. 'I shouldn't be talkin' like this. You shouldn't make me talk like this. It isn't proper, we're . . . we're not married.'

'Don't be daft, we're as good as married. I tell you there's only you, there's only . . .'

'No, Rory, no, not until it's done.' She thrust his hands away. 'I mean proper like in the church, signed and sealed. No, no, I'm sorry. I love you, oh, I do love you, Rory, I've loved you all me life. I've never even thought of another lad an' I'm twenty. I can't tell you how I love you, it eats me up, but even so I want to start proper like so you won't be able to throw anythin' back at me after.'

'What you talking about?' He had her by the shoulders now actually shaking her. 'Me throw anything back at you? Actually thinking I'd do a thing like that?'

'You're a man and they all do. Me grannie . . .'

'Blast your grannie! Blast her to hell's flames! She's old. Things were different in her day.'

'Not that. That wasn't any different. Never will be. It's the only thing a woman's really looked down on for. Even if you were to steal you wouldn't have a stamp put on you like you would have if . . . if you had a bairn.'

'You won't have . . .'

'Rory, no. I tell you no. We've waited this long, what's a few more months?'

'I could be dead, you could be dead.'

'We'll have to take a chance on that.'

'You know, Janie, you're hard; there's a hard streak in you, always has been about some things . . .'

'I'm not.' Her voice was trembling. 'I'm not hard.'

'Yes you are. . . .'

'I'm not. I'm not.'

'All right, all right. Aw, don't cry. I'm sorry, I am. Don't cry.'

'I'm not hard.'

'No, you're not, you're lovely . . . It's all right. Look, it's all right; I just want to hold you.'

When his arms went about her she jerked herself from his hold once more and going to the window, stood stiffly looking down on to the river, and he stood as stiffly watching her. Only his jaw moved as his teeth ground against each other.

She drew in a deep breath now and, her head turning from one side to the other, she looked up and down the river. As far as her eyes could see both to the right and to the left the banks were lined with craft, ships of all types and sizes, from little scullers, wherries and tugs to great funnelled boats, and here and there a masted ship, its lines standing out separate and graceful from the great iron hulks alongside.

Rory now came slowly to the window and, putting his arm around her shoulders and his manner softened, he said, 'Look. Look along there. You see that boat with a figurehead on it—there's a fine lass for you . . . Look at her bust, I bet that's one of Thomas Anderson's pieces, and I'll bet he enjoyed makin' it.'

'Rory!'

He hugged her to him now and laughed, then said, 'There's the ferry boat right along there going off to Newcastle . . . one of the pleasure trips likely. Think on that, eh? We could take a trip up to Newcastle on a Sunday, and in the week there'll always be somethin' for you to look at. The river's alive during the week.'

She turned her head towards him now and said, 'You said the rent's three and six?'

'Aye.'

'You won't get anything from Jimmy, not until he gets set-in.'

'I know, I know that. But we'll manage. I'll still be workin'. I'll keep on until we really do get set-in and make a business of it. I mightn't be able to build a boat but I'll be able to steer one, and I can shovel coal and hump bales with the rest of them. I didn't always scribble in a rent book you know; I did me stint in the Jarrow chemical works, and in the bottle works afore that.'

'I know, I know, but I was just thinkin'. Something the mistress said.'

'What did she say?'

'Well—' she turned from him and walked down the length of the room—'she doesn't want me to leave, I know that, she said as much.' She swung round again. 'Do you know she even said to me face that she'd miss me. Fancy her sayin' that.'

'Of course she'll miss you, anybody would.' He came close to her again and held her face between his hands. 'I'd miss you. If I ever lost you I'd miss you. God, how I'd miss you! Oh, Janie.'

'Don't . . . not for a minute. Listen.' She pushed his hands from under her oxters now and said, 'Would you demand I be at home all day?'

'I don't know about demand, but I'd want you at home all day. Aye, of course I would. Who's to do the cooking and the washing and the like? What are you gettin' at?'

'Well, it was something the mistress said. She said she had been thinking about raising me wage . . .'

'Ah, that was just a feeler. Now look, she's not going to put you off, is she?'

'No, no, she's not. She knows I'm goin' to be married. Oh, she knows that, but what she said was, if . . . if I could come for a while, daily like, until the children got a bit bigger and used to somebody else, because well, as she said, they were fond of me, the bairns. And she would arrange for Bessie to have my room and sleep next to them at night and I needn't be there until eight in the morning, and I could leave at half-six after I got them to bed.'

He swung away from her, his arms raised above his head, his hands flapping towards the low roof, and he flapped them until he reached the end of the room and turned about and once more was standing in front of her. And then, thrusting his head forward, he said, 'Look, you're going to be married,

81

you're going to start married life the way we mean to go on. You'll be me wife, an' I just don't want you from half-past six or seven at night till eight in the morning, I want you here all the time. I want you here when I come in at dinner-time an' at tea-time.'

'She'll give me three shillings a week. It's not to be sneezed at, it would nearly pay the rent.'

'Look. Look, we'll manage. A few more games like last night, even if nothing bigger, and I can spit in the eye of old Kean . . . and your master and mistress.'

'Don't talk like that!' She was indignant now. 'Spittin' in their eye! They've been good to me, better than anybody in me life. I've been lucky. Why, I must be the best-treated servant in this town, or in any other. She's kept me in clothes. And don't forget—' she was now wagging her head at him— 'when things were rough a few years ago with their damned strikes and such, she gave me a loaded basket every week-end. And your own belly would have been empty many a time if I hadn't have brought it. Meat, flour, sugar . . .'

'All right, all right; have you got to be grateful for a little kindness all your life? Anyway, it was nothing to them. The only time that kind of charity has any meaning is when the giver has to do without themselves. She likely throws as much in the midden every week.'

'We haven't got a midden, as you call it.'

'You know what I mean.'

Both their voices were lowering now and in a broken tone she replied, 'No, I don't know what you mean. There's things about you I don't understand, never have.'

He didn't move towards her but turned his head on his shoulder and looked sideways at her for some seconds before saying, 'You said you loved me.'

'Aye, aye, I did, but you can love somebody and not understand them. I might as well tell you I don't understand how you're always taken up so much with cards. It's a mania with you, and I shouldn't be surprised that when we're married you'll be like the rest of them; the others go out every night to the pubs but you'll go out to your gamin'.'

'I'll only go gamin' when I want money to get you things.'

'That'll be your excuse, you'll go gamin' because you can't stop gamin', it's like something in your blood. Even as far back as when we went gathering rose hips you wanted to bet on how many you could hold in your fist.'

They were staring at each other now, and he said, 'You don't want to come here then?'

'Aw yes, yes. Aw Rory.' She went swiftly towards him and leant against him. Then after a moment she muttered, 'I want to be where you are, but . . . but at the same time I feel I owe them something. You don't see them as I do. But . . . but don't worry, I'll tell her.'

He looked at her softly now as he said, 'It wouldn't work. And anyway I want me wife to meself, I don't want her to be like the scum, gutting fish, or going tatie pickin' to make ends meet. I want to take care of you, I want a home of me own, with bairns and me wife at the fireside.'

She nodded at him, saying, 'You're right, Rory, you're right,' while at the same time the disconcerting mental picture of Kathleen Leary flashed across the screen of her mind. Mrs Leary had borne sixteen children and she was worn out, tired and worn out, and she knew that Rory was the kind of man who'd give her sixteen children if he could. Well, that was life, wasn't it? Yes, but she wasn't sure if she was going to like that kind of life. She drew herself gently from him now and made for the trap door, saying, 'I'll have to get started on some sewing, I haven't got all that much in me chest.'

As he took her hand to help her down on to the first step she looked up at him and said, 'The mistress is goin' to give me me bed linen. I didn't tell you, did I?'

'No.'

'Well, she is. And that'll be something, won't it?'

'Aye, that'll be something.'

As he looked down into her face he stopped himself from adding, 'She can keep her bloody bed linen, I'll make enough afore long to smother you in bed linen.'

4

Rory didn't make enough money in a very short time to smother Janie in bed linen. By the third week of the New Year he had managed to acquire only a further eight pounds and this after four Saturday nights' sittings. And the reason wasn't because of his bad play or ill luck, it was because he was playing against fiddlers, cheats, a small gang who worked together and stood by each other like the close-knit members of a family.

Well, he was finished with the Corstorphine Town lot, and he had told little Joe either he got him into a good school or he himself would do a little investigating into No. 3 Plynlimmon Way. He could have told him he had already done some investigating and that the occupier, a Mr Nickle, was a shipowner. Even if not in an ostentatious way, nevertheless he was big enough to be a member of the shipowners' association, known as the Coal Trade Committee, which had its club and meeting room in a house on the Lawe. Moreover, he was understood to have shares in a number of businesses in the town, including those which dealt not only with the victualling of ships with bread and beef but also in ships' chandlery. And then there was the tallow factory, and many other smaller businesses. In his favour it could be said that he subscribed generously to such causes as distressed seamen and their families. And at times there were many of these; the bars along the waterfront were not always full, nor the long dance rooms attached to them in which the sailors jigged with the women they picked up.

Mr Nickle had also been a strong advocate for better sewerage, especially since the outbreak of cholera in '66, and the smallpox outbreak in 1870. He had helped, too, to bring about the new Scavenging Department under the Borough Engineer. Before this the removal of the filth of the town had been left to contractors.

Oh, Mr Nickle was a good man, Rory wasn't saying a thing against him, but Mr Nickle had a failing which was looked at askance by the temperance societies and the respectable members of the community.

And although Rory himself thought none the less of Mr Nickle, for if the crowned heads could gamble . . . and it was well known that Bertie, the Prince of Wales, was a lad at the game, why not Mr Nickle, and why not Rory Connor, or any working man for that matter? But it was the same injustice here, one law for the rich, another for the poor. Yet these sentiments did not deter him from harassing, or even threatening little Joe, nor did little Joe see any injustice in Mr Connor's treatment of him. He had a rough-hewn philosophy: there were gents of all grades, there were the high gents, middle gents, and the lower gents. Mr Connor was of the lower gents, but his money was as good as anybody else's and often he was more generous than the middle gents. The real toffs were open handed, and the waterfront gamblers were free with their money when they had it, but the middle gents were mean, and although Mr Nickle was prominent in the town and lived in one of the best ends he was, to little Joe, a middle gent, in the upper bracket of that section maybe, but still a middle gent. But he was a man who had power, as had those who worked for him, and they could be nasty at times.

Little Joe was worried for Mr Connor, but apparently Mr Connor wasn't worried for himself. In a way Joe admired a fellow like Mr Connor; he admired his pluck because it was something he hadn't much of himself.

So it was that little Joe spoke to Mr Nickle's man. Mr Nickle's man was a kind of valet-cum-butler-cum-doorman, and his wife was Mr Nickle's housekeeper, and his two daughters were Mr Nickle's parlour-maid and housemaid respectively. Altogether it was another close-knit family. There was no Mrs Nickle, she had died some years previously.

Little Joe did not lie about Mr Connor's position, that is not exactly. What he said was, he was a gent in the property business. Also, that he played a good hand and was very discreet. He had known him for some years and had set him on in schools along the waterfront, and he had added that, as he understood that two of Mr Nickle's friends had passed away recently, he had stressed the word friends, he wondered if Mr Nickle was looking for a little new blood. One thing he told Mr Nickle's man he could assure his master of, and that was Mr Connor was no sponger.

Mr Nickle's man said he would see what could be done. What he meant was he would look into Mr Connor's mode of business. He did.

When next little Joe met Rory all he could say was, 'I've got you set-in for a game in a place in Ocean Road, just near the Workhouse.'

'Do you think you'll make it the night, Rory?' Jimmy asked under his breath as he stood near the door watching Rory pull on his overcoat.

'I'll have a damned good try, I can't say better. It's a new place; I'll have to see how the land lies, won't I?'

'You'll find yourself lying under the land if you're not careful.'

Rory turned his dark gaze on to Lizzie where she

sat at one side of a long mat frame jabbing a steel progger into the stretched hessian. He watched her thrust in a clipping of rag, pull it tightly down from underneath with her left hand, then jab the progger in again before he said, 'You'd put the kibosh on God, you would.'

Ruth looked up from where she was sitting at the other side of the frame. In the lamplight her face appeared delicate and sad, and she shook her head at him, it was a gentle movement, before she said, 'Just take care of yourself that's all.'

'I've always had to, haven't I?'

'Aw, there speaks the big fellow who brought himself up. Suckled yourself from your own breast you did.'

Rory now grabbed his hard hat which Jimmy was holding towards him, then wrenching open the door, he went out.

It was a fine night. The air was sharp, the black sky was high and star-filled. He could even make out the gate because of their brightness, and also with the help of the light from the Learys' window. They never drew their blinds, the Learys.

He picked his way carefully down the narrow lane so that he shouldn't splash his boots. He had also taken the precaution of bringing a piece of rag with him in order to wipe them before he should enter this new place because the houses in King Street and down Ocean Road were mostly decent places.

The rage that Lizzie always managed to evoke in him had subsided by the time he reached Leam Lane and entered the docks. And he decided that if there was a cab about he'd take a lift. But then it wasn't very likely there'd be one around the docks, unless it was an empty one coming back from some place.

He didn't find a cab, so he had to walk all the way down to Ocean Road, a good couple of miles.

Although the streets were full of people and the roads still packed with traffic, but mostly flat carts, drays and barrows now, he kept to the main thoroughfare because the bairns seemed to go mad on a Saturday night up the side streets, and in some parts lower down in the town one of their Saturday night games was to see which of them could knock your hat off with a handful of clarts. The devil's own imps some of them were. Once he would have laughed at their antics, but not since the time he'd had a dead kitten slapped across his face.

The market place was like a beehive; the stalls illuminated with naphtha flares held every description of food, household goods, and clothing; the latter mostly second, third and fourth hand. The smells were mixed and pungent, and mostly strong, especially those emanating from the fish and meat stalls.

In King Street the gas lamps were ablaze. People stood under them in groups, while others gazed into the shop windows. Saturday night was a popular night for window-gazing and there was no hurry to buy even if you wanted to; the supplies never ran out and most of the shops were open until ten o'clock, some later.

He stopped within a few yards of his destination. He had come down here last night to make sure of the number. It was a corner house, not all that prosperous looking but not seedy. He stooped and rubbed his boots vigorously with the rag, then threw it into the gutter, after which he straightened his coat, tilted his hard hat slightly to the side, pulled at the false starched cuffs that were pinned to the ends of his blue-striped flannelette shirt sleeves, then, following little Joe's directions, he went round the corner, down some area steps, and knocked on the door.

He was surprised when it was opened by a maid, a maid of all work by the look of her, but nevertheless a maid.

'Aye?' She peered up at him in the fluttering light from a naked gas jet attached to a bracket sticking out from the wall opposite the door, and in answer he said what Joe had told him to say. 'Me name's Connor. Little Joe sent me.'

'Oh aye. Come in.'

He followed her into a room which by its appearance was a kitchen and, after closing the door, she said, 'Stay a minute'; then left him. A few minutes later she returned, accompanied by a man. He was a middle-aged half-caste, an Arab one, he surmised. It was his hair and his nostrils which indicated his origin. He looked Rory up and down, then said in a thick Geordie accent that was at variance with his appearance, 'Little Joe said you wanted a set-in. That right?'

'That's right.'

'You've got the ready?'

'Enough.'

'Show us.'

Rory stared back into the dull eyes; then slowly he lifted up the tail of his coat, put his hand in his inside pocket and brought out a handful of coins, among which were a number of sovereigns and half-sovereigns. Without speaking he thrust his hand almost into the other man's chest.

The man looked down on it, nodded and said briefly 'Aye.' Then turning about, he said, 'Come on.'

As they passed from the kitchen into the narrow passage the man said over his shoulder, 'You'll be expected to stand your turn with the cans. Little Joe tell you?'

Little Joe hadn't told him but he said, 'I'll stand me turn.'

The man now led the way into another room, and Rory saw at once that it was used as a storage place for some commodity that was packed in wooden boxes. A number of such were arrayed along one wall. The only window in the place was boarded up. There was an old-fashioned stove at one side of the room packed high with blazing coals, and the room was lit by two bracket gas lamps. There were six men in the room besides Rory's companion and himself: four of them were in a game at the table, the other two were looking on. The players didn't look up but the two spectators turned towards Rory and the half-caste with a jerk of his head said, 'This's who I was tellin' you about. Connor—' he turned to Rory—'What's your first name?'

'Rory.'

'What!'

'Ror-ry.'

'Funny name. Haven't heard that afore.'

The two spectators at the table nodded towards Rory and he nodded back at them. Then the man with arm outstretched named the players one after the other for Rory's benefit.

Rory didn't take much heed to the names until the word Pittie was repeated twice. Dan Pittie and Sam Pittie. The two brothers almost simultaneously glanced up at him, nodded, then turned their attention to the game again.

Rory, standing awkwardly to the side of the fireplace, looked from one to the other of the men, then brought his attention back to the two Pitties. They looked like twins. They were bullet-headed men, heavy-shouldered but short. These must be the fellows, together with a third one, whom Jimmy said had started the keel business from nothing. They looked a tough pair, different from their partners at the table, who didn't look river-front types; the elder of the two could have been Mr Kean; he wasn't unlike him, and was dressed in much the same fashion.

Well, he had certainly moved up one from Corstorphine Town, because, for a start, they were playing Twenty-Ones, but as yet he didn't know whether he liked the promotion or not; he certainly didn't like the half-caste. But he wasn't here to like or dislike any of them, he was here to double the money in his pocket and then see that he got safely outside with it. On the last thought he looked from

the half-caste to the Pittie brothers again and
thought it would take him to keep his wits about
him. Aye . . . aye, it would that.

5

'You're tellin' me she's in the family way?'

'Don't put it like that, man.'

'How do you expect me to put it? You bloody fool
you, how did you manage it? Where? On the ferry
or in the train? . . . All right, all right.' He thrust
John George's raised arm aside. 'But I mean just what
I say, for you've seen her for an hour or so a week,
so you've told me, when you've taken her around
Newcastle making a tour of ancient buildings. From
the Central Station into Jesmond Dene, there doesn't
seem to be one you've missed, so that's why I ask
you . . . Aw, man . . .'

They were standing on a piece of open land. A
building was being erected to one side of it while at
the other old houses were being knocked down. There
was a thin drizzle of rain falling, the whole scene was
dismal and it matched John George's dejected appearance. His thin shoulders were hunched, his head
hung down, his gaze was directed towards the
leather bag in his hand but without seeing it. He
mumbled now, 'It's all right. Don't worry, I'll manage.
I'm sorry I asked you; you'll want everytning you can
lay hands on to get the yard, I know.'

'It isn't that. You can have the two pounds, but
what good's that going to do you in this fix, I ask
you. It's a drop in the ocean and what'll happen when
she tells her folks?'

John George raised his eyes and looked up into the
grey sky. 'God! . . I just don't know. He'll be for
murdering her. He's an awful man from what I can

gather. I want to get her out of there afore he finds out.'

'How far is she?'

'Over . . . over three months.'

'Well, it won't be long then will it afore he twigs something?'

Rory shook his head, then put his hand into his back pocket, pulled out a small bag and extracted from it two sovereigns, and as he did so his teeth ground tightly together. This was putting him in a fix, he'd had just five pounds left to make a start the night, and it could be a big night, now he was left with only three.

He hadn't won anything that first Saturday night down in the cellar but he hadn't lost either, he had broken even. And the following week he had just managed to clear three pounds ten; the week after he was nine pounds up at one o'clock in the morning, but by the time he left it had been reduced to four pounds, and even then they hadn't liked it. No, none of them had liked it, the Pittie brothers least of all.

Last week when he had cleared six he said he was calling it a day and, aiming to be jocular, had added, and a night. It was the elder of the Pittie brothers who had looked at him and said, 'No, not yet, lad.' But he had risen to his feet, gathered his winnings up and stared back at the other man as he replied, grimly, 'Aye, right now, lad. Nobody's going to tell me when I come or go. I'll be along next week and you can have your own back then, but I'm off now.'

There had followed an odd silence in the room, it was a kind of rustling silence as one man after the other at the table moved in his seat. 'So long,' he had said, and not until he was up the steps and into the street did he breathe freely. For a moment he had thought they were going to do him. He had decided then that that was the last time he would go there.

Three times this week he had tried to find little Joe but with no success. He was keeping out of his way apparently, so there was nothing for it if he wanted a game but to show up in the cellar again the night.

He never went with less than five pounds on him and he'd had a job to scrape that up today because during the week he had, by putting twelve pounds ten down, cleared half the cost of the boat yard, and signed an agreement that the other seventeen pounds ten was to be paid within six weeks, and he knew, his luck holding out and as long as he didn't get into a crooked game, he would clear that. One thing about them in the cellar, they played a straight game. Anyway, they had so far.

But if he went in with only three and lost that in a run, well then, the sparks would fly. He'd have to put his thinking cap on. Oh, this bloody fool of a fellow.

As he handed the two sovereigns to John George and received his muttered thanks he asked himself where he could lay his hands on a couple of quid. It was no good asking any of them back in the house. His dad usually blew half his wages before he got home; by the time he had cleared the slate for the drinks he had run up during the week Ruth was lucky if there was ten shillings left on the mantelpiece for her. There was Janie; she had a bit saved but he doubted if it would be as much as two pounds. Anyway, he wouldn't be able to see her until the morrow and that would be too late. Oh, he'd like to take his hand and knock some damn sense into John George Armstrong.

They were walking on now, cutting through the side streets towards the market and the office, and they didn't exchange a word. When they reached the office door they cast a glance at each other out of habit as if to say, Now for it once again, but when the door didn't move under Rory's push he shook it, then, looking at John George, said, 'That's funny.'

'Use your key. Aw, here's mine.'

John George pushed the key into the lock and they went into the office and looked about them. The door to the far room was closed but on the front of the first desk was pinned a notice and they both bent down and read it. There was no heading, it just said, 'Been called away, my father has died. Lock up takings. My daughter will collect on Monday.' There was no signature.

They straightened up and looked at each other; then Rory jerked his head as he said, 'Well, this's one blessin' in disguise, for I've had the worst morning in years. He'd have gone through the roof.'

'Funny that,' John George smiled weakly; 'my takings are up the day, over four pounds. About fifteen of them paid something off the back and there wasn't one closed door.'

'That's a record.'

'Aye.' John George now went towards the inner office, saying, 'I hope he hasn't forgot to leave the key for the box.'

Standing behind Mr Kean's desk and, having opened the top drawer on the right-hand side, John George put his hand into the back of it and withdrew a key; then going to an iron box safe that was screwed down on to a bench table in the corner of the room he unlocked it. He now took out the money from his bag, put the sovereigns into piles of five and placed them in a neat row on the top shelf with the smaller change in front of them, and after placing his book to the side of the compartment he stepped back and let Rory put his takings on the bottom shelf.

As John George locked the door he remarked, 'One day he'll get a proper safe.'

'It would be a waste of money, it's never in there long enough for anybody to get at it.'

'It'll lie in there over the week-end, and has done afore.'

'Well, that's his look-out. Come on.'

John George now replaced the key in the back of the drawer; then they both left, locking the outer door behind them.

As they walked together towards Laygate, Rory

said stiffly, 'What you going to do about this other business, have you got anything in mind?'

'Aye. Aye, I have. I'm going to ask her the day. I'm going to ask her to just walk out and come to our place. She can stay hidden up there until we can get married in the registry office.'

'Registry office?'

'Aye, registry office. It's just as bindin' as any place else.'

'It isn't the same.'

'Well, it'll have to do for us.'

'Aw, man.' Rory shook his head slowly. 'You let people walk over you; you're so bloomin' soft.'

'I'm as God made me, we can't help being what we are.'

'You can help being a bloody fool, you're not a bairn.'

'Well, what do you expect me to do, leave her?'

'You needn't shout unless you want the whole street to know.'

They walked on in silence until simultaneously they both stopped at the place where their roads divided.

'See you Monday then.' Rory's tone was kindly now and John George, looking at him, said, 'Aye, see you Monday. And thanks Rory. I'll pay you back, I promise I'll pay you back.'

'I'm not afraid of that, you always have.'

'Aw . . . I wish, I wish I was like you, Rory. You're right, I'm too soft to clag holes with, no gumption. I can never say no.'

It was on the tip of Rory's tongue to come back with the retort, 'And neither can your lass apparently.' Janie had said no, and she'd kept both feet on the ground when she said it an' all. But what he said and generously was, 'People like you for what you are. You're a good bloke.' He made a small movement with his fist. 'I'll tell you something. You're better liked than me, especially up in our house. It's John George this, an' John George that.'

'Aw, go on, man, stop pulling me leg. But it's nice of you to say it nevertheless, and as I said—' he patted his pocket—'I won't forget this.'

'That's all right, man. So long, and good luck.'

'So long . . . so long, Rory. And thanks. Thanks again.'

They went their ways, neither dreaming he would never see the other again.

When Rory went into the cellar that same evening he had eight pounds in his pocket.

The Pittie brothers were already at the table, but the two men partnering them were unknown to Rory until he realized that one of them was the third Pittie brother. He was a man almost a head taller than the other two. His nose was flattened and looked boneless. This was the one who was good with his fists, so he had heard, but by the look of him he wasn't all that good for his face looked like a battered pluck. The fourth man looked not much bigger than little Joe and he had a foxy look, but he was well put on. His suit, made of some kind of tweed, looked quite fancy, as did his pearl-buttoned waistcoat. During the course of conversation later in the evening he discovered that he was from across the water in North Shields and was manager of a blacking factory.

Rory kicked his heels for almost an hour before he got set-in at the table, for after the game they spent quite some time drinking beer and eating meat sandwiches. Although he always stood his share in buying the beer he drank little of it and tonight less than usual, for he wanted to keep his wits about him. Some part of him was worried at the presence of the third Pittie brother, it was creating a small niggling fear at the back of his mind.

The big Pittie was dealer. He shuffled the cards in a slow ponderous way until Rory wanted to say, 'Get on with it'; then of a sudden he spoke. 'You aimin' to buy old Kilpatrick's yard I hear?'

Rory was startled, and he must have shown it for the big fellow jerked his chin upwards as he said, 'Oh, you can't keep nowt secret on the waterfront; there's more than scum comes in on the tide . . . Your young 'un works at Baker's, don't he?'

'Aye. Yes, he works at Baker's.'

'What does he expect to do at Kilpatrick's, build a bloody battleship?'

The three brothers now let out a combined bellow and the thin man in the fancy waistcoat laughed with them, although it was evident he didn't know what all this was about.

Rory's lower jaw moved from one side to the other before he said, 'He's going to build scullers and small keel-like boats.'

'Keel-like boats. Huh!' It was the youngest of the Pittie's speaking now. 'Where's he gona put them?'

'Where they belong, on the river.'

'By God! he'll be lucky, you can hardly get a plank atween the boats now. And what's he gona do with the keel-like boats when he gets them on the water, eh?'

'Same as you, work them, or sell them.'

As the three pairs of eyes became fixed on him he told himself to go steady, these fellows meant business, they weren't here the night only for the game. He kept his gaze steady on them as he said, 'Well now, since you know what I have in mind, are we going to play?'

The big fellow returned to his shuffling. Then he dealt. When Rory picked up his cards he thought, Bad start, good finish.

And so it would seem. He lost the first game, won the next two, lost the next one, then won three in a row. By one o'clock in the morning he had a small pile of sovereigns and a larger pile of silver to his hand. Between then and two o'clock the pile went down a little before starting again to increase steadily.

At the end of a game when the man in the fancy

waistcoat had no money in front of him he said he must be going. He had, he said, lost enough for one night and what was more he'd have to find somebody to scull him across the river. And at this time of the morning whoever he found would certainly make him stump up, and what he had left, he thought, was just about enough to carry him over.

When Rory, too, also voiced that he must be on his way there were loud, even angry cries from the table.

'Aw, no, no, lad,' said the big fellow. 'Fair's fair. You've taken all our bloody money so give us a chance to get a bit of it back, eh? We've to get across the river an' all.' There was laughter at this, but it was without mirth.

And so another game started, and long before it finished the uneasy sickly feeling in the pit of Rory's stomach had grown into what he hated to admit was actual fear.

Another hour passed and it was towards the end of a game when things were once again going in Rory's favour that the youngest Pittie brother began speaking of Jimmy as if he were continuing the conversation that had centred around him earlier in the play.

'Your young 'un's bandy,' he said. 'Bandy Connor they call him along the front . . . Saw him from the boat t'other day. Drive a horse and cart through his legs you could.' He now punched his brother in the side of the chest and the brother guffawed: 'Aye, his mother must have had him astride a donkey.'

Any reference to the shape of Jimmy's legs had always maddened Rory; he had fought more fights on Jimmy's account than he had on his own. But now, although there was a rage rising in him that for the moment combated his fear, he warned himself to go steady, for they were up to something. They were like three bull terriers out to bait a bull. He was no bull, but they were bull terriers all right.

The stories of their past doings flicked across the

surface of his mind and increased his rising apprehension, yet did not subdue his rage, even while the cautionary voice kept saying, 'Careful, careful, let them get on with it. Get yourself outside, let them get on with it.'

When he made no reply to the taunt, one after another, the three brothers laid down their cards and looked at him, and he at them. Then slowly he placed his cards side by side on the table.

The three Pitties and the half-caste stared at his cards and they did not lift their eyes when his hand went out and drew the money from the centre of the table towards him. Not until he pushed his chair back and got to his feet did one of them speak. It was the youngest brother. 'You goin' then?' he said.

'Aye.' Rory moved his head slowly downwards.

'You've had a good night.'

'You all had the same chance.'

'I would argue about that.'

'Would you?'

'I think you had a trick or two up your sleeve.'

'What! Then search me if you've got a mind.'

'Aw, no need for that, I wasn't meanin' the actual cards. But you're a bit of a clever bugger, aren't you?'

'I'm bucked that you think so.' He stood buttoning his coat, and noted that the half-caste was no longer in the room. He picked up his hat from a side table and went towards the door, saying, 'So long then.'

The brothers didn't speak. When he pulled at the door it didn't open. He tugged at it twice before turning and looking back into the room. The three men had risen from the table. He stared at them and now the fear swept over him like a huge wave and his stomach heaved.

'What you standing there for? Can't you get out?'

The big fellow was approaching him, his arms hanging loosely at his sides. But strangely it wasn't the fellow's arms or his face that Rory looked at, but his feet. He hadn't noticed them before. They were enormous feet encased in thick hob-nailed boots. The boots had the dull sheen of tallow on them with which they had likely been greased.

When the arms sprang up and grabbed at his shoulders Rory struck out, right, then left; right, then left, but his blows were the wild desperate punches used in the back lanes or among the lads in a scrap, as often happened in a work's yard.

He remembered hearing the big fellow laugh just before the great fist struck his jaw and seemed to snap his head from his body.

He was on the floor now and he screamed when the boot caught him in the groin. Then he was on his feet again, somebody holding him while another belted into him, the big fellow. They left it all to the big fellow. He was still struggling to hit out but like a child swapping flies when the blow came under his chin, and once more he was on his back. But this time he knew nothing about it. He didn't feel them going through his pockets, nor when the three of them used their feet on him. He was quite unaware of being hoisted across the big fellow's shoulder and being carried past the half-caste who was standing in the doorway now and up the area steps into the dark side street, then through the back alleyways towards the river.

That he didn't reach the river was due to the appearance of two bulky figures coming through a cut between the warehouses. One was a dark-cloaked priest who had been to a ship to give the last rites to a dying sailor. The man accompanying him was the dead man's friend who was seeing the priest safely back into the town. But to the three brothers their shapes indicated two burly sailors or night-watchmen, and both types could do some dirty fighting on their own, so with a heave they threw the limp body among a tangle of river refuse, broken spars, boxes, and decaying fruit and vegetable, and minutes later the priest and the sailor passed within six feet of it and went on their way.

6

They were all in the kitchen, Bill Waggett, Gran and Janie—Janie still had her outdoor things on; Collum Leary and Kathleen and with them now was their son Pat; Paddy Connor, Ruth, Jimmy; and lastly Lizzie; and it was Lizzie who, looking at young Pat Leary said, 'Talk sense, lad. 'Tis three o'clock on Sunday afternoon an' he left the house round six last night. Who would be playin' cards all that time I ask you?'

'It's true, Lizzie. 'Tis true. I've heard of games goin' on for twenty-four hours. They win an' lose, win an' lose.'

'He would never stay all this time; something's happened him.'

Nobody contradicted her now but they all turned and looked at Janie who, with fingers pressed tightly against her lower lip, said, 'You should have gone down and told the polis.'

'What should we tell the polis, lass?' Paddy Connor now asked her quietly. 'That me son was out gamin' last night an' hasn't come back? All right, they'll say, let's find him an' push him along the line. Where was he gamin'? I don't know, says I. Lass—' his voice was still gentle—'we've thought of everything.'

Grannie Waggett, who was the only one seated, now turned in her chair and, her pale eyes sweeping the company, she said, 'If you want my advice the lot of you, you'll stop frashin'. It's as Pat there says, he's got into a game. He's gamin' mad, always has been. It affects some folks like that, like a poison in their blood. Some blokes take to drink, others to whorin' . . .'

'Gran!'

The old woman flashed a look on Janie. 'Whorin'
I said, an' whorin' I mean, an' for my part I'd rather
have either of them than one that takes to gamin',
'cos with them you're sure of a roof over your head
some time, but not with a gamer for he'd gamble the
shift off your back an' you inside it. There was this
gentleman who used to come to the house when I
was in service in Newcastle. Real gentleman, carriage an' pair, fancy wife, mansion, he had. One day
he had everything, next day nowt. I tell you, me
girl—' she turned and stabbed her finger towards
Janie—'you want to put your foot down right from
the start or get used to livin' in the open, for I tell
you, you won't be sure of a roof . . .'

'Be quiet, Ma.'

Grannie Waggett turned on her son. 'Don't you
tell me to be quiet.'

'Be quiet all of you, please.' It was Ruth speaking
gently. 'What I think should be done is somebody
should go down to the Infirmary, the new Infirmary.
If anything had happened to him they'd take him
there.'

'And make a fool of themselves askin'.'

Ruth now looked at her husband. 'I don't mind
lookin' a fool, I'll go.'

'No, Ma.' Jimmy who had not opened his mouth so
far went towards the bottom of the ladder now,
saying, 'I'll go, I'll change me things an' I'll go.'

As he mounted upwards Collum said, 'It's odd it is
that he made no mention of whereabouts he'd be,
now isn't it? But then again perhaps it isn't; if he'd
got set on in a big school the least said the soonest
mended, for you can't be too careful: the polis just
need a whisper and it's up their nose it goes like a
sniff to a bloodhound.'

Up in the loft Jimmy went straight to a long
wooden box and took out his Sunday coat and
trousers, but he didn't get into them immediately.
For quite some minutes he stood with them gripped
tight against his chest, his eyes closed, his lips

moving as he muttered to himself, 'Oh dear God! don't let nowt happen our Rory. Please, please, don't let nowt happen him.'

As he came down the ladder again, Janie said, 'I'll go with you.' But he shook his head at her. 'No, no, I'll be better on me own. Well, what I mean is, I can get around the waterfront. If he's not in the hospital I can get around and ask.'

'Be careful.'

He turned to Lizzie and nodded, saying, 'Aye; aye,' and as he went to let himself out, Ruth followed him and, opening the door for him, said quietly, 'Don't stay late, not in the dark, not around there.'

'All right, Ma.' He nodded at her, then went out.

He ran most of the way into Shields and wasn't out of breath. He took no notice of the urchins who shouted after him:

'Bow-legged Billy,
Bandy-randy,
One eye up the chimney, the other in the pot,
Poor little sod, yer ma's given you the lot.'

At one time the rhyme used to hurt him but he was inured to it now. Nothing could hurt him, he told himself, except that something should happen to their Rory. He'd want to peg out himself if anything happened to their Rory. What was more, if it had already happened he would be to blame because if he hadn't yarped on about the boatyard Rory wouldn't have gone gambling . . . But, aye, he would, he would always gamble. But not at this new place, this big place he had gone to these past few Saturdays. He hadn't let on where it was. He had asked him, but the laughing answer had been, 'Ask no questions and you'll get no lies . . .'

The porter at the Infirmary said, 'No, lad, nobody the name of Connor's been brought in the day. Then they don't bring people in on a Sunday less it's accidents like.'

'Well, I was thinkin' it could've been an accident.'

'Well, there's no Connor here, lad. Neither mister nor missis.'

'Ta . . . thanks.' He didn't know whether he was disappointed or relieved.

He was going down the gravel drive when the porter's voice hailed him, saying, 'Just a minute! There's a fella, but I hope it isn't the one you're lookin' for. There was a bloke brought in round dinner-time, no name on him, nothing. He was found on the waterfront. Not a sailor. His clothes were respectable, what was left of them, but I expect by now he's kicked the bucket.'

Jimmy walked slowly back towards the man, saying as he went, 'What's he like?'

'Oh, lad, his own mother wouldn't be able to recognize him, he's been bashed about worse than anybody I've seen afore.'

'Had he brown hair, thick, wavy. . . ?'

'Whatever colour this fellow's hair once was, lad, I couldn't say, but the day it was dark red, caked with blood.'

Jimmy stood looking up at the man, his mouth slightly agape. Then closing it, the words came dredged through his lips as he said, 'Could . . . could I see him, this . . . this fella?'

'Well. Well, I'll ask the sister. Come on back.'

'Sit there a minute,' he said a moment later, pointing to a polished wooden chair standing against the painted brick wall of the lobby.

Jimmy sat down, glad to get off his legs. He was feeling weak, faint, and frightened, very frightened.

The porter came back and beckoned to him. Then with his hand on Jimmy's shoulder, he pointed and said, 'Go down there, lad, to the end of the corridor, turn left, an' you'll see the sister.'

The sister was tall and thin. She put him in mind of John George. He had to put his head back to look up at her. She said to him, 'You're looking for your brother?'

'Aye, miss.'

'How old is he?'

'Twenty-three, comin' up twenty-four next month.'

'There's a young man in there,' she nodded towards the wall. 'He's in a very bad state, he's been badly beaten. But . . . but you may be able to recognize him, if he is your brother.'

She turned away, and Jimmy followed her towards the figure lying on the bed. It was very still. The head was swathed in bandages, the face completely distorted with bruises. He found himself gasping for breath. He had once seen a man taken from the river. He was all blue, bluey black and bloated. He had been dead for days, they said. This man on the bed could be dead an' all. He didn't know if it was their Rory. The sister was whispering something in his ear and he turned and looked dazedly at her. Then he whispered back as he pointed to his thumb. 'He had a wart atween his finger an' thumb towards the front. He'd always had it.'

The sister gently picked up the limp hand from the counterpane and turned it over; then she looked at Jimmy as he stared down at the flat hard wart that Rory had for years picked and scraped at in an effort to rid himself of it.

The sister drew him backwards away from the bed, and when they were in the corridor again she still kept her hand on his shoulder as she endeavoured to soothe him, saying, 'There now. There now.'

The tears were choking him. Although they were flooding down his face they were packing his gullet, he couldn't breathe.

She took him into a room and said, 'Where do you live?'

When he was unable to answer she asked, 'In the town?'

He shook his head.

'Tyne Dock?'

He brought out between gasps, 'Up . . . up Simonside.'

'Oh, that's a long way.'

He dried his face now on his sleeve, then took a clean rag from his pocket and blew his nose. After some minutes he looked up at her and said, 'I'll bring me ma and da,' then added, 'Will he. . . ?'

She said kindly, 'I don't know, he's very low. He could see the morning, but then again I don't know.'

He nodded at her, then walked slowly from the room. But in the corridor he turned and looked back at her and said, 'Ta,' and she smiled faintly at him.

He didn't run immediately, he walked from the gates to where the road turned into Westoe and as he looked down it he thought of Janie. Poor Janie. Poor all of them. In their different ways they'd all miss him, miss him like hell. He had been different from them, different from his da and Mr Waggett and Mr Leary, and all the women had looked up to him. He had become something, a rent collector. There were very few people from their walk of life who rose to rent collectors . . . And himself? He stopped in the street. If Rory went then his own life would come to an end. Not even boats would bring him any comfort. This feeling he had for Rory was not just admiration because he had got on in the world, it was love, because he was the only being he'd really be able to love. He had another love, but that was in a secret dream. He'd never have a lass of his own for no lass would look the side he was on; but that hadn't mattered so very much because there'd always be Rory.

As if he were starting a race he sprang forward and ran. He ran until he thought his heart would burst, for it was uphill all the way after he left the docks, and when finally he staggered into the kitchen he dropped on to the floor and held his side against the painful stitch before he could speak to them all hanging over him. And when he did speak it was to Janie he addressed himself.

They walked quickly, almost on the point of a run,

all the way back with him into Shields in the dark, Paddy, Ruth, Lizzie and Janie, and for hours they all waited in the little side room. It was against the rules, but the night sister had taken pity on them and brought them in out of the cold.

Janie left the Infirmary around eleven o'clock to slip back to her place, and the look on her face checked the upbraiding from the cook and her master and mistress. The master and mistress were deeply concerned over the incident and gave her leave to visit the hospital first thing in the morning.

Fortunately it was not more than five minutes' walk from the house, they said, so she was to go upstairs and rest, as she would need all her strength to face the future.

It was a term that ordinary people used when a man had died and a woman was left to fend for herself and her family with no hope of help but the questionable charity of the Poor House. It was as if Rory were already gone. Well, the family expected he would go before dawn, didn't they? Men in his condition usually went out about three in the morning.

She asked politely if she could go back now because she'd like to be with him when he went.

Her master and mistress held a short conference in the drawing-room and then they gave her their permission.

Rory passed the critical time of 3 a.m. He was still breathing at five o'clock in the morning, but the night sister informed them now that he might remain in a coma for days and that they should go home.

Ruth and Paddy nodded at her in obedience because they both knew that Paddy must get to work; and Ruth said to Janie, 'You must get back an' all, lass. Don't take too much advantage an' they'll let you out again.' And Janie, numb with agony, could only nod to this sound advice. But Lizzie refused to budge. Here she was, she said, and here she'd remain until she knew he was either going or staying. And Jimmy said he'd stay too, until it was time to go to work.

So Ruth and Paddy nodded a silent good-bye to Janie when their ways parted at Westoe and walked without exchanging a word through the dark streets that were already filling with men on their way to the shipyards, the docks, and farther into Jarrow to Palmer's. But when they had passed through the arches and came to where the road divided Paddy said, 'I'd better go straight on up else I'll be late.'

'You've got your good suit on.'

'Bugger me good suit!'

Ruth peered at him through the darkness before she said quietly, 'If he goes things'll be tight, think on that. There'll be less for beer and nowt for clothes. I depended on him.'

'Aw, woman!' He swung away from her now and made for the Simonside road, saying over his shoulder, 'Then stop skittering behind, put a move on. If they dock me half an hour it'll be less on the mantelpiece, so think on.'

Think on, he said. She had thought on for years. She had thought on the pain of life that you managed to work off during the daytime, but which pressed on you in the night and settled around your heart, causing wind, the relief of which brought no ease. She had loved him in the early years, but after Rory was born she hated him. Yet her hate hadn't spread over Lizzie. Strange that, she had always liked Lizzie. Still did. She couldn't imagine life without Lizzie. When Nellie was born a little wonder had entered her life, yet she had actually fought him against the conception. Every time he had tried to touch her she had fought him. Sometimes she conquered because he became weary of the struggle, but at other times after a hard day at the wash tub and baking and cleaning, because she'd had it all to do herself then as Lizzie went out daily doing for the people down the bank, she would surrender from sheer exhaustion. When Jimmy came life ran smoothly for a time. She felt happy she had a son; that he should have rickets didn't matter so much. As he grew his legs would straighten. So she had thought at first. Then came the day when hate rose in her for Paddy again. It was when he tried once more to take Lizzie. She had come in from next door and found them struggling there in the open on the mat and the bairns locked in the scullery. There had been no need for Lizzie to protest 'I want none of him, Ruth, I want none of him,' the scratches on his face bore out her statement.

From then on the dess bed in the kitchen became a battleground. Finally he brought the priest to her; and she was forced to do her duty in the fear of everlasting hell and damnation.

She had never asked herself why Lizzie had stayed with them all these years because where would a single woman go with a bairn? Anyway, it was his responsibility to see that she was taken care of after giving her a child.

And now that child was lying back there battered and on his way to death. What would Lizzie do without him? He had scorned her since the day he learned she was his mother. But it hadn't altered her love for him; the only thing it had done was put an edge to her tongue every time she spoke to him. Funny, but she envied Lizzie. Although she knew she had Rory's affection, she envied her, for she was his mother.

Rory regained consciousness at eight o'clock on the Monday morning. Lizzie was by his side and he looked at her without recognition, and when his lips moved painfully she put her ear down to him and all she could make out was one word, which she repeated a number of times and in an anguished tone. 'Aye. Aye, lad,' she said, 'it is a pity. It is a pity. Indeed it is a pity.'

He would rally, they said, so she must leave the ward but she could come back in the afternoon.

Without protest now she left the hospital. But she didn't go straight home. She found her way to the Catholic church, which she had never been in before; on her yearly visits she patronized the Jarrow one. She waited until the Mass was finished, and then approaching the priest without showing the awe due to his station and infallibility, she told him that her son was dying in the Infirmary and would he see that he got the last rites. The priest asked her where she was from and other particulars. He showed her no sympathy, he didn't like her manner, she was a brusque woman and she did not afford him the reverence that her kind usually bestowed on him, nor did she slip anything into his hand, but she did say that if her son went she would buy a mass for him.

He watched her leave the church without putting a halfpenny in the poor box.

The priest's feelings for Lizzie were amply reciprocated. She told herself she didn't like him; he wasn't a patch on the Jarrow ones. But then she supposed it didn't make much difference who sent you over to the other side as long as there was one of them to see that you were properly prepared for the journey.

It was around half-past one when Lizzie, about to pick up her shawl for the journey back to the hospital, glanced out of the cottage window, then stopped and said, 'Here's John George; he must have heard.'

By the time John George reached the door she had opened it and, looking at his white drawn face, said quietly, 'Come in, lad. Come in.'

He came in. He stood in the middle of the room looking from one to the other; then as he was about to speak Ruth said softly, 'You've heard then, John George?' and he repeated 'Heard?'

'Aye, about Rory.'

'Rory? I . . . I came up to find him.'

'You don't know then?'

He turned to Lizzie. 'Know what, Lizzie? What . . . what's happened him?' He shook his head, then asked again. 'What's happened him?'

'Oh lad!' Lizzie now put her hand to her brow. 'You mean to say you haven't heard? Jimmy was going to tell Mr Kean at break time.'

'Mr Kean?'

'Aye, sit down, lad.' Ruth now put her hand out and pressed John George into a chair, and he looked at her dumbly as he said, 'Mr Kean's not there. Miss Kean, she . . . she came for a while.' He nodded his head slowly now, then asked stiffly, 'Rory. Where is he?'

'He's down in the hospital, John George. He was beaten up, beaten unto death something terrible.'

When John George now slumped forward over the table and dropped his head into his hands both women came close to him and Lizzie murmured, 'Aye, lad, aye, I know how you feel.'

After a while he raised his head and looked from one to the other and said dully, 'He's dead then?'

'No.' Lizzie shook her head from side to side. 'But he's as near to it as makes no matter. It'll be one of God's rare miracles if he ever recovers, an' if he does only He knows what'll be left of him . . . Was Mr Kean asking for him?'

It seemed now that he had difficulty in speaking for he gulped in his throat a number of times before repeating, 'He wasn't there, won't be; won't be back till the night, his father died.'

'Ah, God rest his soul. Aye, you did say he wasn't there. Well, you can tell him when you do see him that it'll be some time afore Rory collects any more rents, that's if ever. It's God's blessin' he hadn't any collection on him when they did him. Whatever they took from him, an' that was every penny, it was his own.'

John George's head was bent again and he now made a groaning sound.

'Will you come in along of me and see him, I'm on me way? It's the Infirmary.'

He rose to his feet, and stared at her, then like someone in a daze, he turned and made for the door.

'Aren't you stayin' for a cup of tea, lad?' It was Ruth speaking now.

He didn't answer her except to make a slight movement with his head, then he went out leaving the door open behind him.

They both stood and watched him go down the path. And when he was out of sight they looked at each other in some amazement, and Lizzie said, 'It's broken him; he thought the world of Rory. It's made him look like death itself.'

'Get your shawl on and go after him.' Ruth pointed to where the shawl was lying across the foot of Lizzie's bed which was inset in the alcove. But Lizzie shook her head, saying, 'He wants no company, something about him said he wants no company.' She moved her head slowly now as she stared back at Ruth. 'God knows, this has hit everyone of us but in some strange way him most of all. It's strange, it is that. Did you see his face, the look on it? It was as if he himself was facing death. Me heart's breakin' at this minute over me own, yet there's room for sorrow in me for that lad. Poor John George.'

7

Janie sat by the bed and gazed down on the face that she had always thought was the best looking of any lad in the town and she wondered if it would ever go back into shape again. Oh, she hoped it would, for, being Rory, he'd hate to be marked for life. And she couldn't stand the thought either of him being disfigured; but as long as he was alive that's all that really mattered. And he was alive, and fighting to keep alive.

He had opened his eyes once and looked at her and she thought that he had recognized her, but she wasn't sure. His lips were moving continuously but all he kept saying was 'Pity. Pity.' There must be something on his mind that was making him think it was a pity, and she thought too that it was the greatest of pities that he had ever gone gaming because she had no doubt but that he had been followed from wherever he had played, and been robbed, and by somebody in the know; likely one of them he had played against. But as Jimmy said last night, they mustn't breathe a word of it because if it got to Mr Kean's ears that would be the finish of his rent collecting. You couldn't be a gambler and a rent collector . . . And then there was this business of John George.

Eeh! she was glad to the heart that Rory didn't know about that because that would really have been the finish of him. Of all the fools on this earth John George was the biggest. She couldn't really believe it, and if the master hadn't told her himself she wouldn't have, but the master's partner dealt with Mr Kean's business. Odd, but she hadn't known that afore. But still, she asked herself, why should she? Anyway, he had pricked his ears up when he heard that one of Mr Kean's men had swindled him because, as he said, he knew that her intended worked for Mr Kean.

Rory's head moved slightly on the pillow, his eyelids flickered, and she bent over him and said softly, 'Rory, it's Janie. How you feelin', Rory?'

'Pity,' he said. 'Pity.'

The tears welled up in her eyes and rolled down her cheeks and she whispered, 'Oh, Rory, come back from wherever you are.' Then she said softly, 'I've got to go now, I've got to get back, but I'll come again the night. The mistress says I can take an hour off in the afternoon and evening. It's good of her.' She spoke as if he could understand her, then she stood up, whispering softly, 'Bye-bye, dear. Bye-bye.'

Five minutes later she was turning off the main road and into Westoe when she saw the two dark-clothed figures of Ruth and Lizzie approaching. She ran towards them, and immediately they asked together, 'You've been?'

'Aye, yes.'

'Any change?'

She looked at Lizzie and shook her head, then said, 'He opened his eyes but . . . but I don't think he knew me, he just keeps sayin' that word, pity, pity . . . Have . . . have you heard about John George?'

'John George? Was he in?'

'No, Mrs Connor—' she always gave Ruth her full title—'he's . . . he's been taken.'

'Taken?' They both screwed up their faces while they looked back at her.

'Yes, for stealin'.'

'John George!' Again they spoke simultaneously.

She nodded her head slowly. 'Five pounds ten, and . . . and he's been at it for some time.'

They were speechless. Their mouths fell into a gape as they listened. 'Mr Kean was away and Miss Kean came early on, earlier than usual to collect the money. She was on her way to some place or other an' she just called in on the off-chance. She had her father's key and she opened the box and . . . and there was five pounds ten short from what was in his book. Apparently he had been doin' a fiddle.'

'No! Not John George.' Ruth was holding the brim of her black straw hat tightly in her fist.

'Yes. Aye, I couldn't believe it either. It made me sick. But the master, he heard it all in the office. The solicitors, you know. He . . . he said he was a stupid fellow. I . . . I put a word in for him I did. I said I'd always found him nice, a really nice fella, and he said, 'He's been crafty, Janie. He's admitted to using this trick every time he was sure Mr Kean wasn't goin' to collect the Saturday takings.' Apparently he would nip something out then put it back on the Monday mornin' early, but this time he was too late. And then he said nobody but a stupid man would admit to doing this in the past, then try to deny that he had taken five pounds ten. He wanted to say it was only ten shillings, and he had that on him to put back . . . He had just been to the pawn. They found the ticket on him.'

'Oh God Almighty! what'll happen next? Rory and now John George, an' all within three days. It isn't possible. But this accounts for his face, the look on his face when he came up yesterday. Eeh! God above.' Lizzie began rocking herself.

'It's this lass that he's caught on to, Lizzie.' Janie nodded slowly. 'Rory said he was barmy about her. He bought her a locket an' chain at Christmas and he takes her by the ferry or train to Newcastle every week, then round the buildings. He's daft about buildings. I never knew that till he told me one night. Then last week he gave her tea in some place. Yes, he did, he took her out to tea. And not in no cheap café neither, a place off Grey Street. An' Rory said Grey Street's classy.'

'Women can be the ruin of a man in more ways than one.' Lizzie's head was bobbing up and down now. 'But no matter, I'm sorry for him, to the very heart of me I'm sorry for him 'cos I liked John George. He had somethin' about him, a gentleness, not like a man usually has.'

Ruth asked quietly, 'Do you know when he'll be tried, Janie?'

'No, but I mean to find out.'

'Somebody should go down and see him, he's got nobody I understand, only those two old 'un's. And you know, it isn't so much laziness with them—' Ruth turned now and shook her head at Lizzie—'it isn't, Lizzie, it's the rheumatics. And this'll put the finish to them, it'll be the House for them. Dear, dear

Lord!'—Ruth never said God—'You've got to ask why these things happen.'

The three of them stood looking at each other for a moment. Then Janie said, 'I've got to go now, but I'm gettin' out the night an' all. The mistress said I can have an hour in the afternoon and in the evenin's. She's good, isn't she?'

They nodded at her, and Lizzie agreed. 'Aye, she's unusual in that way. Bye-bye then, lass.'

'Bye-bye.' She nodded from one to the other, then again said, 'Bye-bye,' before running across the road and almost into a horse that was pulling a fruit cart, and as Lizzie watched her she said, 'It only needed her to get herself knocked down and that would have been three of them. Everythin' happens in threes, so I wonder what's next?'

8

Janie had never before been in a court. She sat on the bench nearest the wall. At the far end of the room, right opposite to her, was the magistrate; in front of him were a number of dark-clothed men. They kept moving from one to the other, they all had papers in their hands. At times they would bend over a table and point to the papers. The last prisoner had got a month for begging, and now they were calling out the name: 'John George Armstrong! John George Armstrong!'

As if emerging out of a cellar John George appeared. The box in which he stood came only to his hips, but the upper part of him seemed to have shrunk, his shoulders were stooped, his head hung forward, his face was the colour of clay. One of the dark-suited men began to talk. Janie only half listened to him, for her eyes were riveted on John George, almost willing him to look at her, to let him know there was someone here who was concerned for him. Poor John George! Oh, poor John George!

. . . 'He did on the twenty-fourth day of January steal from his employer, Septimus Kean, Esquire, of Birchingham House, Westoe, the sum of five pounds ten shillings . . .'

The next words were lost to Janie as she watched John George close his eyes and shake his head. It was as if he were saying, 'No, no.' Then the man on the floor was mentioning Miss Kean's name . . . 'She pointed out to the accused the discrepancy between his entries in the ledger and the amount of money in the safe.'

Rory had always said they hadn't a safe, not a proper one. She looked towards Miss Kean. She could only see her profile but she gathered that she was thin and would likely be tall when she stood up. She wore a pill-box hat of green velvet perched on the top of her hair. She looked to have a lot of hair, dark, perhaps it was padded. Even the mistress padded her hair at the back, especially when she was going out to some function.

'The accused argued with her that he was only ten shillings short and he had the amount in his pocket, and he had intended to replace it. He asked her to recount the money. This she did. He then admitted to having helped himself on various previous occasions to small sums but said he always replaced them. He insisted that there was only ten shillings missing. He then tried to persuade her to accept the ten shillings and not mention the matter to her father . . . When taken into custody he said . . .'

Oh John George! Why had he been so daft? Why? It was that girl. If she ever met her she'd give her the length of her tongue, she would that, and when Rory came to himself and heard this he'd go mad, he would that. But it would be some time before they could tell Rory anything.

The magistrate was talking now about trusting employers being taken advantage of, about men like the prisoner being made an example of; about some men being nothing more than sneak thieves and that the respectable citizens of this town had to be protected from them.

'Do you plead guilty or not guilty?'

'I . . . I didn't take five pounds, sir.'

'Answer the question. Do you plead guilty or not guilty?'

'I didn't take five . . .' John George's voice trailed away. There was talk between the magistrate and one of the men on the floor, then Janie's mouth opened wide when the magistrate said, 'I sentence you to a total of twelve months. . . .'

She shot to her feet and actually put her hand up to try to attract John George's attention, but he never raised his head.

A few minutes later she stood by the door of the Court House. The tears were running down her face. Her hour was nearly up and she wanted to call in at the hospital. That's where she was supposed to be. She didn't know what she would have done or said if the master had been in the court, but he wasn't there. Oh, John George! Poor John George!

A policeman came through the door and looked at her. He had seen her in the court room, he had seen her lift her hand to the prisoner. He said, not unkindly, 'He got off lightly. I've known him give three years, especially when they've been at it as long as he has. He always lays it on thick when he's dealin' with men who should know better. He had the responsibility of money you know an' he should have known better. Anyway, what's a year?' He smiled down at her, and she said, 'Would . . . could . . . do you ever allow anybody to see them for a minute?'

'Well now. Aye, yes, it's done.' He stared at her, then said quickly, 'Come on. Come this way. Hurry up; they'll be movin' them in next to no time. There's more than a few for Durham the day and he'll be among them I suppose.'

She followed him at a trot and when he came to an abrupt stop she almost bumped into his back. He opened a door and she glimpsed a number of men, definitely prisoners, for the stamp was on their faces, and three uniformed policemen.

Her guide must have been someone in authority, a sergeant or someone like that, she thought, for he nodded to the officers and said, 'Armstrong for a minute, I'll be with him.'

'Armstrong!' one of the policemen bawled, and John George turned about and faced the door. And when the policeman thumbed over his shoulder he walked through it and out into the corridor.

The sergeant now looked at him. Then, nodding towards Janie, said, 'Two minutes, and mind, don't try anything. Understand?' He poked his face towards John George, and John George stared dumbly back at him for a moment before turning to Janie.

'Hello, John George.' It was a silly thing to say but she couldn't think of anything else at the moment.

'Hello, Janie.'

'Oh!' Now as the tears poured from her eyes her tongue became loosened and she gabbled, 'I'm so sorry, John George. Why? Why? We're all sorry. We'll come an' see you, we will. There'll be visitin' times. I'll ask.'

'Janie!' His voice sounded calm, then again he said 'Janie!' and she said, 'Yes, John George?'

'Listen. Will you go and see Maggie? She won't know, at least I don't think so, not until she reads the papers. She's . . . she's going to have a bairn, Janie, she'll need somebody.'

She put her hand tightly across her mouth and her eyes widened and she muttered, 'Oh, John George.'

'Time's up. That's enough.'

'Janie! Janie! listen. Believe me; I never took the five pounds. Ten shillings aye, but never the five pounds. You tell that to Rory, will you? Tell that to Rory.'

'Yes, yes, I will, John George. Yes I will. Good-bye. Good-bye, John George.'

She watched him going back into the room. She couldn't see the policeman now but she inclined her head towards him and said, 'Ta, thanks.'

He walked with her along the stone passage and to the door, and there he said, 'Don't worry. As I said, what's a year? And you can visit him once a month.' Then bending towards her he said, 'What are you to him? I thought you were his wife, but I hope not after what I heard . . . You his sister?'

'No, only . . . only a friend.'

He nodded at her, then said, 'Well, he won't need any friends for the next twelve months, but he will after.'

'Ta-rah,' she said.

'Ta-rah, lass,' he said, and as she walked away he watched her. He was puzzled by her relationship to the prisoner. Just a friend, she had said.

She walked so slowly from the Court House that she hadn't time to call in at the hospital and when she arrived in the kitchen she was crying so much that the cook called the mistress, and the mistress said, 'Oh, I'm sorry, I'm sorry, Janie,' and she answered her through her tears, 'No, 'tisn't . . . 'tisn't that, he's . . . he's still as he was. It's . . . it's John George. I know I shouldn't have but I went to the court, ma'am, and he got a year.'

Her mistress's manner altered, her face stiffened. 'You're a very silly girl, Janie,' she said. 'The master will be very annoyed with you. Court rooms are no places for women, young women, girls. I, too, am very annoyed with you. I gave you the time off to visit your fiancé. That man's a scamp, a thieving scamp. I'm surprised your fiancé didn't find it out before. . . . What sentence did he get?'

'A year, ma'am.'

'That was nothing really, nothing. If he had been

an ordinary labouring man, one could have understood him stealing, but he was in a position of trust,
and when such men betray their trust they deserve
heavy sentences. Dry your eyes now. Go upstairs and
see to the children. I'm very displeased with you,
Janie.'

Janie went upstairs and she was immediately
surrounded by the children.

Why was she crying? Had their mama been cross
with her?

She nodded her head while they clung to her and
the girls began to cry with her. Yes, their mama had
been cross with her, but strangely it wasn't affecting
her. Another time she would have been thrown into
despair by just a sharp word from her mistress. At
this moment she did not even think of Rory, for
Rory had turned the corner, they said, and was on
the mend, but her thoughts were entirely with John
George. His face haunted her. The fact that he had
told her that he had got a girl into trouble had
shocked her, but what had shocked her even more
was his mental condition, for she felt he must be
going wrong in the head to admit that he took the
ten shillings but not the five pounds. Poor John
George! Poor John George! And Rory would go mad
when he knew.

9

A fortnight later they brought Rory home in a cab
actually paid for by Miss Kean. Miss Kean had
visited the hospital three times. The last time Rory
had been propped up in bed and had stared at her
and listened silently as she gave him a message from
her father.

He was not to worry, his post was there for him when he was ready to return. And what was more, her father was promoting him to Mr Armstrong's place. Her father had taken on a new man, but he was oldish and couldn't cover half the district. Nevertheless, he was honest and honest men were hard to come by. Her father had always known that but now it had been proved to him.

Miss Kean had then asked, 'Have you any idea who attacked you?' and all Rory did was to make one small movement with his head. He had stared fixedly at Miss Kean and she had smiled at him and said, 'I hope you enjoy the grapes, Mr Connor, and will soon be well.' Again he had made a small movement with his head. It was then she said, 'When you are ready to return home a cab will be provided.'

His mind was now clear and working normally and it kept telling him there was this thing he had to face up to and it was no use trying to ignore it, or hoping it would slip back into the muzziness that he had lain in during the first days of his recovery when they had kept saying to him, all of them, the nurses, the doctor, Ruth, his dad, her, Janie, all of them, 'Don't worry, take it slowly. Every day you'll improve. It's a miracle. It's a miracle.'

Although after the third day he had stopped saying the word 'Pity' aloud it was still filling the back of his mind. Whenever he closed his eyes he saw the big feet coming towards him; that's all he remembered, the big feet. He couldn't remember where they had hit him first, whether it was on the head or in the groin or in his ribs; they had broken his ribs. For days he had found it difficult to breathe, now it was easier. His body, although black and blue from head to foot, and with abrasions almost too numerous to count, was no longer a torment to him, just a big sore pile of flesh. He did not know what he looked like, only that his face seemed spread as wide as his shoulders.

He didn't see his reflection until he reached home.

When they helped him over the step he made straight for the mantelpiece. Although Ruth tried to check him he thrust her gently aside then leant forward and looked at his face in the oblong mottled mirror. His nose was still straight but his eyes looked as if they were lying in pockets of mouldy fat. Almost two inches of his hair had been shaved off close to the scalp above his left ear and a zig-zag scar ran down to just in front of the ear itself.

'Your face'll be all right, don't worry.'

He turned and looked at Ruth but said nothing, and she went on, 'The dess-bed's ready for you, you can't do the ladder yet. We'll sleep upstairs.'

He said slowly now, like an old man might, 'I'll manage the ladder.'

'No,' she said, 'it's all arranged. Don't worry. Now come on, sit yourself down.' She led him towards the high-backed wooden chair, and he found he was glad to sit down, for his legs were giving way beneath him.

He said again, 'I'll make the ladder,' and as he spoke he watched Lizzie go into the scullery. It was as if she could read his mind; he didn't want to lie in the same room with her, although she lay in the box bed behind the curtains. He couldn't help his feelings towards her. He knew that she had been good to him over the past weeks, trudging down every day to the hospital, and he hadn't given her a kind word, not even when he could speak he hadn't given her a kind word. It was odd but he couldn't forgive her for depriving him of the woman he thought to be his mother. But what odds, what odds where he slept; wherever he slept his mind would be with him, and his mind was giving him hell. They thought he wasn't capable of thinking straight yet, and he wasn't going to enlighten them because he would need to have some excuse for his future actions.

Nobody had mentioned John George to him, not one of them had spoken his name, but the fact that he had never been near him spoke for them. Something had happened to him and he had a good idea what it was; in fact, he was certain of what it was. And he also knew that he himself wasn't going to do anything about it. He couldn't. God! he just couldn't.

'Here, drink that up.' Lizzie was handing him a cup of tea, which he took from her hand without looking at her and said, 'Ta.'

'It was good of old Kean,' she said, 'to send a cab for you. He can't be as black as he's painted. And his daughter comin' to the hospital. God, but she's plain that one, stylish but plain. Anyway, he must value you.'

'Huh!' Even the jerking of his head was a painful action, which caused him to put his hand on his neck and move his head from side to side, while Lizzie concluded, 'Aye well, you know him better than me, but I would say deeds speak for themselves.'

When Lizzie took his empty cup from him and went to refill it, Ruth, poking the fire, said, 'I'll have to start a bakin',' and she turned and glanced towards him. 'It's good to have you home again, lad. We can get down to normal now.'

He nodded his head and smiled weakly at her but didn't speak. It was odd. Over the past weeks he had longed to be home, away from the cold painted walls and clinical cleanliness of the hospital, but looking about him now, the kitchen, which had always appeared large, for it was made up of two rooms knocked into one, seemed small, cluttered and shabby. He hadn't thought of it before as shabby, he hadn't thought of a lot of things before. He hadn't thought he was cowardly before. Afraid, aye, but not cowardly. But deep in his heart now he knew he was, both cowardly and afraid.

He had always been afraid of enclosed spaces. He supposed that was why he left doors open; and why he had jumped at the collecting job, because he'd be working outside most of the time in the open. He had always been terrified by being shut in. He could take his mind back to the incident that must have created the fear. The Learys lads next door were always full of devilment, and having dragged a coffin-like box they had found floating on the Jarrow slacks all the way down the East Jarrow road and up the Simonside bank, they had to find a use for it before breaking it up for the fire, so the older ones had chased the young ones, and it was himself they had caught, and they had put him in the box and nailed the lid on. At first he had screamed, then become so petrified that his voice had frozen inside him. When they shouted at him from the outside he had been incapable of answering; then, fearful of what they had done, they fumbled in their efforts to wrench the heavy lid off.

When eventually they tipped him from the box he was as stiff as a corpse itself, and not until he had vomited, after the grown-ups had thumped him on the back and rubbed him, did he start to cry. He'd had nightmares for years afterwards, and night after night had walked in his sleep, through the trap door and down the ladder. But having reached the kitchen door that led outside he would always wake up, then scamper back to bed where he would lie shivering until finally cold gave place to heat and he would fall into sweaty sleep.

But since starting collecting, he'd hardly had a nightmare and he hadn't sleep-walked for years. But what now, and in the weeks ahead?

Jimmy came in at half-past six and stood just inside the door and stared towards the dess-bed where Rory was sitting propped up, and he grinned widely and said, 'Aw, lad, it's good to see you home again,' then went slowly towards the bed. 'How you feelin'?'

'Oh, well, you know, a hundred per cent, less ninety.'

'Aye, but you're home and you'll soon be on your feet again. And you know somethin'?' He sat on the edge of the bed. 'I've seen him, Mr Kilpatrick. I told him how things stood, an' you know what he said?

He said the rest can be paid so much a month. If you could clear it off in a year he'd be satisfied.'

'He said that?'

'Aye.'

'Oh well—' Rory sighed—'that's something. Yes—' he nodded at Jimmy—'that's something. We can go ahead now, can't we?'

'You know, he came to the yard for me 'cos he was down that way on business. And Mr Baker wanted to know what he was about 'cos I had to leave me work for five minutes, and so I told him.' Jimmy pulled a face. 'He wasn't pleased. Well, I knew he wouldn't be. You know what he said? He said he had intended keepin' me on an givin' me a rise . . . That for a tale. He asked what we were givin' for it and when I told him he said we were being done, paying that for the goodwill when it was just a few sticks of furniture and half an old patched sculler. One of the lads told me that he had seen him round there himself lookin', an' what he bet was that the old fellow was after the place for himself. Anyway, we scotched him.' He jerked his head and grinned widely, then added, 'Eeh! man, I'm excited. I never thought, I never thought.' He leant forward and put his hand on Rory's. 'And if it wasn't for what happened you we'd be over the moon, wouldn't we?'

'Aye, well, we can still be over the moon now.'

'Get off the side of that bed with your mucky clothes on!'

'Aw, Lizzie.' Jimmy rose to evade her hand and he laughed at her as he said, 'You're a grousy woman,' and when she made to go for him he ran into the scullery, his body swaying and his laughter touched with glee.

Jimmy was happy, Ruth was happy, and, of course, Lizzie was happy; and Janie would be happy; everybody was happy . . . except himself . . . and John George. John George. God Almighty, John George!

Yes, Janie was happy at the news that they had got

the yard, for this meant she could be married any time now. Yet her excitement seemed to have been stirred rather by the fact that she had been granted a full day's leave next Thursday. She sat by the bed gazing at Rory as she gave him the news. He wasn't actually in bed, just lying on the top of it fully dressed. His legs and ribs still ached, and so the bed was left down during the day so that he could rest upon it.

Janie glanced from him to the Sunday company, all assembled as usual, and she hunched her shoulders at them as she said, 'I told a fib, well, only a little one. I told her, the missis, it would need time to clear up the place an' put it to rights an' suggested like if I could have a full day. But you know what I wanted the day for? I thought we'd go up to Durham and—' She clapped her hand over her mouth, then stared at Rory before looking back at the others again and saying, 'Eeh! I forgot.' Again she was looking into Rory's unblinking stare and, taking his hand, she said softly, 'We . . . we didn't tell you, 'cos you were so bad, and you wouldn't have been able to take it in.' She gave him an apologetic look now. 'I mean, with your head bein' knocked about an' that. And we knew that if you had been all right you would have asked for him, you know. Now, Rory, don't be upset.' She gripped his hands tightly. 'John George's been a silly lad. It's all through that lass. You know, you said he was daft. Well, he was, and . . . and he took some money. He meant to put it back. I don't know whether you knew or not but he had been on the fiddle for a long time and so . . . and so he was caught and'—her head drooped to one side as she shook it—'he was sent along the line. He's in Durh . . . Oh, Rory . . .'

They were all gathered round the bed now looking down on him. The sweat was pouring from him and Lizzie cried at them, 'Get back! the lot of you's an' give him air.' She looked angrily across the bed at Janie. 'You shouldn't have given it him like that.'

'I'm sorry. I know, but . . . well, he had to know some time, Lizzie.'

'He'll be all right. He'll be all right.' Ruth was wiping the sweat from his brow and the bald patch on his head. 'It's just weakness. It's like how he used to be after the nightmares. Go on—' she motioned the men towards the table—'get on with your game.'

'Bad that,' said Grannie Waggett. 'Bad. Don't like it. Bad sign.'

'Anybody can have sweats, Gran.' Jimmy's voice was small, his tone tentative, and she bent forward from her chair and wagged her bony finger at him, saying, 'Nay, lad, not everybody, women but not men. Bad look out if all men had sweats. Always a sign of summit, a man havin' sweats. I remember me grannie when she worked for those high-ups in Newcastle sayin' how the son got sweats. Young he was an' the heir. Lots of money, lots of money. He started havin' sweats after the night he went out to see Newcastle lit up for the first time. Oil lamps they had. Eighteen and twelve was it, or eleven, or thirteen? I don't know, but he got sweats. Caught a chill he did going from one to the other gazin' at 'em, got the consumption . . .'

'Gran!'

'Aye, Ruth . . . Well, I was just savin' about me grannie an' the young fellow an' the things she told me. Do you know what the bloody Duke of Northumberland did with a pile of money? Gave it to buildin' a jail or court or summat, an' poor folks . . .'

'Look, come on in home.' Bill Waggett was bending over his mother, tugging at her arm now, and she cried at him, 'Leave be, you big galoot!'

'You're comin' in home, Rory wants a bit of peace an' quiet.'

'Rory likes a bit of crack, an' I've said nowt.'

'Go on, Gran.' Janie was at her side now pleading.

Spluttering and upbraiding, the old woman allowed her son to lead her from the cottage. And this was the signal for the Learys, too, to take their leave, although it was but six o'clock in the evening, and a Sunday, the day of the week they all looked forward to for a game and a bit crack.

The house free from the visitors, as if at a given signal Jimmy went up the ladder into the loft, and his father followed him, while Lizzie and Ruth disappeared into the scullery, leaving Janie alone with Rory.

She had pulled her chair up towards the head of the bed, and, bending towards him, she asked tenderly, 'You feeling better?'

He nodded at her.

'I knew when it came it would be a shock, I'm sorry.'

He made no motion but continued to stare at her.

'I . . . I thought we should go up and see him on Thursday. It'll be the only chance we have, he's allowed visitors once a month . . . All right, all right.'

She watched his head now moving backwards and forwards against the supporting pillows, and when he muttered something she put her face close to his and whispered, 'What do you say?'

'I . . . I can't.'

'We'd take the ferry up to Newcastle an' then the train. It . . . it might do you good, I mean the journey.'

'I can't; don't keep on.'

She looked at him for a moment before she said, 'You don't want to see him?'

'I . . . I can't go there.'

'But why, Rory? He's . . . he's your friend. And if you had seen him in the court that day, why . . .'

Again he was shaking his head. His eyes, screwed up tightly now, were lost in the discoloured puffed flesh.

She sat back and stared at him in deep sadness. She couldn't understand it. She knew he wasn't himself yet, but that he wouldn't make an effort to go and see John George, and him shut up in that place . . . well, she just couldn't understand it.

When he looked at her again and saw the expression on her face, he said through clenched teeth, 'Don't keep on, Janie. I'm sorry but . . . but I can't. You know I've always had a horror of them places. You know how I can't stand being shut in, the doors and things. I'd be feared of making a fool of meself. You know?'

The last two words were a plea and although in a small way she understood his fear of being shut in, she thought that he might have tried to overcome it for this once, just to see John George and ease his plight.

She said softly, 'Somebody should go; he's got nobody, nobody in the world.'

He muttered something now and she said, 'What?'

'You go.'

'Me! On me own, all that way? I've never been in a train in me life, and never on the ferry alone, I haven't.'

'Take one of them with you.' He motioned his head towards the scullery. And now she nodded at him and said, 'Aye, yes, I could do that. I'll ask them.' She stared at him a full minute before she rose from the chair and went into the scullery.

Both Lizzie and Ruth turned towards her and waited for her to speak. She looked from one to the other and said, 'He won't, I mean he can't come up to Durham with me to see John George, he doesn't feel up to it . . . not yet. If it had been later. But . . . but it's early days you know.' She nodded at them, then added, 'Would one of you?'

Ruth looked at her sadly and said, 'I couldn't, lass, I couldn't leave the house an' him an' them all to see to. Now Lizzie here—'

'What! me? God Almighty! Ruth, me go to Durham! I've never been as far as Shields Market in ten years. As for going on a train I wouldn't trust me life in one of 'em. And another thing, lass.' Her voice dropped. 'I haven't got the proper clothes for a journey.'

'They're all right, Lizzie, the ones you've got. There's your good shawl. You could put it round your shoulders. An' Ruth would lend you her bonnet, wouldn't you, Ruth?'

'Oh, she could have me bonnet, and me coat an' all, but it wouldn't fit her. But go on, it'll do you good.' She was nodding at Lizzie now. 'You've hardly been across the doors except to the hospital—' she paused but didn't add, 'since you came from over the water' but said 'in years. It's an awful place to have to be goin' to but the journey would be like a holiday for you.'

'I'd like to see John George.' Lizzie's voice was quiet now. 'Poor lad. A fool to himself, always was. He used to slip me a copper on a Sunday even though I knew he hadn't two pennies to rub against one another. And I didn't want to take it, but if I didn't he'd leave it there.' She pointed to the corner of the little window-sill. 'He'd drop it in the tin pot. The Sunday there wasn't tuppence in there I knew that his funds were low indeed. Aye, lass, I'll come along o' you. I'll likely look a sketch an' put you to shame, but if you don't mind, I don't, lass.'

Janie now laughed as she put out her hand towards Lizzie and said, 'I wouldn't mind bein' seen with you in your shift, Lizzie,' and Ruth said, 'Oh! Janie, Janie,' and Lizzie said, 'You're a good lass, Janie. You've got what money can't buy, a heart. Aye, you have that.'

It took some minutes before Janie could speak to John George. It was Lizzie who spoke first. 'Hello there, lad,' she said, and he answered, 'Hello, Lizzie. Oh hello, Lizzie,' in just such a tone as he would have used when holding out his hands towards her. But there was the grid between them.

'Hello, Janie.'

There was a great hard lump in her throat. The tears were blinding her but through them the blurred outline of his haggard features tore at her heart. 'How . . . how are you, John George?'

'Well . . . well, you know, Janie, not too bad, not too bad. Rough with the smooth, Janie, you know. Rough with the smooth. How . . . how is everybody back there?'

'All right. All right, John George. Rory, he . . . he couldn't make it, John George, he's still shaky on his legs after the knockin' about, like they told you. Eeh! he was knocked about, we never thought he'd live. He would have been here else. He'll come later, next time.'

John George made no reply to Janie's mumbled discourse but he looked towards Lizzie and she, nodding at him, added, 'Aye, he'll come along later. He sent his regards.'

'Did he?' He was addressing Janie again.

'Aye.'

'What did he say, Janie?'

'What was that, John George?'

He leant farther towards the grid. 'I said what did Rory say?'

'Oh, well.' She sniffed, then wiped her eyes with her handkerchief before mumbling, 'He said to keep your pecker up an' . . . an' everything would work out once you get back.'

'He said that?' He was holding her gaze and she didn't reply immediately, so that when she did say 'Aye,' it carried no conviction to him.

'We've brought you a fadge of new bread an' odds an' ends.' Lizzie now pointed to the parcel and he said, 'Oh, ta, Lizzie. It's kind of you; you're always kind.'

'Ah, lad, talkin' of being kind, that's what's put you here the day, being kind. Aw, lad.'

They both looked at the bent head now; then when it jerked up sharply they were startled by the vehemence of his next words. 'I didn't take five pounds, I didn't! Believe me. Will you believe me?' He was staring now at Janie. 'I did take the ten bob.

As I said, I'd done it afore but managed to put it back on the Monday morning, you know after going to the pawn.' He glanced towards Lizzie now as if she would understand the latter bit. Then looking at Janie again, he said, 'Tell him, will you? Say to him, John George said he didn't take the five pounds. Will you, Janie?'

It was some seconds before she answered, 'Aye. Yes, I will. Don't upset yourself, John George. Yes, I will, an' he'll believe you. Rory'll believe you.'

His eyes were staring into hers and his lips moved soundlessly for a moment before he brought out, 'Did you go and see Maggie, Janie?'

Janie, flustered now, said, 'Why, no; I couldn't, John George, 'cos you didn't tell me where she lived.'

Just as he put his doubled fist to his brow and bowed his head a bell rang, and as if he had been progged by something sharp he rose quickly to his feet, then gabbled, 'Horsley Terrace . . . twenty-four. Go, will you Janie?'

'Yes, John George. Yes, John George.' They were both on their feet now.

'Ta, thanks. Thank you both. I'll never forget you. Will you come again? . . . Come again, will you?'

They watched him form into a line with the others before they turned away.

Outside the gates they didn't look at each other or speak, and when Lizzie, after crossing the road, leaned against the wall of a cottage and buried her face in her hands Janie, crying again, put her arms about her and having turned her from the wall, led her along the street and into the town. And still neither of them spoke.

PART TWO

Miss Kean

1

Rory stood before the desk and looked down at Charlotte Kean and said, 'I'm sorry to hear about your father.'

'It's a severe chill, but he'll soon be about again. As I told you, you are to take Armstrong's place and you will naturally receive the same wage as he was getting . . . You don't look fully recovered yourself, Mr Connor. Are you feeling quite well?'

'Yes. Yes, miss, I'm quite all right.'

'I think you had better sit down.' She pointed with an imperious finger towards a chair, and he looked at her in surprise for a moment before taking the seat and muttering, 'Thank you.'

'As I told you, we took on a new man.'

He noticed that she said 'we' as if she, too, were running the business.

'He was the best of those who applied; with so many people out of work in the town you would have thought there would have been a better selection. If it had been for the working-class trades I suppose we would have been swamped.'

He was surprised to know that rent collecting didn't come under the heading of working-class trade, yet on the other hand he knew that if they had been living in the town, in either Tyne Dock or Shields, he wouldn't have been able to hob-nob with neighbours such as the Learys or the Waggetts; the distinction between the white collar and the muffler was sharply defined in the towns.

'My father suggests that you take over the Shields area completely. Mr Taylor can do the Jarrow district, particularly the Saturday morning collection.' She smiled thinly at him now. 'As he says, it's a shame to waste a good man there . . . He has a high opinion of your expertise, Mr Connor.'

Well, this was news to him. Shock upon shock. If things had been different he would have been roaring inside, and later he would have told John George and . . . Like a steel trap a shutter came down on his thinking and he forced himself to say, 'That's very nice to know, miss.'

She was still smiling at him, and as he looked at her he thought, as Lizzie had said, God! but she's plain. It didn't seem fair somehow that a woman looking like her should have been given all the chances. Education, money, the lot. Now if Janie had been to a fine school, and could have afforded to dress like this one did, well, there would've been no one to touch her.

As he stared across the desk at the bowed head and the thin moving hand—she was writing out his district—he commented to himself that everything she had on matched, from her fancy hat that was a dull red colour to the stiff ribboned bow on the neck of her dress. Her green coat was open and showed a woollen dress that took its tone from the hat, but had a row of green buttons down to her waist. He could see the bustle of the dress pushing out the deep pleats of the coat. It took money to dress in colours and style like that. The old man seemingly didn't keep her short of cash.

When she rose to her feet he stood up, and when she came round the desk she said, 'I can leave everything in your hands then, Mr Connor?' She handed him a sheet of paper.

'Yes, miss.'

'I've got to go now. Mr Taylor should be in at any moment.' She turned the face of the fob watch that was pinned to the breast of her dress and looked at it. 'It isn't quite nine yet, make yourself known to him. And this evening, and until my father is fully recovered, I would like you to bring the takings to the house. You know where it is?'

'Yes, I know where it is.'

Yes, he knew where it was. He had caught a glimpse of it from the gates. He knew that it had been occupied by Kean's father and his grandfather, but that's all he knew about it, for he had never been asked to call there on any pretext. But what he did know was that all the Keans had been men who had made money and that the present one was a bully. More than once, when he had stood in this office and been spoken to like a dog, he'd had the desire to ram his fist into his employer's podgy face.

'Good morning then, Mr Connor.'

'Good morning, miss.'

He went before her and opened the outer door, then stood for a second watching her walking down the alley towards the street. She carried herself as straight as a soldier; her step was more of a march than a walk, and she swung her arms; she didn't walk at all like women in her position usually did, or should.

He closed the door, then looked around the office and through into the inner room. Then walking slowly into it, he sat in the chair behind the desk, cocked his head to the side and, speaking to an imaginary figure sitting opposite, he said, 'Now, Mr Taylor, I will assign you to the Jarrow district.' Oh yes, he would always speak civilly to subordinates because, after all, he was a subordinate himself once, wasn't he? A mere rent collector. But now. He looked round the office. He was master of all he surveyed.

Huh! This was the time to laugh, if only he had someone to laugh with.

When he heard the outer door open he got quickly to his feet and went round the desk.

He looked at the clean but shabbily dressed figure standing, hat in hand, before him, and he said quietly, 'You, Mr Taylor?'

'Yes, sir.' The old man inclined his head, and Rory, now making a derogatory sound in his throat, said, 'You needn't sir me, Mr Taylor, I'm just like yourself, a roundsman. Me name's Connor. The old man—Mr Kean—is in bed with a cold. His daughter's just been along. She says you're to take my district.'

'Anything you say, Mr Connor. Anything you say.'

God! had he sounded as servile as this when he was confronted by Kean? There should be a law of some kind against bringing men to their knees.

As he stared at the old man it came to him that everything in his life had changed. And it was to go on changing. How, he didn't know, he only knew that things would never again be as they were.

It was half-past five when he made his way from the office to Birchingham House in Westoe, and it was raining, a fine chilling soaking rain.

The house was not in what was usually called the village, nor did it stand among those that had sprung up to run parallel with that part of Shields that lay along the river, nor was it one of a small number that remained aloof in their vast grounds. But it was of that section the social standing of which was determined by its size, the number of servants it supported, and whether its owner hired or owned his carriages.

And Birchingham House had another distinction. Although it stood in only two acres of ground it was situated on the side road that led off the main road to Harton and to two substantial estates, one belonging to a mine owner, the other to a gentleman who was known to own at least six iron ships that plied their trade from the Tyne.

The histories of the houses of the notabilities of the town were known to the nobodies of the town; and the notabilities themselves formed a topic of gossip, not only in the bars that lined the river-front, but also in the superior clubs and societies that flourished in the town.

But the situation of his master's house or of his master himself had not up till this moment impressed Rory with any significance. Kean, to him, had been just a money-grabbing skinflint who owned rows of property, particularly in Jarrow, which should have been pulled down years ago, and streets in Shields that were fast dropping into decay for want of repair. Yet in this respect he admitted Kean was no worse than any of the landlords he represented.

Now, as he neared the house in the dark and saw the front steps leading to it lighted by two bracket lamps, he stopped for a moment and peered at it through the rain. It was big. There were ten windows along the front of it alone. Moreover, it was three-storey. He couldn't quite make out the top one, only that there was a gleam of glass up there. Likely attics. There was a carriage standing on the drive at the foot of the steps and he paused near it to look up at the driver sitting huddled deep in a cloaked coat. The man hadn't noticed him; he seemed to be asleep.

He hesitated. Should he go to the front door or the back door? Damn it all, why not the front! Why not!

He went up the steps and pulled the bell.

The door was answered by a maid. She was wearing a starched apron over a black alpaca dress. The bib of the apron had a wide, stiff frill that continued over the straps on her shoulders. She had a starched cap on her head and the strings from it looked as stiff as the cap itself and were tied under her chin in a bow. She was evidently flustered and said, 'Yes, yes. Who is it?'

'I'm Mr Connor. Miss Kean told me to come. I've brought the takings.'

'Oh! Oh!' She looked from one side to the other, then said, 'Well, you'd better come in.' And she stood aside and let him pass her into the small lobby, then opened another door into a hall, which he noted immediately was as big as the kitchen at home.

'Stay there,' she said, 'an' I'll tell her, that's if she can come, the master's had a turn. They've had to send for the doctor again. He's right bad.' She nodded at him, then made for the stairs that led from the hallway in a half spiral and disappeared from view.

He stood looking around him, frankly amazed at what he saw. To the right of the staircase was a side table with a lamp on it. He noted that it was oil, not gas. Yet they had gas outside. The soft light from it illuminated a large oil painting on the wall showing the head and shoulders of a man: he had a broad, flat face, and the high collar was wedged into the jowls below his chin; he had a white fringe of hair above his ears, the rest of his head was bald; his eyes were round and bright and seemed to be looking with stern condemnation at the visitor. Rory did not need to guess that this was an ancestor of Mr Kean, and also that the lamp was there as a sort of illuminated commemoration to do him honour.

A cabinet stood against the wall at the far side of the stairs. He had never seen the like of it before, not even in a picture. It was glass-fronted and made of yellowish wood picked out in gold; the legs were spindly with fancy cross-bars connecting the four of them. It had two shelves. The top one held figures, some single, some in groups; the lower shelf had glass goblets standing on it. From what he could see at this distance they were etched with paintings.

There were a number of doors going off all round the hall, and the thick red carpet he was standing on reached to the walls on all sides except where one door was deeply inset in an alcove and had a step down to it.

He felt his mouth closing when he heard the rustle of a gown on the stairs and saw Charlotte Kean coming down towards him. Her face wore a worried expression. She said immediately, 'My father has taken a turn for the worse, we are very concerned. Will you come this way?'

Without a word he followed her down the step and through the door that was set in the alcove and found himself in an office, but an office very different from the one in Tangard Street. The room in a way was a pattern of the hall, thick carpet, highly polished desk, the top strewn with papers and ledgers. There were paintings on all the walls except that which was taken up with two long windows over which the curtains had not been drawn.

He watched her turn up the gas light; the mantle, encased in its fancy globe gave out a soft light and set the room in a warm glow.

He couldn't understand the feeling he was experiencing. He didn't know whether it was envy, admiration, or respect, that kind of grudging respect the symbols of wealth evoke. He only knew that the feeling was making him feel all arms and legs.

'Sit down, Mr Connor.'

This was the second time in one day she had invited him to be seated.

He hesitated to take the leather chair that she had proffered; instead, looking down at the bag he had placed on the desk, he opened it for her and took out a number of smaller bags and the two pocket ledgers, which he placed before her, saying, 'I've counted everything, it's in order.'

She glanced up at him, saying, 'Thank you.' Then with her hand she indicated the chair again. And now he sat down and watched her as she emptied each bag and counted the money, then checked it against the books.

In the gaslight and with her expression troubled as it was, she looked different from what she had done in the stark grey light this morning, softer somehow.

The money counted, she returned the books to the bag; then rising, she stood looking at him for a moment before saying, 'I'm sure I can trust you, Mr Connor, to see to things in the office until my father is better. I . . . I may not be able to get along. You see'—she waved her hand over the desk—'there is so much other business to see to. And he wants me with him all the time.'

'Don't worry about the office, miss, everything will be all right there. And . . . and Mr Taylor seems a steady enough man.'

'Thank you, Mr Connor.'

'I'm sorry about your father.'

'I'm sure you are.'

He stared back into her face. There was that something in her tone. Another time he would have said to himself, Now how does she mean that?

He opened the door to let her pass out into the hall, and there she turned to him and asked, 'Is it still raining?'

'Yes. Yes, it was when I came in.'

'You have a long walk home. Go into the kitchen and they will give you something to drink.'

Crumbs from the rich man's table. Soup kitchens run by lady bountifuls. Clogs for the barefoot. Why was he thinking like this? She only meant to be kind, and he answered as if he thought she was. 'Thank you, miss, but I'd rather get home.'

'But you don't look too well yourself, Mr Connor.'

'I'm all right, miss. Thank you all the same. Good night, miss.'

'Good night, Mr Connor.'

The maid appeared from the shadows and let him out. He walked down the steps and along the curving drive into the road, feeling like some beggar who had been given alms. He felt deflated, insignificant, sort of lost. It was that house.

He walked through the rain all the way back to the beginning of Westoe, down through Laygate and on to Tyne Dock, through the arches and the last long trek up Simonside Bank into the country and the cottage.

Opening the door, he staggered in and dropped into a chair without taking off his sodden coat, and he made no protest when Lizzie tugged his boots from his feet while Ruth loosened his scarf and coat and held him up while she pulled them from him.

He had no need to pretend tonight that he was ill,

at least physically, for the first day's work had taken it out of him, and the trail back from Westoe had been the last straw.

When later in the evening Jimmy, by way of comfort, whispered to him, 'When we go to the yard it'll be easier for you, you could cut from the office to the boatyard in five minutes,' he nodded at him while at the same time thinking, not without scorn, The boatyard! With thirty-five pounds he could have got himself a mortgage on a decent house. Slowly it came to him the reason why he had allowed himself to become saddled with the boatyard. It wasn't only because he wanted to kill two birds with one stone: marry Janie and give Jimmy something of his own to live and work for; it was because he wanted to get away from here, from the kitchen; and now from their concern for his mental state, which must be bad, so they thought, when he still wouldn't go and see his best friend, and him in prison.

Only last night when he said good-bye to Janie the rooms over the boatyard had appeared to him like a haven. And later, as he lay awake staring into the blackness listening to Jimmy's untroubled breathing, he had thought, Once we get there, once I'm married, I'll see it all differently. Then like a child and with no semblance of Rory Connor, he had buried his face in the pillow and cried from deep within him, 'I'll make it up to him when he comes out. I'll make him understand. He'll see I could do nothing about it at the time 'cos I was too bad. He'll understand. Being John George, he'll understand. And I'll make it up to him, I will. I will.'

But now, after his visit to Birchingham House, he was seeing the boat house for what it was, a tumble-down riverside shack, and he thought, I must have been mad to pay thirty-five pounds for the goodwill of that. Look where it's landed me. And the gate shut once again on his thinking as an inner voice said, 'Aye; and John George.'

They were married on the Saturday after Easter. It was a quiet affair in that they hadn't a big ceilidh. They went by brake to the Catholic church in Jarrow, together with Ruth, Paddy, Lizzie, Jimmy, and Bill Waggett. A great deal of tact and persuasion had to be used on Gran Waggett in order that she should stay behind. Who was going to help Kathleen Leary with the tables? And anyway, Kathleen being who she was needed somebody to direct her, and who better than Gran herself?

Janie's wedding finery was plain but good, for her flounced grey coat had once belonged to her mistress, as had also the blue flowered cotton dress she wore underneath. Her blue straw hat she had bought herself, and her new brown buttoned boots too.

She was trembling as she knelt at the altar rails, but then the church was icy cold and the priest himself looked blue in the face and weary into the bargain. He mumbled the questions: Wilt thou have this man? Wilt thou have this woman? And they in turn mumbled back.

After they had signed their names and Rory had kissed her in front of them all they left the church and got into the brake again, which was now surrounded by a crowd of screaming children shouting 'Hoy a ha'penny oot! Hoy a ha'penny oot!'

They had come prepared with ha'pennies. Ruth and Lizzie and Jimmy threw them out from both sides of the brake; but they were soon finished and when there were no more forthcoming the shouts that followed them now were, 'Shabby weddin' . . . shabby weddin',' and then the concerted chorus of:

> Fleas in yer blankets,
> No lid on your netty,

To the poor house you're headin',
Shabby weddin', shabby weddin'.

The fathers laughed and Ruth clicked her tongue and Lizzie said, 'If I was out there I'd skite the hunger off them. By God! I would.' But Janie and Rory just smiled, and Jimmy, sitting silently at the top end of the brake, his hands dangling between his knees, looked at them, and part of him was happy, and part of him, a deep hidden part, was aching.

Out of decency Jimmy did not immediately go down to the yard. The young married couple were to have the place to themselves until Monday, and on Monday morning the new pattern of life was to begin, for Janie had had her way and was continuing to go daily to the Buckhams'.

Of course, in the back of her mind she knew that the three shillings had been a great inducement to Rory seeing her side of the matter, for now that he wasn't gaming there was no way to supplement his income, and what was more, as she had pointed out, he would be expected to give a bit of help at home since he was depriving them of both his own and Jimmy's money. So the arrangement was that, until Jimmy got some orders, for his sculler was almost finished, then she would continue to go daily to her place . . .

Having clambered up the steps in the dark and unlocked the door and dropped their bundles and a bass hamper on to the floor, they clung to each other in the darkness, gasping and laughing after the exertion of humping the baggage from where the cart had dropped them at the far end of the road.

'Where's the candle?'

'On the mantelpiece of course.' She was still laughing.

He struck a match and lit the candle, then held it up as he looked towards the table on which the lamp stood.

When the lamp was lit he said, 'Well, there you are now, home sweet home.'

Janie stood and looked about her. 'I'll have to get stuck in here at nights,' she said.

'Well, if you will go working in the day-time, Mrs Connor.' He pulled her to him again and they stood pressed close looking silently now into each other's face. 'Happy?'

She smiled softly, 'Ever so.'

'It's not going to be an easy life.'

'Huh! what do I care about that as long as we're together. Easy life?' She shook her head. 'I'd go fish guttin' if I could help you, an' you know how I hate guttin' fish, even when we used to get them for practically nowt from the quay. Do you remember walkin' all the way down into Shields and getting a huge basketful for threepence?'

'Only because they were on the point of going rotten.'

'Ger-away with you . . . Do you want something to eat?'

'No.'

'You're not hungry?'

'Not for food.'

Her lips pressed tightly together; she closed her eyes and bowed her head.

He now put his hands up to her hair and unpinned her hat and throwing it aside, unbuttoned her coat.

'I'll have to get these bundles unpacked and . . . and tidied up.'

He went on undoing the buttons. 'There's all day the morrow and the next day and the next day and the next, all our life to undo bundles . . .'

'Hie! what're you doin'? That's me good coat. Look, it's on the floor.'

'Leave it on the floor; there's more to follow.'

'Rory! Rory! the bed isn't made up.'

'The bed is made up, I saw to it.'

'Oh Rory! . . . An' I'm cold, I'm cold, I'm cold. I'll have to get me nightie.'

'You're not going to need a nightie.'

'Aw, Rory! . . . Eeh!' She let out a squeal as, dressed only in her knickers and shift, he swung her up into his arms and carried her through into the bedroom and dropped her on to the bed. She lay there just where he had dropped her and in the dim light reflected from the kitchen she watched him throw off his clothes.

When he jumped on to the bed beside her she squealed and said, 'Eeh! the lamp.'

'The lamp can wait.'

They were pressed close, but she was protesting slightly, she didn't want to be rushed. She was a bit afraid of this thing. If she could only make him take it quietly—lead up to it sort of. Her grannie had said it hurt like hell. His lips were moving round her face when she murmured, in a futile effort to stem his ardour, 'Oh Rory, Rory, I'll never be happier than I am at this minute. It's been a wonderful day, hasn't it? . . . They were all so good, an' they enjoyed themselves, didn't they? I bet they'll keep up the jollification all night.' She moaned softly as his hands moved over her; then, her voice trailing weakly away, she ended, 'If-only-John-George-had-been-there . . .'

His hands ceased their groping, his lips became still on her breast and she screamed out now as he actually pushed her from him with such force that her shoulders hit the wall as he yelled at her, 'God Almighty! can't you give him a rest? What've you got to bring him up now for, at this minute? You did it on purpose. *You did!*'

In the silence that followed he listened to her gasping. Then she was in his arms again and he was rocking her. 'Oh lass, I'm sorry, I'm sorry. I didn't mean it. Did I hurt you? I'm sorry, I'm sorry. It was only, well, you know, I've waited so long . . . And, and . . .'

When she didn't answer him, or make any sound, he said softly, 'Janie. Janie. Say something.'

What she said was, 'It's all right. It's all right.'

'I love you. I love you, Janie. Aw, I love you. If I lost you I'd go mad, barmy.'

'It's all right. It's all right, you won't lose me.'

'Will you always love me?'

'Always.'

'You promise?'

'Aye, I promise.'

'I'll never love anybody in me life but you, I couldn't. Aw, Janie, Janie . . .'

Later in the night when the light was out and he was asleep she lay still in his arms but wide awake. It hadn't been like she had expected, not in any way. Perhaps she wasn't goin' to like that kind of thing after all. Her grannie said some didn't, while others couldn't get enough. Well she'd never be one of those, she was sure of that already. Perhaps it was spoiled for her when he threw her against the wall because she had mentioned John George.

It was most strange how he reacted now whenever John George's name was mentioned. She could understand him not wanting to go to the prison, him having this feeling about being shut in, but she couldn't work out in her own mind why he never spoke of John George. And when the name was mentioned by anybody else he would remain silent. But to act like he had done the night just because . . . Well, she was flabbergasted.

Her grannie, as part of the advice she had given her on marriage last Sunday, had said, 'If he wants any funny business, out of the ordinary like, and some of them do, you never know till the door's closed on you, you have none of it. An' if he raises his hand to you, go for the poker. Always leave it handy. Start the way you mean to go on 'cos with the best of them, butter wouldn't melt in their mouths afore they get you in that room. But once there, it's like Adam and Eve racing around the Garden of Eden every night. An' if you cross your fingers and say skinch, or in other words, hold your horses, lad, I've had enough, they bring the priest to you, an' he reads the riot act. "Supply your man's needs," he says, "or it's Hell fire and brimstone for you." So off you gallop again, even when your belly's hangin' down to your knees.'

She had laughed at her grannie and with her grannie. She had put her arms around the old woman and they had rocked together until the tears had run down their faces, and the last words she had said to her were, 'Don't worry, Gran, nowt like that'll happen to me. It's Rory I'm marrying, and I know Rory. I should do, there's only a thin wall divided us for years.'

But now they hadn't been hours married afore he had tossed her against a wall, and tossed her he had because he had hurt her shoulder and it was still paining. Life was funny . . . odd.

3

Septimus Kean died, and Rory continued to take the day's collections to the house for some four weeks after Mr Kean had been buried, and each time Miss Kean received him in what she called the office. But on this particular Friday night she met him in the hall and said to him, 'Just leave the bag on the office table, Mr Connor; we'll see to that later. By the way, are you in a hurry?'

He was in a hurry, he was in a hurry to get home to Janie, to sit before the fire and put his feet up and talk with Jimmy, and hear if he had managed to get an order, and to find out if any of the Pitties had been about again . . . The Pitties. He'd give his right arm, literally, if he could get his own back on the Pitties. There was a deep acid hate in him for the Pitties. And it would appear they hadn't finished with him for they had been spying about the place. He knew that to get a start on the river Jimmy would have to take the droppings, but if it lay with the Pitties he wouldn't get even the droppings. They were beasts, dangerous beasts. By God he'd give anything to get one over on them.

He answered her, 'Oh no, not at all.'

'There is something I wish to discuss with you. I'm about to have a cup of tea, would you care to join me?'

Old Kean's daughter asking him to join her in a cup of tea! Well! Well! He could scarcely believe his ears. Things were looking up. By lad, they were.

In the hall she said to the maid, 'Take Mr Connor's coat and hat.'

Then he was following her to the end of the hall, and into a long room. There was a big fire blazing in the grate to the right of them. It was a fancy grate with a black iron basket. It had a marble mantelpiece with, at each end, an urn-shaped vase standing on it, and above the mantelpiece was another large oil painting of yet another past Kean.

At first glance the prominent colour of the room seemed to be brown. The couch drawn up before the fire and the two big side chairs were covered with a brown corded material. The furniture was a shining brown. There were three small tables with knick-knacks on them. A piece of furniture that looked like a sideboard but like no sideboard he'd ever seen before had silver candlesticks on it. The velvet curtains hanging at the windows were green with a brown bobble fringe and were supported from a cornice pole as thick as his upper arm.

'Sit down, Mr Connor.' She motioned him towards one of the big chairs and he sat down, then watched her pull a handbell to the side of the fireplace.

When the door opened she turned to the maid, not the same one who had opened the door to him, and said, 'I'll have tea now, Jessie; please bring two cups.'

The girl bent her knee, then went out.

He noticed that although her tone was uppish, as always, she had said 'Please.'

He watched her as she sat back in the corner of the couch. She made a movement with her legs and for a moment he thought that she was actually going to cross them. But what she did was cross her feet, and as she did so her black skirt rode above her ankles and he saw the bones pressing through what must have been silk stockings . . . She certainly looked after herself in the way of dress did this one. She was in mourning but her mourning was silk.

'I will come to the point, Mr Connor. I have a proposition to make to you.'

'A proposition?' His eyes widened slightly.

'I don't know whether you are aware that property dealing was only one of my father's interests.' She did not wait for him to comment on this but went on, 'Among other things, he had interests in a number of growing concerns and, since my grand-father died, other small businesses have come into the family. Do you know the Wrighton Tallow Works?'

'I've heard of them.'

'Well, my grandfather owned the works and naturally they fell to my father, and unfortunately, I say unfortunately, because of the loss of my father they are now my concern . . . How far have you advanced in book-keeping Mr Connor?'

'Advanced?' He blinked at her. 'What . . . what do you rightly mean, miss?'

'What I mean is, have you studied any further than that which is required to tot up rent accounts? Have you thought of your own advancement in this line, such as that of becoming a fully fledged clerk in a bank, or to a solicitor, say?'

'No, miss.' The answer was curt, his tone cold. 'The opportunities didn't provide themselves.' He knew too late that he should have said present, not provide.

'Opportunities are there for the taking, Mr Connor. This town offers great opportunities to those who are willing to take advantage of them. It isn't only the shipyards and the boat builders and such who offer apprenticeships in particular crafts; there are the arts.'

The arts! He narrowed his eyes at her. What was she getting at? Was she having him on, trying to get a bit of amusement out of him? The arts! Why didn't she come to the point?

She came to the point by saying, 'I have in mind that I need a manager, Mr Connor, someone who is capable not only of taking charge of the property side of my affairs but who could assist me in the running of my other businesses. There are places that need to be visited, books to be gone over. Of course I have my accountant and my solicitor but these are there only for the final totalling at the year's end, and for advice should I need it. But there is so much to be seen to in between times and my father used to attend to this side of affairs, for you know, if a warehouse or business is not visited regularly those in charge become slack.' She stared at him without speaking for almost a full minute before saying, 'Would you consider taking on this post if, and when, you became qualified to do so? You would, of course, need a little training.'

His heart was thumping against his ribs causing his breath to catch in his throat. He couldn't take it in. She was proposing that he should be her manager. He was peering at her through the narrow slits of his eyes now, he was puzzled. Why wasn't she advertising for somebody right away if the burden of the businesses was so great on her?

As if she were reading his thoughts she said, 'I have no doubt I could get someone to fill this post almost immediately, but then the person would be strange to me, and . . . and I don't mix easily. What I mean is, I take a long time in getting to know people.'

154

They were staring at each other through the fading light, and in silence again. It was she who broke it, her voice low now, ordinary sounding, no uppishness to it. 'I . . . I have known you for some time, Mr Connor, and have always thought that you should be capable of much better things than mere rent collecting.'

Before he could answer the door opened and the maid entered pushing a tea trolley.

When the trolley was by the side of the couch she looked at the maid and said, 'I'll see to it, Jessie. I'll ring when I need you.'

'Yes, miss.' Again the dip of the knee.

'Do you take sugar, Mr Connor?'

'No. No, thank you.'

'That is unusual; men usually like a lot of sugar.'

He watched her pour the weak-looking tea from a small silver teapot and add milk to it from a matching jug, and when a few minutes later he sipped at it he thought, My God! dish-water.

'Oh, I'm sorry, I didn't ask what tea you preferred. You see, they're so used to bringing me China; I'll ring and get some . . .'

'Oh·no, please don't. It's nice, it's only different. And'—he grinned now at her—'you can understand I'm not used to havin' China tea.'

She actually laughed now, and he noticed that it changed her face and made her almost pleasant-looking, except that her nose remained just as sharp. 'I hope it will be a taste you will learn to acquire in the future.'

He doubted it but he nodded at her, smiling in return.

He took the buttered scone she proffered him and found it good, and had another, and by the time he had eaten a cake that melted in his mouth he was laughing inside, thinking, By gum! they just want to see me now, all them in the kitchen. They just want to see me now. And wait till I tell Janie. My! who would believe it? She had asked if he was willing to learn to manage her affairs. God! just give him the chance. By lad! he had fallen on his feet at last. It wouldn't matter now if the boatyard never made a go of it. But he hoped it would, for Jimmy's sake. He mentioned the boatyard to her now. It was when she said, 'I mustn't keep you any longer, Mr Connor, you have a long walk home. But I will leave you to think over my proposition. Perhaps tomorrow evening you will tell me what you have decided. If your answer is favourable I can put you in touch with a man who would teach you book-keeping and the rudiments of management. And perhaps you could attend night school. But we can discuss that later.'

He rose to his feet, saying, 'I'm not more than ten minutes' hard tramp from my home now; I'm . . . I'm on the waterfront.'

She raised her eyebrows as she repeated, 'The waterfront?'

'Yes.' He squared his shoulders. 'I became interested in a boatyard, a very small one mind.' He smiled as he nodded at her. 'A pocket handkerchief, some folks would call it, but nevertheless it's big enough to make a keel and scullers and such like. There's a house of sorts attached. I . . . I took it for my brother. He's served his time in boat building, small boats that is, the same line, scullers, wherries and such, and it's always been his dream to have a place of his own where he could build. So I heard of this concern. The man had died, and . . . and it was going reasonable, so I took a chance.'

Her face was stretching into a wide smile, her lips were apart showing a set of strong white teeth. 'Well, well!' She inclined her head towards him. 'I wasn't wrong, was I? You do have business acumen. Where is this place?'

'Oh, it's yon side of the mill dam. It's so small you wouldn't be able to see it, not among all the other yards along there. It used to belong to a Mr. Kilpatrick.'

'Kilpatrick?' She shook her head. 'I don't recall

hearing the name. But . . . but I'm very interested in your enterprise. I must come and see it some time.'

'Yes, yes, do that.'

She walked with him to the door and although the maid was standing ready to open it she herself let him out, saying, 'Good night, Mr Connor. We will reopen this subject tomorrow evening.'

'Yes, as you say, miss. Good night.'

He was walking down the drive . . . no, marching down the drive.

'We will reopen this subject tomorrow evening.'

Indeed, indeed, we will.

Would you believe it?

They said the age of miracles was past.

Would he go to night school?

He'd go to hell and sit on a hot gridiron to please her.

But on the road he slowed his pace and again asked himself why she had picked him. And he gave himself her own answer. She didn't mix and it took her a long time to get to know people. Aye. Aye well, he could understand that. She wasn't the kind that most people would take to. No looks and too smart up top for most men, he supposed, for he had the idea she'd be brainy. And that would apply to her effect on women an' all.

Hip-hip-hooray! He wanted to throw his hat in the air. Things were happening. They were happening all the time. Janie! Here I come . . . A manager!

What wage would he get?

He'd have to leave that to her of course but he'd know the morrow night.

4

Janie left the Buckhams' with the mistress's words racing round in her mind. 'Well, you have a month to think it over, Janie,' she had said. 'It would be wonderful for you and it'll only be for three weeks. And just think, in all your life you might never have the opportunity to go abroad again. And the children would love to have you with them, you know that.'

Yes, Janie knew that, but she also knew that she was being asked to go to keep the children out of the way and let the master and mistress enjoy their holiday in France.

She had said she would talk to her husband about it, but she already knew what his answer would be. He hated the idea of her being out every day and if it wasn't that he had needed her wages he would have put his foot down before now. But with this new development and Miss Kean offering to make him manager, well, she knew that her days at the Buckhams' were numbered; in fact, she could have given in her notice this morning.

There was something else on her mind. She had promised John George she would go and see that lass of his, but with one thing and another she had never had time. But tonight Rory would be late, for even now he'd be in Westoe clinching the matter, and so she told herself why not clear her conscience and go round and see that girl. She must be all of six months' gone.

When she reached the end of the road she did not, automatically, turn right and cut down to the river but went into a jumble of side streets and towards Horsley Terrace.

They were, she considered, nice houses in the terrace, respectable. It was number twenty-four; it had three steps up to the front door and an iron railing cutting off four feet of garden. She went up the steps and rapped on the door with the knocker. When it was opened she stared at the young woman in front of her. She wasn't pregnant. 'Could . . . could I speak with Miss Maggie Ridley please?'

The young woman cast a quick glance over her shoulder, then stepped towards her, pulling the door half closed behind her.

'She's not here.'

'Oh, I had a message for her.'

The girl's eyes widened. 'A message? Who from?'

'Well, he's . . . he's a friend of hers.'

The young woman stared at her for a moment, then poked her face forward, hissing, 'Well, if it's the friend I think it is you can tell him that she's married. Tell him that.'

'Married?'

'That's what I said.'

'Oh, well'—Janie was nodding her head now—'In a way I'm glad to hear it. I . . . I hope she'll be happy.'

The face looking into hers seemed to crumple and now the whispered tone was soft and laden with sadness as she said, 'He . . . he was a friend of, of my father's, he's a widower with a grown-up family.'

In the look they exchanged there was no need to say any more.

Janie now nodded towards the young woman and said, 'Thank you, I'll . . . I'll tell him,' then turned and went down the steps. Poor John George! And the poor lass. A dead old man likely. The very thought of it was mucky, nasty.

Rory hadn't returned when she got in, but Jimmy was there with the kettle boiling and the table set, and immediately he said, 'Sit down and put your feet up.'

'I'm not tired.'

'Well, you should be. And you will be afore the night's out, I've put the washing in soak.'

'Thanks, Jimmy. Any news?'

'Aye, Mr Pearson, you know Pearson's Warehouse, I went in and asked him the day. I said I'd carry anything. He joked at first and said he had heard they were wantin' a battleship towed from Palmer's. And then he said there were one or two bits he wanted sending across to Norway.' He laughed, then went on excitedly, 'But after that he said, "Well, lad, I'll see what I can do for you." He said he believed in passing work around, there was too many monopolies gettin' a hold in the town. I've got to look in the morrow.'

'Oh Jimmy, that's grand.' She took hold of his hand. 'Eeh! you just want a start. And when I'm home all day I could give you a hand, I could, I'm good at lumpin' stuff. And I could learn to steer an' all . . . But I'd better learn to swim afore that.' She pushed at him and he laughed with her, saying, 'Aye, but if they had to learn to swim afore they learned to row a boat on this river it would be empty; hardly any sailors swim.'

'Go on!'

'It's a fact.'

'Eeh! well, I'll chance it, I'll steer for you, or hoist the sail, 'cos have you thought you'll need another hand?' At the sound of footsteps she turned her head quickly away from him and towards the door, and she was on her feet when Rory entered the room, and she saw immediately that he was in great high fettle.

'It's settled then?'

'Out of me way, Mrs Connor.' He struck a pose and marched down the room as if he were carrying a swagger stick, and when he reached Jimmy he slapped the top of his own hat, saying, 'Touch yer peak, boy. Touch yer peak.'

Then they were all clinging together laughing, and he swung them round in a circle, shouting:

'Ring a ring o' roses,
    Keels, scullers and posies,
    Managers, managers,
    All fall down.'

'But we're all going up!' He pulled them to a stop and, looking into Janie's laughing face, he added, 'Up! Up! We're going up, lass; nothing's going to stop us. She's for me, why God only knows, but she's the ladder on which we're going to climb. You take that from me. All of us'—he punched Jimmy on the head—'all of us . . . She's got influence, fingers in all pies, and that includes this river an' all. We're going up, lad.'

Later, when in bed together and closely wrapped against each other, he said to her, 'You haven't seemed as over the moon as I thought you would be. There's something on your mind, isn't there?'

She didn't answer, and when he insisted, 'Come on,' she said, 'There's two things on me mind, Rory, but if I mention them they'll both cause rows, so I'd better not, had I?'

He was quiet for a moment before saying, 'Go on, tell me. I won't go off the deep end, whatever they are . . . I promise, whatever they are.'

It was a long moment before she said, 'Well mind, don't forget what you said.'

He waited, and then her voice a whisper she began, 'The missis, she wants me to go with them to France for a holiday. Of course, it's only to keep the bairns out of the way, I know, but she keeps tellin' me that I won't get the chance again . . .'

'Who says you won't get the chance again? They're not the only ones who can go to France. You're not goin'. You told her you're not going? All right, all right, I'm not going to get me neb up about it, but you did tell her you weren't goin'?'

'I said I didn't think you would hear of it.'

'That's right I won't. And you can also tell her when you're on, that you're putting your notice in . . . Well now, the other thing?' He waited.

'I went the night to take a message to . . . to John George's lass. She's . . . she's married.'

'Married!'

'Yes, to an old man, a widower with a grown-up family.'

'It's . . . it's the best thing.' She could hardly hear his voice but she was relieved that he had kept his promise and hadn't gone for her for mentioning John George or his affairs. And now, a minute later, he was mumbling into her neck, 'When he comes out

I'll set him up. I've . . . I've always meant to do something for him but now I can, I'll set him up properly in something.'

'Oh, Rory, Rory. Aw, that's . . . that's my Rory. I knew you would. Aw ta, thanks, lad, thanks. I'll tell the missis the morrow straight out, I'll tell her me husband's put his foot down and said no France and that I'll have to be givin' in me notice shortly. Oh, Rory, Rory . . .'

In the middle of the night she was wakened by him crying out. His arms were flaying about and when she put her hand on his head it came away wet with sweat and she cried at him, 'Rory! Rory! wake up,' but he continued to thrash about in the bed, gabbling out words from which she could distinguish bits of the conversation that they'd had last night. 'I'll make it up to John George, I will, I will. I always meant to.' Then he began to shout, ''Twas being shut in, 'twas being shut in.'

When she finally managed to wake him he spluttered, 'What's it? What's-the-matter?' Then putting his hand to his head, he added, 'I was dreamin' . . . Was I talking?'

'Just jabbering. It was all the excitement.'

'Aye, yes,' he said, 'all the excitement. By! I'm wringing.'

'Yes, you are. Lie down, right down under the clothes here.' She drew him towards her and held him closely, soothing him as if he were a child, until he went to sleep again.

5

On three afternoons and three evenings of each of the next three weeks Rory visited Mr Dryden, to be coached in the matter of accountancy and business management.

Mr Dryden had in his early years been in accountancy, and later had become a solicitor's clerk, and the reports he gave to Miss Kean on the progress of his pupil were most encouraging. 'He shows great acumen,' he told her. 'I think you have made a wise choice,' he told her. But he also told his friends with a smirk that old Kean's daughter had taken on a protégé. Ha! Ha! they said. Well, she wasn't likely to get a husband, so she had to resort to a pastime. Yet, as some of them remarked, she ought to have known her place and picked her pastime from a grade higher than that of rent collectors, and this one by all accounts wasn't a skin away from a common labouring man. If it wasn't that the fellow was already married you could put another version to it, for as had already been demonstrated in one or two instances she was a strong-headed young woman who took little heed of people's opinions. Look what she was like on committees. She had got herself talked about more than once for openly defying the male opinion. Of course, this was due to the type of education she'd been given. She had been sent away, hadn't she? To the south somewhere, hadn't she? That was her mother's doing. So . . . well, what could you expect?

Rory was not unaware of Mr Dryden's personal opinion of him. He gauged it in the condescending tone the old man used when speaking to him. But what did it matter, he could put up with that.

He was now receiving the handsome sum of twenty-five shillings a week, with the promise of it being raised when he should finally take over his duties. He'd had glimpses into what these would be during the past few days when he had seen the number of properties in Hexham and Gateshead, and the haberdashery and hatters shops that had been left by Grandfather Kean. All this besides the business old Kean himself had had on the side.

He became more and more amazed when he thought of what his late employer must have been worth. Yet never a night had he missed, winter or summer, coming to the office to pick up the takings, except when he was called away to visit his father. He had never, not to his knowledge, taken a holiday all the time he had been there, and yet he was rolling in money.

He wondered what she would be worth altogether. If she ever married, some man would come in for a packet. But apart from her not being the kind to take a man's fancy he thought she was too independent to think that way. No one, he considered, could be as business-like as her without having the abilities of a man in her make-up . . .

It was Saturday morning and he had brought the takings from his two men—he thought of them as his now. She had allowed him to choose the second man himself. This fellow was young and hadn't done any rent collecting before but he had been to school continuously up till he was fourteen, and that was something to start on. Moreover, he was bright and eager and in need of work. He felt he had made a good choice. And he told her so. 'Patterson's doing well,' he said. 'Gettin' round quickly. And so far he's allowed nobody to take advantage of him, you know, soft-soap him.'

'Good.' She smiled at him from across the desk; then she said, 'I would like you to accompany me to Hexham on Monday.'

'Hexham?' He moved his head downwards while keeping his eyes on her. 'Very well.' He sometimes omitted to say miss, but she had never pulled him up for it.

'I think it's time you saw the places you're going to be responsible for.'

'Aye, yes, of course.' He'd have to stop himself saying aye.

'By the way—' she was still smiling at him—'I should like to come and see your boatyard. I'm very interested in it. I may be of some assistance in supplying freight—in a small way. Would this afternoon be convenient?'

He thought quickly. What was the place like, was it tidy? Was there any washing hanging about? No, Janie had cleared the ironing up last night and scrubbed out last thing.

He nodded at her, saying, 'Yes, that'll be all right with me. Me wife won't be in because she works until four on a Saturday, she's nursemaid at the Buckhams in Westoe, but you'll be welcome to see . . .'

'Your . . . wife?' The words came from deep within her chest and were separate as if they were strange and she had never spoken them before.

'Yes. Yes, miss, me wife . . .' His voice trailed off for he was amazed to see the colour flooding up over her face like a great blush.

'I . . . I wasn't aware that you were married, Mr Connor . . . Since when?'

'Well, well—' he moved uneasily in the chair— 'just recently, miss. I didn't like to mention it to you at the time because the date was fixed for shortly after your father's funeral. I couldn't change it, but it didn't seem proper to . . .'

Her eyes were shaded now as she looked down towards the desk and on to her hands which were lying flat on the blotter, one on each side of the ledger that he had placed before her. Her back was straight, her body looked rigid. She said coolly, 'You should have informed me of your change of situation, Mr Connor.'

'I . . . I didn't think it was of any importance.'

'No importance!' She did not look at him, but now her eyes flicked over the table as if searching for some paper or other. 'A married man cannot give the attention to business that the single man can, for instance, he hasn't the time.'

'Oh, I have all the time . . .'

'Or the interest.' She had raised her eyes to his now. The colour had seeped from her face leaving it moist and grey. 'This alters matters, Mr Connor.'

He stared at her, his voice gruff now as he said, 'I don't understand, I can't see why.'

'You can't? Well then, if you can't then I am mistaken in the intelligence I credited you with.'

His back was as straight as hers now, his face grim.

As she held his gaze he thought, No, no, I'd be barmy to think that. I haven't got such a bloody big head on me as that. No! No! Yet it was pretty evident that the fact that he was married had upset her. She was likely one of these people who didn't believe in marriage, there were such about; there was one lived in the end house down the lane. She dressed like a man and it was said that she handled a horse and a boat as well as any man, but she looked half man. This one didn't. Although she had a business head on her shoulders she dressed very much as a woman of fashion might. He couldn't make her out. No, by God! he couldn't.

He said now, 'I can assure you, miss, me being married won't make any difference to my work. I'll give you my time and loyalty . . .'

'But as I have indicated, Mr Connor, only a certain amount of time and an equal amount of your loyalty . . . a married man has responsibilities. We can discuss the matter later. Mr Dryden has been paid in advance for your quarter's tuition, you will continue to go to him. That'll be all at present, Mr Connor. Good day.'

He rose stiffly from the chair. 'Good day . . . miss.'

The maid let him out; she smiled at him broadly. 'Good day, sir,' she said.

He had acquired the title of sir since it was known Miss Kean was sending him for training to be her manager and there was a significant deference in the servants' manners towards him now. She kept six altogether, with the gardener-cum-coachman. He answered her civilly, saying, 'Good day,' but as usual he did not address her by name. His position wasn't such that he felt he could do so yet.

Out on the drive he walked slowly, and at one point he actually stopped and said to himself, No!

No! And before he entered the main thoroughfare he again slowed his walk and exclaimed aloud now, 'Don't be a fool!'

He had no false modesty about his personal attraction. He knew that many a back door would have been left open for him if he had just raised an eyebrow or answered a gleam in a hungry woman's eyes. He didn't class himself as particularly handsome but was aware that he had something which was of greater appeal. If he had been asked to define it he would have found it impossible; he only knew that women were aware of him. And he had liked the knowledge, it gave him what he called a lift. But at the same time he knew there was but one woman for him.

But he couldn't get away from the fact that she had done what she had for him because she thought he was single. Now the question was, why? Why?

Yet again he shook his head at himself and said no, no. Why, the woman must be worth a fortune, and although she was as plain as a pikestaff there were men in the town who, he thought, would more than likely overlook such a minor handicap in order to get their hands on what she owned. Doubtless, some were already trying, for twice of late there had been carriages on the drive and he had seen sombre-clothed gentlemen descending towards them as he approached the house. And he recalled now, they had looked at him pretty hard.

But coming to know her as he had done over the past weeks, he imagined she would have all her wits about her with regard to such suitors who would be only after the main chance. She was the kind of woman who would do the choosing rather than be chosen, and apart from her face she had a lot on her side to enable her to do the choosing . . . *Had she been going to choose him?*

He didn't answer himself this time with, 'No! No!' but walked on, muttering instead, 'God Almighty! it's unbelievable.'

'You're quiet the night. Nothing wrong is there? And what made you go back to the office this afternoon?'

'Oh, I had some work to get through. It's been a heavy week, and I've got that Pittie mob on me mind. Did he say he'd seen them around the day?'

'No. He only stayed in for a few minutes after I got home, I told you. He said he was goin' down to collect some wood he had roped together.'

'But that was this afternoon. It's dark, he should be back by now. I'd better take a walk out and see if he's comin'.'

He looked towards her where she was kneading dough in a brown earthenware dish, then went out and down the steps into the yard. There was a moon riding high, raced by white scudding clouds. He walked to the end of the little jetty and looked along each side of the river where boats large and small were moored. He liked the river at night when it was quiet like this, but he had made up his mind, at least he had done until this morning, that it wouldn't be long before he moved Janie away from this quarter and into a decent house in the town. He had thought Jimmy could stay on here, Jimmy wouldn't mind living on his own, for he was self-sufficient was Jimmy. But now things had changed. This morning's business had blown his schemes away into dust.

He'd had the feeling of late that he was galloping towards some place but he didn't know where. So many strange things had happened over the past months. He wasn't even wearing the same kind of clothes he wore a few weeks ago for she had hinted not only that he should get a new suit but where he should go to buy it. However, he hadn't patronised the shop she suggested; he hadn't, he told himself, enough money as yet for that kind of tailoring. Nevertheless, he had got himself a decent suit, with a high waistcoat and the jacket flared, and the very cut of it had lifted him out of the rent collector's class. But now the rosy future had suddenly died on him. What would she say on Monday? . . . Well, he'd have to wait and see, that's all he could do.

He heard a soft splash and saw the minute figure of Jimmy steering the boat towards the jetty. He bent down and grabbed the rope that Jimmy threw to him, then said, 'You all right? Where you been all day? What's taken you so long?'

'The wood I'd had piled up, it was scattered, some back in the river, all over. I had a job collectin' it again.'

'The Pitties?'

'I shouldn't wonder. I don't think it could be bairns, it would have been too heavy for them.'

'Well, leave it where it is till the mornin', we'll sort it out then.'

When Jimmy had made fast his boat and was standing on the quay he peered at Rory saying, 'What's up? You look as if you'd lost a tanner and found a threepenny bit. Anything wrong?'

'No, no, nothing. How about you?'

'Oh well, they were around early on in the mornin' again, two of them. They moored just opposite and sat lookin' across, just starin'. But I went on with me work, and I stood for a time and stared back. Then they went off.' And he added, 'If they try anything I'll go straight and tell the river polis.'

'It'll likely be too late then. The only thing is be careful and don't be such a bloody fool stayin' out in the dark. They're not likely to try anything in the daylight, but give them a chance in the dark, and you're asking for it.'

All Jimmy replied to this was, 'Aye. By! I'm hungry,' and ran up the steps, and when he opened the door he sniffed loudly and said, 'Ooh! that smells good.'

Janie turned to him from the table, saying, 'Aye well, now you'll have to wait a bit, we've had to wait for you.'

'I'm hungry, woman.'

'Are you ever anything else?' she laughed at him. 'Well, there's some fresh teacakes there, tuck into them.'

As he broke a hot teacake in two, he asked, 'What's for supper?'

'Finny haddy.'

'Good, and hurry up with it.'

She thrust out her arm to clip his ear, but he dodged the blow and went and sat himself on the steel fender with his back to the oven and laughed and chatted as he ate.

Looking at him, Rory knew a sudden spasm of envy as he thought, he was born bowed, but he was born happy. Why can't I be like him? But then the answer to that one was, they had different mothers. He hadn't thought along these lines for some time now; it was odd but it was only when he was faced with trouble that he let his bitterness against Lizzie have rein.

Of a sudden he said to neither of them in particular, 'Will we have to go home the morrow again?'

Both Janie and Jimmy turned a quick glance on him and it was Janie who said, 'Of course we'll have to go home the morrow. We always do, don't we? It's Sunday.'

'That's it, that's what I mean, we always do. Couldn't we do something different, take a trip up the river or something? We've got our own boat.'

'But they'll be expectin' us. It won't be Sunday for them if we don't go up; they'll all be there.'

'Aye, they'll all be there.' His voice trailed away on a sigh and he turned and went into the bedroom while Janie and Jimmy exchanged another look and Jimmy said under his breath, 'Something's wrong. I twigged it right away.'

'You think so?' Janie whispered back.

'Aye, don't you?'

'Well, I did think he was a bit quiet, but when I asked him he said everything was all right.'

'Aye, that's what he says, but there's something up. I'm tellin' you, there's something up.'

When, in the middle of the night, Janie was again woken from her sleep by Rory's voice, not mumbling this time but shouting, she hissed at him, 'Ssh! ssh! Wake up. What is it?'

But he went on, louder now, 'I'll make it up to you, I will . . . I know . . . I know, but I couldn't.'

'Rory! Rory! wake up.'

'Five pounds. I had it, I had it. You're to blame.'

'Rory! do you hear me?' She was trying to shake him.

'Wha'? Wha'?' He half woke and grabbed at her hands, then almost at the same time threw her aside, crying, 'What was the good of two of us doin' time! I'm not goin' in there, so don't keep on. You won't get me in there, not for five pounds, or fifty. Five clarty pounds. Five clarty pounds. If I'd had the chance I'd have put it back, I would. I . . . would . . .' His voice trailed away and he fell back on the pillows.

Janie sat bolt upright in the bed staring down through the darkness, not on to Rory but towards where her hands were gripping the quilt . . . *That was it then. That was it!* It should have been as clear as daylight from the beginning.

She saw John George's face through the grid saying, 'Tell Rory that, will you? Tell him I didn't take the five pounds.' And what John George was actually saying was, 'Tell him to own up.' She couldn't believe it, yet she knew it was true. He had let John George, his good friend, go to that stinking place alone. It was true he couldn't have done much about it at first, but after he regained consciousness in hospital he must have known. That's why he hadn't asked for John George. It should have been one of the first things he mentioned. 'What's the matter with John George?' he should have said. 'Why hasn't he come to see me?'

No, she couldn't believe it, she couldn't. But she had to. She now turned her head towards the bulk lying beside her and instinctively hitched herself away from it towards the wall. But the next move she made was almost like that of an animal, for she pounced on him and, her hands gripping his shoulders, she cried, 'Wake up! Wake up!'

'Wha'? What's-it? What's-up? What's wrong?'

'Get up. Get up.'

As he pulled himself up in the bed she climbed over him, grabbed the matches from the table and lit the candle, and all the while he was repeating, 'What is it? What's the matter?'

The candle lit, she held it upwards and gazed down into his blinking eyes.

'What's up with you? You gone mad or something?'

'Aye, I've gone mad, flamin' mad; bloody well flamin' mad.'

She sounded like Lizzie and her grannie rolled into one. He pushed the clothes back from the bed but didn't get up, he just peered at her. 'What the hell's up with you, woman?'

'You ask me that! Well, you've just had a nightmare an' you've just cleared up somethin' that's been puzzling me for a long time. *You*! Do you know what I could do to you this minute? I could spit in your eye, Rory Connor. I could spit in your eye.'

He now leant his stiff body back against the wall. He'd had a nightmare, he'd been talking. He was sweating, yet cold, it was always cold on the river at night. With a thrust of his arm he pushed her aside and got out of the bed and pulled his trousers on over his linings, but didn't speak; and neither did she. But when he went towards the door to go into the other room she followed him, holding the candle high, and she watched him grab the matches from the mantelpiece and light the lamp. When it was aflame he turned and looked at her and said quietly, 'Well, now you know.'

'Aye, I know. And how you can stand there and

say it like that God alone knows. My God! to think you let John George take the rap for you . . .'

He turned on her. His voice low and angry, he said, 'He didn't take the rap for me, he took it for himself. He'd have been caught out sooner or later; he'd been at it for months.'

'Aye, he might have, but only for a few shillings at a time not five pounds.'

'No, not for a few shillings, a pound and more. I'd warned him.'

'You warned him!' Her voice was full of scorn. 'But you went and did the same, and for no little sum either. It was for your five pounds he got put away for the year, not for the little bits.'

'It wasn't. I tell you it wasn't.'

'Oh, shut up! Don't try to stuff me like you've been doin' yourself. That's what you've been tellin' yourself all along, isn't it, to ease your conscience? But your conscience wouldn't be eased, would it? Remember our first night in this place. You nearly knocked me through the wall 'cos I mentioned his name. I should have twigged then.'

'Aye, yes, you should.' His tone was flat now, weary-sounding. 'And if you had, it would have been over and done with, I'd have gone through less.'

'Gone through less! You talkin' about goin' through anything, what about John George?'

'Damn John George!' He was shouting now. 'I tell you he would have gone along the line in any case.'

'You'll keep tellin' yourself that till the day you die, yet you don't believe it because the other night you promised to set him up when he came out. Eeh!—' she now shook her head mockingly at him —'that was kind of you, wasn't it? And I nearly went on me knees to you for it.'

'Janie—' he came towards her—'try to understand. You . . . you know how I feel about being locked in, and I was bad at the time. I was bad. God! I nearly died. And that was no make game, I couldn't think clearly not for weeks after.'

As his hand came out towards her she sprang back from it, saying, 'Don't touch me, Rory Connor. Don't touch me, not until you get yourself down to that station and tell them the truth.'

'What!' The word carried a high surprised note of utter astonishment. 'You'd have me go along the line now?'

'Aye, I would, and be able to live with you when you came out. It isn't the pinchin' of the five pounds that worries me, an' if nobody had suffered through it I would have said, "Good for you if you can get off with it," but not now, not the way things are; not when that lad's back there. And you know something? When I think of it he could have potched you, he could have said you were the only other one who had a key. He could have said you were a gambling man and would sell your own mother. Oh aye—' she wagged her head now—'you would sell your real mother for less than five pounds any day in the week, wouldn't you? Poor Lizzie . . .'

The blow that caught her across the mouth sent her staggering, and at the same moment Jimmy came rushing down the ladder. Without a word he went to her where she was leaning against the chest-of-drawers, her back arched, her hand across her mouth, and he put his arm around her waist as he looked towards Rory and said, 'You'll regret that, our Rory. There'll come a day when you'll be sorry for that.'

'You mind your own bloody business. And get out of this.'

'I'll not. I've heard enough to make me as sick as she is. I can't believe it of you, I just can't. And to John George of all people. He'd have laid down his life for you.'

Rory turned from the pair and stumbled to the mantelpiece and, gripping its edge, he stared down into the banked-down fire. That he was more upset by Jimmy's reactions than by Janie's didn't surprise him, for he knew he represented a sort of hero to his brother. He had never done one outstanding thing to deserve it but he had accepted his worship over the years, and found comfort in it, but now Jimmy had turned on him.

God Almighty! why did everything happen to him at once? Her, yesterday, blaming him for being married, now this with Janie; and not only Janie, Jimmy. Yet he knew that if, come daylight, he took himself along to the polis station they'd both be with him every inch of the road. But he couldn't, he knew he couldn't go and tell them the truth. Apart from his fear of imprisonment look what he stood to lose, his job; and not only that but the good name that would help him to get another. Never again would he be allowed to handle money once he had been along the line. And this place would go, Jimmy's yard. Had he thought of that? He swung round now, crying at them, 'All right, if I was to give meself up, what would happen? No more yard for you, Jimmy boy, your dream gone up in smoke. Did you think of that?'

'No, but now you mention it, it wouldn't be the end of me, I could always get me other job back. And I can always go home again. Don't let that stop you. Don't you try to use me in that way, our Rory.'

'And her, what's gona happen to her then?' He was speaking of Janie as if she weren't sitting by the table with her face buried in her hands, and Jimmy answered, 'She won't be any worse off than she was afore, she's always got her place.'

'Aw, to hell's flames with the lot of you!' He flung his arm wide as if sweeping them out of the room. 'What do you know about anything? Own up and be a good boy and I'll stand by you. You know nowt, the pair of you, the lot of you, you're ignorant, you can't see beyond your bloody noses. There's swindlin' going on every day. Respectable men, men looked up to in this town twisting with every breath. And you'd have me ruin meself for five pounds.'

'It's not the five . . .'

175

'Be quiet, Jimmy! Be quiet!' Janie's voice was low. 'You won't get anywhere with him 'cos he'll keep on about the five pounds, he'll try to hoodwink you like he's hoodwinked himself. Well—' she rose from the table—'I know what I'm gona do.' She walked slowly into the bedroom and they both gazed after her. When the door banged behind her Jimmy made for the ladder and without another word mounted it and disappeared through the trap door.

Rory stared about the empty room for a moment, then turning towards the mantelshelf again he bowed his head on it and slowly beat his fist against the rough wall above it.

6

'Why, lass, it's the chance in a lifetime. In a boat cruising? My! my! round France. By! the master's brother must have plenty of money to own a boat like that.'

'I think it's his wife who has the money, he married a French lady.'

'And you tell us it's a sort of castle they live in?'

'Yes, that's what the missis says.'

'We'll miss you, lass.' Lizzie sat back on her heels from where she had been kneeling sweeping the fallen cinders underneath the grate and she looked hard at Janie as she said, 'I know it's only for three weeks, but what puzzles me is him lettin' you go at all. Didn't he kick up a shindy?'

Janie turned away and looked towards Ruth where she was coming out of the scullery carrying plates of thickly cut bread, and she answered, 'Yes, a bit. But then he's taken up with his new position an' such, and . . . and often doesn't get in till late.'

'Aye.' Lizzie pulled her bulk upright and bent to her sweeping once again. 'His new position. By! he's fallen on his feet if anybody has. It was a whole day's blessin' when old Kean died, you could say.'

'You're off first thing in the mornin' then, lass?'

Janie nodded towards Ruth and said, 'Yes, we've got to be in Newcastle by eight o'clock; we're goin' up by carriage.'

'Then all the way to London by train.' Ruth shook her head. 'It's amazing, wonderful; the sights you'll see. It would have been a great pity if you hadn't taken the opportunity; such a thing as this only comes once in a lifetime . . . And you won't stay for a bite to eat?'

'I can't, thanks all the same, there's so much to do, to see to you know. And that reminds me. I needn't ask you, need I, to see to me grannie?'

'Aw, lass—' Ruth pulled a face at her—'you know that goes without sayin'. At least you should.'

'Aye, I know. And thanks, thanks to both of you.' She cast her glance between them, then looking at Lizzie, who had now risen to her feet, she said, 'Well, I'd better say ta-rah,' and the next moment she was hugging Lizzie, and Lizzie was holding her tight and saying brokenly, 'Now don't cry, there's nowt to cry about, goin' on a holiday . . . Don't. Don't lass.'

'There, there.' She was enfolded in Ruth's arms now and Lizzie was patting her shoulder. Then swiftly pulling herself away from them, she grabbed up her bag from a chair and ran out of the cottage.

It was Ruth who, having closed the door after her, came back to the centre of the room and looking at Lizzie said, 'Well, what do you make of it?'

'What can I make of it? There's somethin' wrong, and has been for weeks past, if you ask me. He's hardly been across the door. And Jimmy, look what he was like the last time he was here, no high-falutin' talk of boats and cargoes and contracts an' such like.'

'Whatever it is, it doesn't lie just atween the both of them, not when Jimmy's concerned in it.'

'No, you're right there.' Lizzie nodded. 'And it couldn't be just marriage rows. Jimmy would take those in his stride, havin' been brought up on them.' She smiled faintly. 'No, whatever it is, it's somethin' big and bad. I'm worried.'

'In a couple of days' time we could take a walk down and tidy up and do a bit of baking and such like. What do you say, Lizzie?'

'That's a sensible idea. Aye, we could do that, and we might winkle out something while we're there.'

'It could be. It could be.'

'Things are changin', Ruth. Folks and places, everything.'

Ruth came to her now and, tapping her arm gently, said, 'Don't worry about him, he'll straighten things out. Whatever trouble there is he'll straighten things out. He's your own son, and being such he's bound to be sensible at bottom.'

'You're a good woman, Ruth, none better.'

They turned sadly away from each other now and went about their respective duties in the kitchen.

Janie had been gone ten days and his world was empty. If she were to appear before him at this minute he would say to her, 'All right, I'll go, I'll go now, as long as I know you'll be here, the old Janie, waiting for me when I come out.' His mind was like a battlefield, he was fighting love and hate, and recrimination and bitterness.

The recrimination was mostly against his employer. He had seen her only twice in the past three weeks. He still took the takings to the house in the evenings but his orders were to leave them in the study and to call for the books the next morning.

During their two meetings there had been no discussion about future plans of any kind. Her manner had been cool and formal, her tone one that he recalled from her visits to the office years ago. It was the one in which orders were issued and brooked no questions.

But although in one breath he was telling himself that if Janie were here now he would do what she asked, in the next he was asking himself what was going to happen when she did return. After the night of the show-down she had slept up in the loft, and Jimmy had slept on a shaky-down in the kitchen. Would it go on like that until he gave in? He could have asserted his rights as many a man before him had done by well-directed blows, but the fact that he had hit her once was enough; that alone had created a barrier between them. She wasn't the type of girl who would stand knocking about, she had too much spirit, and he was ashamed, deeply ashamed of having struck her. He had acted no better than his father whom, at bottom, he despised.

It was Saturday again. He hated Saturdays, Sundays more so. He hadn't gone up home since she had left, but they had been down here, at least Ruth and she had. They had cleaned up and cooked, and spoken to each other as if they were back in the kitchen. They hadn't asked any questions regarding how he felt about her going away, which pointed more forcibly than words to the fact that they were aware that something was wrong.

Then there was Jimmy. Jimmy was making him wild, sitting for hours at night scratching away with a pencil on bits of paper and never opening his mouth. He had turned on him the other night and cried, 'If anyone's to blame for this business it's you. Who pestered me into buying this bloody ramshackle affair, eh? Who?' and snatching up a miniature wooden ship's wheel from the mantelshelf he had flung it against the far wall, where it had splintered into a dozen pieces, and Jimmy, after looking down on the fragments with a sort of tearful sadness, had gone up the ladder, leaving him to increased misery.

He stood at the window now looking down on to the yard. The sun was glinting on the water; there were boats plying up and down the river; on the slipway Jimmy had set the keel of a new boat in the small stocks and he was working on it now. In the ordinary way he would have been down there helping him, they would have been exchanging jokes about what they would do when they had the monopoly of the river, or grinding their teeth at the Pitties and their tactics.

As he looked down on Jimmy's fair head, he was suddenly brought forward with a jerk, for there, coming round the side of the building, was Ruth and his da and Lizzie. It wasn't the fact that they'd all turned up together to visit him, it was the expression on their faces that was riveting his attention for both Lizzie and Ruth were crying, openly crying as they talked rapidly to Jimmy, and his da was now holding out a paper to Jimmy. He watched Jimmy reading it, shake his head, then put his hand to his brow before turning and looking up at the window. Then they were all looking up at the window.

He didn't step back but stared down at them as they remained still, their postures seemingly frozen into a group of statuary. He noticed that Lizzie was wearing her old shawl, and old it was, green in parts. And Ruth too was in a shawl; she nearly always wore a bonnet. And they both still had their aprons on.

He moved from the window and went to the door and, having opened it, looked down the steps at them. They came towards him. It was his father who mounted first, and he said to him, 'What's up?' But Paddy didn't answer, he just walked into the room, followed by Ruth and Lizzie and, lastly, Jimmy.

Rory's gaze travelled from one to the other, then came to rest on Jimmy who was gripping the paper with both hands and staring at him.

He did not repeat his question to Jimmy, but took the paper from him and began to read.

'It is with deep regret that we hear of the terrible tragedy that has overtaken a Shields family on holiday on the coast of France. Mr Charles Buckham, his wife, three children, and their

180

nursemaid Mrs Jane Connor, together with Mr Buckham's brother, are feared lost, after their yacht was caught in a great storm. Mrs Buckham's body and that of one child were washed ashore, together with pieces of wreckage from the boat. There is little hope of any survivors. Two other boats were wrecked at the same time, with a total loss of twenty-six lives. Mr Charles Buckham was a prominent member . . .'

Someone must have brought a chair forward for him to sit on because when next he looked at them they were standing in a half-circle before him and they were all crying, even his da. His own eyes were dry; his whole body was dry, he was being shrivelled up; his mind had stopped working except for a section which oozed pain and ran like a burning acid down into his heart, and there it was etching out her name: Janie. Janie.

'Janie. Janie,' he said the name aloud and turned and saw Lizzie lift up her white apron and fling it over her head, and when she began to moan like a banshee he made no protest because the sound was finding an echo within himself. 'Janie. Janie. Aw, Janie, don't go, Janie. Don't be dead, Janie. Come back to me, Janie. Don't leave me. Don't leave me. I'll see about John George, honest to God I promise, now, right now. Oh, Janie.'

'Give him a drop out of the bottle.'

Paddy put his hand into his inside pocket and drew out a flat flask of whisky and, picking up a cup, he almost half-filled it. Then handing it to Rory, he said, 'Get it down you, lad. Get it down you. You need to be fortified. God knows you need to be fortified.'

When Lizzie suddenly cried, 'Why does God bring disasters like this to us? What have we ever done to Him?' Paddy turned on her, hissing, 'Whist! woman. It's questions like that that bring on disasters.'

Her wailing increased, and she cried, 'It's the third thing. I said there would be three, didn't I?

Didn't I? An' I told Andrews the polis when he brought the paper up, didn't I, didn't I?'

'Oh Janie, Janie. Come back, Janie. Just let me look on you once more.' It was sayings like that that brought disaster his da had just said. He was ignorant. They were all ignorant. That's what he had said to Janie, they were all ignorant. And he had compared their talk, their ways, and their dwelling, the dwelling that he had known since birth, with Charlotte Kean and her fine house. Yet their ignorance was a warm ignorance, it was something you didn't have to live up to; pretence fell through it like water through a sieve. Their ignorance was a solid foundation on which he could lean. He was leaning against it now, his head tucked against warm, thick flesh, nor when he realized it was Lizzie's flesh, his mother's flesh, did he push it away. In this moment he needed ignorance, he needed love, he needed warmth, he needed so many things to make up for the loss of Janie.

'Aw, Janie, Janie. I'm sorry, Janie. I'm sorry, Janie.'

7

Charlotte Kean did not read the paper until late on the Saturday evening. She had returned from Hexham about seven o'clock feeling tired, irritable and lonely. After a meal she had gone into the office with the intention of doing some work on the mass of papers that always awaited her on the desk, but after sitting down she stared in front of her for a moment before closing her eyes and letting her body slump into the depths of the leather chair.

How much longer could she go on like this? She'd asked herself the same question numbers of times over the past weeks. There was a remedy, in fact two. But the cure offered by either Mr Henry Bolton or Mr George Pearson was worse, she imagined, than her present disease. Henry Bolton was forty-eight and a widower. George Pearson would never see fifty again. She wasn't foolish enough to think that either of them had fallen in love with her. She would go as far as to say that they didn't even like her, considering her ways too advanced by half, having heard her opinions from across a committee table. But since the death of both her father and her grandfather they had almost raced each other to the house.

No. No. Never.

She rose from the desk. She was a spinster and she'd remain a spinster. The wild fantastic dream she'd had was only that, a wild fantastic dream. She had humiliated herself because of her dream; she had been willing to be publicly humiliated because of her dream.

She went from the office and upstairs to her room, the room that until a few weeks ago had been her father's. It was the largest bedroom in the house and faced the garden and shortly after he died she had it completely redecorated and had made it her own. She knew that the servants had been slightly shocked by such seeming lack of respect for the dead but she didn't care what servants thought, or anyone else for that matter.

It was very odd, she mused, as she slowly took off her day clothes and got into a housegown, a new acquisition and another thing that had shocked the servants, for it wasn't black or brown, or even grey, but a startling pink, and its material was velvet. Yes, it was very odd, but there was no one for whose opinion she cared one jot. And more sadly still, there was no one who cared one jot about what happened to her. She hadn't a close relative left in the world, nor had she a close friend. There were those in the town who would claim her as a friend, more so now, but to her they were no more than acquaintances.

She sat before the mirror and unpinned her hair

and the two dark, shining plaits fell down over her shoulders and almost to her waist. As her fingers undid each twist the hair seemed to spring into a life of its own and when, taking a brush, she stroked it from the crown down to its ends it covered her like a cloak.

The brush poised to the side of her face, she stared at herself in the mirror. It was a waste on her; it should have been doled out to some pretty woman and it would have made her beautiful, whereas on her head it only seemed to emphasize the plainness of her features. She leant forward and stared at her reflection. How was it that two eyes, a nose, and a mouth could transform one face into attractiveness while leaving another desolate of any appeal? She was not misshapen in any way, yet look at her. She dressed well, she had a taste for dress, she knew the right things to wear but the impression they afforded stopped at her neck. She had even resorted to the artifice of toilet powder, and in secret had applied rouge to her lips and cheeks with the result that she looked nothing better, she imagined, than a street woman.

She rose and glanced towards the bed. Were she to go to bed now she wouldn't sleep. She couldn't read in bed at all. This was the outcome, she supposed, of being taught to read while sitting in a straight-backed chair. Her father had enforced this rule and the teachers at the school to which her mother had sent her were of a like mind too. When she was young her idea of heaven had been to curl up on the rug before the fire and read a book, but when finally she had returned home from school she had found no pleasure in this form of relaxation.

She decided to go down to the drawing-room and play the piano for a while. This often had the power to soothe her nerves. Then she would take a bath, after which she might get to sleep without thinking.

It was as she was crossing the hall that she noticed the local paper neatly folded, together with a magazine, lying on a salver on the side table. She picked up both and went on into the drawing-room. But before laying them down she glanced at the newspaper's headlines: Shields Family Lost at Sea.

'It is with deep regret that we hear of the terrible tragedy that has overtaken a Shields family on holiday on the coast of France. Mr Charles Buckham, his wife, three children and their nursemaid, Mrs Jane Connor, together with Mr Buckham's brother are feared lost, after their yacht was caught in a great storm. Mrs Buckham's body and that of one child were washed ashore, together with pieces of wreckage from the boat. There is little hope of any survivors . . .'

Mrs Jane Connor, nursemaid.
Mrs Jane Connor, nursemaid.

He had said she was nursemaid to the Buckhams. Yes, yes, it was the Buckhams of Westoe. She knew him, Charles Buckham, and she had met his wife a number of times, and . . . and there couldn't be two nursemaids by the name of Jane Connor.

He hadn't said his wife had gone away, but then she hadn't spoken to him for weeks, not since he had startled her by saying he was married.

She was sorry, very sorry . . .

Was she?

Of course she was, it was a terrible thing. Could she go to him now and tell him? What time was it? She swung round and looked at the clock on the mantelpiece. Quarter-to-nine. It was still light, yet she didn't know exactly where the place was; but it was on the waterfront and would be dark by the time she got there.

She found herself walking up and down the room. Her stomach was churning with excitement. She said again, 'What a tragedy! A terrible tragedy. And those poor young children.'

She suddenly stopped her pacing and, dropping

into a chair, bent her body forward until her breasts were almost touching her knees. She mustn't make herself ridiculous; nothing had altered, things stood as they had done a few minutes earlier.

Slowly she drew herself up and, taking in deep draughts of air, said to herself, 'You can call tomorrow morning. It will be quite in order then for you to go and offer your condolences. He's in your employ and naturally you have his concern at heart. Go and have a bath now and go to bed; you can do nothing until tomorrow.'

She had a bath and she went to bed, but it was almost dawn before she finally fell asleep. And she was still asleep when the maid came in with her early morning tea at eight o'clock.

She hardly gave herself time to drink the tea before she was out of bed dressing, and at nine o'clock she left the house, presumably to go to an early service. She had informed Jessie that she wouldn't need the carriage, it was a fine morning and she preferred to walk.

The only answer Jessie could give to this was 'Yes, miss,' but the expression on her face told Charlotte that she considered that by breaking yet another rule she was letting the prestige of the family down; no one of any importance in this district went to church on foot.

Because the occasion demanded sobriety she had dressed in the black outfit she had worn to her father's funeral and so she wasn't conspicuous as she made her way from the residential quarter of Westoe to the long district lining the waterfront. Yet she did not pass without notice for she was tall and slim and her walk was purposeful as if she knew where she was going. But on this occasion she didn't, at least not precisely.

Having almost reached the Lawe she stopped an old riverside man and asked him if he could direct her to Mr Connor's boatyard.

'Connor's boatyard? Never knew no boatyard by

that name along this stretch, ma'am. No Connor's boatyard along here.'

'It's . . . it's a small yard, I understand.'

'Big or small, ma'am, none of that name.'

'Mr Connor has only recently taken the yard over.'

'Small yard, taken it over?' The old man rubbed the stubble on his chin and said, 'Oh aye, now I come to think of it, it's old Barney Kilpatrick's place. Oh aye, I heard tell of a young 'un startin' up there. Takes some grit and guts to start on your own along this stretch. Well now, ma'am, you turn yourself round and go back yonder till you pass a space full of lumber, bits of boats . . . odds and ends. There's a cut at yon side atween a set of pailings, the gate into Kilpatrick's place is but a few steps down there.'

'Thank you. Thank you very much.'

'You're welcome, ma'am. You're welcome.'

She walked swiftly back along the potholed road, followed the directions the old man had given her and within a few minutes found herself opposite a wooden gate in a high fence of black sleepers.

The gate opened at a touch and she went through and stood for a moment looking at the ramshackle building before her. There were steps leading up to a door and, having mounted them, she knocked gently and waited. After a short interval she knocked again, harder now, and after knocking a third time she tried the handle and found the door locked.

She descended the steps and looked about her. There was evidence of a small boat being built. She walked into the slipway, then out again and stood looking up at the windows. She could see the place as a boatyard, even though it was very small, but as a residence, never. She gave a slight shudder. Being almost on the river's edge it would be overrun with rats and so damp. And he lived here and had spoken of it with enthusiasm!

Where was he now? Most likely at his parents' house. Of course, that's where he would be. Well, she couldn't go there . . . or could she?

'You mustn't. You mustn't.'

She walked out of the yard, closing the gate behind her, and again she chastised herself, sternly now. 'You mustn't. You mustn't. Please retain some sense of decorum.'

But it was such a long time until tomorrow. Would he come to work? Well, the only thing she could do was to wait and see, and if he didn't put in an appearance, then she would go to his home. It would seem quite in order to do so then.

She walked slowly back through the town. People were making their way to the churches. There were a number of carriages in the market place adjacent to St. Hilda's. She wondered for a moment whether she should go in there, then decided not to. What would she pray for? She mustn't be a hypocrite. She'd always prided herself on being honest, at least to herself. She went to church, but she was no church-woman. She knew why more than half the congregation attended her own particular church. Their reasons were various, but had nothing to do with God and worship: to see and be seen; to make connections. It was an established fact that it did one no harm in the business world to belong to a congregation, especially if you paid substantially for your pew and had your name inscribed on a silver name-plate.

In her loneliest moments she warned herself against cynicism knowing that if she didn't want to lose those few people who termed themselves her friends she must keep her radical opinions to herself. But oh, she had thought so often how wonderful it would be, how comforting to have someone with whom she could talk plainly. A male. Oh, yes a male, someone like . . .

When had she first thought of him in that way? All her life seemingly. Don't be ridiculous. Well, four and a half years was a lifetime.

Sunday was a long day, and on Monday morning she

was awake early and dressed for outdoors by eight o'clock, and by a quarter to nine she was seated behind the desk in the inner office in Tangard Street.

If he were coming to work he would come here to see to the men. If he didn't put in an appearance, well she must see to them, and once they were settled she would go on to Simonside and offer her condolences . . .

He came into the office at ten minutes to nine and she was shocked at the sight of him, and sad, truly sad; yet at the same time envious of a woman who, by her going, could pile the years almost overnight on a man.

She rose swiftly from the chair, then came round the desk and stood in front of him, saying, and with sincere feeling, 'I'm so sorry. Now you shouldn't have come, I didn't expect you. You . . . you must go home and stay there as long as you feel it is necessary; there's no hurry, I can see to things . . .'

She watched him wet his lips before saying in a voice so unlike his own in that it was quiet, like that of a sick man bereft of strength, 'I'd . . . I'd much rather be at work, if you don't mind.'

'Well—' she shook her head slowly—'it's as you wish. But . . . but you don't look well. And . . . and haven't you got . . . ? Well, aren't there things you must see to officially?'

'No.' He shook his head. 'We . . . I went on Saturday. The police said they'd let me know if they heard anything further. Mr . . . Mr Buckham's father has gone over, I'm to see him when he comes back.'

'Oh.' She stared into his face. It was grey, lifeless. She realized as she looked at him that his appeal did not come from his looks at all, as one might imagine, as she herself had imagined years ago, but from the vitality within, from the bumptiousness and the arrogance that was part of his nature. At the moment there was no life either in his face or in his body.

But, of course, it was to be understood this was only temporary; he was under shock, he would revive . . . she would see that he revived. The decision he had taken to come straight to work was the best possible thing he could have done.

She said now, 'Then I can leave you?'

'Yes.'

She picked up her bag and gloves from the desk, and turning to him again, she said, 'If you wish you may send Mr Taylor with the collection.'

'Thanks.' He inclined his head towards her.

'Are you staying with your parents?'

'No.' He shook his head. 'I've been with them over the weekend but I'm going back to the boatyard.'

She said with some concern now, 'Do you think it wise for you to be alone at this time?'

'My brother will be with me.'

'Oh.' She stared at him; then again she said, 'I'm deeply sorry.'

He made no reply but turned from her and she had to stop herself from going to him for she imagined he was about to cry, and if she were to see him cry . . . She turned hastily and went out.

Alone now he stood staring down at the desk as if he had never seen it before, as if he were surprised to find it there; then going behind it, he sat down and, drawing a handkerchief from his pocket, wiped it quickly round his face before blowing his nose. He had said he'd be better at work. He'd never be better anywhere, anytime, but being here was better than remaining in the kitchen. He'd go mad if he had to listen to any more talk of Janie. Since Saturday night they had talked about her, wailed about her, cried about her, and he too had cried and wailed, but inside. To them it was as if she were lying in the coffin in the corner of the room. They had drunk their beer and had their tots of whisky as if they were holding a wake. They had sat up all night, the Learys and her da and grannie, and his own father and Ruth and Jimmy . . . and her. Nellie had come and her husband with her. And that had been another thing that had nearly driven him mad, when Nellie announced through her tears that she was pregnant at last, and her, his big slob of a slavering mother, had cried, 'That's God's way. That's God's way, when He shuts one door He opens another.' Another day among them and he would have gone out of his mind.

There was only one good thing that had come out of it, he and Jimmy were back where they were before. Nothing had been said but Jimmy hadn't left his side since Saturday, not even during the night, the longest night of his life. All Saturday night he had sat by his side up in the loft, and last night too, and it was he who had said early this morning, 'Let's get back away home, eh?' It was odd that Jimmy should think of the boatyard as home rather than the place in which he had been brought up. But Janie had made it home.

He thought with shame and guilt of how he had begun to compare it with Charlotte Kean's place. God, he wouldn't swop it for a palace decked with diamonds at this moment if Janie was in it.

Aw Janie. Janie. Oh! God, and they had parted like strangers. The last words he spoke to her were, 'You are hard. I said it afore in this very house and I say it again, there's a hard streak in you.'

She had gazed at him and replied, 'Aye, perhaps you're right.'

Then she was gone, and when the door closed on her he had beaten his fists against his head.

Why the hell was he standing there! Why didn't he go after her and drag her back by the scruff of the neck? He was her husband, wasn't he? He had his rights—was he a man? No other bloody man in the town would have put up with what he had these past two weeks, they would have knocked the daylights out of her. Why was he standing here?

Back in the cottages they referred to him, behind his back, as 'the big fella,' and he had come to think of himself, and not without pride as 'a gambling man.' But what in effect was he? He . . . he was nothing more than a nowt who couldn't keep his wife, a nowt who had let a little chit of a lass best him. Had it happened to John George he would have said, 'Well, what do you expect?'

. . . John George!

This morning he had taken up a jug and hurled it almost at the same place at which he had thrown the ship's wheel. It was because of him he was in this pickle.

Janie! Janie! How am I to go on?

There was a knock on the door and Mr Taylor entered and provided him with the answer . . . work. It was either that or the river.

PART THREE

The Bargain

In 1877 those who were enlightened by reading newspapers discussed among other things such topics as Disraeli proclaiming Queen Victoria Empress of India and seeing to it that she had the adulation of Indian princes and African chiefs. But for the ordinary man and woman in towns such as South Shields, there were other happenings that struck nearer home, very much nearer home.

The sea which provided most of the inhabitants with a livelihood also created havoc and disaster. There was that awful night in December last year when three vessels were wrecked and the sea, still unsatisfied, had engulfed and destroyed another two later in the day, and all under the eyes of horrified townspeople who could only watch helplessly. Even though the Volunteer Life Brigade did heroic work, many lives were lost.

Such tragedies had the power to unite the townspeople, at least for a time. Rich and poor alike mingled in their sorrow until the poor, once again forgetting their place in God's scheme of things, protested against their lot. And how did they protest? They protested through societies called trade unions.

Since the first national union of the Amalgamated Society of Engineers had been founded in 1851, in every town in the country where skilled workers were employed trade unions had sprung up, to the fear and consternation of the middle classes who looked upon them as a network of secret societies, whose sole purpose was to intimidate honest citizens, plot to confiscate their property, cause explosions and mob violence and bring the country to total revolution if they were allowed to get the upper hand.

The County of Durham was a hotbed of such people. They agitated in mines, in steel works, in shipbuilding yards, in factories, and it was even whispered they tried to inveigle young women into their ranks; and not only those, let it be understood, from the common herd, but women of education and property.

Such a one who was suspect in South Shields was Miss Charlotte Kean. She wasn't accused openly of supporting trade unions because then that would be ridiculous, for she not only held shares in some quite big concerns but owned outright a number of small ones. No, they weren't accusing her of giving her sympathy to the quarter that would eventually precipitate her ruin through business, but what they did say was, she pushed her nose into too many cultural activities in the town, activities that had hitherto been inaugurated and worked mainly by gentlemen, such as the Public Library that had been opened four years previously.

This grand building could boast its eight thousand two hundred volumes only because of generous donations from men like the Stephensons, and Mr Williamson, and Mr Moore. What was more, the library had grown out of the Mechanics' Institute and the Working Men's Club, and this joint establishment had its origins in the Literary, Mechanical and Scientific Institution which was one of the earliest mechanics' institutions in the kingdom, having come into being in the November of 1825.

And who had created such places of learning? *Men*, gentlemen of the town, not women, or even ladies. Why the efforts of the gentlemen of the town had made The Working Men's Club and Institution so popular that in 1865 they'd had to seek new premises yet once again, premises large enough to contain now not only a newsroom and library but two classrooms and a conversation and smoking room, besides rooms for bagatelle, chess and draughts, and, progress and modernity being their aim, a large space was set off in the yard for the game of quoits.

For such progress men, and men only, could be given the credit. But now there were people like Charlotte Kean pushing their way into committees and advocating, of all things, that the library should be open seven days a week. Did you ever hear of such a suggestion that the Lord's Day should be so desecrated! She had been quoted as saying, if the wine and gin shops can remain open on a Sunday why not a reading room? One gentleman had been applauded for replying that God's house should be the reading room for a Sunday.

Then there was the matter of education. She would have made a ruling that no fee be charged for schooling and that a poor child should have admission to a high-class teaching establishment merely on his proven intelligence.

Some gentlemen of the town were amused by Miss Kean's attitude and said, Well, at least credit should be given her for having the mentality of a man. However, the majority saw her as a potential danger both to their domestic and business power. To light a fire you needed tinder, and she was the equivalent to a modern matchstick. Look how she was flaunting all female decorum by parading that upstart of a rent collector around the county. Not only had she made him into her manager but she took him everywhere as her personal escort. She was making a name for herself and not one to be proud of. By, if her father had still been alive it would never have happened. He had made a mistake by allowing her to become involved with the business in the first place, because she had developed what was commonly termed a business head. She was remarkable in that way. But they didn't like remarkable women, neither those who were against her nor those who were for her. No, they didn't hold with remarkable women. This was a man's town, a seafaring town; women had their place in it, and they would be honoured as long as they kept their place; but they wanted no remarkable women, at least not the kind who tended to match them in the world of commerce.

Her manager, too, had his reservations about his employer, and the things she got up to. Yet he granted, and not grudgingly, that she *was* a remarkable woman. Odd in some ways, but nevertheless remarkable.

A year had passed since the news of Janie's death and the old saying of time being a great healer had proved itself true yet once again, for Rory, over the past months, had come up out of despair and settled on a plane of not ordinary but, what was for him, extraordinary living.

Though Janie still remained in his heart as a memory the ache for her was less. Even in the night when he felt the miss of her he no longer experienced the body-searing agony and the longing for her presence.

Two things had helped towards his easement. The first was the combination of Jimmy and the yard, and the second—or should he have placed her first?—was Charlotte Kean.

When, six months ago, he had taken up the position as her manager she had raised his wage—salary she called it now—to three pounds a week. It was incredible. Never in his life had he dreamed of ever being able to earn three pounds a week. To get that much and ten times more by gambling, oh yes, he had dreamed of that, but never as an earned wage. And did he earn it? Was the work he was doing worth three pounds a week, going to the town office in the morning, then around ten o'clock up to the house and the office there, he at one side of the table, she at the other?

'What would you advise in a case like this, Mr Connor?'

The first time she had pushed a letter across the table towards him he had stared at her blankly before reading it. It was from her solicitor advising her that a certain new chemical company was about to float its shares, and suggesting that she would do well to consider buying.

Utterly out of his depths Rory had continued to stare at her, for he sensed in that moment that a great deal depended on how he answered her. And so, holding her gaze, he said, 'I can't advise you for I know nothin' whatever about such matters;' but had then added, 'as yet.'

She hadn't lowered her eyes when she replied, 'Then you must learn . . . that is if you want to learn. Do you, Mr Connor?'

'Yes . . . yes, I want to learn all right.'

'Well, that's settled,' she had said. 'We know now where we stand, don't we?' And then she had smiled at him, after which she had rung the bell, and when Jessie opened the door she had said, 'We'll have some refreshment now, Jessie.'

And that was the pattern he followed on the days he didn't go to Hexham or Gateshead or over the water to Wallsend to cast an eye over her interests, until two months ago, when the pattern had changed and she began to accompany him.

Journeying by train, they would sit side by side in the first-class carriage. He helped her in and out of cabs, he opened doors for her, he obeyed her commands in all ways, except that he would refuse her invitation to stay for a meal after he had delivered the takings of an evening, or when they had returned from one of their supervising trips. The reason he gave was a truthful one, his brother expected him, he was alone.

When he first gave her this reason she looked at him with a sideward glance and asked, 'How old is your brother?'

'Coming up twenty.'

'Twenty! And he needs your protection at nights?'

And he answered flatly and stiffly, 'Yes, he does. Only last week a boat he had started to build was smashed up to bits, and it could be him next.'

'Oh!' She showed interest. 'Did you inform the police?'

'No.'

'Have you any idea who did it, and why?'

'Yes, both; I know who did it, and why. There's a family on the river who run the wherries, three brothers called Pittie . . .'

'Ah! Ah! the Pitties.' She had nodded her head.

'You've heard of them?'

'Yes, yes, I've heard the name before. And I also know of some of their activities.'

'Well, you know what they're like then.'

'Yes, I've a pretty good idea. And—' she had nodded and added, 'I can see the reason why you must be with your brother at night. But you, too, must be careful. What they've done once they can do again.'

His head had jerked in her direction as he asked, 'What do you mean?'

'Well, they could break up another boat.'

'Oh. Oh yes; yes they could.'

So he had stayed at home every night, including Saturdays, up till recently when, the urge rearing once more, he had joined a game, not on the waterfront, nor in the town, but away on the outskirts in Boldon.

It was odd how he had come to be reintroduced to the Boldon house for he had forgotten he had ever played there. He was in the train going to Gateshead when a 'find the lady' trickster took him for a mug. He had followed him into the compartment at Shields, then got on talking with a supposedly complete stranger who boarded the train at Tyne Dock, whom he very convincingly inveigled into 'finding the lady,' and, of course, let him win, all the while making a great fuss about his own bad luck, before turning to Rory and saying, 'What about you, sir?' It was then that Rory had turned a scornful glance on the man and replied, 'Don't come it with me. That dodge is as old as me whiskers.'

For a moment he had thought the pair of them were going to set about him. Then the one who had supposedly just won peered at him and said, 'Why I know you, I've played in with you. Didn't you use to go up to Telfords' in Boldon?'

Yes, he had played in the Telfords' wash-house, and in their kitchen, and once up in the roof lying on his belly.

From that meeting the urge had come on him again, not that it had ever really left him. But he had played no games, even for monkey nuts since Janie had gone.

So he had got in touch with the Telfords again and he went to Boldon on a Saturday night, where it could be simply Black Jack or pitch and toss. Sometimes the Telford men went farther afield to a barn for a cock fight, but he himself would always cry off this. He didn't mind a bit of rabbit coursing but he didn't like to see the fowls, especially the bantams, being torn to shreds with steel spurs. To his mind it wasn't sporting.

His winnings rarely went beyond five pounds, but neither did his losses. It didn't matter so much now about the stake as long as he could sit down to a game with men who were serious about it.

But now, at this present time, he was also vitally aware that he was playing in another kind of game, and this game worried him.

He looked back to the particular Saturday morning when, having told her he was married, her reaction had made him jump to conclusions which caused him to chastise himself for being a big-headed fool. But he chastised himself no longer.

He saw the situation he was in now as the biggest gamble of his life. There were two players only at this table and inevitably one would have to show his hand. Well, it wouldn't, it couldn't be him, it could never be him for more reasons than one. *Him* marry Charlotte Kean, a woman years older than himself and looking, as she did, as shapeless as a clothes prop, and with a face as plain as the dock wall! True, she had a nice voice . . . and a mind. Oh aye, she had a mind all right. And she was good company. Yes, of late he had certainly been discovering that. She could talk about all kinds of things, and he had realized that by listening to her he too could learn. She could make a very good friend; yet even so there could be no such thing between him and her for two reasons: on his part, you didn't, in his class, make friends with a woman, oh no, unless you wanted one thing from her: on her part, it wasn't a friend she wanted, it was a man, a husband.

Oh, he knew where things were leading. And he wouldn't hoodwink himself, he was tempted all right. Oh aye, he was both tempted and flattered. At nights he would lie thinking of what it would mean to live in Birchingham House in the select end of Westoe and to be in control of all those properties and businesses, all that money. My God! just to think of it. And he would be in control, wouldn't he? What was the wife's was the husband's surely. And there she was, willing, more than willing, to let him take control, him, Rory Connor, once rent collector from No. 2 The Cottages, Simonside. It was fantastic, unbelievable.

And them up in the kitchen, what would they say if he took this step? Lord! the place wouldn't hold them. No, he was wrong there. It wouldn't affect Ruth. As for her, his mother, after one look at Charlotte Kean she would be more than likely to say, 'My God! everything must be paid for.' She had a way with her tongue of stating plain facts. It would be his da who would brag. Every man in his shop would know, and it would be talked of in every pub in Jarrow from the church bank to the far end of Ellison Street.

But what would Bill Waggett say?

Ah, what the hell did it matter! It wouldn't happen. It couldn't. He couldn't do it. He wouldn't do it. Anyway, he was all right as he was. Jimmy wasn't doing so bad; he'd do better if it wasn't for them blasted Pitties. By, he'd get his own back on them if it was the last thing he did in life. Hardly a day passed but that he didn't think of them, when he would grab at this or that idea to get even with them. And he would, he would. He'd get a lead one day, and by God, when he did, let them look out! . . . He could have a lead now, right away. With money you had power, and it needed power to potch the Pitties. All he had to do was to say, 'Thank you kindly, Miss Kean, I'll be your man,' and he was home, safe home from the stormy sea, with chests full to the top.

But what would he really say? He knew what he'd say. 'I'm sorry, miss, but it wouldn't work.'

And, strangely, he realized that when he should say the latter he would be sorry, for, banter as he would, and did, about her in his mind there was a part of him that was sorry for her, and it had been growing of late. He pitied her lonely state, and he understood it because of the loneliness within himself. But although her kind of loneliness had gone on for years and she was weary of it, she was not yet resigned to it. That was why she had set her sights on him.

But why him? People of her station usually classed the likes of him as muck beneath their feet. And what was more, just think how she'd be talked about if anything should come of it. Lord! any link up with him would set the town on fire.

He was already vaguely aware that sly looks were being cast in their direction. When they were last in Durham to look over some property along the river bank they had gone to an inn to eat. She had chosen it, she said, because she thought he would like it; it was a man's place, oak-trestle tables, hefty beams, meat pudding and ale. And he would have liked it if it hadn't been in Durham . . . the gaol was in Durham.

Well, he had done what he could in that direction. He had tried to make reparation; he had given Jimmy ten pounds and sent him up to visit John

George and to ask him if he would come and see him when he came out. But Jimmy had returned with the ten pounds; John George was already out and they couldn't tell him where he had gone. For days afterwards he had expected a visit from him, but John George hadn't come. So he told himself that the business was closed; he had done his best. It was only in his recurring nightmare, when he would relive the awakening to Janie shouting at him, did he realize that his best hadn't been good enough and that John George would be with him like an unhealed wound until the end of his days.

But on that day in the inn in Durham, two Shields' men—gentlemen—had come to their table to speak to Charlotte Kean, and she had introduced him to them. They were a Mr Allington and a Mr Spencer. He knew of both of them. Allington was a solicitor, and Spencer owned a number of small grocery shops. He had started with one about fifteen years ago, and now they had spread into Jarrow and beyond.

After the first acknowledgment, they hadn't addressed him again until they were bidding her good-bye, and then they had merely inclined their heads towards him. Oh, he knew where he stood with the gentlemen of the town. He was an upstart rent man.

Then came the day when Charlotte Kean showed her hand and brought an abrupt end to the game by laying her cards face up on the table.

They had returned from Newcastle where she had been to see, of all things, an iron foundry with a view to taking a part share in it. The journey had been taken against the advice of her solicitor. The Tyneside foundries, he had said, were unable to produce iron as cheaply as they once had done; the railways had killed the iron trade in this part of the country. But she had explained, and to Rory himself, that she could not follow her solicitor's reasoning, for, as she saw it, people would always want iron stoves, kitchen grates, fenders, and railings of all kinds, from those that enclosed parks to small private gates; and then there were bedsteads and safes and such-like. She went on to say she wasn't thinking of competing with Palmer's and making ships but merely of supplying household requisites. What did he think?

He had answered her bluntly, as always, for he had learned that she preferred the truth, at least in most things. 'I think that I agree with Mr Hardy; he knows what he's talking about.'

'And you think I don't?'

'Well, I wouldn't say that you know very much about the iron trade.'

'You are aware that I read a great deal?'

'Yes, I'm aware of that, but as I understand it it takes more than reading to get an insight into such trades; the workings of them go deeper than books.'

'The workings might, but I would leave the workings to managers and men, of course.'

He shrugged his shoulders slightly and smiled as he said, 'Well, I won't say you know best, but what I will say is, you'll do what you want in the long run.'

That he could speak to her in this fashion was evidence of how far they had travelled in their association over the past year. He now rarely used the term miss, and although from time to time she would call him Mr Connor, it was usually done when in the presence of servants; at other times she addressed him without using his name at all.

Whatever her servants thought of the situation they treated their mistress's new manager with respect, even deference, which at one time would have amused him. At one time, too, such subservient attitudes would have given him material for mimicry and a big joke in the kitchen; in fact, his association with Miss Charlotte Kean would have been one big joke. At one time, but not now. Anyway, Sundays were different now. He did not always visit the cottage on a Sunday, he went up only on Jimmy's urging. He did not ask himself why he had turned against the Sunday gatherings, but he knew that the general opinion was he had become too big for his boots. And that could very well be near the truth, for he admitted to himself that the more he saw of the Westoe side of life the less he liked that in which he had been brought up.

He had, on this day, gone through a mental battle which left him thinking he didn't know which end of him was up. It was the anniversary of Janie's death, and there was no fierce ache left in him, and he felt there should be. He should, in some way, have held a sort of memorial service, at least within himself, but what had he done? Gone up to Newcastle, walked blithely by his employer's side as she paraded around a foundry, sat with her at a meal, which she called lunch, at the Royal Exchange Hotel; then had waited like a docile husband while she went shopping in Bainbridge's. He had sauntered with her through the Haymarket, where they had stopped and examined almost every article in the ironmongery store. Then she had said they would go to the Assembly Rooms and he wondered what her object was, until, standing outside, she looked at the building and said almost sadly, 'My mother once danced in there. She often told me about it. It was the highlight of her life; she was taken there by a gentleman—and they danced the whole evening through.'

When she had turned her face towards him he had ended for her, flippantly, 'And they married and lived happy ever after.'

'No, she married my father.'

What could he make of that?

Her last call was at Mawson & Swan's in Grey Street, where she purchased a number of books.

By the time they reached the railway station he likened himself to a donkey, he was so loaded down under parcels, and he thanked God he wasn't likely to come across anyone he knew. When they arrived at Shields she hired a cab, and they drove through the drizzling rain to the house, and into warmth and comfort and elegance.

Elegance was another new word he had of late added to his vocabulary; it was the only word to describe this house, its furniture and the comforts of it.

'Ah, isn't it nice to be home?' She had returned from upstairs, where she had evidently combed her hair and applied some talcum powder to her face for her chin had the same appearance as Ruth's had when she wiped it with a floured hand.

'It's an awful night; you must have something before you go, something to eat that is. Did Mr Taylor bring the takings?'

'Yes; I've checked them, they're all right.'

This was a new departure; he no longer went to the office to collect the rents. Mr Taylor had been promoted and so came each evening to the house.

On the days she did not send him off on tours of inspection he would receive the money from the old man, count it, then check the books, and never did he hand them back to him but he saw himself as he was a year ago, a younger edition of this man. That was the only difference, a younger edition; the old man's insecurity did not make his own position in comparison appear strong, quite the reverse.

Only a week ago he had felt he could play his hand for a good while yet, but today, the anniversary of Janie's death, he had a feeling in his bones that soon all the cards would be laid face up, and as always they would show a winner and a loser; there could never be two winners in any game . . .

Why not?

Oh my God! He'd been through it all before, hadn't he, night after night? He was what he was, that was why not.

Below his outer covering, his jaunty aggressive air, the look that gave nothing away while at the same time suggesting that what it had to hide was of value, behind all this, only he himself knew the frailties of his character. Yet, in this particular case, he wasn't going to be weak enough—or did he mean strong enough?—to cheat at this game and let her be the winner.

And again he told himself he had to stop hoodwinking himself on this point too, because it wasn't really the moral issue that would prevent him from letting her win, but the fact that he didn't think he was up to paying the stake. It was too high. Yet he liked her. Oh aye, it was very odd to admit, but he liked her. He liked being with her; she was good company, except at those times when she made him feel so small that he imagined she could see him crawling around her feet. Once or twice she had done this when he had dared to contradict her on some point with regard to the business. And yet she never took that high hand with him when they were in company. At such times she always deferred to him as a woman might to her husband, or her boss.

She was a funny character; he couldn't get to the bottom of her. He had never known anyone in his life so knowledgeable or so self-possessed. But then, never in his life had he been in contact with women of her class.

'You will stay for something to eat?'

He hesitated, then said, 'Yes. Yes, thank you.'

'Good.' She smiled at him, put her hand to her hair and stroked it upwards and back from her forehead; then she said, 'Don't sit on the edge of that chair as if you were waiting to take off in a race.'

His jaw tightened, his pleasant expression vanished. This was the kind of thing that maddened him.

'Oh! Oh, I'm sorry.'

Now she was sitting forward on the edge of the couch leaning towards him. 'Please don't be annoyed. I have the unfortunate habit of phrasing my requests in the manner of orders.' She made a small deprecating movement with her head. 'I . . . I must try to grow out of it. All I intended to say was, please

relax, be comfortable . . . make yourself at home.'
The last words ended on a low note.

After a moment he slid slowly back into the chair and smiled ruefully at her.

Settling herself back once again on the couch, she stared at him before saying, still in a low tone, 'I'm going to call you . . . No'—she lifted her hand—'again my phrasing is wrong. What I mean to say is, may I call you by your Christian name?'

He did not answer but stared at her, unblinking.

She was looking down at her hands now where they were joined on her lap, her fingers making stroking movements between the knuckles. 'You see, I . . . I want to talk to you this evening about . . . about something important, if you can afford me the time after dinner. Which reminds me. Would you mind ringing the bell, please?'

He rose slowly to his feet and pulled the bell by the side of the fireplace, and they didn't speak until the maid appeared; then she said, 'Mr Connor will be staying for dinner, Jessie. How long will it be?'

'Well . . . well, it's ready now, miss, but'—The girl cast a glance in Rory's direction, then added, 'Say five minutes' time, miss?'

'Very well, Jessie, thank you.'

When the door was closed on the maid, she said, 'I have never seen you smoke, do you smoke?'

'Yes. I have a draw at nights.'

'My father never smoked. I like the smell of tobacco. About . . . about your Christian name. What does the R stand for . . . Robert?'

'No, Rory.'

'Roar-y. What is it short for?'

'Nothin' that I know of. I was christened Rory.'

'Roar-y.' She mouthed the word, then said, 'I like it. My name, as you know, is Charlotte. My father once said it was a very suitable name for me.' Her head drooped again. 'He was an unkind man, a nasty man, a mean nasty man.'

He could say nothing to this. He was so amazed at

her frankness he just sat staring at her, until she said, 'Would you care to go upstairs and wash?' He blinked rapidly, swallowed, wetted his lips, and as he drew himself up from the chair answered, 'Yes. Yes, thank you.'

She did not rise from the couch but looked up at him. 'The bathroom is the third door on the right of the landing.'

He inclined his head towards her, walked out of the drawing-room, across the hall and up the stairs. This was the first time he had been upstairs and he guessed it would be the last.

After closing the bathroom door behind him he stood looking about him in amazement. A full length iron bath stood on four ornamental legs. At one end of it were two shining brass taps, at the foot was a shelf and, on it, an array of coloured bottles and fancy boxes. To the left stood a wash basin, and to the left of that again a towel rack on which hung gleaming white towels. In the wall opposite the bath was a door, and when he slowly pushed this open he found he was looking down into a porcelain toilet, not a dry midden as outside the cottage, or a bucket in a lean-to on the waterfront, but something that looked too shiningly clean to be put to the use it was intended for.

A few minutes later as he stood washing his hands, not from any idea of hygiene, but simply because he wanted to see the bowl fill with water, he thought, I'm a blasted fool. That's what I am, a blasted fool. I could use this every day. I could eat downstairs in that dining-room every day. I could sit in that drawing-room, aye, and smoke every day. And I could sleep up here in one of these rooms every . . . He did not finish the sentence but dried his hands, gave one last look around the bathroom, then went downstairs.

The meal was over and once again they were sitting in the drawing-room.

He had hardly opened his mouth from the moment he had entered the dining-room until he left it. Talk about arms and legs; he could have been a wood louse, and he felt sure he had appeared just about as much at home too at that table as one might have done. Nor had it helped matters that she had been quiet an' all. She usually kept the conversation going, even giving herself the answers, and now here they were and the game had come to an end, the cards were face up.

He felt sorry. In so many different ways he felt sorry, but most of all he knew that at this moment he was feeling sorry for her because he could see from her face, and her attitude, that she, too, was in a bit of a spot, and he was wishing, sincerely wishing that it could have been possible for him to help her out of it, when she spoke.

Sitting perfectly still, staring straight ahead as if she were concentrating on the picture of her grandfather above the mantelpiece, she said, 'I . . . I really don't know how to begin, but this thing must be brought into the open. You . . . you are aware of that as much as I am, aren't you?' It was some seconds before she turned her head towards him, and now such were his feelings of pity that he couldn't hold her gaze. He looked down on his hands, as she herself had done earlier and, like hers, his fingers rubbed against each other.

She was speaking again, softly now, her voice scarcely above a whisper. 'I am putting you in a very embarrassing situation. I'm aware of that. Even if your feelings were such that you wanted to put a certain question to me, you wouldn't under the circumstances have the courage to do so, but let me tell you one thing immediately. I know that you have no wish to put that question to me. If you agree to what I am going to ask of you, I won't be under the illusion it is through any personal attraction, but that it will be for what my offer can bring to you in the way of advantages.'

His head was up now. 'I don't want advantages that way.'

'Thank you at least for that.' As she made a deep obeisance with her head towards him, he put in quickly, 'Don't get me wrong. What I meant was—' He shook his head, bit hard down on his lip as he found it impossible to explain what he meant, and she said, 'I know what you meant, but . . . but you haven't yet heard my proposition.'

She turned her face away and once again stared at the picture as she went on, 'Suppose I were to ask you to marry me, you would . . . you would, on the face of it I know, refuse, forgoing all the advantages that would go with such a suggestion, but suppose I were to say to you that this would be no ordinary marriage, that I . . . I would expect nothing from you that an ordinary wife would from her husband. You could have your own apartments, all I would ask for is . . . is your companionship, and your presence in this house, of which . . . of which you would be the master.' She again turned her face towards him.

He was sitting bolt upright in the chair now; his eyes were wide and his mouth slightly open. He said under his breath, 'That would be the poor end of the stick for you, wouldn't it?'

'Poor end of the stick?' She gave a short laugh. 'Well, if I would be quite satisfied with the poor end of the stick, shouldn't that be enough for you?'

He shook his head. 'No! No! It wouldn't be right, for as I see it you wouldn't be gettin' any more out of me than you do now. . . . So why not let things be as they are?'

There now came upon them an embarrassing silence, before she said, 'Because I need companionship, male companionship. Not just anyone, someone, an individual, someone whom I consider special, and . . . and I chose you. What is more, I feel I know you, I know you very well. I know that you like this house, you like this way of living, I know that you could learn to appreciate finer things.

Not that I dislike the roughness in you; no, it is part of your attraction, your bumptiousness, your arrogance. It is more difficult to be arrogant when you have nothing to be arrogant about than when you have something.'

His face took on its blank look. This was the kind of clever talk that maddened him, and he had no way of hitting back except by using the arrogance she was on about. He said gruffly, 'You seem to think you know a lot about me, everything in fact.'

'No, not everything, but quite a bit. I've always given myself the credit of being able to read character. I know a lot of things about a lot of people, especially in this town, and I know what a good many of them are saying at this very moment—and about us.'

'About us?'

'Oh yes, yes, about us. Don't you know that we're being talked about? Don't you know they're saying—' she now dropped into the local inflexion which patterned the speech of even many of the better-off of the townsfolk—"What d'you think, eh? Kean's daughter and the rent collector. And her five years older than him and as plain as a pikestaff. She's brazen, that's what she is, she's buying him. And, of course, he's willing to be bought. He's no fool, who would turn down that chance? She should be ashamed of herself though, using her money as bait. You can't blame the fellow. And you know, this didn't start the day, or yesterday; they were going at it when his wife was alive"? . . . That's what they're saying.'

His face was burning, the colour suffusing it was almost scarlet.

'Oh, please don't get upset about it; you must have been aware that our association would cause a minor scandal?'

'I wasn't!' His answer was vehement. 'If . . . if I'd thought they'd been saying that I . . . I wouldn't have gone on. I . . . I was your manager. Anyway, if you

213

knew this, why didn't you put a stop to it? Why did you let it go on?'

'Oh . . . huh! Why? Well, to tell you the truth, it made me all the more determined to go on. I don't care a fig for their chatter. What are they after all, the majority of them? Braggarts, strutting little nonentities, men who have clawed their way up over the dead bodies of miners, or of their factory workers. Oh, there are a good many hypocrites in this town. I could reel them off, sanctimonious individuals, leading double lives. You know, you'd think New-castle was at the other end of the world, and it is for some of them, keeping their second homes . . . It is very strange you know but women talk to me, they confide in me; perhaps it's because to them I'm unfeminine. But anyway—' she tossed her head to the side—'I have no room to speak, at least on the point of clawing one's way up, for what did my father do for anyone except himself? And for that matter what have I done but talk? But this is where you come in. I have thought that with you I might begin to do things for other people. I—' her voice dropped—'I might become so at peace with myself that I could turn my thoughts on to the needs of others, and there are many in need in this town. And you know that better than I do, because you have been on that side of the wall. You have had to say "Yes, sir," and "No, sir," and of course—' she nodded at him—' "Yes, miss," and "No, miss," and it's only recently and only through you that I have realized how people such as you, in your position, must feel.'

She now rose from the couch abruptly and, going to the mantelpiece, she put her hands on it and looked down into the fire as she muttered, 'I am not saying this in order to make the future appear more attractive. If . . . if closer association with me would be intolerable to you, very well, you have only to say so.'

'And what if I did, what then?' The question was

quiet, soft, and her answer equally so. 'I don't know, because . . . because I haven't allowed myself to look into the future and face the desolation there.'

As he stared up at her he thought, She's remarkable. By aye, she's a remarkable woman. He had never imagined anyone talking as frankly as she had done; no man would ever have been as honest. He said softly, 'Will you give me time to think it over?'

'No!'

The word was barked and it brought him to his feet as if it had been the crack of a gun. He watched her march down the room, then back again towards him. At the head of the couch she stopped, and he saw her fingers dig into the upholstery as she said tersely, 'It must be now, yes or no. I . . . I cannot go on in uncertainty. I . . . I'm not asking anything from you but to come into this house and stay with me as a . . . a friend, a companion. You don't believe it now, but you'll find out there's more lasting happiness stems from friendship than has ever done from love. I know you don't love me, couldn't love me, and never will . . . No! No! Don't protest.' She lifted her hand. 'Let us start from the beginning being honest. When you lost your wife I knew that you must have loved her deeply, and that kind of love only happens once, but there are other emotions comparable with love. A man can have them towards a woman and be happy. That can also apply to a woman, although' —She swallowed deeply in her throat here before ending, 'In most cases she needs to love even if she's not loved in return.'

God, he was hot, sweating. What could he say? What could he do? Strangely, he knew what he had the desire to do, and it was scattering to the winds all his previous decisions, for at this moment he wanted to go behind that couch and put his arms about her, comfort her. Just that, comfort her. Nothing else, just comfort her. Then why wasn't he doing it?

He was surprised to hear himself saying in a voice

that sounded quite ordinary, 'Come and sit down.' He was holding his hand out to her, and slowly she put hers into it. Then he drew her round the head of the couch and on to its seat, and still with her hand in his he sat beside her, and as he looked at her an excitement rose in him. He seemed to be drawing it from her. Aye yes, that was the other word he wanted for what he felt for her, excitement. It was almost akin to the feeling he got when he was in a good game. He hadn't been aware of it, but that was why he had liked to be in her company, liked to hear her talk; even when she was getting her sly digs in at him, she was exciting.

If she hadn't been so tall and thin and plain what was happening now would likely have happened months ago. But now he realized that her thinking, her voice, her manner, the way she dressed, all the things she did were in a way a compensation for her looks. In fact, they formed a kind of cloak over them because there had been times lately when in her company that he had forgotten how she looked. He hadn't realized this until now. Suddenly he felt at ease with her as he'd never done before. He knew he could talk to her now, aye and comfort her. He bent towards her and said, 'Can I tell you something?'

Her eyes had a moisture in them when she answered, 'I'm eager to hear whatever you have to say, Rory.'

'It's going to be difficult for me to put into words 'cos you see I haven't your gift, your gift of the gab.' He wagged the hand that was within his. 'You know you've got the gift of the gab, don't you? But there's one thing, when you open your mouth something meaningful always comes out. That's the difference between you an' me . . . and the likes of me. But I . . . I want to tell you, I've been learnin' these months past. There's not a day gone by when I've been with you but I haven't learned something from you. It mightn't show, it still hasn't covered up me aggressiveness.' Again he shook her hand. 'And I want to

tell you something more. I've liked being with you
. . . I mean, I do like being with you. You won't
believe this, but well, I . . . I find you sort of exciting.
I've never known any other woman like you. Well, I
wouldn't, would I, not coming from my quarter?
Mind, I must say at this point that Janie was a fine
girl and I was happy with her. I've got to say that;
you said a minute ago let's be honest. Yet, at the
same time, I've got to admit she wasn't excitin'.
Lovable aye, but not excitin'. Looking back, I see that
Janie had little to teach me, only perhaps thought-
fulness for others; she could get really worked up
over other people's problems, you know, and after all,
that's no small thing, is it?'

'No, it isn't . . . Rory.'

'Yes?'

'What is the answer you're giving me? I . . . I want
to hear it in . . . in definite terms. You are being kind
now but I don't know whether it is merely to soothe
me. I want to hear you say, "Yes, Charlotte," or "No,
Charlotte." '

Their hands were still joined, their knees almost
touching, their faces not more than two feet apart,
and he knew that if he said no, his life would in
some way become empty, barren, and not only
because he might no longer have admittance to this
house.

'. . . Yes . . . Charlotte.'

He watched her close her eyes. When she opened
them they were bright; in any other face they would
have been starry.

'It's a bargain.'

'Aye, it's a bargain.'

As he uttered the words he again had a vivid
mental picture of the kitchen. He could see his dad,
Ruth, her, and Jimmy, all staring at him, all saying,
'What, her, Miss Kean! Never! . . . What about Janie?'

He said suddenly, 'I'm not going to make any
excuses about me people; I'm not going to hide them;
you'll have to meet them.'

'I'll be pleased to, very pleased to. I've never had any people of my own.'

He said suddenly on a laugh, 'You know something? I'll never make excuses to you, I'll always tell you the truth. That's a promise. It'll likely not always please you . . .'

'It won't.' She was pulling a long face at him now and her laughter was high, slightly out of control as she said, 'It certainly won't if you tell me you are going out gambling every night.'

When his eyes widened and his lips fell apart her laughter increased and she cried with the air of a young teasing girl, which lay awkwardly on her, 'Didn't I tell you I know most things about most people in this town?'

His face straight and his voice flat, he asked, 'How did you know about that?'

'Deduction, and the one word you kept repeating when you were in hospital. When I first saw you, you said again and again, "Pittie. Pittie. Pittie." The second time I visited you you were still saying it.'

'I was?'

'Yes, and you know when a man gets beaten up as you were there's nearly always something behind it. A footpad might have hit you on the head and knocked you senseless, but then I don't think he would have kicked you within an inch of death's door. After thinking about it, I realized you were telling everyone the name of your assailants, but no one seemed to be taking any notice, they thought you were saying, "Isn't it a pity?" when what you were really doing was giving them the name of the men who attacked you, the Pittie brothers. The Pittie brothers are well-known scoundrels, besides being dirty gamblers. They were fined for gambling some short time ago.'

'Huh! Huh!' A smile was spreading over his face, widening his mouth. He now put his head back on his shoulder and laughed until his body shook, and she laughed with him.

His chest was heaving and he was still laughing when he looked into her face again and said, 'I've thought it, but now I'll say it, you're a remarkable woman.'

'Oh, please don't judge my intelligence on the fact that I recognized something that should have been staring everyone in the face, the police into the bargain. Yet at the same time I don't think the police were as stupid as they made out to be, but when they asked you had you seen the assailant or assailants, I was given to understand you said no, you had been attacked while walking down a side street.'

He screwed up his eyes at her now and, his face serious, he asked, 'But . . . but how could you know that I gambled?'

She stared at him for a long moment before saying, and seriously now, 'A short while ago you said you'd always tell me the truth. I understood, of course, that you were referring to the future, but now I'm going to ask you: Is there anything further you want to tell me, anything, about your past say?'

For a moment he wondered if she were referring to his birth. He stared into her eyes, then gulped in his throat as he thought, She can't know about the other business, else I wouldn't be here now.

'Think hard before you answer.'

He felt the colour flooding his face again. They were staring into each other's eyes. His body was sweating; it was as if he were having a nightmare in broad daylight. His voice was a gruff whisper when he said, 'Well, knowin' what you know, or think you know, why am I sitting here now?'

Her voice was equally low as she replied, 'I'll answer that in a moment when you answer my question.'

His gaze riveted on her, he pondered. If she didn't know, if she wasn't referring to John George's business then what he was about to say would likely put the kibosh on her proposal. But if it was that she

219

was hinting at, then indeed, aye, by God! indeed she was a remarkable woman.

He closed his eyes for a moment, lowered his head, and turned it to the side before he muttered, as if he were in the confessional box: 'I took the five pounds that John George did time for. I went back that night and helped meself, but like him I expected to be there first thing on the Monday morning to return it. If . . . if I had been there and you had caught me I would have stood me rap along of him, but by the time I knew what had happened I was sick and weak, and petrified at the thought of prison.' His head still to the side, he jerked his neck out of his collar before going on, 'I . . . I have a fear on me, always have had since I was nailed down in a box as a child. I fear being shut in, I can't stand being behind closed doors of any kind. I . . . I should have come forward, I know, but there it is, I didn't . . . Is that what you want to know?'

There was a long pause and when she made no reply he looked at her again and said 'You knew this all along?'

'No, not from the beginning,' she shook her head slowly. 'But in the court I felt the man was speaking the truth and I recalled his amazement when I mentioned that not ten shillings but five pounds ten was missing. He was so astonished he couldn't speak. But in any case, five pounds ten or ten shillings he had to be brought to book, for, as he admitted, he had been tampering with the books for some long time, and as he also admitted, not only for ten shillings at a time either.'

All this time their hands had been joined and he looked down on them as he asked quietly, 'Why am I here now? Tell me that. Knowing all this about me, why am I here now?'

She now withdrew her hands from his and, rising to her feet, went towards the fire and once again looked at the picture above the mantelpiece. Then she wetted her lips twice and drew in a long breath before she said softly, 'I . . . I happen to care for you . . . This, of course, wipes out all my fine talk about friendship et cetera, but you see—' again she wetted her lips—'I've loved you since the first time I saw you in my father's office. It was just like that, quickly, the most sudden thing in my life. I remember thinking, that's the kind of man I would like to marry if it were possible. I knew it was a preposterous desire, quite hopeless, utterly hopeless. My father would never have countenanced it. Strangely, he didn't like you. But then he liked so few people, and if I'd shown the slightest interest in you, even mentioned your name in a kindly fashion, he would have dismissed you.'

She turned and looked at him. 'I'm a fraud, but I really did not intend that you should know this. I . . . I was going to acquire you under false pretences. But . . . but it makes no difference to the bargain. That can remain as it stands. But—' she laughed self-consciously—'so much for all my fine platonic talk. You know, Rory, the emotions are not measured in proportion to one's looks: if that were so all the beauties in the world would be passionate lovers, but from what I have gauged from my reading they're often very cold women. My . . . my emotions don't match my looks, Rory, but as I said the bargain stands: you give me your friendship and protection as a husband, I will give you what . . . well, what I cannot help giving you.'

He rose from the couch and went slowly towards her, and he stared into her face before he said softly, 'There must be a dozen men in this town who'd be only too glad to have married you, and would serve you better than I'll ever be able to.'

'Doubtless, doubtless.' She nodded slowly at him. 'But you see, and here we come to the question of truth again, they would have been marrying me for one thing, my money, and they would likely have been men with whom I couldn't bargain. In their cases I would most assuredly have wished them to have their own apartments, but in their cases they would assuredly not have complied, for let us face the fact that most men's needs do not require the stimulus of love. . . .'

Slowly and firmly now he put his arms about her and drew her thin form towards him, and when he felt her taut body relax against him, and her head bury itself in his shoulder, he put his face into the dark coils of her hair and murmured, 'Don't. There, there, don't cry. Please don't cry. I'll . . . I'll make you happy, Charlotte. I promise I'll make you happy.'

He didn't know how he was going to do it. The only thing he was sure of in this fantastic moment was that he'd have a damned good try.

2

He stood in the kitchen at the end of the long table, while they, like a combating force, stood at the other end, Ruth, his father, and Lizzie. Jimmy stood to the side towards the middle of the table, his face pale, anxious, his eyes darting between them like a troubled referee.

'Well, you can say something, can't you?' His voice re-echoed through the timbers in the roof.

It was his father who spoke. Quietly he said, 'Janie's hardly cold.'

'Janie's been dead over a year, a year and three weeks to be exact.'

'Huh! Well.' Paddy broke away from the group and walked towards the fireplace and, picking up a clay pipe from the mantelpiece, he bent and tapped it on the hob, knocking out the doddle as he said, 'You're doin' well for yersel, there's that much to be said. Aye, aye. They used to say old Kean could buy Shields, that is the parts Cookson hadn't bought up. Money grabbers, the lot of them! . . .'

'It wasn't the money . . .'

'Well, begod! it couldn't be her face.'

Rory swung round and glared at Lizzie. It looked for a moment as if he would spring down the table and strike her. Their eyes held across the distance before she snapped her gaze from his and, swinging round, went towards the scullery, muttering, 'My God! My God! What next!'

The anger in him blinded him for a moment. Any other family in the town, any other family from here to Newcastle, would, he imagined, have fallen on his neck for making such a match, but not his family, aw no. In their ignorance they thought you must keep loyal to the dead, if not for ever, then for a decent period of years.

His vision clearing, he glared now at Ruth. She was usually the one to see both sides of everything, but she wasn't seeing his side of this, there was a stricken look on her face. He put his hands on the table and leant towards her now as he cried, 'You didn't condemn her da, did you—' he jerked his head back in the direction of the cottage next door—'when he went off and lived with his woman in Jarrow after Gran died. He couldn't wait. Six weeks, that's all he stayed there alone, six weeks. But you said nothin' about that. And I'm marrying her. Do you hear?' He flashed a glance towards his father's bent head. 'I'm not taking her on the side. And one at a time'll be enough for me.'

There was no sound in the kitchen. Paddy hadn't moved, Ruth hadn't moved, Lizzie hadn't burst into the room from the scullery. He stood breathing deeply. Then looking at Jimmy, he yelled, 'I came here, you know I came here to say that she wanted to meet them. My God! she didn't know what she was askin' . . . Well, it doesn't matter. I know where I stand now; you'll want me afore I'll want you, the lot of you.' And on this he turned round and marched out of the room.

Before the door had crashed closed Lizzie appeared

in the kitchen. Paddy turned from the fireplace, and Ruth, putting her hand out towards Jimmy as if she were pushing him, said quickly and in a choked voice, 'Go after him. Stay with him. Tell . . . tell him it'll be all right.'

She was now pressing Jimmy towards the door. 'Tell . . . tell him I understand, and . . . and she'll be welcome. Tell him that, she'll be welcome.'

Jimmy didn't speak but, grabbing up his cap, he pulled it tight down on his head, then ran wobbling down the path and out of the gate, calling, 'Rory! Rory!'

He was at the top of the bank before he caught up with Rory.

'Aw, man, hold your hand a minute. It's . . . it's no use gettin' in a paddy. I . . . I told you afore we come it would give them a gliff; it gave me a gliff, not only . . . not because of Janie, but . . .'

'But what?' Rory pulled up so suddenly that Jimmy went on a couple of steps before turning to him and looking up at him and saying fearlessly, 'You want the truth? All right, you'll get it. She's different, older, plain, as Lizzie said, plain an' . . .'

'Aye, go on.' Rory's voice came from deep within his throat.

'Well . . . All right then, I'll say it, I will, I'll say it, she's a different class from you. You'll . . . you'll be like a fish out of water.'

Rory, his voice a tone quieter now, bent over Jimmy and said slowly, 'Did you feel like a fish out of water last night when you met her?'

Jimmy tossed his head, blinked, then turned and walked on, Rory with him now, and after a moment, he answered, 'No, 'cos . . . 'cos I felt she had set out to make me like her. But I won't be livin' with her.' He now turned his head up to Rory. 'That's the difference, I won't have to live her life and meet her kind of people. I won't have to live up to her.'

'And you think I can't?'

Jimmy's head swayed from one side to the other following the motion of his body, and he said, 'Aye, just that.'

'Thanks. Thanks very much.'

'I . . . I didn't mean it nasty, man, no more than they meant to be nasty.'

'Huh! They didn't mean to be nasty? My God! You must have ten skins. You were there, you were there, man, weren't you?'

Jimmy didn't answer for a while, and then he said quietly, 'Me ma says she'll be welcome; you can bring her and she'll be welcome.'

'Like hell I will! Take her up there among that bigoted tribe? Not on your bloody life. Well—' he squared his shoulders and his step quickened and his arms swung wider—'why should I worry me head, they're the losers, they've potched themselves. I could have put them all on their feet, I could have set them all up, set them up for life.' He cast a hard glance down now on Jimmy and demanded, 'Do you know how much I'll be worth when I marry her? Have you any idea? I'll be a rich man, 'cos she's rollin', and I'll be in control. Just think on that.'

'Aye well, good for you, I hope it keeps fine for you.'

The colloquial saying which was for ever on Lizzie's tongue caused Rory to screw up his eyes tightly for a moment.

I hope it keeps fine for you.

Would he ever do anything right in this world? Would he ever do anything to please anybody? . . . Well, he was pleasing her, wasn't he? He had never seen a woman so openly happy in his life as he had her these past three weeks. Her happiness was embarrassing; aye, and humbling, making him say to himself each night when he left her, I'll repay her in some way, and he would, he would, and to hell with the rest of them. The kitchen had seen him for the last time, he'd go to that registry office whenever she liked and he'd show them, by God! he'd show them. He would let them see if he could live up to her or not.

I hope it keeps fine for you.

And Janie was dead!

3

He let himself in through the front door, but as he opened the door leading from the lobby into the hall Jessie was there to close it for him.

'What a night, sir. Eeh! you are wet.' As she took his hat and thick tweed coat from him he bent towards her and said in a conspiratorial whisper, 'Well, don't shout it out, Jessie, or I'll have to take cough mixture.'

'Oh, sir.' She giggled and shook her head, then said, 'The mistress is upstairs,' and as he nodded at her and went towards the staircase she hissed after him, 'Your boots, sir.'

He looked down at his damp feet, then jerking his chin upwards and biting on his bottom lip like a boy caught in a misdemeanour he sat down on the hall chair and unlaced his boots. He then took his house shoes from her hand and pulled them on, and as he rose he bent towards her again and said in a whisper, 'Between you all I'll end up in a blanket.'

Again she giggled, before turning away towards the kitchen to inform the cook that the master was in. She liked the master, she did; the house had been different altogether since he had come into it. He might have come from the bottom end of nowhere but he didn't act uppish. And what's more, he had made the mistress into a new woman. By! aye, he had that. She had never seen such a change in anybody. Nor had she seen such a change in the house. Everybody was infected; as cook said, they'd all got the smit . . .

On opening the bedroom door he almost pushed her over and he put out his arm swiftly to catch her, saying, 'Why are you standin' behind the door?'

'I wasn't standing behind the door, Mr Connor, I was about to open the door.'

She put her face up to his and he kissed her gently on the lips.

'I didn't hear you come in.'

'Well, you wouldn't.' He shook his head from side to side. 'Jessie carried me from the front door to the foot of the stairs, made me put my slippers on, and told me to be a good boy.'

She shook his arm and smiled at him; then she unloosened his tie as she asked, 'How did things go?'

He now pressed her from him and on to the long padded velvet stool set before the dressing table, and as he stood back from her he took off his coat and tugged the narrow tie from his high collar; then turned and as he walked towards the wardrobe that filled almost one entire wall, he pulled his shirt over his head, saying, 'Very well. Very well. I've enjoyed meself the day.' He looked over his shoulder.

'More so than usual?'

'Oh, much more so than usual.'

He now took from the wardrobe drawer a silk shirt with a wide soft collar, put it on, then divested himself of his trousers and, after selecting another pair from a rack, he stepped into them, while she watched him in silence and with seeming pleasure. Lastly, he donned a matching coat, then returned towards her, saying, 'I met someone I've been hoping to meet for a long time.'

'Lady or gentleman?'

He gave her a twisted smile now before answering, 'Gentleman.'

'Oh—' She placed her hand on her heart now, saying, 'My rage is subsiding, please proceed.'

He gave a small laugh, then sat down beside her on the stool. 'Do you know a man named Nickle?'

'Nickle? I know two men by the name of Nickle,

Mr Frank Nickle and Mr John Nickle, but they're not related. Which one did you meet?'

'Oh, I'm not sure. This one lives in Plynlimmon Way.'

'Oh, that's Mr Frank Nickle. Why have you wanted to meet him? I'm sure you would have nothing in common.'

'That's where you're wrong . . . What do you know of him?'

She put her head on one side as if considering, then said, 'I know I don't care much for him, yet I have nothing against him except that I don't think he was kind to his wife. I met her twice. It was shortly after I came back from school, Mother was alive. We went to dinner there once, and she came here. She was a sad woman. I think she was afraid of him. Yes—' she nodded—'looking back, I think she was afraid of him. I don't think Mother had much time for him either, but they were all members of the same church and . . . What are you laughing at?'

'Oh, there's the bell for dinner. I'll tell you after.'

'You'll tell me now.'

He stared at her for a moment, then said quietly, 'I'll tell you later, Mrs Connor.'

She bit on her lip to stop herself from laughing, bowed her head slightly, then, holding her hand out to him, rose from the seat. When he didn't immediately follow suit she said, 'Would you mind accompanying me down to dinner, Mr Connor?'

'Not at all, Mrs Connor.' He did rise now and gave her his arm, and she laid her head against his for a moment and they went out and down the stairs and into the dining-room like a young couple who were so in love that they couldn't bear to be separated even while going into a meal . . .

They had been married for five months now and Rory had grown so used to this way of life that it was hard at times for him to imagine he had ever lived any other. He was dressed as became a man of means; he ate like a man of means; he was beginning to enter the society of the town as should a man of means, because twice lately they had been asked out to dinner, and only four days ago he had played host to ten guests at this very table.

As day followed day he became more surprised at himself; he had never thought he would have adapted so quickly and so easily. Even Jimmy had said recently, 'It's amazing how you've learned to pass yourself. You'll be hobnobbing with Lord Cole next.'

He had laughed and said, 'I shouldn't be at all surprised at that either, lad,' at the same time knowing that while he might have gained access to certain houses in the town, there were still those whose doors would never be open to the one-time rent man, and among the latter were certain members of her church.

She'd tried to get him to church. He should attend for two reasons, she had laughingly said, in God's cause, and the cause of business. But no, he had put his foot down firmly here. He couldn't be that kind of a hypocrite. He had been brought up a Catholic and although he had never been through a church door for years, except when the banns were called and on the day he was married, he'd been born one and he would die one, he wasn't going to become a turncoat.

He was happy as he had never expected to be happy again in his life. It was a different kind of happiness, a steady, settled sort of happiness; a happiness made up partly of material things, partly of gratitude, and . . . and something else. It wasn't love, but at the same time it came into that category, yet he couldn't put a name to it. But he liked her, he liked her a lot, and he admired her. Strangely, he had ceased to be sorry for her. He couldn't imagine now why he'd ever been sorry for her. And strangely too, he was more at ease in her company than he had ever been with anyone in his own family, apart from Jimmy that was . . . He hadn't always been at ease with Janie. It was funny that, but he hadn't.

No, he couldn't put a name to the feeling he had for Charlotte, he only knew that he liked being with her and that this was the life for him. He had fallen on his feet and he meant to see that they carried him firmly into the future . . .

The meal over and in the drawing-room, she sat by his side on the couch and watched him begin the process of filling his pipe—This liberty had even shocked the servants. No gentleman smoked in a drawing-room, but there, the mistress allowed it—and now she said, 'Well, I'm waiting. What have you discovered about Mr Nickle that has filled you with glee?'

'Glee?'

'Yes, glee. It's been oozing out of you since you came in.'

'He's a good churchman, isn't he?'

'Yes, as churchmen go, he's a good churchman.'

'A highly respected member of the community.' He pressed the tobacco down into the wide bowl of his red-wood pipe.

'What is it?' She put her hand out and slapped his knee playfully, and he looked at her steadily for a minute before he said flatly, 'He's a two-faced hypocrite.'

'Oh, is that all? Well, he's not alone in this town, is he?'

'He runs a gaming house.'

Now she was startled. 'Mr Nickle running a gaming house? You're dreaming, Rory.'

'Oh no. Oh no, Charlotte, Rory isn't dreaming,' he mimicked her. 'Rory once tried to get into Mr Nickle's gaming house, but he was politely warned off, then recommended to a house in King Street. And you know what happened to Rory in King Street, don't you?'

'You can't mean it?' Her face was straight and his also, and his tone was deep and bitter when he answered, 'I do. And it's not only gaming he's interested in when he can frighten little Joe . . .'

'Who's little Joe?'

'He's a bookie's runner, you know, one who goes round taking bets. But he's many more things besides, some things that it would be dangerous to look into. Not that he could do much on his own. But those who hire him could, such as our Mr Nickle. You know—' he now rose and went to the fire and lit a spill and after drawing on his pipe came back towards her, saying, 'You know, I wouldn't have told you. I mean I wouldn't have given him away, only I met him the day across the water in Crawford's. He was doing the same as I was, getting the lay of the land, seeing if the place was worth buying, and he talked loudly to Crawford for my benefit about the stupidity of competing against rope works just farther up the river, such as Haggie's. And all the while he eyed me. Yet he ignored me, completely ignored me. Then Crawford, who's as blunt as an old hammer, said, "Aw well, if that's your opinion of the place you're not interested, are you? So what about you, Mr Connor, you think the same?" "No," I said, "I'm here to talk business." And on that the old fellow turned his back on our Mr Nickle and walked with me into the office, leaving his highness black in the face. And that's why I'm oozing glee, as you call it, 'cos Crawford's askin' much less than we thought. I told him we weren't thinking of rope, but a foundry, at least material from it to make household goods.'

'Good. Good.' She put her hand out towards him, and he held it and went on, 'And later, I saw his highness in the hotel when I was having a meal, and again he cut me dead. Now I could've understood such an attitude from any number of men in this town, and took it, but not from him, not knowin' what I know about him. Because it isn't only gambling, it's lasses.'

'Lasses?'

'Yes, there's quite a number of lasses disappear now and again.'

'Oh no! Rory, he . . . he wouldn't.'

'He would, and he does. Little Joe, the fellow I
mentioned, was very much afraid of our Mr Nickle,
and a game on the side wouldn't have caused him to
sweat so much so that he got washed and cleaned
up afore going to his back door. I'd never known
little Joe so clean in his life as when I saw him that
day, the day I found out about Nickle . . . Look.' He
tugged her towards him. 'I've thought of something.
Do you think you could invite him here to dinner?'

'Invite him here?'

'That's what I said. Say your husband would very
much like to meet him.'

'But after he's cut you, do you think . . . ?'

'Aye. Aye, I do. Invite him in a way that he'll think
twice about refusing . . . Put that something in your
voice . . . You can do it.'

'Blackmail?'

'Aye. Yes, if you like.'

She began to smile slowly, then she nodded at him.
'Yes, I see your point. Yes, I'll invite him. If I'm not
mistaken I'll be meeting him next week; he's a
member of the Church Council. We'll likely be sitting
side by side in the vestry. Yes—' she laughed outright now—'I'll invite him here, and enjoy it . . .
that's if he accepts the invitation.'

'He will, after you've put it over in your own way
. . . Huh! it's a funny life.' He leant back in the couch
and she twisted her body round and looked fully at
him.

'How are you finding it?'

'Finding what?'

'Life, this funny life.'

Taking the pipe from his mouth, he said, 'I'm
liking this life fine, Mrs Connor. I never dreamed I'd
like it so well.'

'I wish I were beautiful.' Her voice was low, and
he pulled her suddenly towards him and encircled
her with his arm, saying, 'You've got qualities that
beat beauty any day in the week. You're the best-

dressed woman in the town, too. Moreover, you've got something up top.'

'Something up top?' Her face was partly smothered against his shoulder. 'I'd willingly be an empty-headed simpering nincompoop if only I . . . I looked different.'

Quickly now he thrust her from him and said harshly and with sincerity, 'Well, I can tell you this much, you wouldn't be sitting where you are now, or at least I wouldn't be sitting where I am now, if you were an empty-headed nincompoop.'

'Oh, Rory.' She flung herself against him as any young girl might, and he lay back holding her tightly to him.

Hardly a week passed but he had to reassure her with regard to her looks. It seemed that she was becoming more conscious of her plainness as time went on, and yet strangely, he himself was actually becoming less aware of her lack of beauty as the days passed; there were even times when her whole face took on an attractive quality. Then there was her voice. Her voice was beautiful. He never tired listening to it, even when she was in one of her haughty moods, which were becoming rarer.

She was saying, 'You've never asked what I've been doing all day today?'

'What have you been doing all day today?'

'Nothing. Nothing much. But . . . but I have two things to tell you.'

'Two things? Well, get on with them. What are they?'

She pulled herself gently from his arms, saying now, 'Don't be disturbed, but Jimmy came this afternoon. One . . . one of the boats has been sunk . . .'

He was sitting on the edge of the couch now. 'Why . . . why, didn't you tell me this afore?'

She placed her hands on his shoulders, saying, 'Be quiet. Don't get agitated. I've seen to it.'

'Where's Jimmy now?'

'Where he always is, in the boathouse.'

233

'Look, I'd better go down, he shouldn't be there alone. I'll . . .'

'I told you I've seen to it. Mr Richardson is staying there with him.'

'The boat . . . what happened to the boat?'

'A plank had been levered from the bottom.'

'And it would have been full. He was transporting for Watson yesterday.'

'Yes, it had on the usual cargo.'

'And it all went to the bottom?'

'They salvaged it. I went back with Jimmy; you hadn't been gone half an hour.'

He pulled himself up from the couch and began to pace back and forth in front of the fire, grinding out between his teeth, 'Those bloody Pitties!' He never apologized for swearing in front of her, nor did she ever reprimand him. 'If they're not stopped they'll do murder. Something's got to be done.' He was standing in front of her, looking down at her now, and she said quietly, 'Something will be done; I've seen to that as well. I . . . I called on the Chief Constable. I told him of our suspicions. Of course you cannot accuse anyone unless you have absolute proof, but I knew by the little he said that he was well aware of the Pitties' activities and would be as pleased as us to convict them. And he said something that I found very interesting. He ended by saying it was difficult of course to catch little fish when they were protected by big fish. What do you make of that?'

He rubbed his hand tightly along his jawbone. 'What do I make of it? Just that it links up with what I was saying earlier: there are some respectable people in this town leading double lives . . . big fish behind little fish.' He narrowed his eyes at her. 'Who would be protectin' the Pitties? Only somebody who wants to use them. And what would they use them for? What's their job? Running freight, anything from contraband whisky, silk, baccy, or men . . .'

'Or maidens? As you were saying earlier.'

234

He nodded at her. 'Aye, men or maidens, anything.' He bowed his head and shook it for a moment before saying, 'What I'm really frightened of is, if they should go for Jimmy. He's no match for any of them, although he's got plenty of guts. But guts aren't much use against them lot, it's guile you want.'

'If you are so worried about him then you must make him come here to sleep.'

He gave a weak smile and put his hand out and touched her shoulder, saying, 'That's nice of you, kind, but I doubt if he would.'

'Why not? He's got over his shyness of me, he's even, I think, beginning to like me. It gives me hope that your family may well follow suit.'

He turned from her and went towards the mantelpiece. And now he looked up into the face of her great-grandfather, and he thought, That'll be the day. That pig-headed lot. Even Ruth was included in his thoughts now.

Jimmy, acting as a kind of go-between, had arranged that he should take her up one Saturday, and because she also demanded it, but much against the grain, he had complied. And what had happened? Nothing. She had sat there trying to talk her way into their good books, and how had they responded? By staring at her as if she were a curio.

Later, she had remarked, 'I think your mother is a gentle creature.'

His mother. That was one secret he had kept to himself. She knew everything about him but that, and he couldn't bring himself to tell her that the slight, quiet, little woman, with a dignity that was all her own, was not his mother. His mother was the woman he had introduced to her by merely remarking, 'This is Lizzie,' and explaining later that she was his father's cousin. Why was it that some things were impossible to admit to? He felt as guilty at being Lizzie's son as if it were he himself who had perpetrated the sin of his conception.

Damn them! Let them get on with it. It was

Jimmy he was worried about, and those bloody Pitties were beginning to scare him. Little fish protected by big fish!

He turned to her. 'I'm goin' down,' he said.

'All right.' She rose from the couch. 'I'll go with you.'

'You'll do nothing of the sort. It's coming down whole water now.'

'If you're going down there tonight I'm going with you.'

He closed his eyes for a moment; he knew that tone. 'Well, get your things on.' His voice was almost a growl.

As she was walking towards the door, she said, 'I'll tell Stoddard.'

'No, no.' He came to her side. 'You don't want to get the carriage out at this time of night. And he'll be settled down. I meant to walk.'

'All right, we'll walk.'

'Oh, woman!'

'Oh, man!' She smiled at him and tweaked his nose, then left the room smiling.

Half an hour later they went up the steps and into the boathouse and startled Jimmy and Mr Richardson who were playing cards.

'Oh, hello.' Jimmy slid to his feet; then looking from one to the other, he asked, 'Anything wrong?'

'Not at our end; what about this end? What's this I'm hearin'?'

'Oh that.' Jimmy nodded, then said, 'Well, it's done one thing.' He was looking at Charlotte now. 'The river polis have been past here three times to my knowledge this afternoon. That's . . . that's with you going down there. Hardly seen them afore. That should warn the bug . . . beggars off for a bit.'

'Aye, for a bit.' Rory pulled a chair towards Charlotte. She sat down, and what she said was, 'Have you plenty to eat?'

'Oh aye.' Jimmy smiled at her. 'Lizzie's been down

this afternoon an' baked. She feeds me up as if I was carryin' tw . . .' He swallowed and the colour flushed up over his pale face as he amended Lizzie's description of pregnancy, carrying twins for eighteen months, with 'cartin' coals to Newcastle.'

As he looked at Charlotte he saw that her eyes were bright, twinkling. She had twigged what he was about to say. It was funny but he liked her, he liked her better every time he met her. He could see now what had got their Rory. When you got to know her you forgot she was nothing to look at. He had said so to Lizzie this very afternoon when she was on about Rory, but she had come back at him, saying, 'You another one that's got a short memory? I thought you used to think the world of Janie.' Well, yes he had, but Janie was dead. And he had said that to her an' all, but what had she come back again with, that the dead should live on in the memory. She was a hard nut was Lizzie, she didn't give Rory any credit for making life easier for the lot of them. Three pounds every week he sent up there; they had never been so well off in all their lives. New clothes they had, new bedding, and they ate like fighting cocks. If Lizzie kept on, and his ma too didn't really soften towards Charlotte—he wasn't concerned about his da's opinion—he'd give them the length of his tongue one of these days, he'd tell them straight out. 'Well,' he'd say, 'if you think like you do, you shouldn't be takin' his money.' Aye, he would, he'd say that. And what ·would they say? 'It isn't his money, it's hers' . . . Well, it didn't matter whose it was, they were taking it and showing no gratitude. For himself he was grateful. By lad! he was grateful. Three boats he had, but one without a bottom to it.

He said to her, 'Will you have a cup of tea?'

'No, thank you, Jimmy. We . . . we just came to see that everything was all right.' She smiled from him to Mr Richardson.

Mr Richardson was a burly man in his forties. He had worked in Baker's yard alongside Jimmy but had gladly made the move to here when Rory offered him five shillings a week more than he was getting there. He was a married man with a family, so the arrangement of keeping Jimmy company at nights could not be a permanent one.

'We're grateful for you staying, Mr Richardson,' she said.

'Do anything I can, ma'am.'

'Thank you. We won't forget it, Mr Richardson.'

The man nodded and smiled widely. Then she rose to her feet and, looking at Rory, said, 'Well now, are you satisfied?'

Before he could answer she turned her head towards Jimmy, saying, 'The trouble with your brother, Jimmy, is he won't recognize the fact that you are a young man and no longer an apprentice.'

Jimmy laughed back at her, saying, 'Well, we'll have to show him, won't we? You tell him when you see him I'll take him on any day in the week an' knock the stuffin' out of him. You tell him that, will you?'

Rory now thrust out his fist and punched Jimmy gently on the head, saying, 'You've always been a daft lad; you always will be.'

'Daft? Huh! Who's daft comin' down this end in the black dark an' it pourin'. Don't you think you're askin' for trouble yourself, walking along the dockside, an' not alone either?' He nodded towards Charlotte.

'She came along to protect me. Can you imagine anybody tacklin' me when she's there?' He now took hold of Charlotte's arm and led her towards the door as she tut-tutted and cast a reproving glance up at him.

'Keep that door bolted, mind.'

'Aye. Don't you worry.' Jimmy smiled quietly at Rory.

The farewells over, they took the lantern and went down the steps and made their way through the stinging rain on to the road and along the waterfront, and as they hurried through what, even in daytime, was known to be an unsavoury thoroughfare Rory thought. He was right, I was crazy to let her come, and at this time of night.

And so he didn't breathe easily until they emerged into the main street, and there she said to him, 'Now you can relax.'

He did not reply, only heaved a telling sigh as he thought for the countless time, There's no doubt about it, she's remarkable.

His mind more at ease now with regard to Jimmy, he said, 'There were two things you were going to tell me the night. Well, let's have the second one now.'

'No, not now; it will have to wait until we get out of this, the rain is choking me.'

'Serves you right; you would have your own way.'

'Far better have my own way than sit worrying until you returned.'

'You're a fool of a woman. You know that, don't you?'

'Yes, I know that, I've known it now for five months and three days.'

'Oh, Charlotte!' He pressed her arm closer to his side.

She had taken a bath and was now dressed in a pale grey chiffon nightdress with matching negligee. It was night attire which one might have expected to see on a picture postcard such as sailors brought over from foreign countries, like France, on which were painted ladies in flowing robes, their voluptuousness alone signifying their lack of virtue.

He had now become used to seeing her dressed, or undressed, like this. His own night attire not only would have caused the women in the kitchen to throw their aprons over their heads, but would have raised the eyebrow of many a smart gentleman in the town, for his nightshirt was of a pale blue colour, the flannel being so fine as to be almost like cashmere.

239

Moreover, it had cuffs that turned back and were hemmed with fancy braid, as was the deep collar. It, and a dozen more like it, were one of the many presents she had given him. And to hide his embarrassment he had made a great joke the first time he had worn one, but now he never even thought of his nightshirts, even when a fresh one was put out for him every other night.

As he pulled this one over his head he called to her, 'I'm waiting.'

'So am I.'

When her flat reply came back to him he bit on his lip, closed his eyes, tossed his head backwards and laughed silently. She was a star turn really. Who would have thought her like it?

He went from the dressing-room into the bedroom smiling. She wasn't in bed but was sitting on the edge of it, and at this moment she looked ethereal in the soft glow of the lamplight. He had the idea that if he opened the windows the wind that was blowing in gusts around the house would waft her away. He sat down beside her on the bed and, adopting an attitude of patience, he crossed his slippered feet, crossed his arms and stared ahead.

'Are you feeling strong?'

'Strong? In what way?' He turned his head sharply to look at her.

'Oh, in all ways.'

'Look, what is it?' He twisted his body round until he was facing her. 'Stop beating about the bush; what have you got up your sleeve now?'

She gave a little rippling laugh that might have issued from the lips of some dainty creature, then said, 'Nothing up my sleeve. No, decidedly not up my sleeve; I happen to have become pregnant.'

'Preg . . . *pregnant*?'

As his mouth fell into a gape she nodded at him and said, 'Yes, you know, "A woman with child" is how the Bible puts it.'

He drew in a long breath that lifted his shoulders

240

outward. She was pregnant, she was with child, as she had said. Well, well. He had the desire to laugh. He stopped himself. She was going to have a bairn. Charlotte was going to have a bairn. And he had given it to her . . . Well, what was surprising about that? With all that had happened these past months why should he be surprised, for if anyone had worked for a bairn she had? He would never forget the first night in this bed. He had thought to treat her tenderly because right up to the moment they had first stood outside that door there, she had given him the chance to take advantage of the agreement she had first suggested; in fact, she had stood blocking his way into the room as she said, 'I won't hold it against you. Believe me, I won't hold it against you.' And what had he done? He had put his hand behind her and turned the knob. And she had entered with her head down like some shy bride, and he had told himself again that it was as little as he could do to be kind to her, to ease her torment, and make her happy. And he had made her happy. Aye by God! he had made her happy. And himself too. She had been surprising enough as a companion, but as a wife she had enlightened him in ways that he had never thought possible, because she had loved him. Aye, it was she who had done the loving. Up till then he hadn't been aware that he had never been loved. He had loved Janie. A better term for it would be, he had taken Janie. And she had let him, but she had never loved him in the way he was loved now. Perhaps it was his own fault that things had not worked out that way with Janie, it was the business of John George coming between them on that first night. He had known a few other women before Janie. On his first year of rent collecting there had been one in Jarrow—her man went to sea—but what she had wanted was comfort not love. Then another had been no better than she should be, she had given him what she would give anybody at a shilling a go.

No, he had never been loved until Charlotte loved him. It was amazing to him how or from where she had gained her knowledge, for one thing was certain, he was the first man she'd had in her life. Perhaps it was instinctive. Whatever it was, it was comforting. And now, now she was saying . . . 'Huh! . . . Huh! . . . Huh!'

He was holding her tightly to him. They fell backwards on to the bed and he rolled her to and fro, and they laughed together; then, his mouth covering hers, he kissed her long and hard.

When finally he pulled her upright the ribbon had fallen from her hair and it was loose about her shoulders and he took a handful of the black silkiness and rubbed it up and down his cheek.

'You're pleased?'

'Oh! Charlotte, what more can you give me?'

'One every year until I grow fat. I'd love to grow fat.'

'I don't want you fat, I want you just as you are.' And in this moment he was speaking the truth. He now took her face between his hands and watched her thin nostrils quiver. Her eyes were soft and full of love for him, and he said, 'You're the finest woman I've ever known, and ever will know.'

And she said, 'I love you.'

He could not say, 'And me you,' but he took her in his arms and held her tightly.

PART FOUR

The Resurrection

The foreign-looking young woman handed her ticket to the ticket collector, stared at him for a moment, then passed through the barrier. She was the last of a dozen people to leave the platform and his look followed her. She was a foreigner. He could tell by her dress; she had strange-looking clogs on her feet and a black cloak hung from her shoulders right down to the top of them. She had a contraption on her head that was part hat, part shawl, with a fringe, and strings from it, like pieces of frayed twine, were knotted under her chin. Another odd thing about her was, although her skin was brown her hair was white and frizzy, like that of an old Negro's, yet her face was that of a young woman. She reminded him of a man that used to live near him who had white hair and pink eyes. They said he was an albino. He had been an oddity.

When the young woman reached the main thoroughfare she seemed slightly bemused; the traffic was so thick, and the Saturday evening crowd were pushing and shoving. She stepped into the gutter and the mud went over the top of her clogs. She stared at one face after another as if she had never been in a crowd before, as if she had never seen people before.

She walked on like someone in a daze. She skirted the stalls in the market place and when she heard a boat horn hooting she stopped and looked down the narrow lane that led to the ferry, then she went on again.

She was half-way down the bank that dropped steeply to the river when again she stopped. And now she put her hand inside her cloak and pressed it against her ribs. Then she turned her head upwards and gazed into the fading light.

Two men paused in their walking and looked at her, and she brought her head down and stared back at them. And when they looked at each other in a questioning way she ran swiftly down the bank away from them, her clogs clip-clopping against the cobbles.

On the river-front now, she hurried in a purposeful way along it until she came to where had stood the square of waste land, and here she looked about her in some perplexity, for the ground was now railed in, its railings joining those which surrounded the boatyard. Her steps slowed as she approached the alleyway; the light was almost gone, and when she went to open the gate and found it locked, she rattled it, then knocked on it, waited a moment, and, now almost in a frenzy, took her fist and banged on it.

When there was still no reply she looked up and down the alleyway before hurrying towards the far end where it terminated at the river wall; and now she did what she had done a number of times before when Jimmy had bolted the gate from the inside, she gripped the last post of the fence where it hung out over the river and swung herself round it, and so entered the boatyard.

Now she stood perfectly still looking up towards the house. There was a light in the window of the long room. Again she put her hand inside her cloak and placed it over her ribs, then slowly she went towards the steps and mounted them. She didn't open the door but knocked on it.

She heard the footsteps coming across the wooden floor towards it, but it didn't open. A voice said, 'Who's there?'

She waited a second before answering, 'Open the door, Jimmy.'

There was complete silence all about her now, no movement from inside the room. She said again, 'Open the door, Jimmy, please. Please open the door.'

Again there was no answer. She heard the steps moving away from the door. She turned her head and saw the curtains pulled to the side; she saw the outline of Jimmy's white face pressed against the pane. She held out her hand towards it.

She didn't hear the footsteps return to the door; nor was there any other sound, not even any movement from the river. It seemed to her that she was dead again. Her voice high now, beseeching, she called, 'Jimmy! Jimmy, it's me. Open the door. Please open the door.'

When at last the door opened it seemed it did so of its own accord; it swung wide and there was no one in the opening. She stepped over the threshold and looked along the room to where Jimmy was backing slowly along the side of the table towards its far end, and she stood, with her hand on the door and said, almost in a whimper, 'Don't be frightened, Jimmy, I'm . . . I'm not a ghost. It's . . . it's me, Janie. I . . . I've been bad. I . . . I wasn't drowned.' She closed the door, then leant her back against it and slowly slid down on to the floor and slumped on to her side.

Jimmy gazed at the crumpled figure but didn't move. He had never been so terrified in all his life, he wanted to run, jump out of the window, get away from it . . . her. Yet . . . yet it was Janie's voice, and she said she was Janie. That's all he had to go on, for from what he could see of her, her skin was like an Arab's and her hair was white. Janie had been bonny, and her skin was as fair as a peach and her hair brown, lovely brown.

When she moved and spoke again, he started.

'Give me a drink, Jimmy, tea, anything.'

As if mesmerized now, he went to the hob and picked up the teapot that had been stewing there for the past hour, and with a hand that shook he filled a cup, spooned in some sugar, then slowly advanced towards her.

He watched her pulling herself to her feet, and as he stood with the cup in his hand, staring wildly at her, she passed him and went towards a chair, and after a moment she held out her hand and took the cup from him, and although the tea was scalding she gulped at it, then asked, 'Where's Rory?'

The gasp he gave brought her leaning towards him, and she asked softly, 'Nothin' . . . nothin's happened him?'

His head moved as if in a shudder and then he spoke for the first time. 'Where've you been?' he said.

'I . . . I was washed up there. I don't remember anything about it but they told me . . . at least after a long time when the priest came over the hills; he could speak English. The fishing-boat, it found me off Le Palais. I was clinging to this wood and they thought I was dead. I must have been in the water for a long time swept by a current, they said, and . . . and when I came to meself I didn't know who I was. I . . . I never knew who I was till a month ago.'

'Just a month ago?'

'Aye.' She nodded slowly.

He gulped twice before he asked, 'Well, how did you get on? Who did you think you were?'

'Nobody; I just couldn't remember anything except vaguely. I seemed to remember holding a child. I told the priest that, and when he came next, he only came twice a year, he said he had inquired along the coast and he'd heard of nobody who had lost a wife and child. There had been great storms that year and lots of boats had been sunk. He told me to be patient an' me memory'd come back and I'd know who I was. It . . . it was Henri who brought it back.'

'Who's Henry?'

'He was madame's son. They're all fisherfolk, she looked after me. Life was very hard for them all, so very hard, much . . . much harder than here.' She looked slowly around the room. 'I . . . I remember how I used to talk about guttin' fish as being something lowly. I had to learn to gut fish. They all worked so hard from mornin' till night. It was a case of fish or die. You don't know.' She shook her head in wide

248

movements. 'But they were kind and . . . and they were happy.'

Jimmy gulped. His mind was racing. This was Janie. It was Janie all right. Eeh! God, what would happen? Why couldn't she have stayed where she was? What was he saying? He muttered now, 'How did you get your memory back?'

'It was through Henri, he couldn't understand about me not wantin' to learn to swim. The young ones swam, it was their one pleasure, and this day he . . . he came behind me and pushed me off the rock. It . . . it was as I hit the water it all came back. He was sorry, very sorry I mean that it had come back.' She looked down towards the table and up again suddenly. 'Where's Rory? Is he up home?'

Jimmy turned from her. He was shaking his head wildly now. He lifted up the teapot from the hob, put it down again, then, swinging round towards her, he said, 'You've . . . you've been away nearly . . . nearly two years, Janie, things've happened.'

She rose slowly to her feet. 'What things? What kind of things?'

'Well . . . well, this is goin' to be another shock to you. I'm . . . I'm sorry, Janie. It wasn't that he wasn't cut up, he nearly went mad. And . . . and it was likely 'cos he was so lonely he did it, but—' now his voice faded to a mere whisper, and he bowed his head before finishing, 'he got married again.'

She turned her ear slightly towards him as if she hadn't heard aright; then her mouth opened and closed, but she didn't speak. She sat down with a sudden plop, and once more she looked around the room. Then she asked simply, 'Who to?'

Jimmy now put his hand across his mouth. He knew before he said the name that this would be even harder for her to understand.

'Who to?' She was shouting now, screaming at him.

If he had had any doubts before that this was Janie they were dispelled.

'Miss . . . Miss Kean.'

'*What!*' She was on her feet coming towards him, and he actually backed from her in fear.

'You're jokin'?'

'No, no, I'm not, Janie. No.' He stopped at the foot of the ladder and she stopped too. With one wild sweep she unhooked the clasp of her cloak and flung it aside, then she tore the bonnet from her head and flung it on to the cloak. And now she walked back to the table, and she leant over it as she cried, '*Money!* *Money!* He married her for money. He couldn't get it by gamin', but he had to have it some way.'

'No, no, it wasn't like that . . .'

She swung round and was facing him again, and he noted with surprise that her figure was no longer plump, it was almost as flat as Charlotte Kean's had been before her body started to swell with the bairn. Eeh! and that was another thing, the bairn. Oh my God! Where would this end? He said now harshly, 'It's nearly two years, you've got to remember that. He . . . he was her manager, and . . . and she was lonely.'

'Lonely? *Lonely?*' She started to laugh; then thrusting her white head forward, she demanded, 'Where's he now? Living in the big house? Huh! Well, his stay's goin' to be short, isn't it, Jimmy? He can't have two wives, can he?'

'He didn't know, you can't blame him.'

'Can't blame him? Huh! I was the only woman he'd ever wanted in his life, the only one he would ever love until he died. You . . . you know nowt about it. Can't blame him, you say!'

'You should never've gone; it was your own fault, you going on that holiday. I . . . I told him he shouldn't have let you.'

'But he did, he did let me, Jimmy. What he should have done the day I left was come after me and knock hell out of me an' made me stay. But he didn't, did he? He let me go.'

'You know why he let you go. It was because of

250

John George, that business, an' you sticking out and wanting him to go and give himself up. You're as much to blame as he is, Janie, about that. But he's not to blame for marryin' again, 'cos how was he to know? He waited a year, over a year.'

'That was kind of him. Well now, what are we going to do, Jimmy, eh? You'll have to go and tell him that his wife's come back. That's it . . . just go an' tell him that his wife's come back.'

He stared at her. This was Janie all right, but it was a different Janie; not only was she changed in looks but in her manner, her ways, and as he stared at her he couldn't imagine any disaster great enough to change a woman's appearance as hers had been changed.

She saw his eyes on her hair and she said quietly now, 'I mean it, Jimmy. You'd better go and tell him. And . . . and tell him what to expect, will you?' She put her hand up towards her head. 'I . . . I lost all me hair. I was bald, as bald as any man, and . . . and they rubbed grease in, fish fat, an' . . . an' this is how it grew. And . . . and living out in the open in the sun and the wind I became like them, all brown 'cos of me fair skin likely.'

She sat down suddenly on a chair and, placing her elbows on the table, she lowered her face into her hands.

'Don't cry, Janie, don't cry.' He moved to the other side of the table. And now she looked up at him dry-eyed and said, 'I'm not cryin', Jimmy. That's another thing, I can't cry. I should cry about the children and the master and mistress and how I look, but something stops me . . . Go and fetch him, Jimmy.'

'I . . . I can't, Janie. It would . . .'

'It would what?'

'He'd . . . he'd get a gliff.'

'Well, if he doesn't come to me, I'll have to go to him. He'll get a gliff in any case, and he'd far better meet me here than . . . than up home . . . What's the matter? . . . What is it now?'

'Your grannie, Janie, she's. . . .'

'Aw no!' She dropped her head to the side and screwed up her eyes, then after a moment said, 'When?'

'Last year, after . . . shortly after she heard the news.'

'And me da?'

'He . . . he went to Jarrow to live with . . . he took lodgings in Jarrow. There's new people in the house, an old couple. An' the Learys have gone an'll. I never thought they'd ever move but he started work in St Hilda's Colliery, and it's too far for him to trek in the winter. They live down here now in High Shields. It's all changed up there.' He wanted to keep talking in a hopeless effort against what she was going to say next, but she stopped him with a lift of her hand as she leant back in the chair and drew in long draughts of breath, then said, 'I don't think I can stand much more. And I'm so tired; I haven't been to sleep for . . . aw, it seems days . . . Go and fetch him, Jimmy.'

The command was soft, but firm and brooked no argument. He stared at her for a moment longer; then grabbing his coat and cap from the back of the door, he dragged them on and rushed out. But once down in the yard he didn't run; instead, he stood gripping the staunch post that supported the end of the house as he muttered to himself, 'Eeh! my God! What's gona happen?'

2

Charlotte straightened the silk cravat at Rory's neck, dusted an invisible speck from the shoulder of his black suit, and finally ran her fingers lightly over the top of his oiled hair, and then, standing slightly back from him, she said, 'To my mind you're wasted on a gaming table.'

'I'm never wasted on a gaming table.' He pressed his lips together, jerked his chin to the side and winked at her.

Her face becoming serious now, she said, 'Be careful. The more I hear of that man, Nickle, the more perturbed I become.'

'Well, you couldn't ask for a quieter, better mannered or refined gentleman, now could you?'

'No; that makes him all the more sinister. It's really unbelievable when you think of it, but I'm glad that he knows I'm aware of what he is. I wish I had been there when he put his tentative question: "Your wife, of course, knows nothing of our little . . . shall we say excursions into chance?"'

He took up a haughty stance and mimicked, ' "Sir, my wife knows everything; she's a remarkable woman." And she is that.' He put out his hand and slapped the raised dome of her stomach, and she laughed and tut-tutted as she in return slapped at his hand. Then her manner becoming serious again, she said, 'Well, there's one thing I can be assured of, he won't try any of his underhand business on you, because if he wants to silence you he'll also have to silence me. Who are you expecting tonight?'

'Who knows! My, my! It gets more surprising. You should have seen the look on Veneer's face when he saw me there, in the Newcastle rooms I mean. I thought he was going to pass out. I nearly did meself an' all. I couldn't believe me eyes. Him, a staunch supporter of the Temperance League! They would burn him at the stake if they knew. Just imagine the ladies of this town who wave the banners for temperance getting wind of what their Mr Veneer's up to . . . And you know something? I'd gather the kindling for them; I never could stand him. I remember your father once sending me on some business to his office. He spoke to me as if I were so much clarts. Sorry, madam.' He pulled a face at her. 'Mud from the gutter.'

She was now standing in front of him holding his face firmly between her hands, and she said with deep pride, 'Well, we've shown them. You've out-witted two of them already in business deals, and that's only a beginning. What's more, you're the most fashionably dressed, best-looking man in the town, or the county for that matter.' She tossed her head.

He didn't preen himself at her praise, but he said, 'I keep sayin' you're a remarkable woman, and you are. Every day that passes I discover something more remarkable about you. The very fact that you raised no protest at my gaming amazes me.'

'What is one evening a week? As long as your failings only embrace cards and wine I'll be content.'

He bent towards her now and kissed her gently on her lips, then said, 'You can rest assured, Mrs Connor, that these shall be the limit of my failings. But now for orders.' His manner changed, his voice took on a sterner note. 'You are not to wait up for me, do you hear? Stoddard will pick me up at twelve, and when I get in I shall expect to find you in bed and fast asleep. If I don't, then there's going to be trouble.'

'What will you do?'

He stared at her for a moment before replying, 'I'll take up the other vice.'

'No, don't say that.' There was no flippancy in her tone now. 'Not even in joke say you'll take up the third vice. That's something I couldn't bear.'

'You silly woman, don't you ever believe anything I say?'

'I want to.'

'Well, what can I say to make you believe it?'

She looked into his eyes. They were smiling kindly at her and she only just prevented herself from blurting out, 'Say that you love me. Oh, say that you love me.'

'Go on.' She pushed him from the room and into

the hall. It was she who helped him into his coat and handed him his hat and scarf. Then she stood at the top of the steps and watched him go down them and into the carriage, and she waved to him and he waved back. Then stretching out his legs, he leant his head against the leather upholstery and sighed a deep contented sigh.

They were nearing the gate when the carriage was brought to an abrupt halt and he heard Stoddard shouting, 'Whoa! Whoa, there!' then add, 'Who's you?'

He pulled down the window and looked out, and there in the light of the carriage lamps he saw Jimmy. Quickly opening the door, he called to the driver, 'It's all right, Stoddard,' then to Jimmy, 'Get in. What's up? What's happened?'

As the carriage jerked forward again Jimmy bounced back on the seat, and again Rory demanded, 'What is it? What's happened now? Have they sunk another one?'

'No.' Jimmy shook his head. 'It's nowt to do with the boats.'

'Well, what is it? Something wrong at home?' Rory's inquiry was quiet, and when again Jimmy shook his head, he said almost angrily, 'Well, spit it out, unless you've just come for a chat.'

'I haven't just come for a chat, and . . . and I've been hangin' around for nearly an hour waitin', waitin' to see if you'd come out on your own.'

'Why?' Rory was sitting forward on the seat now. Their knees were touching. He peered into Jimmy's white face, demanding, 'Come on, whatever it is, tell us.'

'You're going to get a gliff, Rory.'

'A gliff?'

'Aye, you'll . . . you'll never believe it. You'd . . . you'd better brace yourself. It's . . . it's something you won't be able to take in.' When he stopped, Rory said quietly, 'Well, tell us.'

'It's . . . it's Janie.'

Jimmy's voice had been so soft that Rory thought he couldn't possibly have heard aright; Jimmy's words had been distorted, he imagined, by the grinding of the carriage wheels, so he said loudly, 'What did you say?'

'I said, it's Janie.'

'Janie?' A sudden cold sweat swept over his body and his own voice was scarcely audible now when he asked, 'What . . . what about Janie?'

'She's . . . she's back. She's . . . she's not dead, she wasn't drowned . . .'

Rory didn't utter a word, no protest, nothing, but his body fell back and his head once more touched the upholstery, and as if he had been shot into a nightmare again he listened to Jimmy's voice saying, 'I was petrified. It was her voice, but . . . but I wouldn't open the door at first. And then . . . and then when I saw her, I still didn't believe it was her. She's . . . she's changed. Nobody . . . nobody would recognize her. It . . . it was the shock. Her hair's gone white, and her skin, her skin's all brown like an Arab's in Corstorphine Town. It's the sun, she said. She's . . . she's been in some place in France miles off the beaten track. She talks about a priest comin' once every six months. She's changed, aye. I knew you'd get a gliff but . . . but I had to come. If . . . if I hadn't she would have turned up herself. Eeh! she's changed. What'll you do, Rory? What'll you do?'

His world was spinning about him. He watched it spiralling upwards and away, taking with it the new way of living and the prestige it had brought to him. Sir, he was called, Master. She had given him everything a woman could possibly give a man, a home, wealth, position, and now a child. He had never been so happy in his life as he had been since he married her; and his feelings for her were growing deeper every day. You couldn't live with a woman like that and receive so much from her and give nothing in return; something had been growing in him, and last night he had almost told her what it was, he had almost put a name to it. He had never thought he would be able to say to another woman, I love you. That kind of thing didn't happen twice, he had told himself. No; and he was right, that kind of thing didn't happen twice. But there were different kinds of love. It was even appearing to him that what he was feeling now would grow into a bigger love, a better love, a fuller love. Charlotte had said there were better marriages based on friendship than on professions of eternal love.

He had once sworn eternal love for Janie, but he knew now that that had been the outcome of a boy's love, the outcome of use, the outcome of growing up together, seeing no one beyond her . . .

She couldn't be back. She couldn't. No! No! Life couldn't play him a trick like that. He had gone to the Justice before he married Charlotte and the Justice had told him it was all right to marry again. "Drowned, presumed dead," was what he had said. And she was dead. She had been dead to him for nearly two years now, and he didn't want her resurrected.

God Almighty! What was he saying? What was he thinking? He'd go mad.

'Rory. Rory.' Jimmy was sitting by his side now, shaking his arm. 'Are you all right? I . . . I knew it'd give you a gliff; she . . . she scared me out of me wits. What are you gona do?'

'What?'

'I said what are you gona do?'

He shook his head. What was he going to do?

'She's back in the boathouse; she wants to see you.'

He stared dumbly at Jimmy for a time, then like someone drunk he leant forward and tapped on the roof of the carriage with his silver-mounted walking stick, and lowering the window again, he leant out and said, 'We'll get off here, Stoddard; I . . . I've a little business to attend to.'

A few minutes later Stoddard was opening the carriage door and pulling down the step, and when they alighted he said, 'Twelve o'clock, sir?'

'What? Oh. Oh yes; yes, thank you.'

'Good night, sir.'

'Good . . . Good night, Stoddard.'

He walked away, Jimmy by his side, but when the carriage had disappeared into the darkness he stopped under a street lamp and, peering down at Jimmy, said, 'What, in the name of God, am I going to do in a case like this?'

'I . . . I don't know, Rory.'

They walked on again, automatically taking the direction towards the river and the boatyard, and they didn't stop until they had actually entered the yard, and then Rory, standing still, looked up at the lighted window, then down on Jimmy, before turning about and walking towards the end of the jetty. And there he gripped the rail and leant over it and stared down into the dark, murky water.

Jimmy approached him slowly and stood by his side for a moment before saying, 'You've got to get it over, man.'

Rory now pressed a finger and thumb on his eyeballs as if trying to blot out the nightmare. His whole being was in a state of panic. He knew he should be rushing up those steps back there, bursting open the door and crying, 'Janie! Janie!' but all he wanted to do was to turn and run back through the town and into Westoe and up that private road into his house, *his house*, and cry, 'Charlotte! Charlotte!'

'Come on, man.'

At the touch of Jimmy's hand he turned about and went across the yard and up the steps. Jimmy had been behind him, but it was he who had to come to the fore and opened the door. Then Rory stepped into the room.

The woman was standing by the table. The lamplight was full on her. She was no more like the Janie he remembered than he himself was like Jimmy

258

there. His heart leapt at the thought that it was a trick. Somebody imagined they were on to something and were codding him. They had heard he was in the money. He cast a quick glance in Jimmy's direction as if to say, How could you be taken in? before moving slowly up the room towards the woman. When he was within a yard of her he stopped and the hope that had risen in him flowed away like liquid from a broken cask for they were Janie's eyes he was looking into. They were the only recognizable things about her, her eyes. As Jimmy had said, her skin was like that of an Arab and her hair was the colour of driven snow, and curly, close-cropped, curly.

Janie, in her turn, was looking at him in much the same way, for he was no more the Rory that she had known than she was the Janie he had known. Before her stood a well-dressed gentleman, better dressed in fact than she had ever seen the master, for this man was stylish with it; even his face was different, even his skin was different, smooth, clean-shaven, showing no blue trace of stubble about his chin and cheeks and upper lip.

Her heart hardened further at the sight of him and at the fact that he didn't put out a hand to touch her.

'Janie.'

'Aye, it's me. And you're over the moon to . . . to see me.' There was a break in the last words.

'I thought . . . we all thought . . .'

'Aye, I know what you thought, but . . . but it isn't all that long, it isn't two years. You couldn't wait, could you? But then you're a gamblin' man, you couldn't miss a chance not even on a long shot.'

He bowed his head and covered his eyes with his hand, muttering now, 'What can I say?'

'I don't know, but knowin' you, you'll have some excuse. Anyway, it's paid off, hasn't it? You always said you'd play your cards right one day.' She turned her back on him and walked to the end of the table and sat down.

He now drew his hand down over his face, stretching the skin, and he looked at her sitting staring at him accusingly. Jimmy had said she had changed, and she had, and in all ways. She looked like some peasant woman who had lived in the wilds all her life. The dark skirt she was wearing was similar to that worn by the fishwives, only it looked as if she had never stepped out of it for years. Her blouse was of a coarse striped material and on her feet she had clogs. Why, she had never worn clogs even when she was a child and things were pretty tight. Her boots then, like his own, had been cobbled until they were nothing but patches, but she had never worn clogs.

Aw, poor Janie . . . Poor all of them . . . Poor Charlotte. Oh my God! Charlotte.

'I'm sorry I came back.' Her voice was high now. 'I've upset your nice little life, haven't I? But I am back, and alive, so what you going to do about it? You'll have to tell her, won't you? Your Miss Kean . . . My God! You marryin' her of all people! *Her*! But then you'd do anything to make money, wouldn't you?'

'I didn't marry her for . . .' The words sprang out of his mouth of their own volition and he clenched his teeth and bowed his head, while he was aware that she had risen to her feet again.

Now she was nodding at him, her head swinging like that of a golliwog up and down, up and down, before she said, 'Well, well! This is something to know. You didn't marry her for her money. Huh! You're tellin' me you didn't marry her for her money. So you married her because you wanted her? You wanted *her*, that lanky string of water, her that you used to make fun of?'

'*Shut up*! My God! it's as Jimmy said, you're different, you're changed. And yet not all that. No, not all that. Looking back, you had a hard streak in you; I sensed it years ago. And aye, it's true what I said, I . . . I didn't marry her for her money, but it's also true that I didn't marry her 'cos . . . 'cos I was in love with her.' He swallowed deeply and turned his head to the side and, his voice a mutter now, he said, 'She was lonely. I was lonely. That's . . . that's how it was.'

'And how is it now?'

He couldn't answer because it was wonderful now, or at least it had been.

'You can't say, can you? My God, it's a pity I didn't die. Aye, that's what you're thinkin', isn't it? Eeh! I wouldn't have believed it. I wouldn't, I wouldn't.' She was holding her head in her hands now, her body rocking. Then of a sudden she stopped and glared at him as she said, 'Well, she'll have to be told, won't she? She'll have to be told that you can have only one wife.'

As he stared back at her he was repeating her words, 'I wouldn't have believed it,' for he couldn't believe what he was recognizing at this moment, that it could be possible for a man to change in such a short time as two years and look at a woman he had once loved and say to himself, 'Yes, only one wife, and it's not going to be you, not if I can help it'—What was he thinking? What was he thinking?

He was trapped. Standing before him was his wife, his legal wife, and he'd have to tell Charlotte that his wife had come back and that she herself had no claim to him and the child in her couldn't take his name. He couldn't do it. What was more, he wouldn't do it. He heard his voice saying now, clearly and firmly, 'I can't tell her.'

'You what!'

'I said I can't tell her, she's going to have a ch . . . bairn.' He had almost said child, so much had even his vocabulary changed.

There was complete silence in the room, until Jimmy moved. He had been standing at the side of the fireplace and now his foot jerked and he kicked the brass fender, which caused them both to look towards him. And then she said, 'Well, it's going to be hard on her, isn't it, bringing up a bairn without a father? But then, her way will be smoothed, money's a great compensation. Oh yes, money's a great compensation. You can make things happen when you've got money. I had four sovereigns. The mistress give them to me to buy presents for you all to bring home. I put them in me little bag, an' you know me an' me little bag. Whenever I changed I used to pin it under me skirt, and when they found me there was me little bag still pinned under me skirt. But I didn't know anything about it until I got me memory back. Madame, the old woman I lived with, had taken it, but when I came to meself and wanted to come home and didn't know how, the son put the bag into me hand. He was very honest, the son, and so I travelled in luxury all the way here. First, in the bottom of a cart with pigs; then for miles on foot, sleeping on the floors of mucky inns; then the boat; and lastly, the back end of the train, like a cattle-truck; and—' and now she screamed at him—'you're no more sorry for me than you would be for a mangy dog lying in the gutter. The only thing you're worried about is that I've come back and your grand life is to be brought to an end. Well, if you don't tell her, I will; I'm not gona be pushed aside, I'm gona have me place.'

'Janie. Janie.' His voice was soft, pleading, and she stopped her ranting and stared at him, her face quivering but her eyes still dry. 'I'll . . . I'll do what I think is right. In . . . in the end I'll do what I think is right. But give me a little time, will you? A few days, time to sort things out, to . . . to get used to—' He gulped in his throat. 'You can have what money you want . . .'

'I don't want your money. Anyway, 'tisn't *your* money, you've never worked for it, it's her money.'

'I do work for it, begod! and hard at that.' His voice was loud now, harsh. 'I work harder now than ever I've done in me life. And now I'm goin' to tell you something, an' it's this. Don't push me; don't drive me too far. This . . . this has come as a surprise. Try to understand that, but remember I'm still Rory Connor and I won't be pushed.' He paused for a moment, then ended, 'I'll . . . I'll be back the morrow night,' and on this he swung round on his heel and went out.

Jimmy, casting a look at Janie, where she was standing now, her hands hanging limply by her side and her mouth open, turned and followed him. In the yard he saw the dim outline of Rory standing where he himself had stood earlier in the evening against the stanchion post, and he went up to him and put his hand on his arm, and held it for a moment before saying, 'I'm sorry, Rory. I'm sorry to the heart of me, but . . . but you can't blame her.'

'What am I going to do, Jimmy?' The question came out as a groan.

'I don't know, Rory. Honest to God, I don't know. Charlotte 'll be in a state. I'm sorry, I mean I'm sorry for Charlotte.'

'I . . . I can't leave her, I can't leave Charlotte. There's her condition and . . . Oh dear God! what am I goin' to do? Look, Jimmy.' He bent down to him. 'Persuade her to stay here out of the way, don't let her go up home. Look, give her this.' He thrust his hand into an inner pocket and, pulling out a chamois leather bag, emptied a number of sovereigns on to Jimmy's palm. 'Make her get some decent clothes; she looks like something that's just been dug up. I could never imagine her letting herself go like that, could you?'

'No. No, Rory. I told you, she's . . . she's changed. She must have gone through it. You'll have to remember that, she must have gone through it.'

'Aye, and now she's going to make us all go through it.'

As he moved across the yard Jimmy went with him, saying, 'Where you makin' for? Where were you going?'

'To a game.'

263

'Game? Does Charlotte know?'

Rory stopped again and said quietly, 'Aye, Charlotte knows and she doesn't mind. As long as I'm happy, doing something that makes me happy, she doesn't mind; all she minds is that she'll ever lose me. Funny, isn't it?'

They peered at each other through the darkness. 'Where you goin' now, back home?'

'No, no, I'll . . . I'll have to go on to the game. They're expecting me, and if I didn't turn up something would be said. Anyway, I've got to think. I'm . . . I'm nearly out of me mind.'

Jimmy made no reply to this and Rory, touching him on the shoulder by way of farewell, went up the yard and out of the gate.

He did not go straight to Plynlimmon Way but walked for a good half-hour, and when at last he arrived at the house Frank Nickle greeted him with, 'Well, Connor, we thought you weren't coming, we've been waiting some—' he drew from the pocket of his spotted grey waistcoat a gold lever watch attached to a chain across his chest—'three quarters of an hour.'

'I . . . I was held up.'

'Are you all right? Are you unwell?'

'Just . . . just a bit off colour.'

'No trouble, I hope?'

'No trouble.'

'Then let us begin.'

Nickle's tone was peremptory, it was putting him back into the servant class as far as he dared allow it. That the man hated him he was well aware, for he knew he was cornered, and had done since the night he came to dinner. But he also knew that he'd have to be careful of him in all ways. However, at this moment Nickle and his nefarious doings seemed of very minor importance.

They went into what was known as the smoking room. It was part office and part what could be considered a gentleman's rest room, being furnished mostly with leather chairs, a desk, and a small square table, besides four single chairs.

The two men present were smoking cigars and they greeted Rory cordially, speaking generally, while Frank Nickle lifted a china centrepiece from the square table, laid it aside, then opened the top of the table which was cut in the shape of an envelope, each piece being covered with green baize. This done, they all took their seats around the table and Nickle, producing the cards from a hidden drawer underneath, the game began . . .

Three hours later Rory rose from the table almost twenty pounds poorer. At one time in the evening he had been thirty pounds to the good.

He left before the others, and at the door Frank Nickle, smiling his thin smile, said, 'You weren't your usual brilliant self tonight, Connor.'

'No, I think I'm in for a cold.'

'That's a pity. Give my regards to your lady wife.' The large pallid face now took on a slight sneer. 'Tell her not to slap her little boy too hard for losing.'

He had the urge to lift his hand and punch the man on the mouth. But wait, he told himself, wait. Give him time, and he would do it, but in another way. He left without further words, went down the pathway through the iron gate and to the road where the carriage was waiting.

Nickle had suggested covertly that it was unwise to come by carriage, servants talked . . . ordinary servants, and to this Rory had replied that Stoddard was no ordinary servant, he was as loyal as Nickle's own. And anyway, wasn't he visiting the house for a 'Gentlemen's Evening'? They were common enough. How could one discuss the finer points of business if it weren't for 'Gentlemen's Evenings'?

When he arrived home Charlotte was in bed, but she wasn't asleep, and when, bending over her, he kissed her she pushed him slightly away from her, but holding him by the shoulders, she said, 'What is it? What's happened?'

'Nothing.'

'Oh, come, come, Rory, you . . . you looked strained. Something happened at Nickle's?'

'No.' He pulled himself from her. 'Only that I lost . . . twenty pounds.'

'Oh!' She lay back on her pillows. 'Hurt pride. Twenty pounds, quite a sum. But still I suppose you must let them have their turn. If you won every time they would say you were cheating.'

'Yes, yes.' When he went into the adjoining room to undress she called to him anxiously, 'There's nothing else wrong, is there? I mean, he didn't say anything, there wasn't any unpleasantness?'

'No, no; he wasn't more unpleasant than usual. He was born unpleasant.'

'Yes, yes, indeed.'

In bed he did not love her but he held her very tightly in his arms and muttered into her hair, 'Oh, Charlotte. Charlotte.'

It was a long time before he went to sleep, but even then she was still awake, although she had pretended to be asleep for some time past. There was something wrong; she could sense it. By now she knew every shade of his mood and expression. Her love for him was so deep that she imagined herself buried inside him.

At four o'clock in the morning she was woken up by his screaming. He was having a nightmare, the first he had had since his marriage.

3

Three days passed before Charlotte tackled him openly and very forcibly. 'What is it?' she said. 'Something is wrong. Now—' she closed her eyes and lifted her hand upwards—'it's no use you telling me, Rory, that there's nothing amiss. Please give me credit for being capable of using my eyes and my ears if not my other senses. There *is* something wrong, and I must know what it is. Rory, I must know what it is.'

When he didn't answer but turned away and walked down the length of the drawing-room towards the window she said, 'You're going out again tonight; you have been out for the last two nights supposedly to see Jimmy. When I was passing that way today I called in . . .'

'You what!' He swung round and faced her.

She stared at him over the distance before rising to her feet and saying slowly, 'I said I called in to see Jimmy. Why should that startle you? I have done that before, but what puzzled me today, and what's puzzling me now, is that you are both reacting in the same way. I asked him if he was feeling unwell and he said, no. I asked him if there had been any more tampering with the boats, he said, no . . . Rory, come here.'

When he made no move towards her, she went swiftly up the room and, putting her arms about him, she demanded, 'Look at me. Please, look at me,' and when he lifted his head, she said, 'Whatever it is, it cannot be so awful that you can't tell me. And whatever it is, it's leaving its mark on you, you look ill. Come.' She drew him down the room and towards the fire, and when they were seated on the couch she said, softly now, 'Tell me, Rory, please. Whatever it is, please tell me. You said once you would always speak the truth to me. Nothing must stand between us, Rory. Is it that man, John George? Is he blackmailing you? After all I did for him is he . . . ?'

'Oh no! No! Oh God, I wish I could say he was, I wish that's all it was, John George. John George wouldn't blackmail anybody, not even to save his life. I know that, don't I? . . . Charlotte—' he now gathered her hands tightly between his own and held them against his breast—'I've . . . I've wanted to say this to you for some time past, but . . . but I didn't

267

think I could convince you because, to tell you the truth, when . . . when all this first started between you and me, I never thought it would ever be possible, but Charlotte . . . Charlotte, my dear, I . . . I've grown to care for you, love you . . .'

'Oh Ror-y, Ror-y.' She made a slow movement with her head, then pressed her lips tightly together as he went on, 'I want you to know this and believe it, for . . . for what I'm going to tell you now is going to come as a great shock. If it were possible to keep it from you I would, especially now when the last thing in the world I want you to have is worry, or shock, but . . . Aw God! how can I tell you?' When he turned his head to the side she whispered. 'Rory. Rory, please; whatever it is, listen to me, look at me, whatever it is, whatever you've done, it won't alter my feelings for you, not by one little iota.'

He was looking at her again. 'I haven't done anything, Charlotte, not knowingly. It's like this.' He swallowed deeply on a long breath. 'The other night, Saturday, when you sent me out so gaily to the game, Jimmy was waiting at the bottom of the drive. He . . . he had news for me . . .'

He stopped speaking. He couldn't say it but gazed at her, and she didn't say, 'What news?' but remained still, very still as if she knew what was coming.

. . . 'He told me something amazing, staggering. I . . . I couldn't believe it, but . . . but Janie, she had come back . . . *Charlotte! Charlotte!*'

As she lay back against the couch he watched the colour drain from her face until she had the appearance of someone who had just died, and he took her by the shoulders and shook her, crying again, 'Charlotte! Charlotte! it's all right. Listen, listen, it's all right, I won't leave you, I promise I won't leave you. I know she can claim through law that . . . that she's still my wife, but . . . but after seeing her, hearing her . . . I don't know, I don't know.' He lowered his head, 'She's no more like the woman I married than . . .'

Charlotte had made a small groaning sound, and now he gathered her limp body into his arms and, stroking her hair, he muttered, 'Believe me. Believe me, Charlotte, I'll never leave you. No matter what happens I'll never leave you unless . . . unless you want me to . . .'

. . . 'Unless I want you to?' Her voice was scarcely audible. 'How . . . how can you say such a thing? I'd want you near me even if I knew you were a murderer, or a madman. Nothing you could do, nothing, nothing would ever make me want to be separated from you.'

'Oh my dear! My dear!'

They were holding each other tightly now and, her mouth pressed against his cheek, she was murmuring, 'How . . . how are you going to go about it? Does . . . does she know?'

He released her and sat slowly back against the couch. 'I'm . . . I'm going down to tell her tonight.'

'Where is she?'

'In the boathouse.'

'Yes, yes, of course, she would be there. That is why Jimmy was so concerned. It is strange but . . . but already I seem to have lost a family. I liked Jimmy, I liked him very much indeed. I . . . I had great plans for him, a new yard. I had been looking about on my own. It . . . it was to be a surprise for you, and your . . . your people. I thought they were coming to accept me, particularly your aunt, for it was she who from the beginning appeared the most distant. But these past few weeks, in fact only last Thursday when I met her in the boathouse, she was cooking for Jimmy, and she made a joke with me, and for the first time she didn't address me as ma'am . . . and now . . . Oh! Oh, Rory!' She turned and buried her face in his shoulder, and when her body began to shake with her sobbing his heart experienced an agony the like of which hitherto he hadn't imagined he was capable of feeling. It was only the second time he had heard her cry. She wasn't the weeping type; she was so strong, so self-assured; she was in command of herself and of him and of everyone else.

As he held her tightly to him he dwelt for a moment on the strangeness of life and what two years could do to a man's feelings, and he realized that no man could really trust himself and say that what he was feeling today he would still feel tomorrow. A few moments ago he had told Charlotte he loved her and would never leave her; two years ago he had told Janie that he loved her and she would always and ever be the only one in his life. What was a man made of when he could change like this? It was past him, he couldn't understand it. Yet there was one thing at the moment he was certain of, and that was that he no longer wanted Janie but he did want Charlotte, and that what he felt for her wasn't mere gratitude but love, a love that owed nothing to externals but sprang from somewhere deep within him, a place that up till now he hadn't known existed.

4

Janie had refused to take the money that Rory had left. Not until she was back in her rightful place, she had said, would she take a penny from him.

'But Janie,' Jimmy had pleaded, 'you can't go round looking like that, and . . . and all your clothes . . . well, they were given away, the Learys got them.'

'Why can't I go round like this, Jimmy? This is what I've worn for the last two years, and as I said, when I'm back in me rightful place then I'll take money from him for clothes.'

On that night one of the first things she asked when he had come back into the room was, 'What's happened to John George?'

'Oh,' Jimmy had answered, 'John George's all right.

He has a newspaper shop in Newcastle . . . and that lass is with him. When he got out he came back and saw her, and she left the man. Her father went after her and threatened both of them, but she said it was no good she wouldn't go back. They're all right,' he had ended.

She had looked at him hard as she asked, 'How did he come by the paper shop?'

'Well.' Jimmy had brought one foot up on to his knee and massaged his ankle vigorously while he said, 'It was her . . . Charlotte, she saw to it.'

'*She* saw to it? You mean to say, after sendin' him along the line she set him up in a shop?'

'Aye.'

'And he let her?'

'Oh aye, he held no grudge. That's John George, you know. He's too good to be true really, or soft, it's how you take him. But she found out where he was, and she went up to him and talked with him and . . . and well, that was that . . . She's kind, Janie.'

She had looked hard at him as she said, 'I don't know about kind, but one thing's clear, she's wily. She's bought the lot of you. You're for her, aren't you, Jimmy? Hook, line and sinker you're for her. And I'll bet you'll be telling me next that all them in the kitchen are at her feet an' all.'

'Oh no, Janie, oh no. There was hell to pay. They . . . they didn't speak to him for ages.'

Slightly mollified, she held out her hands towards the blaze, then said quietly, 'He doesn't want me now, Jimmy. You can see it; he doesn't want me.'

And Jimmy could make no reply to this by way of comfort . . .

Nor could he the next night after Rory had gone, nor last night, because each time they met they seemed to become further apart. They were like two boxers who hated each other. Even if Rory were to leave Charlotte he couldn't see them ever living together again. He began to wonder why she was insisting on it.

He had just come in from the yard and the sight of her cooking a meal caused him to say, 'Lizzie . . . Lizzie 'll be down the morrow; she . . . she comes to bake. What you gona do, Janie?'

'What do you think?' She went on cutting thick slices from a piece of streaky bacon.

'Well, you'll give her a gliff.'

'We've all had gliffs, Jimmy.' Still continuing slicing the bacon, she didn't look up as she said, 'You didn't mention it, but I suppose her ladyship's been supportin' them up there an' all?'

It was some seconds before he answered, 'Rory has, and it's his own money, 'cos as he said he works hard for it. And he does, Janie. He travels about a lot, seein' . . . seein' to different businesses and things . . . and he studies . . .'

'Studies!' She raised her head and looked at him scornfully. 'Rory Connor studies! What? New tricks in the card game?'

'Don't be so bitter, Janie.'

She flung the knife down so hard on to the table that it bounced off on to the floor, and, leaning towards him, she cried, 'Jimmy, have you any idea how I feel, comin' back here and finding I'm not wanted by nobody? *Nobody*. Oh—' she moved her head slowly from shoulder to shoulder—'how I wish I'd never got me memory back. Do you know something? I was happy back there. The life was hard, but they were good people, jolly, and they took to me.' She now looked down towards the table. 'There's something else I'll tell you. There was a man there, the son . . . he wanted to marry me. There were few young ones in the village and they had to go miles and miles to reach the next settlement. But . . . but I still had me wedding ring on'—she held out her hand—'and I said I must be married to somebody. They all worked it out that I'd been with me husband and child and they must have been both drowned 'cos I kept talking about the child afore I came round, so the priest said. He was on one of his visits when I was picked up. It was Miss Victoria. And . . . and then Henri pushed me off the rock and when I came up out of the water I remembered. They were all strange to me. I looked at them an' saw them as I hadn't afore, rough fisherfolk, rougher than anything you see round here, livin' from hand to mouth. They only had two old boats atween the lot of them. It was his, Henri's boat, that picked me up. He'—Her voice trailed away now, as she ended, 'He sort of felt I belonged to him 'cos of that.'

When she raised her eyes again to Jimmy she said softly, 'They all came and saw me off. They walked the five miles with me to where we met the priest and he took me on to the next village in the cart. And you know something? He warned me, that priest. He warned me that things would've changed. And do you know what I said to him, Jimmy? I said to him, "Well I know, Father, of one who won't have changed, me husband . . ."'

It was half an hour later when they'd almost finished the meal that Jimmy, scraping the fat up from his plate with a piece of bread, said tentatively, 'What'll happen, Janie, if . . . if he won't leave her?'

'He's got to leave her. He's got no other option, it's the law.'

'Janie—' He chewed on the fat-soaked piece of bread, swallowed it, then said, 'Rory's never cared much for the law. I mean he hasn't bothered about what people think. What if he says, I mean 'cos of the bairn comin', "To hell with the law!" and stays with her, what then?'

'What then? Well, she'll be living in sin won't she? And she's prominent in the town, and the gentry won't stand for that, not in the open they won't. Things can happen on the side, but if it came out in court that he wouldn't take me back, and me his wife, and he went on living with her, why neither of them would dare show their faces. There's things that can be done and things that can't be done, especially in Westoe; it isn't like along the riverfront here. And he'll find that out. Oh aye, he'll find that out.'

It was at this point in the conversation that the door opened and Rory entered. She did not turn and look at him, and he walked slowly towards the fireplace.

Jimmy, rising flustered from the table, said, 'Hello there.'

Rory nodded towards him, but gave him no reply. He had taken off his hat and was holding it in one hand which was hanging by his side; then looking at Janie he said, 'Do you think we could talk quietly?'

'That's up to you.' She did not even glance towards him.

'I've . . . I've made a decision.'

She said nothing, but waited, and he glanced towards Jimmy, whose eyes were tight on him. Before he spoke again he stretched his chin up out of the collar of his overcoat. 'I'm not going to leave her, Janie.'

She made no move in any way, no sign.

'You'll take me to court as is your right, and I'll maintain you, and well too, as is also your right, but . . . but she's carrying my child and I'm not leaving her.'

Now she did turn towards him and, like a wild cat, she spat her words at him. 'You're a swine! Do you know that? You're a rotten, bloody swine, Rory Connor! And, as I said to Jimmy, you do this and you won't be able to lift your head up in this town. Aye, and I'll see you don't, I'll take you to court. By God! I will. It'll be in all the papers; both you an' her'll have to hide yourselves afore they've finished with you. And her money won't save you, not from this disgrace it won't . . .'

As he stared back into her face which was livid with passion, he thought, even if Charlotte were to die at this minute I wouldn't go back to her; I could never live with her again. His thoughts, swirling back over the past, tried to find the man he had been,

274

the man who had loved this woman, the man who had sworn always to love her, but in vain. And so he said, 'Do what you think you have to do; if it'll make you feel any better go the whole hog; but I'd like to remind you that Shields isn't the only town on the planet. The world is wide and when you have money you can settle where you like.' He felt no compunction now at throwing his money at her.

He stared at her a moment longer. She was not recognizable to him; the white hair, the brown skin, even her eyes were no longer Janie's. He pulled on his hat, saying, 'Well, that's that; the rest is up to you,' and, turning, went out; and as he always did on these visits, Jimmy followed him into the yard.

It was a bright evening; the twilight was long in passing. They walked side by side down to the end of the yard and stood against the railing bordering the river. The moored boats were bobbing on the water beneath them. They stood looking down into them, until he asked, 'Do you blame me?'

There was a short pause before Jimmy answered, 'No, not really, Rory, no. But . . . but I'm sorry for her. I can see her side of it an' all.'

'Well, I would expect you to 'cos she has got a side. And I'm sorry for her too. At this moment I'm sorry for us all.'

He looked up and down the river as he said, 'Things were going so fine. I was riding high, I was me own man. Even with Charlotte's money I was me own man, because I knew I was making meself felt in the business.' He looked down at Jimmy. 'You know, as I said, we could go away. I thought of that as I came along. We could move to any place in the country, but somehow I don't want to leave this town. And I know she doesn't. But anyway, no matter where we go we'll see you're all right.'

'Aw . . . aw, don't worry about me, Rory, I'll get through. And you've done more than enough already. By the way, I didn't tell you, 'cos you've got enough on your plate, but those buggers down there must have been up to something last night. I heard somebody in the yard, more than one. I . . . I thought they were comin' under the house, and then a patrol boat came up and stopped—it stops most nights—and I heard nothing after that. I . . . I was a bit scared.'

'Get Richardson to come along and stay with you.'

'Aye, I will, but I think I must look for somebody else, somebody single. You see, he's got his wife and family.'

'You do that. Tell them they'll be well paid.'

Jimmy nodded; then he asked quietly, 'What's going to happen her . . . Janie? I mean, will she want to go on livin' here? It's awkward. She says she's going up home the night or the morrow. Well, if she does she might decide to stay up there.'

'Home? Huh!' Rory tossed his head back. 'They'll have a field day with this. Our dear Lizzie will come out with all the sayings back to Noah: As ye sow so shall ye reap; Pride goes before a fall; Big heid small hat. Oh, I can hear her.'

'I . . . I don't think so, Rory. You know, I've always meant to say this to you, but you don't see Lizzie as she really is. She's all right is Lizzie, and I've never been able to understand why you still hold it against her. And I look at it this way: after what's happened to you if you don't see her side now you never will.'

'Aye. Aye, I suppose you're right . . . Well, I'll be off. I . . . won't come back as long as she's here. Come up, will you, whenever you can and let me know how things are going? I'll want to know when I'm to expect the authorities.'

'All right, Rory, I'll let you know. Tell Charlotte I wish her well, and I'm sorry . . .'

'I will; she'll be grateful. So long then.'

'So long, Rory, so long.'

They looked at each other for a moment longer, then Rory turned away and walked slowly out of the yard.

Jimmy waited a while before returning to the

house, and it was as he mounted the steps that he heard her crying. When he entered the room he saw her, her face buried in her arms on the table, her body shaking.

He did not go to her but went and sat by the side of the fire and, following his habit, he brought his foot on to his knee again and stroked his ankle vigorously. It would do her good, he told himself, to cry it out. Perhaps it would wash away some of the bitterness in her.

After a moment he slid his foot off his knee and looked down at the triangular shape made by his legs; he had always hated them for from the beginning they had erased any hope of him ever finding a lass of his own; no lass wanted to be seen walking the streets alongside him. He had gone through a lot of body torment, and occasionally he still did, but these feelings he mostly sublimated in his affection for the family and his love for Rory . . . Aye, and her sitting behind him there.

But now at this particular moment as he looked down at his legs he was in a way grateful to them, for because of them he would never experience the agony that Rory, Janie and Charlotte were enduring at this minute.

Life was funny, it handed out compensations in very odd ways.

5

'You're sure, darling, quite sure?'

'I'm as sure as I will be of anything in me life.'

'You won't regret it. I'll never let you regret it for one moment.'

'There'll be a hell of a rumpus. As she said, we won't be able to lift our heads up in the town . . . Should we leave?'

'No, no, we won't leave . . . we won't leave. We married in good faith; she has no children by you, I'm to have your child. We are as it were the victims of circumstance.'

'They won't look at it that way. You know as well as I do what they'll say. He's on to a good thing, that's what they'll say. He's not going to give all that up and go back to rent collectin', or some such.'

'Do you mind very much what they say?'

He thought for a moment before answering, 'Yes, I do, because . . . because it won't be true. I'm staying with you now for one reason only, although I can't say I haven't got used to all this—' he spread his arms wide—'but if I had retained any feeling for her, as it once was, say, this wouldn't have mattered.'

'I know that . . . Oh, why had this to happen? We were so happy, so content; there was only one thing missing in my life.'

'One thing?'

'Yes, and then you gave it to me earlier this evening . . . You said you loved me.'

'Oh, Charlotte!' He put his hand out and caught hers.

'When do you think she'll take proceedings?'

'Tomorrow likely. The mood I left her in, she'll waste no time. But you know something? In spite of all I know is going to happen, the scandal, the gossip, the papers, the lot: "Woman returns from the dead. Husband, married again, refuses to acknowledge her"—You can see them, can't you, the headlines?— Well, in spite of it all, the moment I came back, the moment I stepped through the door and saw you sitting there I had the oddest feeling. It was strange, very strange. I can't remember feeling anything like it before. It was a feeling . . . well, I can't put a name to it, a sort of joy. No, no—' he shook his head—'I shouldn't say joy . . . Certainty? No, I really can't put a name to it, but I knew that everything was going to turn out all right. I thought, in a way it's a good job it's happened; we'll start a new life, you and me and him—or her.' He placed his hand gently across the mound of her stomach, and she put her two hands on top of his and as she pressed them downwards she looked into his face and said, 'I love you, I adore you. Blasphemy that, isn't it? But to me you are my God.'

He now dropped on to his knees and, burying his face in her lap, murmured, 'Charlotte, Charlotte, I'll want no other but you ever, believe me . . .'

When there came the tap on the drawing-room door he turned round hastily and knelt before the fire and busied himself attending to it as Charlotte called, 'Come in.'

Jessie closed the door softly behind her, came up the room, and, standing at the edge of the couch, she said, 'There's . . . there's a man at the door, sir. He . . . he says he would like to speak to you.'

'A man?' Rory got to his feet thinking, My God she hasn't lost much time. 'Did he give you his name?'

'No, sir. He just said it was important, and . . . and he must speak with you. He's a little man, very little, sir.'

A little man, very little. Who did he know who was very little? Only little Joe.

'Where is he now?'

'I've . . . I've left him in the lobby, sir. He's . . . he's a workman type.'

He looked down towards Charlotte. Then went swiftly past Jessie.

When he opened the hall door and looked into the lobby he was looking down on to little Joe.

'Evenin', Mr Connor.'

'Hello, Joe. What's brought you here?' His voice was stiff.

'Mr Connor, I'd . . . I'd like a word with you.'

'I don't need to be set-on any longer, Joe, you should know that.' His tone held a slight bitterness.

'Tisn't about that, Mr Connor. I . . . I think you'd better hear me, and in private like; it's . . . it's important, very, I should say.'

Rory hesitated a moment, then said, 'Come away in.' He opened the door and let the little fellow pass him. He watched him as his eyes darted around the hall. Then he led the way to the office. Once there, he seated himself behind the desk and, motioning to a chair, said, 'Sit yourself down,' and when Joe was seated he said, 'Well, let's have it.'

'I thought you should know, Mr Connor, but . . . but afore I tell you anythin' I want you to believe that I wasn't in on the other business when they done you over. They're a dirty crew an' they've got me where they want me, the Pitties an' him—Nickle. But . . . but there's some things I don't stand for, and if they knew I was here the night me life wouldn't be worth tuppence. But . . . but I thought you should know.'

'Know what?'

'Well.' Joe stretched his feet downwards until his toes touched the carpet; then he leant forward towards the desk and, gripping it, he said under his breath, 'They're up to something. I just got wind of it a while ago. They're gona get at you through your brother. I've . . . I've seen him. He's not much bigger than me, and he's got his own handicap, and . . . and I didn't think it was fair 'cos of that, so I thought I'd come and tell you, 'cos you always played straight by me, never mean like some of them. And . . . and after that business when you didn't drag me into it, and you could 'ave, oh aye, you could 'ave, I thought to meself, if ever . . .'

'Get on with it, Joe. What are they up to?'

Joe now brought his hands from the table and, joining them together, he pressed them between his knees before he announced, 'They're gona burn you out.'

'*Burn me out*? Here?'

'Oh no, not here; they wouldn't dare come up this way. No, the boatyard and the boathouse. Steve Mackin let it drop. They'd been to him for paraffin.'

'What!' Rory was on his feet and around the desk. 'When?'

'Oh, late on's afternoon. I . . . I was payin' him a bet and he said, "Poor little bastard."' Joe now looked from one side to the other as if to apologize to someone for his language, then went on, 'I said, "Who?" and he said, "Connor. Little bandy Connor. But what can you do against those three buggers?"'

Rory was going towards the door now. 'What time was this?'

'Oh, an hour gone or more. I took a stroll by that way 'cos I thought if I saw him, I mean your brother, I would tip him off to keep clear like, but I saw big Pittie standing at the corner. He was talking to a fellow, just idling like, standing chattin'. But he doesn't live down that end, and so I thought it wasn't fair, Mr Connor, an' so I came . . .'

They were in the hall now and the drawing-room door was opening.

'What is it?'

'I . . . I've got to go down to the boatyard. Nothing, nothing.'

Charlotte came up to him as he was taking his coat from the hall wardrobe and again she asked, 'What is it?' then added, 'Oh, what is it now, Rory?'

'Nothing.' He turned to her, a faint smile on his face. 'This chap here, well—' he thumbed towards Joe—'he's been kind enough to come and give me a warning. The Pitties mean business; I think they're going to loosen the boats.'

'Don't go.' Her voice was stiff now. 'Don't go, please. Let us go straight to the station; the police will deal with it.'

'Now, now.' He put his hands on her shoulder and turned her about, then led her towards and into the drawing-room. Once inside he closed the door, then whispered to her, 'Now look, it's nothing. All right, all right—' he silenced her—'I'll get the police. I promise I'll get the police.'

'It's dark; anything could happen; it's dark.'

'Look, nothing's going to happen. Richardson'll be

there with him. He's a tough fellow is Richardson. Now look, I've got to go. You stay where you are.'

'No, let me come with you. Please let me . . .'

'No. No. Now don't you dare move out of here.' He opened the door and called, 'Jessie!' and when the maid appeared he said, 'See that your mistress doesn't leave the house until I get back. Now, that's an order.'

The girl looked from one to the other, then said, 'Yes, sir. Yes, sir.'

He turned again to Charlotte and, putting his hand out, he cupped her chin and squeezed it before hurrying towards the door, where little Joe was standing.

The little fellow cast a glance back towards Charlotte, touched his forelock and said, 'Evenin', ma'am,' and she replied, 'Good evening.' Then he sidled out quickly after Rory.

They hadn't reached the bottom of the steps before Charlotte's voice came after them, crying, 'Wait for the carriage!'

'I don't need the carriage. Go back inside. Do what you're told.' His voice trailed away as he hurried down the drive.

Once in the lane, he began to run and little Joe kept up with him, but by the time they had reached Westoe village the little fellow was lagging far behind.

Fire. It only needed a can of oil and a match and the whole place would go up like dried hay lit by lightning, and they mightn't be able to get out in time. If Jimmy was up in the loft he could be choked with smoke. There were so many books and papers up there, and all that wood, oiled wood inside and out, and the tarred beams underneath in the covered slipway . . . He'd kill those Pitties; one or all of them he'd kill them. It had to come sooner or later; it was either them or him. If they hurt Jimmy . . . And she was there an' all, Janie. To come back from the dead and then be burned alive. And that's what could happen, if they'd both gone to bed. Those buggers! They were murderers, maniacs.

He was racing down the bank towards the market. Dark-clothed figures stopped and looked after him, then looked ahead to see if he was being chased.

It was as he turned into the Cut that he smelt the smoke, and then he looked up and saw the reflection of the flames. Like a wild horse he tore down to the waterfront and along it. But he was too late. He knew before he reached the crowd that he was too late.

The place was alive with people. He pushed and thrust and yelled to try to get through them. But they were packed tight and all staring upwards towards the flaming mass inside the railings.

Dashing back, he climbed the stout sleepers that he'd had put up to encase the spare land they had bought only a few months earlier. When he dropped on to the other side he saw men dragging a hawser from a river boat, and he ran, scrambling and falling over the debris, yelling, 'Jimmy! Jimmy!'

He grabbed hold of a man's arm. 'Are they out?'

'Who, mate?'

'Me . . . me brother.' He was looking wildly around him. 'And . . . and Janie.'

'There's nobody in there, man. Anyway, look at it, nothin' could live long in that, they'd be choked with the smoke afore now.'

'Jimmy! Jimmy!'

He was hanging over the rail yelling down into the wherries when a woman appeared. She swung round the end post from the passage and he stared into her face, made pink now by the reflection from the fire. 'Janie!' He gripped her arms. 'Where's . . . where's Jimmy?'

'Jimmy? I . . . I left him. I left him here, I've been up home.'

'Oh my God!'

He turned now towards the house and gazed upwards. It looked like a huge torch. Flames were coming out of the two bottom windows but only smoke out of the upper one. As he stared there came the sound of breaking glass. It could have been caused by the heat but instinctively he swung round to Janie, and there flashed between them a knowing glance. Then she put her hand over her mouth as she cried, 'God Almighty, Jimmy!'

He raced towards the steps, but as he attempted to mount them the heat beat him back. To the side of him two men were playing a hose that spurted intermittent water into one of the bottom windows. His hand was gripping the stanchion of the balustrade over which a sack was lying; it was the hessian hood that Jimmy wore when working in the rain. Tearing it from the railing he dashed towards the men and pulling the hose downwards he saturated the sack; then, throwing it over his head, he went up the steps again, and into the house.

Everything that was wood inside was alight. The floor felt like slippery wet mush beneath his feet. Blindly he flew over it and to the ladder. One side of it was already burning but he was up it in a second and had thrust the trap-door open.

The room was full of smoke, but through it he saw the glow of the burning bookcase at the far end. Coughing and choking he dropped flat on the floor and pulled himself towards the window, and there his groping hands touched the limp body, and it wasn't until he went to drag it towards the trap door that he realized that both Jimmy's hands and feet were bound. There was no time to unloosen them. So gripping him under the armpits, he pulled him backwards towards the trap-door, but there he had to pause and stuff the wet hessian into his mouth and squeeze the water down his throat to stop himself from choking.

To descend the ladder he had to get on to his knees, then hoist Jimmy's slight body on to his shoulder. By now he wasn't really conscious of his actions, one followed the other in automatic frenzy. Even the agony of gripping the burning rungs didn't penetrate his mind.

The room now was one inferno of hissing flame and smoke; his coat was alight, as was Jimmy's guernsey. Half-way along the room he felt the floor giving way, and as his feet sank he threw himself and his burden in the direction where he thought the door was. His lungs were bursting, his whole body seemed to be burning as furiously as the room.

One hand groping blindly, he felt for the opening, and found it. The steps were below. He let Jimmy slide to the ground. He was choking. He was choking. Dimly he was aware of yells and screams and at the same time he felt the whole building shudder. That was all he remembered.

He was alive when they raised the burning beam from him, then beat the fire out of his clothes.

When they carried him to where Jimmy was lying covered with coats, Janie stumbled by his side, and when she went to take his blackened hand, his skin came away on her palm.

As if totally unconscious of the turmoil in the yard she knelt between the two men with whom she had been brought up, and she groaned aloud.

Someone went to raise her up but she pushed the hands aside. The voices were floating over her: 'We must get him to the hospital. Get a stretcher, a door, anything.' Then there followed a period of time before a voice said, 'Here, Mrs Connor. He's here, Mrs Connor,' and she lifted her head to see a tall figure dropping on to her knees at the other side of the man who was her husband. She stared at the woman who was putting her arm under Rory's shoulders and crying to him, such words, endearing words that she had never heard said aloud before. 'Oh my darling, my darling, dearest, dearest. Oh Rory, Rory, my love, my love.' Such private words all mixed up with moans.

Janie felt herself lifted aside, almost pushed aside

285

by a policeman. He was directing the lifting of Jimmy on to a stretcher. When they went to take up Rory they had to loosen the woman's hands from him, and she heard the voices again saying, 'We must get him to hospital.' And now the woman's voice, 'No, no, he must go home. Both of them, they must come home. I . . . I have the carriage.'

'They'll never get in a carriage, ma'am.' It was a policeman speaking.

'A cart then, a cart, anything. They must come home.'

There were more voices, more confusion, then a discussion between three uniformed men.

When they carried the two still forms out of the yard Janie followed them. They crossed the waste land to avoid the fire which was now merely a mass of blazing wood to where, on the road stood a flat coal cart that had been commandeered. She watched them putting the two stretchers on to it, and as it moved away she saw the woman walk closely by its side. Then the driver got down from a carriage that was standing by the kerb in the road and ran to her. She watched her shake her head at him, and he went back and mounted the carriage and drove it behind the cart. And Janie followed the carriage.

Even when it turned into the drive and up towards the house she followed it. She stopped only when it moved away to the side, past the cart and towards the stables. She watched the men who had accompanied the cart lifting the stretchers off it. She watched the servants running up and down the steps. Then everyone disappeared into the house, and for a few minutes she was standing alone looking at the lighted windows, until the coachman came racing down the steps, rushed into the yard, turned the carriage and put the horses into a gallop and went past her.

Then again she was alone for a time and she stood staring unblinking at the house. She did not move when the carter and three other men came down the steps and mounted the cart and rode away.

She did not know how long she stood there before she saw the carriage return and the doctor, carrying his leather bag, get out and hurry into the house, but she imagined that it was near on two hours before he came out of the house again.

As he went to get into the carriage she seemed to come out of a trance and, stumbling towards him, asked, 'Please, please. How is he? How are they?'

The doctor looked her up and down, her odd hat, her cloak, her clogs. She looked like a field peasant from the last century, and not a peasant of this country either. He peered at her for a moment before he answered, 'The young man will survive but Mr Connor is very ill, seriously so.' He made an abrupt movement with his head, then stepped up into the carriage, and the driver, after giving her a hard stare, mounted the box, turned the carriage and was about to drive away when a servant came running down the steps, calling, 'Will! Will!' When the coachman pulled the horses up, the servant, gripping the side handle, looked up at him and said quickly, 'The mistress, she says, you're to go straight on after dropping the doctor and . . . and bring the master's people. You know where.'

'Aye. Aye.' The coachman nodded and cracked his whip and the horses once again sped down the drive.

The servant now looked at the woman standing to the side of the balustrade. 'Do you want something?' she asked.

Janie shook her head.

'Did . . . did you come with them?'

Janie nodded once.

The servant now looked her up and down. She had never seen anyone dressed like her, she looked a sketch, like a tramp, except that her face didn't look like that of a tramp for it was young, but she looked odd, foreign, brown skin and white hair sticking out from under that funny hat. She said, 'What do you want then?'

'Just to know how they are.'

The voice, although low and trembling, was re-assuring to the servant. She might look foreign but she was definitely from these parts.

'They're bad. The master's very bad and . . . and the mistress is demented. The master's brother, he'll pull through. Come back in the mornin' if you want to hear any more. Do . . . do you know them?'

'Aye.'

'Aw . . . well, come back in the mornin'.'

As the servant went up the steps Janie turned away, but only until she had heard the click of the door; then she stopped and took up her position again, staring at the two upper brightly lit windows.

6

Rory lay swathed in white oiled linen. His face was the same tone as the bandages. At five o'clock this morning he had regained consciousness and he had looked into Charlotte's face, and she had murmured, 'My dearest. Oh, my dearest.'

As yet he wasn't conscious of the pain and so had tried to smile at her, but as he did so it was as if the muscles of his face had released a spring, for his body became shot with agony. He closed his eyes and groaned and turned his head to the side, and when he opened his eyes again he imagined he was dreaming, because now he was looking into Lizzie's face. And he could see her more clearly than she could him, for her face was awash with tears. But she was crying silently.

Vaguely he thought, she generally moans like an Irish banshee when she cries . . . then, What's she doing here? He turned his head towards Charlotte again and her face seemed to give him the answer. He was that bad. Yes, he was bad. This pain. He couldn't stand this pain. He'd yell out. Oh God! God! what had happened him? The fire. The Pitties! The Pitties. They were murderers. He had always meant to get the Pitties but they had got him and Jimmy . . . Jimmy . . . Jimmy . . .

He said the name a number of times in his head before it reached his lips. 'Jimmy.'

'He's all right, darling. Jimmy's all right. He's . . . he's in the other room, quite close. He's all right. Go to sleep, darling, rest.'

'Char-lotte.'

'Yes, my dear?'

The words were again tumbling about in his mind, jumping over streams of fire, fire that came up from his finger nails into his shoulders and down into his chest. His chest was tight; he could hardly breathe but he wanted to tell her, he wanted to tell her again, make her understand, make her believe, press it deep into her that he loved her. He wanted to leave her comfort . . . What did he mean? Leave her comfort. Was he finished? Had they finally done for him? Was he going out? No. No. He could put up a fight. Aye, aye, like always he could put up a fight, play his hand well. If only the burning would stop. If he could jump in the river, take all his clothes off and jump in the river.

'Char-lotte.'

'Go to sleep, darling. Rest, rest. Go to sleep.'

Yes, he would go to sleep. That's how he would fight it. He would survive; and he'd get the Pitties. Little Joe, he'd make Little Joe speak out . . . and about Nickle. God! Nickle. It was him who was the big fish, aye he was the big fish . . . Aw, God Almighty. Oh! oh, the pain . . . He only needed thirty-five pounds to get the boatyard for Jimmy. If he could get set into a good game he'd make it in two or three goes. He wanted to give Jimmy something to make up for those lousy legs he was stuck with . . . Somebody was scorching him . . . burning him up . . .

'Drink this.'

The liquid sizzled as it hit the fire within him, then like a miracle it gradually dampened it down . . .

'He'll sleep for a while, lass.'

Lizzie took the glass from Charlotte's hand and placed it on a side table and, coming round the bed, she said, 'Come away and rest yourself.'

'No, no; I can't leave him.'

'He doesn't need you now, he needs nobody for the time being. It's when he wakes again and that won't be long, come away.'

Charlotte dragged her eyes from the face on the pillow and looked up into the round crumpled face of the woman she had come to think of as Rory's aunt. Then obediently she rose from the chair and went towards the other room, and Lizzie, following her, said, 'I would change me clothes if I was you and have a wash, then go downstairs and have a bite to eat. If you don't, you'll find yourself lying there along of him, and you won't be much use to him then, will you?'

Charlotte turned and stared at the fat woman. She spoke so much sense in her offhand way. She nodded at her but didn't speak.

Lizzie now closed the door and walked back to the bed and, sitting down, stared at her son, at the son who hadn't given her a kind word for years. As a boy he had liked her and teased her, as a man he had insulted her, scorned her, even hated her, but all the while, through all the phases, she had loved him. And now her heart was in ribbons. He was the only thing she had of her own flesh and he was on his way out.

On the day he was born when he had lain on her arm and first grabbed at her breast she had thought, He's strong; he'll hold the reins through life all right. And everything he had done since seemed to have pointed the same way, for he had earned a copper here and there since he was seven. And hadn't he been sent to school? And hadn't he been given full-time work afore he was fourteen? And then to jump from the factory into the high position of a rent man. Moreover he had been the best dressed rent man in the town because he made enough out of his gaming to keep himself well rigged out and still have a shilling or two in his pocket. Then his latest bit of luck, marrying into this house. Who would ever have believed that would have come about? He'd always had the luck of a gambling man.

Aye, but she hadn't to forget that a gambling man's luck went both ways. And she had thought of that at tea-time yesterday when that ghost walked in the door. How she stopped herself from collapsing she'd never know. Only the fact that Ruth was on the verge of it herself had saved her, for to see Janie standing there, the Janie that wasn't Janie, except when she spoke. God in heaven! Never in all her born days had she had such a shock. And nothing that would happen to her in this life or the next would equal it. But a couple of hours later, as she watched Janie go down the path looking like something from another world, she asked God to forgive her for the thoughts that were passing through her mind, for there had been no welcome in her heart for this Janie, whose only aim in life now seemed to be the ruin of the man she had once loved, and whose wife she still was. Aye, that was a fact none of them could get over, whose wife she still was. And that poor soul back there in the room carrying a child. Well, as she had always said, God's ways were strange but if you waited long enough He solved your problems. But dear, dear God, she wished He could have solved this one in some other way than to take her flesh, the only flesh she would ever call her own.

When the door opened behind her she rose to her feet, and going towards Charlotte, she said, 'I'll call Ruth and the young maid, an' I'll come down along of you and put me feet up for a short while.'

Charlotte passed her and walked to the bed, and, bending over it, she laid her lips gently on the white sweat-laden brow, and as she went to mop his face Lizzie took her arm and said, 'Come. No more, not now. And them nurses should be here by daylight.'

Out on the landing, Jessie was sitting on a chair by the side of the door, and Charlotte said to her, 'Sit by the bed, Jessie, please. I'll . . . I'll be back in a few moments.'

'Yes, ma'am.'

The girl disappeared into the room and Charlotte crossed the landing and gently opened the door opposite, and Ruth turned from her vigil beside Jimmy's bed and asked in a whisper, 'How is he?'

'Asleep.' She went to the foot of the bed and, looking at Jimmy, she said softly, 'His hair will grow again, it's only at the back. He's sleeping naturally.' Then she asked, as if begging a favour, 'Would you sit with Rory just in case he should wake? Jessie's there, but . . . but I'd rather—' She waved her hand vaguely. 'You could leave the door open in case Jimmy calls.'

Ruth stared up at her for a moment, then looked at Lizzie before she said, 'Aye, yes, of course' . . . .

In the drawing-room, Charlotte sat on the couch, her hands gripped tightly in front of her, and stared at the fire, and when the door opened and Lizzie came from the kitchen carrying a tray of tea and a plate of bread and butter she did not show any surprise.

The time that had passed since nine o'clock last night was filled with so many strange incidents that it seemed to have covered a lifetime, and that this woman should go into her kitchen and make tea seemed a natural thing to do; it was as if she had always done it.

It seemed to Charlotte from the moment she had knelt beside Rory last night that she had lived and died again and again, for each time she thought Rory had drawn his last breath she had gone with him. That he would soon take his final breath one part of her mind accepted, but the other fought hysterically against it, yelling at it, screaming at it: No, no! Fight for him, will him to remain alive. You can't let him go. Tell him that he must not go, he must not leave you; talk to his spirit, get below his mind, grasp his will, infuse your strength into him. He can't. He can't. He must not die . . .

'Here, drink that up and eat this bit of bread.'

'No, thank you. I . . . I couldn't eat.'

'You've got to eat something. If nothin' else you need to keep the wind off your stomach when you're carryin' or you'll know about it.'

'I'm sorry, I couldn't eat. But you . . . please, please help yourself.'

'Me? Aw, I've no need to eat.' Lizzie sighed as she sat down on the edge of a chair. There followed a few moments of silence before Charlotte, wide-eyed, turned to her and said, 'What do you think?'

'Well, lass, where there's life there's hope they say. As long as he's breathin' he's got a chance, but if you want my opinion, it's a slim one. He was always a gamblin' man, but he's on a long shot now.' She put her cup down on a side table and her tightly pressed lips trembled.

Again there was silence until Lizzie said quietly, 'It's not me intention to trouble you at this time, for God knows you've got enough on your plate, but . . . but I think there's somethin' you should know 'cos there's only you can do anything about it . . . Janie. She's been outside all night sittin' in the stables, your coachman says. He doesn't know who she is of course. He told one of your lasses that there was a strange woman there and she wouldn't go, she was one of his relatives he thought.'

Lizzie now watched Charlotte rise to her feet and, her hands clasped tightly in front of her, go towards the fire and stand looking down into it, and she said to her, 'When she walked into the kitchen last night I was for droppin' down dead meself.'

Charlotte's head was moving in small jerks. The woman, the girl, his wife . . . his one-time wife in her stables? She had a vague memory of seeing a black huddled figure kneeling at Rory's side in the yard, then again when they had lifted him on to the cart, and for a moment she had glimpsed it again in the shadows of the drive. What must she do? Would Rory want to see her? He had once loved her . . . She couldn't bear that thought; he was hers, wholly hers. The happiness she had experienced with him in the months past was so deep, so strong, that the essence of it covered all time back to her beginning and would spread over the years to her end, and beyond. And he loved her, he had said it. He had put it into words, not lightly like some unfledged puppy as he had been when he married his childhood playmate, but as a man who didn't admit his feelings lightly. So what place had that girl in their lives? What was more, he had told her he wanted none of her . . .

'If he had been taken to the hospital she would have seen him, she would have claimed the right.'

Charlotte swung round. Her face dark now, she glared at the fat woman, and for a moment she forgot that she knew her as Rory's aunt. She was just a fat woman, a common fat woman, ignorant. What did she know about rights?

'Don't frash yourself, 'cos you know as well as I do the law would say she had a right. They would take no heed that his feelings had changed.' She nodded now at Charlotte. 'Oh, aye, Janie told me he wouldn't go back to her, he had told her so to her face, and that must have been hard to stomach. So havin' the satisfaction that he wanted you, and seemingly not just for what you could give him, it should be in your heart, and it wouldn't do you any harm, to let her have a glimpse of him.'

'I can't.'

Lizzie now got to her feet and heaved a sigh before she said, 'Well, if you can't, you can't, but I'd like to remind you of one thing, or point it out, so to speak. As I see it, you should be holding nothing against her. You've got nothin' to forgive her for except for being alive She's done nothin' willingly to you. The boot's on the other foot. Oh aye—' she dropped her chin on to her chest—'it was all done in good faith, legal you might say, but nevertheless it was done. How would you feel this minute if you were in her place? Would you be sitting all night in the stables hoping to catch a glimpse of him afore he went?'

Charlotte sat slowly down on the couch again and, bending her long body forward, she gripped her hands between her knees.

It was some time, almost five minutes later when she whispered, 'Take her up. But . . . but I mustn't see her; I . . . I will stay here for half an hour. That is, if . . . if he doesn't need me.'

She was somewhat surprised when she received no answer. Turning her head to the side, she saw Lizzie walking slowly down the room. She was a strange woman, forthright, domineering, and she had no respect for class . . . of any kind. Yet there was something about her, a comfort.

She lay back on the couch and strained her ears now to the sounds coming from the hall. She heard nothing for some minutes, then the front door being closed and the soft padding of footsteps across the hall towards the stairs brought her upright. She was going up the stairs, that girl, his wife, she was going up to their bedroom, to hers and Rory's bedroom. And she would be thinking she was going to see her husband. *No! No, not her husband*, never any more. Hadn't he told her she could do what she liked but he'd never return to her?

She'd be by his bedside now looking at him, remembering their love, those first days in the boathouse.

'*My wife won't be there, miss, but you're welcome.*'

She was back sitting behind the desk again looking at him as he told her he was married.

She almost sprang to her feet now. She couldn't bear it, she couldn't bear that girl being up there alone with him. She must show herself. She must let her see that she was the one he had chosen to stay with, not someone who was seven years her junior, or young and beautiful, but her, as she was . . . herself.

She was out of the drawing-room and running up the stairs, and she almost burst into the bedroom, then came to a dead stop and stared at the three women standing round the bed, his mother, his aunt and the person in the black cloak who wasn't a beautiful young girl but a strange-looking creature with dark skin and white frizzy hair; she was young admittedly, but she could see no beauty in her, no appeal.

She walked slowly up to that side of the bed by which Ruth stood and she stared across into the eyes of the girl called Janie. The eyes looked sad, weary, yet at the same time defiant.

A movement of Rory's head brought their attention from each other and on to him. He was awake and looking at them.

If there had been any doubt in Rory's mind that he was near his end it was now dispelled. Janie and Charlotte together. Through the fire in his body was now threaded a great feeling of sadness. He wanted to cry at the fact that this was one game he was going to lose. The cards were all face up, and his showed all black . . . dead black. But still he had played his hand, hadn't he? The game had been short but it hadn't been without excitement. No, no, it hadn't. But now it was over . . . almost. He wished the end would get a move on because he couldn't stand this pain much longer without screaming out his agony. Why didn't they give him something, a good dose, that laudanum . . . laudanum . . . laudanum . . .

He was looking into Janie's eyes now. They were as he remembered them in those far-off days before they were married when she was happy, because she had never really been happy after, had she? It was funny, but in a way Janie hadn't been made for marriage. She looked it, she had the body for it, but she hadn't been made for marriage, whereas Charlotte. Ah! Charlotte.

Charlotte's face was close above his. He was looking up into her eyes. Charlotte. Charlotte was remarkable. Charlotte could forgive sins. She was like all the priests rolled into one. There'd been a priest here last night, hadn't there? He couldn't really remember. Well, if there had been he knew who would have brought him . . . A dose . . . Why didn't they give him something?

'Darling.'

It was nice to be called darling . . . Oh God! the pain. Why the hell didn't they give him something? . . . Janie had never called him darling. She had said she loved him, that was all. But there was more to love than that, there was a language. Charlotte knew the language. Charlotte . . . Should he fight the pain, try to stay? He could hardly breathe . . . If only they'd give him something.

He closed his eyes for a second; when he opened them again he was looking at Lizzie. There was something in her face that was in none of the others. What was it? Why had he hated her so? It seemed so stupid now. Why had he blamed her as he had done? If there had been anybody to blame it was his father. Where was his father? He was surrounded by women. Where was his father? Where was Jimmy? They'd said Jimmy was near. Jimmy was all right. And his father? His father had a bad leg; his father had been burnt at the blast furnace . . . He had been burnt . . . *Burnt. Burnt*. He was back in the boathouse gasping, struggling. The floor was giving way. He slid Jimmy from his shoulder. He was getting out, he was getting out . . .

'He's asleep again. Leave him be, let him rest.' Lizzie moved from the bed as she spoke, and Ruth followed her, leaving Janie and Charlotte standing one on each side.

Janie looked down on the man whose face was

contorted with agony. She did not see him as the virile young man she had married, nor yet as the boy she had grown up with, but she saw him as the stranger, dressed as a gentleman, who had confronted her in the boathouse. Not even when he had looked into her eyes and recognized her a moment ago had she glimpsed the old Rory, but had seen him as someone who had transported himself into another world and made that world fit him—and having won that world, so to speak, and being Rory Connor, he was determined to hang on to his winnings.

She was the first to turn away from the bed. She knew she had looked at the face on the pillow for the last time and she could not, even to herself, describe how she felt.

As Charlotte watched her walking towards the door she was amazed that the turmoil in her mind had disappeared; she was feeling no jealousy against this girl now, no hate. Amazingly she was experiencing a feeling of pity for her. As Lizzie had said, put yourself in her place; she was the one who had been rejected.

She bent over Rory now and, the tears blinding her, she gently wiped the sweat from his face, murmuring all the while, 'Oh my dearest, my dearest.'

When the door opened and Jessie entered she said brokenly, 'I . . . I won't be a moment. If the master should wake call me immediately,' and Jessie whispered, 'Yes, ma'am,' and took her seat beside the bed once more.

On the landing she stood for a moment drying her face and endeavouring to overcome the choking sensation that was rising from the anguish in her heart, as it cried, 'Oh Rory, what am I to do without you? Oh my darling, how am I to go on now? Don't leave me. Please, please don't leave me.' Yet as she descended the stairs she knew it was a hopeless cry.

In the hall she showed her surprise when she saw Ruth in her cape and tying on her bonnet. Going to her, she murmured, 'You're not leaving? You, you can't . . .'

Ruth swallowed deeply before she said, 'Just for . . . for a short while; I'm takin' Janie back home. And there's me husband, he's got to be seen to. He can do nothing with his leg as it is. I'll be back later in the mornin'.'

'I'll call the carriage for you then.' There was a stiffness in her tone.

'That would be kind.'

'But why?' Charlotte was now looking at Ruth with a deeply puzzled expression. 'I . . . I should have thought you'd have let Lizzie go back and take care of things . . . Being his mother, you would have—' she paused as Ruth, nodding at her now, put in quietly, 'Aye, yes, I know what you're thinkin', it's a mother's place to be at her son's side at a time like this. Well, he'll have his mother with him. For you see, lass, I'm not his mother, 'tis Lizzie.'

'What!' The exclamation was soft.

'Yes, 'tis Lizzie who's his mother.'

'But . . . but I don't understand. He's never, I mean he's got such a regard for you, I'm . . .'

'Aye, it is a bit bewilderin' and it's a long story, but put simply, me husband gave Lizzie a child when she was but seventeen. Rory regarded me as his mother for years and when he found out I wasn't and it was Lizzie who had borne him he turned against her. I'm not surprised that you didn't know. It's something very strange in his nature that he should be ashamed of her, for she's a good woman, and she's suffered at his hands. I shouldn't say it at this stage, but to be fair I must; many another would have turned on him as he did on her, but all she did was give him the length of her tongue. Her heart remained the same towards him always. She's a good woman is Lizzie . . . So there it is, lass, that's the truth of it. Well, I'll be away now, but I'll be back.'

When the door had closed on her Charlotte remained standing. The hall to herself, she looked about it; then in a kind of bewilderment she walked down the step into the office and, sitting behind the desk, she put her forearms on it and patted the leather top gently with her fingers. He had admitted to her the theft of the five pounds; he had told her everything about himself; he had confessed his weaknesses, and boasted of his strength; yet he had kept the matter of his birth to himself as if it were a shameful secret. *Why*? Why couldn't he have told her this? She felt a momentary hurt that he should have kept it from her. She had wondered at times at him calling his mother, Ruth. He had appeared very fond of the gentle-voiced, quiet little woman, even proud of her. And yet of the two women she was the lesser in all ways, body, brain, intelligence. She remembered that Rory had once referred to Lizzie as ignorant, and she had replied that she should imagine her ignorance was merely the lack of opportunity for her mind always seemed lively.

It was strange, she thought in this moment, that he could never have realized that all the best in him stemmed from Lizzie—for now she could see he was a replica of her, in bulk, character, obstinacy, bumptiousness . . . loving. Her capacity for loving was even greater than his, for, having been rejected, she had gone on loving.

There came a knock on the door and when she said, 'Come in,' it opened and Lizzie stood on the threshold.

'I was wondering where you were, I couldn't see you. You mustn't sit by yourself there broodin', it'll do no good. Come on now out of this.'

Like a child obeying a mother, Charlotte rose from the chair and went towards Lizzie. Then standing in front of her, she looked into her eyes and said quietly, 'I've just learned that you're his mother. Oh, Lizzie. Lizzie.'

'Aye.' Lizzie's head was drooping. 'I'm his mother an' he's always hated the fact, but nevertheless, it was something he could do nowt about. I am what

I am, and he was all I had of me own flesh and blood an' I clung to him; even when he threw me off I clung to him.'

'Oh, Lizzie, my dear.' When she put her arms around Lizzie, Lizzie held her tightly against her breast, and neither of them was capable of further words, but they cried together.

It was three days later when Rory died. He was unconscious for the last twelve hours and the final faint words he spoke had been to Charlotte. 'If it's a lad, call him after me,' he murmured.

She didn't know how she forced herself to whisper, 'And if it should be a girl?'

He had looked at her for some time before he gasped, 'I'll . . . I'll leave that to you.'

It was odd but she had hoped he would have said, 'Name her Lizzie,' for then it would have told her of his own peace of mind, but he said, 'I'll leave it to you.' His very last words were, 'Thank you, my dear . . . for everything.'

Through a thick mist she gazed down on to the face of the man who had brought her to life, who had made her body live, and filled it with new life—his life. She was carrying him inside of her; he wasn't dead; her Rory would never die.

When she fainted across his inert body they thought for a moment that she had gone with him.

7

Rory's funeral was such that might have been accorded to a prominent member of the town for the sympathy of the town had been directed towards him through the newspaper reports of how he had been fatally injured in saving his brother from the blazing building, and the likelihood that charges, not only of arson, but of murder or manslaughter as well, would soon be made against local men now being questioned by the police.

No breath of scandal. No mention of former wife reappearing.

Other reports gave the names of the town's notable citizens who had attended the funeral. Mr Frank Nickle's name was not on it. Mr Nickle had been called abroad on business.

Two of the Pittie brothers had already been taken into custody. The police were hunting the third. And there were rumours that one of the brothers was implicating others, whose names had not yet been disclosed. Not only the local papers, but those in Newcastle as well carried the story of how there had been attempts to monopolize the river trade, and that Mr Connor's boats had not only been set adrift, but also been sunk when they were full of cargo.

The reports made Jimmy's little boats appear the size of tramp steamers or tea clippers, and himself as a thriving young businessman.

The private carriages had stretched the entire length of the road passing Westoe village and far beyond. The occupants were all male. In fact, the entire cortège was male, with one exception. Mrs Connor was present at her husband's funeral and what made her presence even more embarrassing to the gentlemen mourners was that it was whispered she was someway gone in pregnancy. She wore a black silk coat and a fashionable hat with widow's weeds flowing low down at the back but reaching no farther than her chest at the front. She was a remarkable woman really . . . nothing to look at personally, but sort of remarkable, a kind of law unto herself.

Another thing that was remarkable, but only to the occupants of the kitchen, was that John George had been present at the burial, but had not shown his face to condole with them nor had he spoken with Paddy who had struggled to the cemetery on sticks. All except Jimmy said they couldn't make him out. But then prison changed a man, and likely he was deeply ashamed, and of more than one thing, for was he not now living with another man's wife?

Poor John George, they said. Yet in all their minds was the faint niggling question, Who was the poorer? John George was alive; Rory, the tough gambling man, was dead.

And this was exactly what had passed through Jimmy's mind when he had seen John George standing against the wall of an outbuilding in the cemetery.

It happened that as they left the grave-side he had become separated from Charlotte. He'd had to make way for gentlemen who had ranked themselves on each side of her. He could not see his father, and so he walked on alone, weighed down with the pain in his heart and the sense of utter desolation, and wondering how he was going to live through the endless days ahead.

It was as he crossed an intersecting path that he saw in the distance the unmistakable lanky figure of John George. He was standing alone, head bowed, and his very stance seemed to be portraying his own feelings.

Without hesitating, he went towards him; but not until he was almost in front of him did John George raise his head.

For almost a full minute they looked at each other without speaking. Then it was Jimmy who said, 'I'm glad you came, John George.'

John George swallowed deeply, wet his lips, sniffed, then brought out a handkerchief and rubbed it roughly around his face before mumbling, 'I'm sorry, Jimmy, sorry to the heart.'

'Aye, I knew you'd feel like that, John George. In spite of everything I knew you'd have it in your heart to forgive him.'

'Oh, that.' John George shook his head vigorously, then bowed it again before ending, 'Oh, that was over and done with a long time ago.'

'It's like you to say that, John George. You were always a good chap.'

'No, not good, just weak, Jimmy. And you know, in a funny sort of way I feel responsible for . . .'

'No! Don't be silly, John George.' Jimmy cut in. 'Now don't get that into your head. It's me, if anybody, who should shoulder the blame for Rory's going. It's me. If I hadn't wanted the damned boatyard he'd be here the day. Aye, he would.'

'No, no, don't blame yourself, Jimmy. It was just one of those things. Life's made up of them when you think about it, isn't it?' He paused, then asked softly, 'How's she, Miss . . . I mean his wife? How's she taking it?'

'Oh, hard, though she's puttin' a face on it to outsiders. She was more than fond of him you know.'

'Aye. Yes, I guessed that. Yet it came as a surprise when I heard they'd married. But I got a bigger surprise when she sought me out. I couldn't take it in. After all . . . well, you know, doing what I did, and the case and things. I'd imagined she was like her father. You knew about what she did for me, like setting me up?'

'Yes, John George.'

'And you didn't hold it against me for taking it?'

'Why, no, man. Why, no; I was glad; it showed you held no hard feelings.'

'Some wouldn't see it that way. What did they think about it in the kitchen?'

'Oh, they just thought it was kind of her; they don't know the true ins and outs of it, John George.'

Again they stared at each other without speaking. Then John George said, 'Well, they'll never hear it from me, Jimmy. I've never let on to a soul, not even to Maggie.'

'Thanks, John George. You're one in a thousand.'

'No, just soft, I suppose. He used to say I was soft.'

He turned and looked over the headstones in the direction of the grave, but there was no rancour in his words. Then looking at Jimmy again, he said, 'It's eased me somewhat, Jimmy, to have a word with you. I hope I'll see you again.'

'Me an' all, John George. Aye, I'd like that. I'll come up sometime, if you don't mind.'

'You'd be more than welcome, Jimmy, more than welcome.'

'Well, I've got to go now, they'll likely be waiting and I'll be holding up the carriages. So long, John George.' Jimmy held out his hand.

John George gripped it. 'So long, Jimmy.'

They now nodded at each other, then simultaneously turned away, John George in the direction of the grave and Jimmy towards the gates, the carriage and Charlotte, and the coming night, which seemed the first he was about to spend without Rory, for up till now his body had lain in the house.

It was as he crossed the intersecting path again that he saw Stoddard hurrying towards him.

'Oh, there you are, sir. The mistress was wondering.'

'I'm sorry. I saw an old friend of . . . of my brother's. I . . . I had to have a word . . .'

'Yes, sir. Of course, sir.'

It was funny to be called sir, he'd never get used to it like Rory had.

They were making their way through small groups of men in order to reach the gates and the carriage beyond when he saw her. Perhaps it was because of the strong contrast in dress that the weirdly garbed figure standing in the shadow of the cypress tree stood out. Both Jimmy and Stoddard looked towards it, and Jimmy almost came to a stop and would once again have diverted had not Stoddard said quietly, 'The mistress is waiting, sir.'

'Oh yes, yes.' Poor Janie. What must she be feeling at this moment? Rory's wife, his real wife after all was said and done, hidden away like a criminal. But she had come; despite the protests she had come. Her presence would surely cause comment.

So thought Stoddard. But then, as he told himself yet again what he had said to the staff last night, it was a lucky family that hadn't someone they were ashamed to own because of their oddities. It happened in the highest society, and certainly in the lowest, and you couldn't blame the master or his folks for not wanting to bring that creature to the fore.

8

They were gathered in the kitchen. Paddy sitting by the fire with his leg propped up on a chair; Ruth sitting opposite to him, a half-made shirt lying on her lap, her hands resting on top of it; Jimmy sitting by the corner of the table, and Lizzie standing by the table to the side of him, while Janie stood at the end of it facing them all.

She was dressed as she had been since she came back; even, within doors she kept the strange hat on her head. She looked from one to the other as she said, 'You're blamin' me for taking it, aren't you? After the stand I made you think I should have thrown the money back in her face?'

'No, no.' They all said it in different ways, shakes of the head, movements of the hands, mutters, but their protests didn't sound convincing to her, and now, her voice raised, she said, 'You took from her. It was all right for you to take from her, all of you. And what had she done to you? Nowt.'

'Nobody's sayin' you shouldn't 've taken it, Janie. We're just sad like that you still feel this way about things.'

She turned and looked at Jimmy, and her body

seemed to slump inside the cloak. She said now flatly, 'How would any of you have felt, I ask you? Look at yourselves. Would you have acted any differently? And don't forget, I could have gone to the polis station, I could have said who I was? I could have blown the whole thing into the open, but I didn't, I kept quiet, I didn't even go and see me da. I kept out of his way even when I saw him at the funeral. And I won't see him now, 'cos he'd open his mouth. It would only be natural. But . . . but when she sent for me and . . . and she knew I was going back there, she asked if she could do anything for me and I said aye, yes, she could. I told her, I told her what it was like there. They had nothing or next to nothing. The boats were dropping to bits. It . . . it was she who named the sum. Five hundred, she said, and I didn't say, yes, aye, or nay.'

'You mean she gave you five hundred straight-away like that?' Paddy was peering at her through narrowed lids.

'No, she gave me a paper. I've . . . I've got to go to a French bank. She's puttin' four hundred and fifty pounds in there; she gave me the rest in sovereigns.'

'And after that, lass, you still haven't got a good word in yer belly for her?'

She dropped her eyes from Lizzie's gaze, then said, 'I can't be like you all, fallin' on her neck.'

'Nobody's fell on her neck.'

She turned and looked at Jimmy. 'No, you didn't fall on her neck, Jimmy, just into her arms. You were as bad as Rory. I've got to say it, it's funny what money can do, by aye, it is. I wouldn't 've believed it.'

'Well, you're not turnin' your nose up at it, are you, Janie?'

'No, no, I'm not, Jimmy, but as I look at it now I'm only takin' what's due to me, 'cos as things were he would have had to support me. And in the long run it would have cost him more than five hundred pounds 'cos I'm likely to live a long time.'

They all stared at her, Ruth, Lizzie, Paddy and

Jimmy. This was the little girl who had grown up next door. This was the young lass, the kindly young lass, who had cared for her grannie, who had been full of high spirits and kindliness. Each in his own way was realizing what life could do to any one of them. Each in his own way knew a moment of understanding, and so it was Ruth who spoke first, saying, 'Well, wherever you go, lass, whatever you do, our good wishes 'll go with you. Our memories are long; we'll always remember you.' She did not add 'as you once were.'

'Aye, that goes for me an' all.' Paddy was nodding at her. 'We've had some good times together, Janie, and in this very kitchen. I'll think back on 'em, Janie.'

Lizzie's face and voice was soft as she said, 'As you say, you'll live a long time, lass, and you'll marry and have a sturdy family, an' when you do, name some of them after us, eh?'

Janie's head was up, her lips were tight pressed together, her eyes were wide and bright; then as the tears sprang from them, they came around her, patting her, comforting her; even Paddy hobbled from his chair, saying, 'There, lass. There, lass.'

'I've . . . I've got to go.'

'Yes, yes, you've got to go.' Ruth dried her eyes and smiled. 'And have a safe journey, lass. It's a long way to go, across the sea to another country. Aren't you feared?'

'No.' Janie shook her head as she blew her nose. 'I know me way, an' I won't have to ride in the cattle trucks.' She smiled weakly, and Lizzie said somewhat tentatively now, 'Why didn't you get yourself a decent rig-out, lass, to go back with?'

'No, Lizzie, no.' Again she shook her head. 'I came like this and that's how I'm goin' back. And . . . and you see, they wouldn't understand, not if I went back dressed up. I'll . . . I'll be one of them again like this. But at the same time I've seen things, and I know things what they don't, and I'll be able to help . . . It's funny, isn't it, how life works out?'

As she looked from one to the other they saw a glimpse of the old Janie, and they smiled tenderly at her.

'Eeh! well, I'll be away. I've got to get the train.'

She backed from them now and, with the exception of Jimmy, they didn't move towards her, not even to come to the door. Jimmy opened the door for her, and with one backward glance at them she went out, and he followed her down the path. At the gate he said, 'Look, wait a minute, I'll go back and get me coat and come down with you to the station.'

'No. No, Jimmy. Thanks all the same. Anyway, you're in no fit state to be about yet, never mind walking to the station.'

He took her hand and they stared at each other. 'Be happy, Janie. Try to forget all that's happened. And . . . and another thing I'd like to say, thank you for not letting on to them'—he jerked his head back towards the cottage—'about, well, you know what, the John George business.'

She stared at him blankly. This was the second time those very words had been said to her within a short space.

Yesterday she had stood in that beautiful room and thought to herself with still remaining bitterness, I can see why he didn't want to come back, for who'd want to give up all this for a boathouse, ignoring the fact that it was the tall black-garbed, sad-looking woman facing her who had been the magnet that had kept him there. Nor had she softened towards her when, in open generosity Charlotte had said, 'I understand how you feel for he was such a wonderful man,' but she had blurted out before she could check herself, 'You didn't know him long enough to know what he was like . . . really like.'

'I did know what he was really like.' Charlotte's tone had altered to tartness.

She had stared hard at the woman before retorting, 'I shouldn't say it at this time, but I doubt it,' and the answer she received was, 'You needn't, for I knew my husband'—the last word was stressed— 'better than most. I was aware of all his weaknesses. I knew everything about him before I married him . . . with the exception of one thing . . .'

'Yes, and I know what that was,' she had said. 'He wouldn't let on about that.'

It had appeared as if they were fighting.

'Do you?'

'Aye.'

'Well, tell me what you think it was,' said Charlotte.

She had become flustered at this. 'It was his business,' she said. 'It's over, it's best left alone.' Then she had stood there amazed as she listened to the woman saying, 'You are referring to the John George Armstrong affair and Rory taking the five pounds and letting his friend shoulder the blame for the whole amount, aren't you?'

She had gaped at her, then whispered, 'He told you that?'

'Yes, he did, but I already knew all about it. I had pieced things together from the events that followed the court case.'

'And you did nothin', I mean to get John George off?'

'He had been stealing for some time. His sentence would have been the same . . .'

She had stared open-mouthed at the woman, she couldn't understand her. She was a lady yet such were her feelings for a fellow like Rory that she had treated as nothing something that she herself had thought of as a crime and condemned him wholesale for. In fact, so big was it in her eyes that she saw it now as the cause of all that had happened to her— all the heartache and the hardship.

She hadn't been able to understand her own feelings at that moment for strange thoughts had galloped about in her mind. She had made a mistake somewhere. Had she ever loved Rory? Of course, she had. But not like this woman had loved him.

Perhaps her own mistake lay in that she had liked too many people, and it had sort of watered down her love; whereas this woman had concentrated all her feelings in one direction and had gained Rory's love in return . . . she hadn't bought him. It seemed to be the last bitter pill she had to swallow.

. . . 'The only thing he kept from me was the fact that Lizzie is his mother.'

'That?'

'Yes.'

'Well, he always was ashamed of it. Yet I couldn't understand why 'cos Lizzie's all right.'

'Yes, Lizzie's all right.'

She had asked her to sit down after that, and then she had offered her the money. But even when she took it she still couldn't like her, or soften towards her . . .

. . . 'You all right, Janie?'

'Aye, Jimmy.'

'Try to forgive and forget.'

'Aye, I will. It'll take time, but I will, Jimmy. I'll marry. I'll marry Henri. I liked him well enough, but that isn't lovin'. Still, we've got to take what we get, haven't we?'

'You'll be happy enough, Janie.'

'Aye, well, think on me sometimes, Jimmy.'

'There'll never be a time when I won't, Janie.' He leant towards her and they kissed quietly, then, her head bowed, she turned swiftly from him and went through the gate and down the narrow path and became lost from his view in the hedgerows.

For quite some time he stood bent over the gate-post. He had been in love with her since he was a lad. During the time Rory courted her he had lived with a special kind of pain, but when he had lain in the loft above them he had suffered an agony for a time because he had loved them both. Now in a way they were both dead, for the Janie he had loved was no more. She hadn't just disappeared down the road; paradoxically she had died when she had come back to life and showed herself as a strange creature that night in the boathouse. Her resurrection had freed him. Life was odd. Indeed it was. As she had said, it was funny how it worked out.

He knew that a different kind of life lay before him. Charlotte was setting him up in a new boatyard and, what was more, she wanted him to take an interest in business.

Yes, a new kind of life was opening up before him, but whatever it offered it would be empty, for Rory was no longer in it. He ached for Rory, and night following night he cried silently while he wished that God had taken him too . . . or instead. Aye, instead. Why hadn't he died instead, for he wouldn't have been missed like Rory was? He had emptied so many lives by his going, Charlotte's, Janie's, Lizzie's, his ma's, aye and even his da's, all their lives were empty now . . . Yet free from the scandal that his living would have created. It was funny, weird. In a way it was like the outcome of Lizzie's saying, leave it to God and He'll work it out.

He went up the path and into the kitchen that housed the old life.

9

They were all in the kitchen again, but now they were waiting for the carriage to take them on what had become for all of them, up till now, one of their twice-weekly visits to Birchingham House.

Ruth stood facing Lizzie and Jimmy as, spreading her hands wide, she said, 'Don't worry about me, I'll have me house to meself for once an'—' she nodded towards Paddy—'I've got your dad to look after.'

'But both of us goin', ma?' Jimmy screwed up his face at her.

'Well, now look at it this way, lad.' Ruth's tone was unusually brisk. 'You're goin' into business, and it's on the waterfront, practically at the end of it. Now, unless you're going to have a carriage and pair for yourself, you can't make that trek twice a day. Now Westoe's on your doorstep so to speak. And there's always the week-ends, you can come home at the week-ends. As for you, Lizzie.' She turned her gaze on Lizzie. 'You know, if you speak the truth, you're breakin' your neck to stay down there; you can't wait for that child to be born.'

'What you talkin' about, woman? Breakin' me neck!' Lizzie jerked her chin upwards.

'I know what I'm talkin' about and you know what I'm talkin' about. And you've lost weight. The flesh is droppin' off you.'

'Huh!' Lizzie put her forearms under her breasts and humped them upwards. 'That should worry you. You've told me for years I'm too fat. And anyway, what do you think Charlotte will have to say about all this?'

'Charlotte will welcome you with open arms, the both of yous, she needs you. Remember the last time we saw her as we went out the door, remember the look on her face? She was lost. She's no family of her own, she needs family.'

'The likes of me?' Lizzie now thumped her chest.

'Yes, the likes of you. Who better? Now stop sayin' one thing and thinkin' another. Go and pack a few odds and ends. And you an' all, Jimmy. Now both of yous, and let me have me own way for once in me own house with me own life. I've never had much say in anything, have I? Now, have I?' She turned and looked towards her husband who was staring at her, and he smiled; then nodding from Lizzie to Jimmy, he said, 'She's right, she's right, she's had the poor end of the stick. Do what she says and let's have peace.'

Stoddard was a little surprised when the two leather-strapped bass hampers were handed to him to be placed on the seat beside him, but then so many surprising things had happened of late that he was taking them in his stride now.

Three quarters of an hour later, when the carriage drew up on the drive, he helped Mrs O'Dowd, as she was known to the servants, down the steps; then taking up the hampers, he followed her and the young gentleman up towards his mistress who was waiting at the door. As the greetings were being exchanged he handed the hampers to the maid, and she took them into the hall and set them down, and when Charlotte glanced at them, Lizzie, taking off her coat, said, 'Aye, you might look at them; you're in for a shock.'

A few minutes later, seated in the drawing-room, Lizzie asked softly, 'Well, how you feeling now, lass?' and it was some seconds before Charlotte, clasping and unclasping her hands, replied, 'If I'm to speak the truth, Lizzie, desolate, utterly, utterly desolate.' Her voice broke and she swallowed deeply before ending, 'It gets worse, I, I miss him more every day. I was lonely before but, but never like this.'

Lizzie, pulling herself up from the deep chair, went and sat beside her on the couch and, taking her hand, patted it as she said, 'Aye, and . . . and it'll be like this for some time. I know. Oh aye, I know 'cos I've a world of emptiness inside here.' She placed her hand on her ribs. 'But it'll ease, lass; it'll ease; it won't go altogether, it'll change into something else, but it'll ease. We couldn't go on livin' if it didn't. So in the meantime we've put our heads together, haven't we, Jimmy?' She looked towards Jimmy, where he sat rubbing one lip tightly over the other and he nodded, 'And this is what we thought. But mind, it's just up to you, it's up to you to say. But seeing that in a short while Jimmy'll be working on the waterfront, well, as Ruth pointed out, it's a trek and a half right back to the cottage twice a day, and in all weathers. And—' she gave a little smile now—

'she also reminded him that he hadn't got a carriage and pair yet, and that he'd have to shank it, so she wondered if you wouldn't mind puttin' him up here for a while, 'cos . . .'

'Oh, yes. *Oh, yes*, Jimmy.' Charlotte leant eagerly towards him, holding out her hand, and Jimmy grasped it. And now with tears in her voice she said, 'Oh, I'm so grateful. But . . . but your mother?'

'Oh, she's all right.' Jimmy's voice was a little unsteady as he replied. 'She has me da, and I'll be poppin' up there every now and again. She's all right.'

'Oh, thank you. Thank you.' Now Charlotte looked at Lizzie, and Lizzie said, 'An' that's not all, there's me.' She now dug her thumb in between her breasts. 'I've got nothin' to do with meself, I'm sittin' picking me nails half me time, an' I thought, well, if she can put up with me I'll stay until the child comes 'cos I've a mind to be the first to see me grandson, or me granddaughter, or twins, or triplets, whatever comes.'

'Oh, Lizzie! Lizzie!' Charlotte now turned and buried her face in the deep flesh of Lizzie's shoulder, and Lizzie, stroking her hair, muttered, 'There now. There now. Now stop it. It's the worst thing you can do to bubble your eyes out. Grannie Waggett used to say that you should never cry when you're carryin' a child 'cos you're takin' away the water it swims in.' She gave a broken laugh here, then said, 'There now. There now. Come on, dry your eyes. What you want is a cup of tea.' She turned towards Jimmy, saying, 'Pull that bell there, Jimmy, an' ring for tea.' Then with the tears still in her eyes, she laughed as she lifted Charlotte's face towards her, saying, 'Did you ever hear anythin' like it in your life? Me, Lizzie O'Dowd, saying ring for tea. What's the world comin' to, I ask you?'

Charlotte stared back into the face of the mother of her beloved. Two years ago she had been alone, but since then she had experienced love, and such love she knew she would never know again. But on the day she had bargained for Rory's love she had

315

said to him that there were many kinds of love, and it was being proved to her now at this moment.

When Lizzie said to her, 'If you don't watch out I'll take over, I'm made like that. Ring for tea, I said, just as if I was born to it. I tell you!' Charlotte put out her hand and cupped the plump cheek, and what she said now and what she was to say for many years ahead was, 'Oh, Lizzie! Lizzie! My dear Lizzie.'

THE END

Catherine Cookson

TILLY TROTTER
TILLY TROTTER WED
TILLY TROTTER WIDOWED

Beginning in the reign of the young Queen Victoria, the three Tilly Trotter novels tell the story of a beautiful girl growing to womanhood amid hardship and despair. Pitting her wits against the local Tyneside villagers, who hate her and accuse her of witchcraft, Tilly's strong instinct for survival leads her to become, in turn, the loving mistress of a wealthy man, and then the wife of his son, travelling to the strange and perilous land of America.

When her husband is killed, Tilly returns to take possession of his estate. The villagers prove ever hostile and suspicious, but Tilly is supported by faithful friends and warm memories. Life still has much in store for Tilly Trotter, old loves and enmities providing fresh challenges to a woman as spirited as ever.

Tilly Trotter	0 552 11737 4	£1.95
Tilly Trotter Wed	0 552 11960 1	£1.95
Tilly Trotter Widowed	0 552 12200 9	£1.95

CORGI BOOKS

THE WHIP

Emma Molinero's dying father, a circus performer, had sent his beloved daughter to live with an unknown grand-mother, not realizing that he had sentenced her to a life of misery.

But the graceful Emma, mistrusted by the local people for her beauty and her "foreign blood", nevertheless became a woman who mystified and fascinated men because of her fiery independence and her skill at performing with the whip – her father's only legacies.

The Whip is an affecting and irresistible novel – Catherine Cookson at the height of her powers.

0 552 12368 4   £2.50

CORGI BOOKS

CATHERINE COOKSON NOVELS IN CORGI

WHILE EVERY EFFORT IS MADE TO KEEP PRICES LOW, IT IS SOME-
TIMES NECESSARY TO INCREASE PRICES AT SHORT NOTICE. CORGI
BOOKS RESERVE THE RIGHT TO SHOW AND CHARGE NEW RETAIL
PRICES ON COVERS WHICH MAY DIFFER FROM THOSE ADVERTISED IN
THE TEXT OR ELSEWHERE.

THE PRICES SHOWN BELOW WERE CORRECT AT THE TIME OF GOING
TO PRESS (APRIL '85).

☐	08700 9	The Blind Miller	£1.75
☐	11160 0	The Cinder Path	£1.25
☐	08601 0	Colour Blind	£1.75
☐	09217 7	The Dwelling Place	£1.95
☐	08774 2	Fanny McBride	£1.75
☐	09318 1	Feathers in the Fire	£1.95
☐	08353 4	Fenwick Houses	£1.75
☐	08419 0	The Fifteen Streets	£1.75
☐	10916 9	The Girl	£1.95
☐	08849 8	The Glass Virgin	£1.95
☐	12451 6	Hamilton	£1.95
☐	10267 9	The Invisible Cord	£1.95
☐	09035 2	The Invitation	£1.75
☐	08251 1	Kate Hannigan	£1.75
☐	08056 X	Katie Mulholland	£2.50
☐	52141 8	Lanky Jones	85p
☐	08493 X	The Long Corridor	£1.75
☐	08444 1	Maggie Rowan	£1.95
☐	09720 9	The Mallen Streak	£1.75
☐	09896 5	The Mallen Girl	£1.95
☐	10151 6	The Mallen Litter	£1.95
☐	11350 6	The Man Who Cried	£1.95
☐	08653 3	The Menagerie	£1.75
☐	08980 X	The Nice Bloke	£1.95
☐	09373 4	Our Kate	£1.95
☐	09596 6	Pure as the Lily	£1.95
☐	08913 3	Rooney	£1.75
☐	08296 1	The Round Tower	£1.95
☐	10630 5	The Tide of Life	£2.50
☐	11737 4	Tilly Trotter	£1.95
☐	11960 1	Tilly Trotter Wed	£1.95
☐	12200 9	Tilly Trotter Widowed	£1.95
☐	08561 8	The Unbaited Trap	£1.75
☐	12368 4	The Whip	£2.50
☐	08821 8	A Grand Man	£1.25
☐	08822 6	The Lord and Mary Ann	£1.50
☐	08823 4	The Devil and Mary Ann	£1.50
☐	09074 3	Love and Mary Ann	£1.50
☐	09075 1	Life and Mary Ann	£1.50
☐	09076 X	Marriage and Mary Ann	£1.50
☐	09254 1	Mary Ann's Angels	£1.25
☐	09397 1	Mary Ann and Bill	£1.50

Writing as Catherine Marchant:

All these books are available at your bookshop or newsagent, or can be ordered direct from the publisher. Just tick the titles you want and fill in the form below.

CORGI BOOKS, Cash Sales Department, P.O Box 11, Falmouth, Cornwall.

Please send cheque or postal order, no currency.

Please allow cost of book(s) plus the following for postage and packing:

U.K. CUSTOMERS – Allow 55p for the first book, 22p for the second book and 14p for each additional book ordered, to a maximum charge of £1.75.

B.F.P.O. & EIRE – Allow 55p for the first book, 22p for the second book plus 14p per copy for the next seven books, thereafter 8p per book.

OVERSEAS CUSTOMERS – Allow £1.00 for the first book and 25p per copy for each additional book.

NAME (Block letters) ....

ADDRESS ....

....